FAUX FINISHED

A Mystery

by

Dawn Dixon

FAUX FINISHED

A Mystery
by Dawn Dixon

Published in the United States by
CLASS LLC
Publishing Division
P.O. Box 2884
Pawleys Island, SC 29585
www.ClassAtPawleys.com

Cover design by Steven T. Ellsworth

ISBN 978-1-955095-00-6

Dedications

To my beautiful daughter, Alexandra,
and all mothers and daughters who love unconditionally.

And, to my doting partner, Nicholas,
who spun in a "happy dance" with me after I typed
"The End."

Acknowledgments

The University of North Carolina at Chapel Hill gave me the wings to fly and proved that the words “alma mater,” which means nourishing mother, are indeed true. Hence, I set the book in that southern part of heaven.

I am eternally grateful to the long-suffering and kind authors who read the book and advised on law, life and how to go to jail. Cathy Pickens, Terry Hoover, Ann Wicker and Dr. Paula Connolly, all mystery mavens extraordinaire, plowed through chapters, drafts, phone calls, text messages, emails and some really dumb questions. I celebrate y’all.

Terri Valentine, author and teacher, started me on the way in an online novel writing course. I treasure her encouragement and sagacity.

My dear family, friends and fellow Tar Heels – Jean Elizabeth Rudo, Cindy Klausmeyer, Alexandra Wilkins, Laura Leach, Rebecca Dixon, Sophie Ambrose, Sonia Lyall, Sara Robinson, Lynne West, Francine Graillot, Gail Golightly, Pamela Overcash, Jennifer Yount, and Greg Hendricks (hope I didn’t forget anyone, but if I did, I apologize) slogged through 300-plus pages, and they still love me.

Jean Elizabeth Rudo gave me the inciting kick in the pants. I told her I wasn’t afraid to fail or succeed. I was just plain afraid. She said, “Just do it, Dawn. Just publish it. Forget queries and rejection letters. It’s not about the money. It’s about getting it done.”

My patient publisher, Linda Ketron at CLASS Publishing, and her excellent editor, Annie Pott, read and marked up a story they knew nothing about by an author they knew nothing about and said, “Go for it.”

Bless them!

Any errors in the novel are entirely of my doing. After all, I am a flawed human being. But a nice person just the same.

Chapters

Above all, be the heroine of your life,
not the victim.

– Nora Ephron

Follow your bliss and the universe
will open doors….

– Joseph Campbell

One

Until I stumbled on a corpse, my greatest fear was climbing ladders. Naïve, huh?

Monday began badly and spiraled down from there. Literally. Angels twirled in a golden fog above my head when things went black. I couldn't be dead, though, because the butterflies mating in my stomach were making me queasy. The Lord wouldn't taketh life and giveth nausea, would He? I came to with my arms entwined in the top rail of a fifteen-foot, metal platform ladder. So, at least I wasn't on Jacob's Ladder in Genesis. The Bible was drummed into me at an early age, what with Sunday School attendance as mandatory as iced tea. Sweet tea. I grasped my parched throat with a purple latex glove and tried to focus.

Of course. The flying angels on the ceiling medallion. Hallelujah! I'd been gilding the carved cherubs when I must've suffered a mini blackout. Probably from a combination of adhesive fumes and the copulating butterflies. I was in the ballroom of Magnolia Blossom Country Club on the big ladder, a recent purchase for my new company, Faux Finish.

As a height-challenged faux painter, I usually left tasks dreaded by acrophobics to my business partner, a former paratrooper with the Airborne Division during Operation Desert Shield/Desert Storm. But today Chica had ordered me up the ladder to defeat my phobia.

I agreed with her method, at least in theory. So, why did the angels persist in fluttering above my head?

Someone coughed. I peered down through the rungs.

"Bridget?" A familiar pair of devilish dark eyes glinted up at me. "You okay?"

Randy La Russo, my second – and thankfully – ex-husband flashed a smug grin as he clutched the ladder.

"Got a bad wheel here." He kicked it with a pristine running shoe. "I promise I wasn't pushing it in circles on purpose." He placed his hand on his heart like the good Eagle Scout his mama always said he was. "I swear." Had he released the brake and pushed me around as a joke?

Right. We'd done the rides at the state fairgrounds in Raleigh enough times for him to know that continuous revolving motion of any kind yielded dire results in my case. I was giving him the old slitty eye when my poor innards rebelled. I jettisoned my stomach contents at the shiny parquet floor. Randy jumped aside at warp speed.

"Jesus H. Christ! Being wimpy about heights shouldn't make you puke," he called from several feet away.

"I can't even do Ring Around the Rosie, you jerk. Remember the Tilt 'a' Whirl? What'd you expect?" I flung my long braids behind me and looked down at the expressionistic splatter reminiscent of Jackson Pollock.

"Still bingeing on Froot Loops, I see," Randy said. He pointed at the mess and closed his eyes. "What's the brown stuff?"

"Oatmeal raisin cookie."

"I should've known."

I took a deep breath and crept down the ladder like an amputee spider. I counted one million rungs, repeating aloud "never again, never again."

"This isn't an ordinary ladder," he said. "It's got handrails and a platform. What're you afraid of?"

"You don't outgrow a fear of heights." I considered kissing the floor when I touched down. "Like you've outgrown your thirty-two-inch waist."

"Touché," he said, but pronouncing it "touchy" in a voice from the past that made the screech of nails down a blackboard preferable. "But thirty-six inches ain't all that bad. Life is short. I'm gonna eat and drink what I want."

Dang if I'd tell him he was still attractive. On the outside, anyway. However, he seemed to live for confrontation. Like the Michael Jordan of arguments, he always sank the basketball no matter where he stood on the court.

After unfurling a mile or so of paper towels, I wiped up my breakfast while Mister Squeamish quaked in his tennies. I threw away my gloves and pulled on a second pair from the box of fifty I'd bought yesterday.

"What're you doing in Chapel Hill? The Carolina-Duke game isn't for five days yet," I said, eyeing his newish gray sweats. "Remember, Thomas Wolfe wrote *You Can't Go Home Again*?"

March 4, 2006, was indelibly stamped in all alumni and fan minds as the second meeting of the men's basketball teams for the season. Still, that didn't explain Randy's presence in town so early in the week.

"Yeah, but Wolfe might've been wrong. And, darlin', he also wrote *Look Homeward, Angel*," Randy replied with a sensitivity noticeably absent during our short marriage. "Besides, I'm hoping this will be another good year for the team, and March Madness is coming up soon."

As much as I would've liked to talk about the basketball team and the upcoming game on Saturday night, I didn't want to have a fun chat with someone who irritated me beyond belief.

"The club is closed on Mondays," I said, introducing a neutral topic. "Not to mention that you can't use the exercise room if you're not a member."

"Not glad to see me? Going on five years since I saw you and Dare at that Duke game I've tried so hard to forget."

Top-ranked Duke whipped our basketball team like a yard dog that day with 87 points to our humiliating 58 in Chapel Hill's Dean Smith Center, popularly referred to as the Dean Dome. I blamed the loss on the icky karma generated by seeing Randy and his latest bubble-gum-chomping toddler slut. As usual, he'd ignored his ex-stepdaughter, Dare.

"Didn't Malcolm tell you?" he added. "I've been an out-of-town member for a couple months now."

"Why should the club manager tell me that? I'm just the hired help." I spread my arms to indicate my light-blue coveralls with the Faux Finish logo embroidered on the left breast pocket. Numerous other pockets held a turkey feather, sponge brush, rags, cell phone and other tools of my trade. "You interrupted me tip-gilding the angels on the ceiling."

He glanced up at the enshrouded chandelier tied to one side for easier access to the unfinished medallion and then sidled over and took one of my braids in his hand as if it were a holy relic. He picked a few gold leaf flakes from my hair.

"You still look like an angel to me, Bridget O'Brien."

Uh-oh.

"Think I'll throw up again," I said.

"You never could take a compliment." He curled the brush end of the braid around his finger.

"They're just words with you, Randy." I slapped his hand away. "Did you come here to aggravate me?"

"Business." He folded his arms and regarded me with amusement. "Thought you might want to take a stroll down Memory Lane today. Walk on campus."

"You once said that looking back was a waste of time."

"I once said a lot of things," he muttered.

"Why not walk with whoever you're shacked up with? Probably some blonde bimbette."

"You're a blonde."

"An intelligent one, though."

"As a matter of fact, Miss Smarty Pants, I'm staying at Mom's. She's tootling around in Daytona Beach on her annual NASCAR pilgrimage. Thought she'd be back by now, though."

His smile was forced. He looked troubled, the usual bravado gone flat.

Stop it, Bridget. Don't imagine things. You haven't seen him in years. You don't know him anymore.

"Yes, well, I've got to get back to work," I said.

I rolled the ladder toward the wall. Not in a straight line, of course. Damned wonky wheel. Trust me to buy a defective ladder. It was the same with grocery carts. The art of picking a wobbly one was a gene that ran on my father's side of the family. Never happened with my mother, who wouldn't be caught dead with an off-kilter buggy.

"That your baby blue hippie van outside?" Randy hooked a thumb over his shoulder and smirked.

"According to Winsor & Newton, it's a pale French ultramarine blue," I said somewhat snootily. "However, never mind that now. I bought it for my business when I got back to town last fall. It's a '79 Chevy. Classic Americana. But being a yuppie snob, you wouldn't see that. Just because you grub for money with the rest of the financial zealots doesn't mean the rest of us have fallen among thieves."

Chica had been driving the van with its "For Sale" sign on Franklin Street when I'd spotted it on my first day back in Chapel Hill last autumn. I'd just returned from a few glorious weeks in Tuscany where I'd indulged in an identity crisis. But missing Dare and feeling massive guilt for leaving her finally poisoned the European idyll. Then Dare's father, my first husband, Marcus Benedetto, died unexpectedly in Chapel Hill, so, I left Italy earlier than I'd planned. As breathtaking as Tuscany was, I'd been homesick by then anyway. The golden light of the Italian landscape couldn't hold a candle to college basketball season in my hometown, and I missed the majestic oaks and cerulean skies of what we natives call the southern part of heaven.

"Earth to Bridget," Randy said, waving a hand in my face and dragging me back to the present. "Being true to your school and driving the Dean Dome around in public are two different things," he added. "You painted clouds on it, too, for Christ's sake."

"I didn't paint them, but I wish I had. Right after my grandfather died, Dare told me she could see PopPop in the cumulus clouds. That he must be in heaven. When I first saw the van, it seemed like some kind of sign."

"You never told me she said that."

"It was after the divorce. You'd moved to Charlotte, and I didn't think stories about PopPop would interest you."

Randy reddened and pointed at the medallion.

"Yeah, well…speaking of Winsor & Newton, it looks like you've given up trying to paint the perfect portrait of Dare. What's with all this fake art crap you're doing now?" He stared at the angels. "I always thought you wanted to be a serious artist."

My developing trigger finger twitched. This would have pleased Chica, who despaired of my ever learning how to shoot a gun. Trouble was I dreaded even touching the Smith & Wesson .38 Special she'd given me. Most of the time, it lurked, bereft of bullets, at the bottom of my thong drawer.

To keep from slapping Randy's jaw, I knelt on a drop cloth beside a bucket of water and stack of clean rags. I dipped a rag in the water and swiped at one of the wainscot panels.

"Sheesh, you aren't the maid here, too, are you? Talk about a comedown."

"If you must know, I've got to clean these before we marbleize, for heaven's sake," I said as Guns 'n Roses' "Sweet Child of Mine" wailed from the neighborhood of Randy's stomach.

"Really? Your ring tone is Axl Rose?"

Randy made a face as he fumbled in the front pocket of his sweatshirt. He waved his cell phone at me and disappeared from the room to take the call.

"Sweet Child of Mine"? How was that for irony? Maybe he'd just leave now. One could only hope. I concentrated on the panel for several undisturbed minutes.

"By the way," he said, reappearing and squatting beside me, "how is Dare these days?"

I dropped my rag.

He looked at me like I was doomed. The last time I'd seen that expression, we were strolling down King Street in Charleston trying to rekindle our flickering union before the final separation. I'd stopped to peek into an antique shop window and in the reflection saw Randy smile at an old man shuffling by. He stopped and slapped Randy on the back.

"La Russo, ain't it?" the man bellowed, adjusting a hearing aid. "About time for you and that cute trick of a wife to head on back to the B&B. Still got the big, canopied bed, you know." He chuckled.

Randy pursed his lips as if sucking a lime.

"She not with you this trip?" the man persisted, looking at me and then up and down the street. "Pretty little thing. No bigger'n a squirrel. My wife is redheaded, too, by the way. From a bottle now, though. Word of warning, son, they all get long in the tooth eventually."

I stepped up to them with all of my five-foot eight-inches, blonde curly hair and bigger'n-a-squirrel hiney. I wasn't sure about the length of my teeth. Guess the old guy didn't recognize me as Randy's wife.

The cackling fool.

Randy steered him away with some hail-fellow-well-met hoo-ha then faced me. Like he was doing now. Like I was doomed. Funny, the average cheating husband would've assumed he was the guilty party, but I'd never explained this theory to Randy.

"Doomed," I said, trying to refocus on the panel.

Randy stared at me like I'd lost it but thought better than to comment.

"Why're you asking about Dare?"

"Because she's…"

I clapped my hand over his mouth and checked for eavesdroppers.

He slapped my hand away. "My ex-stepdaughter? That what you want me to say?"

If I hadn't been so upset, I would've enjoyed his ire.

"Can't I ask about my own ex-stepdaughter?"

"Nope. Ix-nay. Not after all this time. She's none of your business."

"The hell she isn't. We need to talk, Bridget. Now. C'mon outside for a minute."

"Where've you been in the year since her father died? No, never mind. Just go away. I can't deal with your crap right now. We're too busy."

With less than a week to complete the wainscoting, ceiling medallions, and various other small jobs at the club, Chica and I had to hustle. According to Malcolm Jones, a snooty flock of designers and florists were driving him crazy about decorating for the upcoming wedding reception for the mayor's daughter. Besides, I always tried to postpone doom whenever possible.

"Yes, very busy," said Chica as she flitted into the ballroom like Elton John's tiny dancer, Cuban-style. Her gray-streaked black hair bounced in a fat ponytail and her black eyes raked over Randy as she swung a big orange hammer through the air with her right hand and carried a brown bundle in the crook of her left arm.

"Chica, meet Randy, the ex. Randy, meet my business partner, Isabella DeMoya. She goes by Chica. The brown fur ball is Bubba. Dare's dog. Miniature dachshund and spawn of Satan."

The dog's lip rippled along with a throaty growl as Randy moved to pet him. Randy took a step back.

"He's lovely," he said.

"He adores Dare."

"Uh-huh. So, what in the world is that, then?" He pointed at the hammer, Faux Finish's favorite tool. "A traffic cone?"

Chica swung the oversized mallet again.

"Technically speaking," I said, "it's our big, orange, Stanley, non-marring, composite-finish, dead-blow hammer from The Home Depot. Good for banging on paint can lids."

"Also, a good smasher," Chica added with a significant glance at Randy, as she thumped at an imaginary roach scuttling across the floor before dropping the hammer into one of our supply crates and releasing Bubba, who immediately began sniffing around the ballroom. "I pounded our hubcap after I changed the flat tire on the van. Like I said this morning, Mercury goes backwards in a couple days, and things go crappy. Bummer."

Randy raised an eyebrow.

"Astrology," I explained. "When Mercury seems to be moving backward in the sky – even though it really isn't – things go haywire. It's called retrograde, and it's a fact. It starts on March second this year but sometimes it leaks into right before and right after."

"God's truth," Chica said.

Randy dimpled at her as if she were the only person in the world. It was one of his irritating habits, as I knew that the only person who ever captured Randy's full attention was Randy himself.

"This is the wizard who makes big money, I hear?" Chica batted her lashes and extended a graceful hand that he kissed.

Puh-leeze.

"Bridget says much about your pesos." She winked at me.

"I have my little ways." He tried to look modest until he saw my frown.

"Not going there," I said. "Damn, Randy. Okay, I'll give you five minutes." I nodded at Chica. "Back in a minute."

She donned the glasses she swore she didn't need and inspected the unfinished medallion.

"You did not finish the angels?" She said, all businesslike now.

"Got sick up there." I nodded at the ceiling and strode toward the front doors, motioning for Randy to follow.

"No problem," Chica called after us. "I will stamp out this fear someday. Go. Talk. I leave soon for A.A. They'll wait for me before starting to drink."

I walked back and whispered in her ear.

"You're not falling off the wagon, are you? And what's with all the Cuban cha-cha behavior for Randy?" I said. Chica could be as tough as a CIA operative, so when she went into silly mode, I knew something was up.

"Just like to keep them guessing, amiga. Better to be underestimated, no? Don't worry. We only drink coffee at the meetings." She laughed, but I saw her frown before I followed Randy from the ballroom.

"She an alkie?" Randy whispered.

Instead of answering, I glanced at the empty sign-in sheet near the front door. Members were required to sign in and out on Mondays when most of the club's services were closed.

"You didn't sign in, Randy."

"No one ever does."

"Some people do."

I felt that the past had come back to haunt me, and every little thing he did, or didn't do, annoyed me for no good reason.

"The list keeps track of how many members use the club," I said. "It's not meant to stifle your freedom."

"Whatever. You the list police now?" He pushed open one of the double doors.

Still a handsome devil. A bit jowlier these days, but that only emphasized the dimples. How fair was that? With a do-rag, hoop earring and cutlass, he'd make one authentic-looking swashbuckler in some Hollywood blockbuster.

Creep.

Thankfully, we emerged outside where a cooling rush of lemony air bathed my burning cheeks. Fragrant, starred daphne bushes in huge earthen pots flanked the doors, and magenta camellia hedges flourished on both sides of the entrance. We passed white columns and topiary urns of holly trees spilling over with ivy and velvety pansies. Savoring the scene, I almost forgot who stood beside me.

Almost.

"About Dare. Why all this fake concern?" I said.

"Look, I know I haven't been there for her since Marcus died," Randy said with mind-boggling sincerity.

That shut me up until we got to the long gravel drive lined on either side by lofty magnolias. As we stood beneath them, I peered through the umbrella-like cluster of leaves to a blue linen sky. I loved these newly cleansed days right before springtime in Chapel Hill.

Maybe the weather signaled the winding down of another successful basketball season. The team had worked hard to come back from a disappointing four-point loss to Duke in the Dean Dome early in February. Like most people in town as well as alumni across the country, my family and I maintained a drop-dead rabid Carolina Tar Heel passion and believed the old bumper sticker on the back of my van, "If God Is Not a Tar Heel, Then Why Is the Sky Carolina Blue?"

Randy used to feel this way, too. I looked at him now, missing that other Randy. In the old days, our main topic of conversation this week would have been the Carolina-Duke game to be played eight miles down the road this Saturday night in Cameron Indoor Stadium. Instead, he'd brought us full speed into an emotional place we'd both avoided for years.

"Think we can beat Duke in Durham?" I asked, changing the subject to what now seemed unimportant. What the hell. I mainlined on nostalgia. "I can't believe we lost the last one at home."

"Yeah, but what I'm remembering is Dare years ago, all excited in the little Carolina cheerleader outfit we bought her," he said with moist eyes.

That was it. I'd plunged into *The Twilight Zone.*

His face puckered with worry. Was this the same man sucked in by a shower of junk bond gold and the faster-paced, high-rise condo lifestyle of uptown Charlotte? He seemed oblivious to his surroundings.

Hold up. Must be weak from losing my cookies. No way would I let myself feel sympathy for this selfish, womanizing wretch.

I jogged ahead. Randy puffed to keep up. About halfway to the street, I turned to face the entrance of the club in all of its gone-with-the-wind splendor.

"For the last time, what's this about?" I demanded, the skin prickling on the back of my neck. "You haven't kept up with Dare for years except for the obligatory Christmas and birthday checks, when what she needs now is to bond with – a father figure."

"Why a father 'figure?'"

"What d'you mean?" But I already knew.

"I want to tell her."

"Never," I was enraged beyond thought.

I raised my arm to slap him, but he blocked it in midair.

"Did you forget that I'm her real father, Bridget?"

The once soothing breeze now stung my eyes.

"Biology," I said. "Marcus did the real fathering. You just had a lucky rogue sperm."

"But she needs me. This is her future we're talking about." He shook me, only letting go when Hermann Salazar and his daughter Pilar pulled into the main driveway in her little blue Dodge Neon. Remembering I was out in public, I swallowed and tried to calm down, forcing my face into more placid lines.

As the car passed, Hermann removed his steel-rimmed glasses and acknowledged me with a nod but only stared at Randy, who waved at him and Pilar. Hermann had been the quiet, hardworking head maintenance engineer at the club for about ten years. Pilar, who moonlighted as a club waitress during school breaks, was a business major at Carolina. A widower, Hermann had struggled to give his little girl a good life after arriving in the United States, and it had paid off. He grew two inches taller every time he mentioned her name.

Pilar was always happy and affectionate. She'd maintained a big-sister relationship with Dare even after she'd finished babysitting her. Today, however, she stared straight ahead.

The car stopped at the small service lot where the club's shiny, hunter green pickup truck with the big white magnolia blossom and gold lettering on the doors was parked. Hermann proudly drove it for job-related tasks and always made sure it was in pristine condition.

He emerged slowly from Pilar's car, his eyes on us. He kissed his daughter goodbye and disappeared through the service door. Pilar sped off.

I felt my anger simmering beneath the surface as other vehicles began to arrive, but I didn't want to make a scene. What would my mother think if she heard? Wouldn't do to freak out anyway; even though the facility was closed today, members were allowed to use the exercise rooms while a skeleton crew and security maintained a presence. Might as well put on the best face until Randy and I could battle it out in private.

I turned to go back just as Dudley Floyd's battered, silver 1969 Oldsmobile Delta 88 stole into the driveway like a huge bottom-feeding shark. I scooted out of the way in case he hadn't had his cataract surgery yet.

"I'm not sure which one suffers more from arthritis, Dudley or the Olds," said Randy as the car creaked to a stop alongside us. Dudley wouldn't hear of any criticism of his car, bragging that he'd paid it off the same day in 1970 that the Beatles disbanded.

He lived next door to Randy's mother, Grace. Winning the 1965 Magnolia Blossom Men's Golf Tournament remained his claim to fame in club geezer lore.

"I can't remember the last time I laid eyes on you, boy," said Dudley, all overlapping wrinkles and speckled pate that barely cleared the top of the steering wheel. He squinted at me. "That Richard's daughter there?"

"Yessir," Randy said. "Isn't she something?"

I waved at Dudley. At times, Southern politeness was a mighty burden.

"Glad you're finally taking an old man's advice," Dudley said to Randy. "Shouldn't ought to of let this one get away."

"Yeah…um, so, what you up to today, Duds?"

"Getting young Andrew Holly to caddie so I can hack

away at a few holes," Dudley replied. "Wanna join us? What's your handicap these days?"

"Six when I'm cooking. Thanks for the invite. Maybe another time. I've got meetings lined up."

"That's all you young folks do. Meet. In my day, we swung. Well, I'll look forward to it when you have a chance, son."

Randy stepped back expecting the car to pull away. Instead Dudley gave me the once-over. For heaven's sake, how old did a man get before he stopped doing that?

But he wasn't admiring me. He frowned at my coveralls and hair.

"I ain't getting that fashion statement, young lady," he said. "Look like a garbage man in that get-up. You kids of the new millennium can't hold a candle to my generation. We were a lot groovier."

"Maybe he has a point," Randy said. "About us, I mean."

"I'd rather have my gums scraped on a daily basis than reconcile with you," I hissed.

A red Lexus convertible zoomed into the parking lot. Even Dudley heard the screeching.

"Wonder who belongs to that fine vehicle," Dudley croaked before easing off the brakes and continuing his three-mile-per-hour journey toward handicapped parking and the red car.

The female driver wore black sunglasses with her hair stuffed under a Carolina ball cap. Silly woman had the top down, and it was freezing.

This seemed to be right up Randy's ladies' man alley, so I was surprised when he only glanced at her and grimaced. He ran his fingers through his hair, pulled on a pair of Ray Bans and laughed.

He looked like a movie star. I felt like a slug.

"You can't ignore what I've been saying about Dare," he said.

Movie star? What was I thinking? Dracula, more like.

"You won't tell her a thing, dammit." I backed away from him. "She loved Marcus, and he thought she hung the moon."

"I was a kid."

"God, that's so typical. This isn't about you. This is about her. She was your child, and you wanted none of the responsibility. She'll be fourteen in September, and she's complicated as hell right now. I don't need you messing with her head to satisfy a selfish whim."

He laughed again.

I stormed off toward the club, finally unable to tolerate him and the people popping up everywhere. Randy stayed close behind me.

A uniformed landscape worker stopped weed-whacking a monkey grass border to stare at me through safety glasses. He shifted a wad of chewing tobacco to his empty cheek and spit a stream of brown juice into a flower bed. His shirt patch showed the name "Virgil." He grinned before turning back to his work.

Pervert.

Andrew, Dudley's caddie for the day, waved as he jogged past me heading toward the club. Andrew was sixteen, a point guard on his high school basketball team and the object of Dare's secret admiration.

"He's got the most amazing sky blue eyes, Mom," Dare was apt to say with a sigh, after which I'd roll mine in mock exasperation. Then we'd both laugh. I couldn't remember the last time we'd bantered like that.

Randy grabbed my arm as I slowed down under the portico.

"How did Dare feel when you dumped her to roll in the Tuscan hay with your Italian stallion?" He was breathing hard from the exertion.

Never being adept at the quick rejoinder when I needed one, I kept my mouth shut. Besides, Randy had a point. In the midst of a roaring midlife crisis, I'd met my third husband, Alessandro Calabria, in Florence at the foot of Michelangelo's David. While studying the statue's marble unmentionables, my gaze drifted down to a young man who could've been the artist's model. But unlike the sightless eyes of David, Sandro's shone green like the sun through extra virgin olive oil. Over the next week or so, things heated up. Well, what did a sane woman do when a hot Latin male ten years younger proposed in a windswept vineyard? I mean, really.

I shoved my finger in Randy's face.

"I'm not saying you're wrong. But at least I've regretted it, and I'm trying to make it up to her. But I know you. Thinking only of yourself. Dare doesn't need to know that her natural father lived with her all that time and couldn't even pretend to be a decent stepfather. She doesn't even like you, Randy."

"It'll be different this time around. I want to get close to her. She needs to know where to find her future."

That sounded a bit strange to me, but I didn't ponder it for long. Instead I wrenched open the heavy front door with the strength of an Amazon. Chica stood on the threshold with her purse dangling from her shoulder and Bubba in her arms. She gaped in surprise. Several people milled about in the foyer behind her. I sensed rather than saw their interest in my little scene. But it didn't matter because I didn't care who saw or heard.

I faced my ex-husband, the biological father of my beloved daughter.

"I swear I'll kill you if you tell her. I mean it, Randy."

His dark eyes widened in shock before I slammed the door in his face.

Two

After bright daylight, the windowless corridor loomed black as I stormed up the short flight of steps with Chica on my heels carrying the yipping dachshund. My peripheral vision caught people scattering like filmy Toulouse-Lautrec figures, as a hefty cleaning woman in a gray uniform lunged at them with a deafening vacuum cleaner.

I stomped into the ballroom. I say I stomped but, in my lightweight hiking boots, a series of plops better described it. I halted under the half-gilded cherubs and looked up.

"Make that dog hush," I said.

She grabbed his snout, and silence prevailed.

"Can I pray to angels?" I asked Chica as she huffed up behind me.

"Pray to el Numero Uno," she said, grabbing my coveralls and spinning me around into her face. Toting an M60 machine gun and ammo in Saudi Arabia had given her one hell of an arm.

"You mean God?"

"Yes," she said. "What happened with Randy?"

Hmmm. How to mention that the scumbag was in essence blackmailing me?

"First things first," I said. I shook her off when I spotted our cadmium orange first aid case on top of the crate where she'd dropped the hammer. What could I say? With Chica it was fiesta-hued equipment or nothing.

I opened the case and snagged my second homemade oatmeal raisin cookie of the day from the freezer bag kept endlessly filled by my mother. I bit off half of it. Oh dear Lord, the aphrodisiac of baked brown sugar, butter and flour rolled over my tongue. After a moment, I relaxed.

"Pitiful," Chica said, observing the chemical transformation. "And you whine of your grande booty."

Bubba's eyes were popping out of his head at the cookie smell.

"It's almost lunchtime," I squeaked. A little nausea never quelled my appetite for long. So I'm an oatmeal cookie junkie. So shoot me. Dastardly ex-husbands demand drastic measures.

Chica made off for the ladies' powder room with the dog.

As I munched, I inventoried our emergency supplies. One unsealed tin of bandages, a blue foam mini Carolina basketball, latex fingers sticking out of an opened the box of purple disposable gloves, waterproof mascara, a half-squeezed tube of antibiotic cream, burn ointment, baby wipes, cherry lip gloss, a new pack of Camel cigarettes with matches, two mini bottles of vodka (not my idea; it was Chica's, to test her self-control, she said), a Hollywood fashion police magazine and my latest journal, a small, leather-bound volume. I scribbled in journals when the mood struck and always kept one nearby. After confronting Randy, I felt the need for therapy and sugar, so I thumbed to the first entry, grabbed another cookie and read.

Thursday, January 12, 2006

I saw Honey Kimball today after more than a year's absence. When

I started seeing her in 1992, I told her I wanted to murder Randy. I was living in a world of controlled fury. Morning sickness, exams and Randy, who was like a wolf biting his leg off to get out of a trap. A marriage trap, according to him. Bastard. But Honey did her magic therapy and life moved on. She told me to write my thoughts in a journal, which I did, sporadically, even though I'd not been that good at the diary bit as an adolescent. And now I'm back. Probably not a good thing to go this long between mental health sessions. Honey still looks like her name, like she did 14 years ago. If you were to conjure up a Chapel Hill therapist, it would be Honey with her flowing honey-colored hair (dyed to match her name), honey-colored clothes, an anything-but-honey-tongued liberal Democrat.

"You OK now?" Chica asked, tearing me away from journal world by tilting my chin up to look into her eyes. "Always reading and writing in diaries. Waste of time. You think you escape, but it is no good escaping. You must face things. And see, now you look verde…green, green."

"Just reading about being pregnant," I said, stuffing the little book into a big pocket in my coveralls. I grabbed one of the mini bottles from the crate and waved it at Chica.

"We ought to get more real supplies in here. Didn't we have more of these?"

She sniffed at me and frowned.

"Just asking, don't get in a snit."

"I still ride the wagon, amiga, and it is very dry. Bubba is my witness."

"Sorry. I worry about…never mind. Besides, we're probably violating some kind of OSHA regulations with booze in our medical kit." Best to change the subject rather than be hit by a female Cuban missile crisis.

"Vodka is like medicine. You can sterilize wounds with it. And I do not give a damn about crappy army rules no more."

"OSHA isn't the army."

"So you say," she snapped.

"I thought you were in a hurry to get to your meeting."

"I will get there. No worries."

"Well, before you go, help me with this." I grabbed one end of the supply crate. "Let's move it. I reckon I've tripped over it a dozen times, and we don't need this stuff right now."

I threw the ball onto the ballroom floor. It was a toy to kick around during work breaks to relieve stress. Bubba wriggled out of Chica's arms and went after it as we dragged the crate through one of the sets of French doors that rimmed the room. We settled it on the hall floor near the staff offices, ladies' restroom and men's locker room.

"Now you tell me what Randy said before I go," said Chica, as we wandered back into the ballroom.

"He's screwing me again," I said, "but not literally."

"And what is new of this behavior?"

Loud measured footsteps echoed behind us as all six-foot six-inches of the club's general manager, Malcolm Jones, headed our way, stooping and clapping his big hands like a basketball player urging on his team, which is what he'd been twenty years ago at Duke. I'd long forgiven him for that mistake because he'd sat on the bench most of the time anyway.

"Ladies, ladies, how goes it?" He scrutinized the bucket and rags beside the one panel I'd started. He scanned the eleven others and gazed heavenward at the unfinished cherubs and untouched medallions. His sharp eyes narrowed under heavy brows.

Typically, gold-leafing was applied to medallions before installation. However, when he hired us, Malcolm explained that he'd been out of town and Long Johnson, the club's assistant manager, had not understood that process. So, the installers attached the medallions to the ceiling and rehung the chandeliers. According to my father, Malcolm was grateful to find a company that would do the gilding despite the awkward access.

"I'm kinda slow out of the gate today, Malcolm." I spoke through my teeth like a ventriloquist. I faked a smile, but he didn't seem to notice.

"You've been here for hours." He checked his gold Rolex watch. He glanced over at Bubba shredding the ball. "And you'd better get that dog out of here. Hermann is scared to death of them. Especially yappy ones that bite."

"He has very small teeth," said Chica. "Makes very small holes only."

"Malcolm is right," I said. "Pilar told me her dad is terrified of dogs and won't let her have one."

"So, we gonna get it done around here?" asked Malcolm, looking at his watch and sighing.

"Sorry, mea culpa. I got Bridget up the ladder, but it is not working." Chica gazed up at him like a tourist at Mount Rushmore. She excelled at this ass-kissing thing, which she said she'd learned from her Cuban granny who'd beguiled Castro into letting some of her family emigrate to the United States.

"It is in her cabeza. I am doctoring her there." She tapped her temple.

Malcolm folded his arms, rolled his eyes over at me. "Should I see if Hermann is available to help this morning? After the dog is gone, I mean? I'm not sure what he could do. Heavy lifting, basic painting? He'll be gone for the day soon, though. Doctor's appointment."

"We're fine."

"You will be able to handle all this, right, missy?"

Missy? He'd once called me Miss O'Brien when etiquette demanded that the staff address members and their families as Miss, Mister or Missus So-and-So. Of course, my finances and job description precluded my own membership these days. My father had wrangled this job for me due to his position on the club's board of directors. At first, I was annoyed at the parental interference.

"I wish you'd let me get my own clients, Daddy," I'd said three weeks earlier in the immaculate designer kitchen of the perfect blue Victorian house on Rosemary Street where I grew up.

Daddy had been near the sink holding Bubba as Mother sat at the island, pursing her lips and pretending to read the paper as we waited for Dare to come home from school. For the dozenth time since returning from Italy, I told them I was there to persuade Dare to come back and live with me in Chica's house. She'd temporarily moved in with my parents while I was out of the country. Then her father, Marcus, had died and, combined with her anger at me for what she termed as "your desertion," she had refused to return home with me.

So, that day I'd brought over Bubba as bait because I knew Dare missed him. My mother highly disapproved of Dare leaving her custody because she thought my lifestyle was now somewhat suspect and Dare needed proper looking after.

I paced in the kitchen and occasionally glanced out the window.

"Grrrrrr," Bubba growled deep in his throat, wriggling in my father's arms.

Daddy peered at the pointy mug as he held him up over his head.

"Feisty little imp, isn't he?" he said, grinning.

"Maybe you think I can't handle things myself," I said as I snatched Bubba and put him on the floor. "But I'm thirty-six years old, for heaven's sake."

Daddy's smile caved in on itself. He fumbled in the pocket of his worn gray cardigan and then, mumbling something about preparing an Anglo-Saxon quiz, shuffled from the room.

Shit. Why'd I do that? I adore the man. Shit.

"Bridget Eve O'Brien, ever since your very first cry in the hospital, your father has lived and breathed to smooth your path," my mother said. "As he has done for Dare." She drummed the granite countertop with flawless buffed nails, an eyebrow raised as she studied my stained, ragged cuticles.

I dropped my hands into my lap and waited for the *coup de grâce.*

"You owe him something after breaking his heart. Your father almost starved to death from grief after you hightailed it to Italy and abandoned us all."

No one could say she wasn't dramatic. During her senior year at Carolina, my mother, the former Miss Sarah Landry Selwyn, played a Valkyrie-like storm goddess in a mindless skit for sorority rush. Daddy still kept a photo of her from that night on his desk. In the snapshot, she is hurling thunderbolts, her lips in a patrician snarl and slender white arms akimbo.

Perfect casting, and she was still at it.

When Daddy reentered the kitchen with a pasted-on smile, I all but fell at his feet to thank him for the job he'd gotten for me. We settled for a hug.

"I only want what's best for you, sugar," he said, patting my head.

So, three weeks later, and for Daddy's sake, I sucked in the smart-assed retort I would've given Malcolm in the ballroom.

"My fault, not Chica's," I said to him. "That no-good ex of mine showed up out of the blue and …"

"Randy's here?" Malcolm's booming voice echoed in the ballroom. "Where?"

But he didn't wait to find out. He did a 180-degree

basketball pivot and marched toward his office, kicking the blue foam basketball out of his way.

"What's that's about?" I muttered.

"No more laddering for you, amiga. I might finish it later." Chica hitched her bag on her shoulder. "It is not your business when Malcolm is pissed off."

I nodded as if I appreciated this wisdom and would take her advice. Always the skeptic, she frowned at my feigned cooperation. I squeezed into yet another pair of latex gloves and hefted a can of semi-gloss called "Black as Pitch." I shimmied and shook the can like a good little worker, set it on a drop cloth and pried the lid off with a metal opener.

After I gave her a rubbery finger wave and toothy grin, Chica compressed her lips and left, with Bubba still sniffing for oatmeal raisin cookie.

I counted to one hundred by fives, grabbed the deadblow hammer and tamped the lid back onto the paint can. Jogging to the door, I peeked out as Chica spun in the gravel and the Faux Finish logo vanished in a cloud of dust.

A man cleared his throat behind me, and I turned with the hammer raised.

Hermann backed off and raised his hands in mock terror, a plastic trash bag in one hand.

We both laughed.

"Lordy, Hermann, I almost nailed you."

"Sorry, miss," he said. "Give you a fright, me and this bin bag? I'm just off to the shops and the doctor. Do you or Miss Chica need anything before I leave?"

According to Pilar, her father hailed from Argentina but had lived in London and learned English from a Church of England vicar. His crisp accent was flavored with a tiny bit of Latin rounding out of certain words.

"No, you go on. We're good. Thanks for asking."

After he left, I strolled toward the ladies' powder room,

which, coincidentally, was one door down from Malcolm's office.

Loud angry voices erupted into the corridor.

Edging past the empty receptionist's office, I pressed against the wall next to Malcolm's open door.

"I know what you've been doing," Randy snarled. "I want in on the action."

For a long minute, it sounded like someone was violently stacking papers on a desk. A couple of drawers slammed.

"What're you talking about?" Malcolm demanded in a deep rumble and Darth Vader sucking-in of his breath.

"Playing games, Malcolm?" Randy said in his light but cutting conversational style. "And speaking of games, did I mention that I played golf with Fred Scaley down at Myrtle Beach? You know, Scaley Seafood Suppliers?"

"Why should I care?"

"You find out a lot about a person at the nineteenth hole over a couple brewskis. About how his business operates. How he gets contracts."

Malcolm choked on whatever he'd been about to say. Poor guy. Randy seemed to have him by the short curlies. For several seconds, it sounded like Malcolm might strangle.

"Now I get it," Malcolm whispered fiercely when his throat cleared. "You…you probably don't even work for a living. You blackmail hard-working people instead. I'd bet my season basketball tickets that you don't pay enough tax on your income. I've a mind to make an anonymous call to the I.R.S."

"You're all hot air, man." Randy said.

I slid sideways toward the powder room door.

"Who'd want Duke season tickets anyway, except to see Carolina play them twice?" Randy added. "So, listen up. You might line your pockets while mine are empty, but that might need some fixing."

"Unbelievable how dense you are," Malcolm said. "I don't suppose you know the concept of gratitude either. It was me who talked the board into not blackballing your membership. Not Richard O'Brien's favorite, are you? Not to mention that I also, shall we say, handle your dues. I never took you for such a greedy, no-class bastard, Randy."

Ouch.

"Mister La Russo to you," Randy said. "Besides, I just handed you my dues check so I don't know what you're talking about. And here's something to chew on. Why do you think you've been here in this position all these years? Can you say 'token' in one of society's liberal lily-white bastions?"

Malcolm sputtered. "We have staff and members of all races at Magnolia Blossom."

"More tokens. You might have a Duke M.B.A.," Randy said dead cold, "but you're still Uncle Tom."

Yikes.

Heat flooded my face, as did horror at Randy, who had never been racist, in fact just the opposite when we were younger. Guess he felt the need to really stick it to Malcolm.

I backpedaled into the powder room and smack into my mother.

***

"Bridget!"

"What're you doing here?" we both cried simultaneously.

"I didn't see your name on the sign-in sheet," I said.

"No one ever signs that thing," she replied.

"So I've heard." I rolled my eyes.

Mother gave me the head-to-toe once-over and winced at the orange hammer. "I forgot. You're staff now."

"Am not."

"Sit here, and put that thing down. You look like a construction worker." She sat on the chintz sofa and patted the cushion as I dropped the hammer on the floor next to the wall.

"Don't pout," she said. "It's most unbecoming. I can't help but…. I'm just glad your Nana Blanche isn't here to see this. And to see you working with that chicken woman. Does she even have a green card?"

I flung myself down hard on the sofa, on purpose, to make Mother bounce.

"D'you hear yourself? And you too, Nana Blanche, wherever you are," I called toward the ceiling. "I'm a business woman, not the club toilet scrubber. And her nickname is Chica. Her real name is Isabella, and her family has been in this country for decades."

"Quibbling over semantics," she said, putting the finishing touches on that topic.

There was no future in staying angry with my mother. Better to go for a slam dunk.

"My, my," I remarked, fingering her black cashmere hoodie. "Prada or Dolce & Gabanna?"

She blushed for probably the third time in her whole life.

"I just had a session with my personal trainer. Mature women needn't look tacky, you know."

She plucked at my coveralls and shuddered.

"Or immature women, for that matter."

With that dig, she negated my two points with a three-pointer from beyond the arc.

"There's no danger of tacky where you're concerned," I said.

She looked me in the eye. For once, I wasn't sarcastic.

I snuck a look at the slim straightness that Dare had inherited, and then examined my thighs encased like sausages in my uniform. Which Neanderthal ancestress had passed these legs down to me?

Mother and I sat in polite silence.

"I've got three tables of bridge at two," she finally said, stood up and ended another intimate mother-daughter conversation.

As we walked toward Mother's car, I was relieved not to run into either Malcolm or Randy after their office shootout. However, I forgot about them when I saw Marla Ann Furr bubble up from the red Lexus roadster I'd seen earlier in the day. She wriggled her pencil skirt down and yanked her tight sweater left and right to emphasize some massive new bodaciousness. In college, she'd been as flat as a fritter.

"Haven't seen you for ages, dear," said Mother, doing the ventriloquist thing through a smile – at least I came by this skill honestly. "How are you keeping?"

"Doin' fine, Miz O'Brien. Just fine." Marla Ann gave me the fish eye despite a pseudo-embrace and air kisses. "You back in town for good, Bridget?" She took in my stained coverall and braids. "You workin' here?"

"Sure as hell am and lovin' it." When necessary, I could yee-haw as well as the next rebel.

"Real estate business must be booming," Mother said, patting the hood of Marla Ann's convertible while examining the E-sized ta-tas.

Hailing from Bunn, North Carolina, Marla Ann drove the elementary school activity bus until, by the age of nineteen, she'd married and buried a wealthy pickle magnate. Once rid of Old Dill, as she called him, she dyed her dishwater brown hair black and attended business school at Carolina. She didn't graduate, but it wasn't necessary. Daddy said that, according to one of her bewitched professors, she could sell, sell, sell with the best of them.

"Gotta go jiggle this on the treadmill again." She slapped her tush with a Louis Vuitton duffle bag. "I came earlier but didn't get it done then. "Had to turn right around for an unscheduled client."

Show-off.

"Y'all didn't see Miz Ruffin in the club, did you?" she asked.

"Muffin?" Mother asked.

"Yes, ma'am. Mike Ruffin's arm candy strumpet. I mean, his wife." Marla Ann giggled and gouged my ribs with an elbow.

"She and Mike are hitting practice balls on the driving range," Mother said.

We all looked beyond the tennis courts to where a man stood behind a curvy redhead with his arms around her, guiding her golf club. Reminded me of Kevin Costner and Rene Russo in *Tin Cup*.

"From what I've seen, she has a lovely swing," Mother said.

"Some folks think so." Marla Ann wrinkled her nose as Botox fought for dominance on her forehead.

My mother's eyebrows rose.

"It's nothin'," Marla Ann added. "Can't stand the dried-up bitch, is all. Pardon my cussin', ma'am."

"I've heard it before," Mother said, unflappable as usual.

"I reckon so. Well, see y'all. Let's do lunch, Bridget."

For heaven's sake, did people still say that with a straight face?

"Old Mr. Ruffin remarried?" I asked as Mother and I approached her light blue Volvo wagon.

"Afraid so. She's an infant, of course. In her twenties," Mother said. "Barely potty trained. I always knew that man did his thinking from below the belt."

A reply seemed unnecessary.

Mother zapped her car lock with the key thingy, and I opened the door for her.

"I don't think Marla Ann was thrilled to see me," I said.

Mother swung her legs in a graceful arc under the steering wheel. When I slammed the door, she eyed me as if I'd done it on purpose. Which I had. She hated slamming doors. I smiled innocently though.

"Not surprising." Mother said. "What with her shacking up with Randy until a couple of weeks ago."

"Really?"

"She probably thinks you might want him back."

"No worries from me there," I said. "What happened to them anyway?"

"I bumped into Grace at Narcissus Nails before she left for that ghastly trip to the Daytona 500. She got long acrylic talons painted flamingo pink with little palm trees. Her toes were aqua or some such thing. Imagine. It's easy to understand Randy's wild streak. My mother always said blood will tell. Anyway, Grace said he broke up with Marla Ann and the silly girl reverted to type. Went all to pieces and trashy in public, Grace said. Calling, crying and threatening to kill herself or both of them."

"Randy can bring out the worst in a person sometimes," I said, recalling my parting words to him that morning.

"By the way, Dare might walk over to the ladies' exercise room after she and Ellie play tennis at the park," she said. "I'd really rather she didn't come here though, with Randy running loose. Did you know he was here today?"

"Uh, no, I didn't," I lied. "Wait a minute. Dare's not in school?"

"Watch that tone, Bridget. You're still my child." Mother clicked the seatbelt and pulled on Jackie-O sunglasses. "Dare felt poorly this morning. That time of the month, you know."

"No, I don't know. How would I when she lives with you?" I struggled to keep my voice down. "You know how bitchy she's been lately. Looks like the bride of Beetlejuice most of the time. She pulls the wool over your eyes. Sick enough to stay home from school but well enough for tennis? She should be with me. I'm her mother. As for my tone, I'm a grown…"

"You should have thought of that before you flew halfway around the world to feed grapes to your Roman gladiator."

"Never forgive me for that, will you?" Full rant now, and in public.

Mother peeked in the rearview mirror and fluffed her smooth flaxen pageboy – a human decompression chamber in the flesh. I itched to jump up and down in the parking lot but that would only have reinforced her notion of my immaturity.

"She gets away with some things," my mother admitted. "But sometimes one must give a little here to get something there."

I blinked. She didn't "give" an inch when she raised me.

"Must run. Don't you have a lot of work to do, dear? All those panels."

Although usually a sedate driver, she peeled out of the parking lot.

***

As it turned out, Chica returned from her A.A. meeting, but Dare never showed up at the club that afternoon. Chica and I worked uninterrupted for a while. I hummed to the soundtrack of *Amadeus* on my iPod after Chica left for the second time to tend to our dogs. Besides Bubba, there was Big Foot, Chica's galumphing Samoyed. As unlikely as it seemed, the gentle white giant and Bubba, the tiny brown terrorist, got along like Scooby-Doo and Scrappy-Doo. Because of this and because Dare and Bubba were soul mates, I resisted shopping the wiener schnitzel to the dog catchers who constantly cruised the streets in an ominous animal control truck.

After finally finishing a thin primer coat on all of the panels, I began the more serious business of taking a dry panel to completion. All of the final steps required concentration and rapid handling. Marbleizing developed in stages, with crucial timing. Letting a layer dry, or not, could mean starting over from scratch.

A little more than halfway through, I reached a point where some veining needed to set. Feeling cramped and achy, I changed the play list on my iPod from the eighteenth century to random shuffle play. "Safety Dance" by Men Without Hats cranked up and a shot of adrenaline rushed through me. Besides being a favorite song of mine back in what Dare called the black days before cell phones, its beat demanded arm and leg movement. I imitated the Maypole bobbing and weaving of the characters in the 1980s Renaissance-themed music video. I ended by lofting the blue foam basketball toward the portrait of an English dandy on a nearby wall. For heaven's sake, an air ball. I dropped to the floor puffing when the song ended.

Ah, catharsis.

Resuming my task, I set the iPod aside to rest my eardrums.

Two aching shoulder blades and one stiff neck later, I stuck the turkey quill in my hair, paint and all, and sat back on my heels to admire the completed panel in the evening stillness and muted light.

As I closed my eyes savoring the quiet, a far door slammed. Pounding feet preceded a zooming blur in the corridor. I rolled onto my rear end, and my heartbeat kicked into alarm mode, a primordial reaction probably absorbed *in utero*.

"One doesn't slam doors, Bridget, unless there is a dire emergency," Mother had said for the umpteenth time after I'd done just that in the pro shop after a miserable and sweaty nine holes of junior golf. "It's very low class and shows bad sportsmanship. Especially in public. And definitely not here."

At Magnolia Blossom Country Club, portals clicked softly shut or, if they were double doors, came together like praying hands accompanied by the whoosh of the proper hydraulic mechanism.

Unless something was wrong.

"Chica?" I hollered even though Mother ranked hollering a notch above slamming in the ill-bred behaviors category.

Duh. Chica was gone. I massaged a shoulder blade. Doors slammed all the time, right? Quiet reasserted itself, and I turned back to the panel.

Not quite happy with the veins I'd applied with the turkey feather, I rubbed a badger brush over them to give a bit more depth and then closed my eyes, which probably showed more visible veins than the panel. As good luck would have it though, the batch of "Curdled Cream White" glaze mix was about gone.

I plucked the feather from my hair, cleaned it and the brush and then looked for the dead-blow hammer. Not finding it on the floor, I schlepped to the hall to check the crate. I always felt like a bona fide professional, albeit a blue-collar one, when I hammered lids back onto paint cans. Don't know why.

No hammer in the crate. I could've sworn that was where I last saw it. I scanned the ballroom with no luck. Did Chica move it? Back I went to the paint can. Kneeling before the panel, I banged the lid shut with my fist.

Another door slammed in the distance.

Oh boy. Two slams. Someone probably running late? I shook my head to clear my anxiety. No go. My heart rate ratcheted up, so I took a couple of deep breaths. Before I'd left him harvesting grapes in his family's Chianti vineyard, Sandro used to say I stressed out too much about trivialities. So, he taught me, among other things, the benefits of deep breathing.

I glanced at my watch. Good Lord, seven already? I'd promised Daddy to watch the Carolina-Maryland game that he'd recorded yesterday. I didn't tell him that I'd seen the game already. He'd missed it because Mother had invited guests for lunch without checking the basketball schedule. Whatever was she thinking? Poor Daddy. Only a Southern gentleman would tolerate a non-Atlantic-Coast-Conference couple from his wife's garden club while his beloved Tar Heels played round ball. That Carolina gave the Terrapins hell, winning 81-57, consoled him somewhat. He so loved to rattle off play-by-play to his loving family. In Chapel Hill, watching Tar Heel basketball constituted a sacred ritual. Two kinds of people lived in this town – fans and the mutants who didn't care about the games. An earlier message from Mother on my dying cell stated we would all watch the game together. No mutants in my family. I had to get over there.

Something or someone screamed.

I bolted upright and smeared a ruinous white blob on the panel with my hand. So much for my lovely marbleizing.

Breathing like a hound snuffling for fox, I ran in circles seeking the hammer. No luck. My cell phone. I slapped my coveralls with paint-smeared hands, finally ripping a seam as I yanked it from some ill-contrived pocket. I mashed buttons and held it up in the air. Dead. I never remembered to charge the little mutha. Shit. For a reason only my therapist could've interpreted, I snatched the turkey feather and darted through the ballroom. I stopped in the hall underneath a dimly lit chandelier and tried to calm my ragged breaths.

"Please no asthma," I whispered.

Quiet didn't seem so good now.

To the right, the closed door to the men's locker room looked innocent enough. Just an ordinary white-paneled door.

Oh God, is it breathing?

I stamped my foot. No more Stephen King books for you, Bridget.

Inhale, exhale.

I sure could've used my inhaler. I tiptoed to the door and knocked timidly.

"Malcolm? Is that you? Malcolm?"

No one could have heard my warble. Not that anyone was around to do so. Right?

Why am I alone?

Didn't a security guard patrol the building and grounds at night?

I glanced at the window down the corridor. God, so dark outside.

Make noise. Don't show fear.

I pounded louder. I nudged the door open a crack. I might've been scared to death but, after all, this was the men's locker room and I'd been brought up a lady.

"Not funny!" I yelled through the slit into the darkened interior. "If you're trying to scare me, congratulations! But I'm warning you. I'm off my Prozac. It could get ugly."

No answer.

Scrabbling with shaking fingers on the inside wall, I found the light switch and flipped it up. Why'd I do that? I didn't really want to see. I avoided haunted houses at Halloween because I hated sudden scares.

I insinuated myself through the door and crept down the short hallway. I'd never been in here, but I reckoned it might be configured like the women's exercise area with the steam room and showers beyond the equipment room.

I took two-and-a-half more steps, stopping with my left foot in midair as I remembered those scary movies about stupid girls who investigate a suspicious noise only to be discovered chopped up like stew beef the next day.

I put my left foot down.

The key word was stupid.

Am I stupid?

Had I sniffed too much craft glue? Inhaled too much paint thinner? Smoked too much wacky tobaccy under the Tuscan moon?

Stiffening my spine, I marched past the weight machines in a fake take-no-prisoners strut. Thankfully, no naked codgers with dangling doo-lollies quivered nearby.

I rounded a corner where the carpet ended and bleached tile floor began. It was darker in here. The silence boded ill in the eucalyptus-infused white-out. Someone had left the steam room door open. I peered through the mist.

On the tile, the handle of my dead-blow hammer glowed orange, the head of its non-marring composite surface wrapped in a white towel with stains the color of burnt sienna.

I continued onward because apparently I was stupid. I stumbled blindly against a large object on the slippery floor, ramming my head against the glass of the open steam room door. As I flailed to right myself, I grabbed wet, hairy skin.

I should have died of fright, but I swallowed hard several times and put off the vertigo lurking behind my eyes.

A man lay on his back halfway out of the steam room with a bath towel knotted around his waist. His body propped the door open.

I glanced back at the towel stains, now appearing more red than brown. Heart thudding into overdrive, I knelt beside the man and waved away the steam.

Randy's once-brilliant dark eyes were cloudy, his thick dark hair wet and swept back off a pale lifeless forehead. I smoothed his hair and drew back bloody fingers.

"No," I moaned, "I didn't mean what I said."

Numbness enshrouded me with the mist. A wave of nostalgic love made me close Randy's eyelids. I grabbed his hand, felt the pruned fingers.

"Because I could not stop for Death, he kindly stopped

for me," I whispered and brushed his cheek with my turkey feather like a blessing. "Damn you, Randy."

I closed my eyes remembering.

We'd giggled so many times in freshman English over this first line of Dickinson's poem about death that the professor assigned extra homework. Later, we'd recited Miss Emily's clipped metaphors, with Randy bombastic and me sweetly defensive, and ridiculed the eccentric spinster who'd saved her letters to the world for posterity. Who at that age could understand her?

It was Frost who had obsessed Randy. Even though the poet wasn't on the syllabus, Randy had begged to study his work in class. When the professor told him to do it on his own time, Randy had gone straight to the student store and bought a small paperback of Frost's poems, which had worn itself ragged in his book bag for the next four years.

It was a season of prowling the leafy alleys of the arboretum and the woods around campus, reciting Frost's crisp yet enigmatic stanzas. Still innocent of life's diverging paths, we'd celebrated "Bob F." (as Randy called him) and speculated on the roads he'd taken.

For the halcyon days, I bowed my head. Then I stood on wobbly legs and stumbled from the locker room.

Get out, Bridget. You need air.

Although sirens wailed outside and engines roared as if the vehicles they heralded would crash through the building, I never hesitated. I flung the doors open and blinked into a flashing kaleidoscope of colored lights from approaching police cruisers, unmarked cars, anonymous-looking vans, an emergency medical services vehicle and a sky-blue fire truck.

Who called them?

Davey McKenzie jumped out of his Jeep. The family lawyer here already? He removed a Tar Heel ball cap and ran his fingers through his hair before pulling it back on and hurrying over to a police panda car. He opened the door as Daddy unfolded himself from the back seat. They shook hands briefly. A shapely, uniformed policewoman hurried over to them. Davey introduced her to Daddy. Eventually, all three of them looked my way. My head felt like a helium balloon, my neck a useless string. I forgot to be sad as a spurt of anger shot through me.

Well, howdy, a party I didn't know about?

"What the hell!" I shouted through the citrus-scented night air, through the echo of dying sirens, car doors closing and boots clumping on pavement.

Everyone stared at me – a wild-eyed woman in braids, smudged with paint and clutching a striped turkey feather. Pippi Longstocking all grown up.

Beyond the chaos, my precious Carolina-blue van sprayed gravel as Chica plowed up the tree-lined drive. Big Foot took up the entire passenger seat, his huge polar bear head looking almost human through the windshield.

A forty-something man in a battered trench coat exited the passenger side of a dark sedan. He spoke first to the policewoman and then to Davey and my father before heading into the club with other police officers and crime scene investigators in white overalls.

Daddy stooped to look into the black-and-white. When he straightened up, he had my daughter by the hand. My beautiful troubled thirteen-year-old daughter.

And Randy's.

Mercifully, everything went black just as I was about to scream the F-word in all its grammatical variations, which would, no doubt, have mortified Mother had she been there to hear it.

***

Mmmmmm. That special late afternoon Italian sunlight

penetrated my closed eyelids. Sandro, that horny devil, nuzzled my ear.

Phew! He needed a bath.

"She's coming around," a male voice shouted.

"Not so loud, carissimo," I murmured, all warm and cozy, grateful to be waking from a nightmare in Alessandro's arms.

"Think she's in shock, Miss Jones?" quavered someone who sounded like Daddy.

Daddy in Italy? Miss Jones?

Sandro licked in a frenzy now, nibbled my ear and … Ouch. He bit me.

I opened my eyes and came nose to snout with Bubba.

"Mom!" cried Dare. She wriggled past Chica and someone who was either a fireman or the front man for the Village People. Dare wrestled one of my braids from Bubba's teeth. "You okay, Mom?"

Bless her, she looked so worried. I smiled at the spiked burgundy-streaked hair. Her dark eyes so like…so like….

Randy's.

I pulled the blanket over my head and howled.

"Cry, amiga. Is good for you," Chica murmured through the blanket.

"Why's she crying, Granddad?" Dare demanded in a strident tone I'd never heard her use with him. "She didn't do anything."

"Dare, honey," said my father as I peeked over the edge of the blanket. He tried to smile as he loomed above me, wringing his hands. He pulled Dare up by the shoulders. "She'll be fine," he said. "We have to go now."

After handing Bubba to Chica, Daddy and Dare headed to the police car.

"Wait," I cried. "Randy's inside. He's…."

I tried to scramble to my feet but got tangled up in helping hands and the fire department blanket.

"We know," Chica said.

"Someone needs to tell her about Dare," Davey said to Chica.

"Tell me what?" I shouted.

Everyone looked at me, but no one answered. I might as well have been a turnip.

Bunch of tongue-tied morons.

"Tell me what?" I struggled to my feet as Chica followed my father and daughter to the police car.

The man in the trench coat reappeared, holding up a police I.D. badge.

"Bridget O'Brien?" he asked, shoulders slumped. "I'm Lieutenant Hendricks."

"How'd this all happen so fast? Who called you?"

The lieutenant rubbed his reddened hands together, his breath blending in with the misty night. "I hate the cold," he said.

As if that mattered, for heaven's sake.

The policewoman came and stood beside Hendricks.

"Jennifer," Hendricks said, "I'd like you to meet Miz Bridget O'Brien. Miz O'Brien, Officer Jennifer Jones."

Slim. Smooth dark hair. About my age. Okay – younger.

"Please let me know if there is anything I can do for you," she said with the accent of a New Jersey mafia wife. I had visions of cannoli and cement overshoes.

In my crumpled, besmirched get-up, I gawped at her. She could've stepped out of a Brooks Brothers' police academy catalog, if one had existed. There was an awkward pause.

"Yes. Well. I'll make sure the press isn't trampling all over the crime scene." She turned to Davey. "Call me later," she said, with a hint of something. Yearning? She squeezed his arm before heading toward a restive herd of photographers on this side of the police tape.

Davey coughed in embarrassment as we all watched her swing through the crowd.

Her butt was smaller than mine. I didn't like her.

"Jennifer, uh, Officer Jones, is a fine gal for a Yankee," Hendricks said to Davey. "Mind you, call her if you need to, Miz O'Brien. In case you need to speak to a woman about anything."

"Oh, I will," I said, lying through clenched teeth. Was this a sexist comment? I was too befuddled to think it through.

Hermann and Long threaded their way through the crowd.

"Be right back," Hendricks said, heading toward them. He waved at an officer standing beside the fire truck and pulled his coat tight about him. He motioned Long and Hermann into the club.

"I didn't know you had a girlfriend," I said to Davey.

"Who says I do?" He sounded a bit testy as an engine started up nearby.

My father and Dare climbed into the back seat of Hendricks's car. The driver nodded at Daddy.

"Where are they going?" I started to move toward them. "I'm going, too."

"I've got to tell you something," Davey said. He dragged me a few feet away for privacy.

"What's Dare doing here?" I asked. "She shouldn't be here. That's her…um…in there, I mean, Randy's in there and …"

"You need to get a hold of yourself."

That had better not be pity in his eyes.

"I know, I know," I cried. "Looks bad for me, my hammer and all. But you know me. I put crickets outside when I find them in the bathtub. Even spiders. Granddaddy long legs. Tell them. I couldn't kill a thing. I swerve for road kill, much less a live animal. Listen, I can explain everything, well not really everything. Well, close except for … crap, wait, I need to make a list. You got a pen? I didn't do it, Davey. I just need to talk to them. It all started when Randy came in..." I gulped in night air and probably a bug or two what with all the blazing lights. "You don't know about Randy, but..."

"For God's sake, will you just shut up for a minute?" Davey shook me so that I wobbled like a rag doll. His blue eyes sparked in the artificial illumination.

I turned away, but he held tight.

"Damn," he said. "I'm sorry, Bridget. I didn't mean that. But sometimes you go on and on..." He released me.

"Yes?" I crossed my arms, planted my feet and met his stare. "Well?"

Davey and I shared a long history of ship-passing in the night. He'd carried a torch for me years ago when he was my father's teaching assistant. When I married Marcus, my art history professor, Davey dropped liberal arts for law school. We'd run back into each other working at a Habitat for Humanity house after my return from Italy.

"As your attorney, I'm advising you to be careful what you say."

"The right-to-remain silent thingy? The police are supposed to do that."

"Don't say more than necessary, is all I'm saying. Kind of."

Used to his annoying articulated speeches, I wondered at this uncharacteristic mumbo jumbo as I looked past him.

A big uniformed policeman crossed his arms over a massive chest and glared at Hall Hooper from *The Chapel Hill Chronicle.* Hooper appeared to argue with him and pointed at the club doors. Although I'd never met him, I'd seen his photo enough to recognize the lowlife. The more sensational a thing was, the better he liked it. The cavalry arrived in the form of Officer Jones, who tapped him on the shoulder.

Hooper gave her an appreciative smile. She had the magic touch, all right.

The crowd in the parking lot started thinning. The baby blue fire truck eased out of the jumble of vehicles and rolled down the drive like a chunk of sky on wheels. The EMS van backed up toward the front doors.

"Are you listening to me, Bridget? Dare called nine-one-one," Davey said.

"Dare?"

"There's no easy way for me to say this."

"Well, I can see that because you haven't said a thing," I broke his grip. "Never mind. Daddy will tell me."

Hendricks hurried out of the club.

"Miz O'Brien, reckon y'all should come down to the station for questioning," he said, puffing, as he reached us. "I'll be down there directly."

As if I had a choice.

"But what are my father and daughter doing in your car? You giving them a ride home?"

"Get on with it, pardner. Tell her." Hendricks said to Davey. "Y'all all need to follow us." The lieutenant climbed into the front passenger seat.

Chica opened Dare's door to let her hug Bubba.

I stumbled to the car and grasped it for support.

"Sugar, listen to me. Listen," Daddy said, opening the door on his side. "Just come down to the station." He looked ten years older than the last time I'd seen him.

"Punkin?" I leaned over Daddy and grabbed Dare's arm.

She wore black gloves with cut-out fingers. My very own goth drama queen.

The driver started the car.

"I did it, Mom." Dare's brown eyes ringed with black eyeliner bored through my skull as I stared at the brownish stains on her arm. "But I don't want to talk about it, so don't wig out."

I let go of her and backed off. Daddy closed the door and loved me with his eyes. The car pulled slowly away.

Davey kept me upright.

"Let's go," he said as Chica grabbed my other arm. Bubba, squashed in the middle, licked my hand but then looked up with beady eyes as if deciding whether to nip out a chunk of flesh.

I finally found my strength and pushed Davey toward his Jeep.

"Go, go, hurry. Stay with Dare."

"I'm supposed to bring you with me."

"I'm coming, for God's sake. I'm fine. Chica'll bring me." But I needed to talk privately with her first. "We'll catch you up. Go on."

He jumped in his vehicle and roared off. Officer Jones watched him leave, and I watched her watching him.

"She is boring, amiga. Not to worry."

I shook my head at Chica because, after all, what did such things matter when my daughter was in such trouble?

"Don't know what you mean," ashamed that I'd let my focus shift to trivial matters. I snatched the weenie dog from her. "Come on, Bubba. Let's go get Dare out of this."

We ran to the van. Chica gunned it even though cops were still thick on the ground. We barreled out of the parking lot and down the road amid Bubba's yips and Big Foot's woofs.

"You flash those dangerous eyes, amiga," Chica yelled over the uproar. "Hush, doggies." They ceased their crooning. Amazing how she could do that.

"Never mind my eyes," I said. "I've got to get organized." I pulled my journal out of my pocket and tore out a blank page. "Got something to write with?"

"You make a list now? Jesus Maria." She dug a pen out of her bag and tossed it over.

"If I get home tonight, assuming I'm not arrested or lethally injected, I'll need your help."

I scribbled on the paper and then stuffed it and my journal into her bag just as the van began to cough and stutter. About a mile from the police station, the vehicle gasped to a halt. Chica twisted the key in the ignition and dropped her head on the steering wheel.

Out of gas. Incredible. We sat perfectly still.

"Didn't I tell you?" she wailed. "Mercury is almost retrograde and life goes to…."

"Shit. You're right," I said. "I'm leaving it with you. Read that list. See you later at home."

I jumped from the van onto the road and, following Alessandro's advice, sucked in a couple of deep breaths. For one of the few times in my life, I ran without a thought for my asthma or bum knees.

Three

Just as I reached for the knob, Daddy burst through the front door of the police station and knocked me on my butt.

"Oh, sweet Jesus," he said, helping me up and hugging me so hard I couldn't breathe. He dragged me inside to a vinyl sofa in the reception area and tried to make me sit.

"Daddy, stop it!" I skipped out of his persistent reach.

His arms dropped to his sides, a dazed look in his eyes.

"So, what do we do, where do we go?" I said, appealing to his take-charge side. "I've never been in a police station before."

The interior was clean though nondescript. Dun-colored flooring and white paint completed the design statement – no glitzy glass walls like its television counterpart *C.S.I.: Miami* or messy squad room like *Law & Order*.

"I'll find the lieutenant," Daddy said, "but first I need to talk to you."

"Where's Dare? What did she mean she did it? Ridiculous. She's just a baby."

"Do you know who did it?" My father sounded like the voice of God giving Moses the skinny on the Ten Commandments.

Sheesh, he got back to being the dad pretty fast, which

was a relief. But I bristled at his subtext and was glad I didn't have to lie to him. I'm much better at lying to strangers.

"No, Daddy. No way. It wasn't me."

His blue-gray eyes x-rayed my soul for several seconds before he clutched me in another stranglehold.

"Thank the Lord. I didn't think so."

"You know me better than that. I'm harmless," I mumbled into his front breast pocket. I pushed him away. "But Dare didn't do this either. A kid like her? Besides, Randy is… was… her..."

Daddy's eyes searched mine for several seconds.

"Hendricks," he muttered, "…find him." He began to pace in the corridor. Up and back. Around the corner.

My father circumnavigated with stress, be it good or bad. During the final game of the 2005 NCAA basketball tournament a year earlier, he'd worn a path in the den carpet before Carolina finally won. Must be how he stayed so thin.

Deciding to let him deal with this situation the best way he could, I hurried to the reception window. A policewoman punched buttons and jiggled the earpiece of a complicated telephone system. I banged on the glass. She slid the pane open and raised a stubby index finger for me to wait.

"Yes?" she asked when free. If frowns are a gauge, she was a tad annoyed. She disconnected from one call and another came through. She raised her eyebrows at me and mouthed, "Can I help you?"

"Where's my daughter? Dare Benedetto?"

The woman stuck that blasted finger up again and slid the glass closed in order to communicate with everyone except me.

Daddy reappeared.

"They're about to interrogate her," he said. "Don't worry. I'll be in there as a legal guardian. Davey's there. And a woman intake counselor, too," he said, hollow-voiced, as if he didn't know what he was saying.

"Intake? As in taking her in somewhere? Where are they? I'm going in there, too. She doesn't know anything but her iPod and MTV. Intake? Shit."

"The lady has a nice face. She knows what she's doing."

For heaven's sake. My parents sometimes latched onto the weirdest criteria for making their decisions.

"Dare doesn't want you in there, sugar." He looked at the floor.

"Bullshit. She's a minor child. Never mind, I'll find her myself."

Daddy assumed his Abe Lincoln expression and tsk-tsked at my language. Courtly manners still thrived in his post-World-War-II generation.

I flew down the hall, rounded a corner and collided with a young policeman escorting a grungy, stringy-haired man who looked familiar.

"Sorry," I said to the officer. "But can you point me to the interrogation room. My daughter…"

"You can't go in there, ma'am," he said.

Jeez, was I getting that old? Bad enough that teenaged bag boys called me "ma'am." Obviously, he was clueless. He didn't look much older than Dare.

He stepped around me and continued on with his charge, who grinned with brown teeth while trailing an odor of tobacco and rancid sweat.

"You the lady doin' the paintin' at the club?" he called over his shoulder.

Now I recognized him: the man with the weed whacker. "Virgil?"

"Excuse me, ma'am," the policeman said. "We need to get on." He gave Virgil a shove.

"Yeah, yeah," Virgil said. "Easy on the jacket there. I ain't goin' nowhere, and I ain't done nothin'." They disappeared down another corridor.

Daddy put his arm around my shoulders.

"Bridget, listen to me. Davey said that thirteen- to sixteen-year-olds have the right to waive the presence of a parent or guardian during questioning, but he's convinced her to let me sit in there. They're waiting for me. That's where I'll be."

"I know I made you her legal guardian, but I'm her mother."

"You could insist on being in there, but she's kicking up a fuss about it, stubborn as a mule. It would be counterproductive. Just let me do it." His gentleness overpowered me, and I knew she couldn't be in better hands, but …

"Stupidest thing I've ever heard of," I muttered overwhelmed by all the authoritarian obstruction and because I was "minding" my daddy.

I trudged back to reception and onto the couch for what seemed like forever.

"Surely no one thinks that a skinny little girl like Dare could…." I said aloud. "Freaking unbelievable, how the hell anyone could think that…What has gotten into everybody?"

Speaking of the infernal regions, epithets uttered in evangelical rhythm whooshed in on a wave of cold air from the front door. A silver-haired geezer, handcuffed and bedraggled in a stained powder blue polyester suit, preceded a middle-aged officer into the station.

"Where there is no vision, the people perish," the old gentleman cried, quoting from Proverbs. The orator was Preacher Bobby Bullard, better known as "Pit" Bullard, a self-ordained itinerant spreader of the Word. On weekends, Pit praised the Lord in The Holy Prophet's Pentecostal Rectification Assembly, a converted doublewide off of Highway 54 outside of Carrboro. On weekdays, he was one of several preachers who ranted righteously in the campus Pit, a sunken brick-paved gathering place located outside of the Student Store. Hence the nickname. Pit Bullard distributed his religious tracts, designing them to look like ransom notes because he claimed to be "kidnapping souls for the Lord." My daddy and Pit were friends, and Daddy often bought lunch for Pit at the Carolina Coffee Shop on Franklin Street. My mother wasn't too crazy about this, but Daddy said Pit was a blast of fresh air on campus.

"Yeah, yeah, old man," the officer said with a sigh. "You say the Lord called you to provide underage kids with fake I.D.s?"

"Better me than the drug-infested criminal element or the Communists on this campus," Pit said with dignity. "Kids'll get likkered up no matter what."

"You may be onto something there, Pit. But you forgot to mention illegal aliens."

"I forgive you, Sergeant…" he squinted at the officers nameplate,"… Justice, is it? ... for your evil thoughts. Do not let your name be an oxymoron, Sergeant Justice. Remember what our Lord said to the criminal on Calvary Hill, 'I assure you, today you will be with me in Paradise.'"

"Never heard the county jail called paradise," said Justice. "But it's rent-free, compliments of the taxpayers." He paused and pointed at his prisoner. "You just call me a moron?"

"A travesty," Pit cried, shaking his fist. "Who better to protect the young from Satan than a messenger from God?"

As their voices faded down the hall, Pit turned to the sergeant and said, "By the way, Bill, when do I get my cell phone back? I gotta check my minutes."

At least Pit would get room and board and maybe even a shower, harmless old fool.

Finally, Hendricks strolled up, still ensconced in his coat.

"Miz O'Brien? Ready for you now."

"What have you done with my daughter?"

"She's fine. A lady intake counselor and a policewoman from our juvie division are shuffling through some paperwork with her. Miss Dare wants her grandfather to go with her to the youth home. Interesting name Dare. Wonder if the heat's on in here. It's freezing."

"Youth home? Jesus Christ on the cross, what's going on?"

"Well, ma'am, your daughter says she up and killed the deceased. And we're gonna have to book her for the…" He stopped and must have decided not to mention the charge, and I didn't push it. Denial is a wonderful state in which to reside.

Hendricks glanced at his notepad. "Well, for this situation with one Randall La Russo. Reckon she might have done it, too. Very insistent about that fact before she clammed up. And taking the Lord's name in vain sure won't help none, Miz O'Brien, if you get my drift."

Davey and my father appeared at my elbow.

"Where have you been?" I cried.

"What he says is true," Davey said. "She confessed to … well, she admits to the crime. And because of the violent nature of … well, she'll have to be detained, at least for now."

"We can keep her at home," said my father to Hendricks. "She's a child."

"Orange Youth Home is close by, Richard," Davey said. "You can go with her to the facility, but you can't go in. For now, anyway. They'll let you know about visiting hours. There'll be a hearing on Wednesday morning."

"What kind of lawyer are you? You're supposed to help us," I shouted. "They can't take her away like this. There's no proof. She's making it up. She's never been in the men's locker room, for God's sake."

"Yes, she has," he said, before following my father down the hall.

***

I sat in one of the orange plastic bowl chairs in the small interrogation room and tried to meditate. The vibes felt wrong. A tape recorder was on the table and a camera angled down from the ceiling. Shit. Close eyes. Breathe in. Breathe out.

When I finally looked up, Davey, armed with legal pad and pen, loomed in the doorway like one of the fine Highland ancestors he bragged about. Reluctantly, I rejoined the nightmarish reality show of murder and mayhem.

"Hendricks should be here in a minute." A jean-clad, buttoned-down warrior, he flicked back his lion's mane of hair. I'd never thought of him in a prurient way before, and this bothered me, especially on this night of all nights. Probably some kind of escape mechanism. Davey'd always just been Davey, the long-drink-of-water hanging around the house years ago. True, his hair was the color of fine brandy, but one didn't pledge troth for hair alone. Besides, he'd been a pest. But that was then, and I was tripping on fantasy now. Maybe I needed to stalk the corridors like Daddy to cool my jets. Or maybe my mother was right in thinking I was not mature enough to raise a teenager.

Good Lord, I need to shake some sense into my kid. Whatever made her confess? A wacky adolescent bid for attention? She didn't do it, of course.

Did she?

"Well?" I asked Davey. "You coming in?"

Fatigue showed in his bloodshot blue eyes. He pulled up a chair beside me and scanned some chicken-scratch notes.

"From a cursory examination of the evidence and from what Dare says, it seems possible that she could've done it."

He held up a hand as I began to sputter. "But the police aren't finished processing the scene yet, so, we wait and see."

"Why do they think she was in the men's locker room? She never showed up at the club like Mother said she was going to." I put a hand up to my hair curling out of its braids and wondered if I could be taken seriously in my present state of dishevelment. Not that I cared.

"They found her cell phone just inside the door to the locker room."

I thunked my forehead on the table and stared cross-eyed at the worn surface. Only God could have pried that phone from her adolescent fingers. Since I'd given it to her at Christmas, it ranked second only to her right arm as her most important appendage.

"And she had blood on her."

"So did I, and I didn't kill him. I mean, isn't this all circumstantial?" I grasped for a straw. "Even if she was in there, it doesn't mean she did it."

"But she confessed," he said. "Until they get some forensic evidence that clears her …."

"What exactly did she say during questioning? Did Daddy say anything?"

"Not much, and that goes for both of them." He shook his head in amusement. "Your dad was the usual rock of dependability. But she's one cool customer. Hendricks read the child her rights. In this case, it was the regular Mirandizing with the juvenile addendum that she has the right to have a parent or guardian present during questioning."

What a pill she was. Where did this nerve come from? Then I remembered Mother.

"What happened then? You weren't in there long."

"He asked her if she understood her rights. She said she did. Then he asked her if she wanted to talk to him, and she said yes."

His mouth turned up at the corners at the memory and lightened my heart just a tad until his next words, which he delivered as gently as possible.

"She said, 'Like, I killed him. With Mom's orange hammer.'" Davey's brow clouded. "When the lieutenant asked her why, she turned to me and said, 'I don't want to talk anymore.' And that was that. Interrogation over."

"Thank God you all were there. My poor baby."

"Didn't seem like a baby to me. More like a scary adult."

"She puts on, you know. Always been good at that. Daddy said she didn't want me in there. Do you know why?"

"Beats me."

I grasped his arm and looked into his eyes.

"She didn't do it, Davey. I know she didn't. I'm her mother, and I'd know. Right here, I'd know." I pounded my heart with my fist.

"No, I don't think so, either," he said, but his expression was speculative.

"What?" I asked, stung. I slapped his arm. "I already said I didn't do it, if that's what you're thinking."

"Problem is, a lot of folks heard you say you were going to kill him," he said. "It seems he still pushes some of your buttons."

"He hasn't pushed them in ages. I've threatened Randy with bodily harm at least a million times since I met him. So have a lot of other people. But this time, he went too far. He ...," I stopped.

Davey leaned back as if to get a better look at me.

I bolted from the chair and began to circle the room.

"I always say I'm going to kill people in the heat of the moment. Everyone does."

"I don't. Never have."

"Well, la-di-da. Do you think he'll read me my rights?"

"Not unless he arrests you. But if it turns out you're the

murderer, they'll want to use whatever evidence you give them in court."

"I'm not the murderer, so tell them to bring it on," I said with more bravado than I felt.

"That's my girl." He smiled like in the old college days, only with a few more eye crinkles for character.

"How are the troops in here?" interrupted Officer Jones. She pranced in freshly powdered and lip-glossed, and set a paper sack on the table. She ignored me to concentrate on Davey.

"I'm fine," I said loud enough for her to remember my presence.

"Course you are," she said almost like an aside. "Davey, Lieutenant Hendricks will be with you shortly."

"Thanks," Davey said.

She winked at him and patted my hand. "A change of clothes is in this bag. Your friend, Miss DeMoya, brought them to the station for you."

She went through the door as Hendricks, still in his trench coat, plodded in with three cups of coffee.

"Hope black coffee suits y'all," he said, carefully placing the containers on the table and closing the door behind Officer Jones.

Hendricks kept one hand wrapped around his steaming cup as he started the tape recorder.

"This is Lieutenant Greg Hendricks and I'm interviewing Miz Bridget O'Brien. It's Monday, February twenty-seventh, eleven-thirty in the p.m. Miz O'Brien, first let me tell you that you are free to go anytime during this interview. You aren't under arrest. But you're an important witness and you discovered the body. So, please think carefully about what you say. Is that clear?"

Miami Vice's Detective Sonny Crockett couldn't have said it any better.

"Yes," I squeaked an octave above my normal range.

Deep breath in. Breathe out.

"Good." He plucked a small notebook and pen out of his shirt pocket, careful not to dislodge his cigarettes.

"Did you kill Randall La Russo?" he asked as if discussing the weather, pen poised above the notepad.

My heart turned a somersault.

"I most certainly did not."

For heaven's sake, did I look like a maniacal killer? It made sense for the lieutenant to ask, but I wasn't about to give him or Davey the Four-One-One on my last chat with Randy, what with blackmail being on the short list for motives.

Shouldn't Davey protest that I didn't have to answer that question or something? A big help he was. I hoped that this was pro bono work for him because I wouldn't pay a penny unless he stepped up.

"Well, ma'am, it's still a bit early to say officially. But it looks to me like the cause of death was multiple compound fractures of the skull, or blunt trauma, as they like to say on all the C.S.I. shows. The murder weapon most likely being your orange mallet. Fine tool, by the way. You get it at a hardware store? Could use one myself."

And here I thought I'd left *The Twilight Zone*.

"If I tell you what I know, you'll see that there are other suspects. My girl didn't do it."

"How do you know?"

"She's my daughter."

He sipped his coffee.

"And she's … I mean I know my own flesh and blood, that's all."

Hmph, let him chew on that.

I straightened in the plastic chair, only to slide back down as if I had gelatin for a backbone.

"You know your daughter was at the country club this afternoon?"

"I never saw her. My mother told me she was coming but …."

"Witnesses saw her."

"Who did? What witnesses?"

He leafed through his notepad, reading aloud.

"I swear I'll kill you if you tell her. I mean it, Randy," he read. "That ring a bell?"

"Well, yeah, but you're ignoring my questions?" I hedged, frantic to be alone to think and plan.

"I'm asking the questions here, ma'am. Besides, we got a dead man en route to a refrigerated drawer. Seems to me manners aren't of particular importance."

Christ, he's talking about the man who fathered my child. The child who now had confessed to his murder. But she didn't know he was her real father. What a tangled web.

Hendricks said, "We seem to be getting nowhere. Tell you what, ma'am, how about you tell me what happened starting from this morning."

Although it wasn't easy for me to stay on track when telling a story, I related how Randy showed up asking for a reconciliation.

That was Lie Number One. He'd asked for no such thing.

I continued. "When he got angry and wouldn't take no for an answer, he threatened to tell Dare we were engaged to be married anyway."

Lie Number Two, but who was counting?

"That's when I said what you said I said about killing him."

Usually I couldn't lie worth a damn, but this was an emergency.

"Seems like overkill, if you'll pardon the expression, to

say you're aiming to kill the poor man when all he wanted to do was marry you again," Hendricks said.

"I didn't know he was going to die, did I? Or I wouldn't have said that."

"Know where he was staying?"

Might as well go whole hog with Lie Number Three and not mention his mother's house at this stage. They'd find out soon enough. Even as a lapsed Catholic, I foresaw hours in a confessional on my knees.

"He hates it here. He lives in Charlotte. He was only in town for the day."

Davey glanced up from his notes.

"Go on," Hendricks said.

I told him about Randy's scene with Malcolm, my workday and the later discovery of the body. I ended with my appearance in the glare of Chapel Hill's finest emergency services.

"Reckon it was Malcolm Jones, do you?"

"Well, I couldn't find him."

"Mr. La Russo was what we call a low-risk victim. Guy who lives a normal life and is assaulted in daylight or in his home. In this case, in his club."

"It's hard for me to believe it might've been Malcolm, but I don't know who else could've done it." I slumped farther down in my chair. Might as well throw Malcolm to the wolves for now, just so the police would investigate all the possibilities. I could apologize to him later and explain that I was just trying to save Dare.

"We sent officers to his house. Says he had to leave the club for a family crisis. Says he planned on going back. He's there right now, matter of fact."

"I heard he's going through a nasty, expensive divorce," Davey said.

"Or maybe it could've been Marla Ann," I said. "Or the

Tooth Fairy. Randy is … had a knack for being abrasive and arrogant. All I know is that it wasn't Dare, and it wasn't me."

"We're talking to the other staff members, *et cetera.* Most of 'em weren't even there and have alibis for the time in question. Don't know about the Tooth Fairy though."

Ha-ha.

"Take anything out of his car?"

"Why would I do that? I don't even know what he drives – or drove."

"Silver Lexus sedan," Hendricks said. "No briefcase. No appointment book. No cell phone. I expect he had one, don't you?"

"I haven't laid eyes on the man in five years."

"No need to get snippy."

"Sorry. Nerves."

"Yeah, well. By the way, I heard about the mayor's big reception this coming weekend from Mr. Jones. He's antsy about you and Miz DeMoya getting back to work. I expect the ballroom to be available by late morning or so. We should be wrapped up in there by then," he said. "Y'all go on by after lunch."

"Catch whoever did it real quick, so Dare can come home."

He leaned toward the tape recorder.

"Hendricks here. It's now Tuesday one thirty-seven a.m. on February twenty-eighth. Ending this interview with Bridget O'Brien." He shut off the machine and stood. "For now."

"You remind me of Columbo in that coat, you know that? In a down-home sort of way."

He brightened immediately.

"Never thought of that." He examined his coat as if seeing it for the first time. "Bought this at the Belk in Gaston

Mall. On sale. I'm very cold-natured. My mama says it's because I was born during a snowstorm."

"That'd do it." At least I'd connected with him on some level, which might be helpful down the road.

He touched the paper bag left by Officer Jones.

"I took the liberty of asking Miz DeMoya to drop off some clothes for you."

"What for?"

"We'd like you to give us what you're wearing, if that's not too much trouble. Just to eliminate you from our inquiries, you understand. Officer Jones will have to be present when you change."

I squinted down at my clothing for trace evidence. If paint, hair and the victim's blood counted, the police had struck gold.

"That's it for the time being," Hendricks added. "Not going anywhere are you, ma'am? Leaving town? I wouldn't if I was you. I'll get Officer Jones."

He pulled cigarettes out of his shirt pocket and strolled out, leaving the door open.

So much for connecting.

At that moment, Pit Bullard shuffled past the interrogation room with Sergeant Justice and bellowed in righteous wrath, "I raise my eyes toward the mountains. From whence will come my help?"

"Hey, preacher, hold on," I called, grabbing the bag containing my clothes, and hurried into the hallway with Davey.

Pit dropped to his plump knees and gazed at the ceiling. After a protracted examination of the acoustical tiles, he spotted me and Davey.

"Why, Miss Bridget, was that you a-calling my name? I figured it was an angel in heaven answering my plea. What brings you to this exalted law enforcement center? Your daddy know you're here?"

"It feels like the world knows I'm here," I said. "But I can't find Daddy. Have you seen him around here? We're in such trouble, and I want someone to tell me what I should do," I said. A ball of emotion closed my throat.

"You do have a way with words, Pit," Davey said as he hoisted the old man to his feet via his armpits. "You'll have to teach me sometime."

"Be a pleasure, son. And I'll pray for you, daughter. Prayer is the thing. The Lord will listen." Pit reached up with his manacled hands and tweaked one of my braids.

"You can pray in jail, Pit," Sergeant Justice said as he nudged him forward.

Officer Jones showed up to accompany me to the ladies' room. I guess to make sure I didn't do anything to taint the evidence on my clothes.

"I forgot to tell Greg something, Bridget," Davey said. "I'll be right back. Wait in reception when you're done changing. I'm taking you home."

"Yessir!" I saluted him.

"I'll make sure she waits there, Davey," Officer Jones said obligingly as we walked into the bathroom.

No time to be modest at this point even if this policewoman seemed to be enjoying my discomfort. I scowled at her, and she turned away slightly to give me a bit of privacy. I kicked off my boots and stepped out of my coveralls. I slid my cell phone into my bra and hid the turkey feather behind my back. Pulled on the jeans and yanked an ancient Carolina sweatshirt over my head. Boots, socks and coveralls went into the paper bag. Slipping into tennis shoes, I handed the bag to Officer Jones and hurried into the hallway, rushing to the reception area. As I waited for Davey, my father, a middle-aged woman, and Dare walked into the room.

"Dare." Blinded with tears, I raced over and smushed her in a bear hug.

She held herself stiff and straight. It was baffling. All teenagers ran hot and cold with their parents, but she and I reveled in touchy-feely, instinctively curling about each other for comfort and love. At least we had before Italy. Had we been that close since I came back? I couldn't think clearly at the moment.

"There, there, Bridget," Daddy said with glistening eyes.

"Mom, chill," Dare added in a teenage creature from outer space persona. "I'm not a baby."

"I want to come with you, punkin. To talk." I sought her eyes, but she turned from me.

I pulled my father away.

"Did you get in touch with Mother? Why isn't she here?"

He gazed at the ceiling.

"Did you hear me? Where's Mother?"

"You know she would hate this sort of thing."

He always made excuses for her.

"God forbid she should be seen in a police station," I replied.

"You don't understand, sugar."

"Oh, I think I do." To my notion, my respectable family seemed to be going to hell in a hand basket.

The woman standing next to my father patted my arm. It was a measure of my father's distress that he had forgotten his manners and failed to introduce her.

"Miz O'Brien," she said with kind country sincerity as she shook my hand, "I'm Miz Breedlove, the intake counselor." She was solid and comforting in a jogging suit and turtleneck. "I think it's important that we get this young lady settled. It's been quite a day."

No kidding.

I kissed Dare lightly on the cheek and hugged my father. "Take care of her, Daddy?" I stepped back, tears spilling down my face.

"Don't fret now, sugar." He pecked me on the forehead. "Remember the Sistine Chapel?"

I nodded, even though I didn't get what he meant by that.

"Good girl."

He put his arm around Dare and followed Mrs. Breedlove out the door.

I shuffled to the sofa to wait for Davey. Sitting cross-legged, I suddenly itched to get something down on paper but my journal was in Chica's purse. I spotted some questionnaires and pencils on a nearby table. I grabbed one of each. The paper was blank on the back.

Honey would be so pleased, I thought as I started to write.

Tuesday, February 28, 2006, (real, real early in the morning)

Here I sit in the Chapel Hill Police Station. Unbelievable. Tonight, my child confessed to a murder she DID NOT, COULD NOT have committed. Daddy told me not to worry, to remember the Sistine Chapel. What did he mean by that? He took me to Italy when I was 15 to see the Creation of Adam up close and now was the time to do it with the restoration in progress. He had a friend who would give us a private tour. So, up the scaffolding we went with Professor Luigi. Daddy said, "Remember to always look straight ahead. Don't look down." Was this the message of the Sistine Chapel Daddy wanted me to remember? Anyway, I'd been shocked to see Adam's privates, itty bitty compared to the rest of him. Then Professor Luigi told me we were six stories high. I forgot to stare straight ahead like Daddy said and looked down. OH MY GOD! I jerked my head up and Adam's little pee-pee started going round and round. My eyes rolled back in my head, and I slunk and then thunked onto the platform. The professor said it sounded like someone had dropped a large head of cabbage. They practically had to roll me off the scaffold. Poor Michael Angel – that's what I called him – painting on his back for four years, 68 feet in the air. After that, I vowed to remain earthbound forever. But as this morning on the ladder showed, vows were made to be broken. Note: Must ask Honey if I'm avoiding the real issues here. Daddy bought me a lovely little diamond cross necklace to mark the occasion, which was eventually lost.

I folded the piece of paper and tucked it into my jeans pocket to insert in my journal later. I was no closer to understanding Daddy's mention of the incident when someone walked up and blocked the light. Thinking it was Davey, I stood and grabbed his arm. Unfortunately, it belonged to Hall Hooper.

After I dropped it, we continued to stare at each other. About my age, give or take a few. Had kind of a Jack Nicholson swagger. A newspaperman you'd better not turn your back on. I took a step back, stuck out my hand.

"I'm Bridget O'Brien. Nice to meet you."

This lying gig was getting easier by the minute.

"I was going to see if Hendricks was in, but I think I hit the jackpot," Hooper said, pumping my hand.

Davey finally turned up. I could've kissed him.

"Sorry, my ride's here," I said, rewarded by Hooper's frown as Davey and I left the building.

Four

Davey eased his SUV into the semicircular drive behind Chica's vintage black BMW convertible. Muffled barking erupted from inside the house.

"Guard pooches hard at work," I said.

"You're not going to do anything stupid, are you?" he asked.

"Excuse me?" I bristled.

"You know what I mean," he said. "Just let the police handle this. You'll only make things worse if you go poking your nose into it. In fact, my advice to you is to go to bed now and get some rest. This will all look clearer in daylight."

Hello? This type of male remark is precisely why there are no men in my life at the moment. Breathe in. Blow out.

"I can handle myself, thank you very much."

What had happened to the Scottish hero I'd envisioned at the police station?

Bossy So-and-So.

"You might think I'm a bossy so-and-so," he said. "But I'm concerned for your safety. There's a killer out there."

"We should meet for lunch tomorrow," I said. Cussing out my lawyer wasn't a good idea even if he was a friend.

"Actually, it's tomorrow already, isn't it? Whatever day it is, we'll talk then."

He stared straight ahead, his jaw twitching.

"If you're a very good boy, I'll bring you a fried bologna sandwich and a cookie. You are formulating a plan, right? This is my Dare we're talking about."

"Don't you work at the club tomorrow? I wasn't paying close attention when you and Greg discussed it. What's the big to-do there soon?"

"Mega wedding reception for Miss Alexandra Holroyd-Wyatt. Club gossip has it that Bad Seed might be a better name."

"The mayor's daughter?"

"Yep. We'll be back in the ballroom working sometime tomorrow. But I'll be beside the Davie Poplar around noon waiting for my esteemed counsel."

"You sound way too sincere." He lowered his brows. "Or was that sarcasm?"

Maybe he wasn't so dumb after all.

I climbed out of the Jeep. Dang yapping dogs would wake the whole street.

Davey lowered his window. "Y'all have done a piss-poor job of training those dogs, and don't roll your eyes at me."

The barking stopped as Chica stuck her head out the door and wedged her body in the few inches of open space.

"Jesus Maria. The doggies go crazy when they hear cars in the driveway," she said. "What's going on? Did you people die out there?" Bubba wriggled in her arms, and Big Foot shoved against her legs.

Davey powered up the window. He smiled at me – a bit of a heart-stopper with that big white smile, as he waved goodbye.

I followed Chica into the house.

When first entering her foyer months ago, I'd expected

a mirror image of her personality – bright, Latin, and flamboyant. Okay, I'd stereotyped her. But, instead of dodging a piñata, I found polished hardwoods, a dainty crystal chandelier, and a side table that screamed Colonial Williamsburg.

"Wow," I'd said. "Are you a Republican or something? This looks like the White House."

"I love bright colors. But it's all about resale value, amiga." She tapped her temple. "I know the market."

The market wasn't on our minds tonight, though.

Chica set Bubba on the floor and straightened to reveal a skintight, all-black ensemble.

"Wait! Don't tell me. You're Cat Woman?"

She waved the piece of paper I'd scribbled on earlier in my face. "Your list says to wear black like a thief. So, here is the thief."

The spandex bodysuit hugged her petite figure. On top she wore a black ball cap with her signature ponytail pulled through the back. She did a little dance in her combat boots. With her olive skin and black eyes, she'd be invisible at night unless she grinned. Around her waist, a black web belt held a big flashlight, a penlight and two cell phones.

"Why two phones?"

She pointed to the bigger one. "A stun gun I bought last year that looks like a phone, no? Very sexy. Six hundred thousand volts, the man says."

She twirled slowly. Her other equipment included the sheathed Swiss Army knife that we used for peeling apples and a small can of super-duper-rigid-hold hairspray buttoned into the holster.

"Hairspray?"

"Better than nothing. The pepper spray exploded, remember?"

"Where's the gun?"

"I forgot to tell you. I took it from your thong drawer

and put it in the supplies the other day. It should be protection for working women, not for underpants."

"With the paint cans and brushes? Cripes. Where's the box?"

"I put it in the box that has doggie toys in it. The gun looks like a doggie toy. Good camouflage."

"I've yet to see a .38 caliber puppy toy. They got those in Cuba or something?"

"You don't know much."

"Dear Lord, is it in the van, or at the club?"

"Not sure. At the club, I think. We have too many boxes. I wanted to show you where I hid it yesterday before I left. For our protection, like I said, OK? Before...before Randy got killed. But I forgot."

"It must be in the van, else the police would've found it."

Being that I'd breached the sanctity of the men's locker room armed with a turkey feather, it would have been nice to have known about the gun. Probably a good thing she hadn't told me. I'd have shot up the whole place and myself to boot. One lesson at Harley's Guns & Ammo hadn't improved my attitude toward firearms. They scared the crap out of me.

"Your thief clothes." Chica pointed to black jeans, black turtle-neck, latex gloves, and a black hat of sorts stacked on the foyer chair. "For the amiga of Cat Woman."

I picked up Dare's old Mickey Mouse toboggan complete with ears.

"You're kidding." I rammed my hair into it. The mirror reflected a 36-year-old mouseketeer. Pitiful.

"Yellow hair is bright at night. Was the only black hat I could find to cover it." She tucked in a few strands, stepped back and patted Mickey's ears.

"It's the latest thief fashion."

***

At my direction, Chica parked her black car down the block from the La Russo home. The dense evergreen shrubbery and pines made up in cover for the leafless oaks and maples. Several parked cars lined the hilly street, so one more wouldn't stand out. A sliver of moon guided us past an eclectic mix of 1960s ranch houses and wooden structures resembling mountain lodges. No porch lights glowed, no dog barked and, luckily, the street light appeared to be broken.

We approached Randy's mother's brown, two-story wooden house, crouching as we hurried around to the back.

"Cross your fingers," I muttered as we reached the worn wooden steps. I scrabbled under the decking and found a key hanging on its nail. So much for security. Randy once told me it had been there since the Johnson administration. I squinted at the dark rusty object in my latex glove. Chica knelt so close behind me that I now fully understood the phrase "monkey on your back."

"Stop panting in my ear," I rasped.

"Grumpy girl." She moved all of an inch backward. "You sure his mama is in Florida? I don't like this B and E."

I'd already explained to her that we weren't really breaking and entering because the dwelling belonged to my former mother-in-law or, even better, my daughter's biological grandmother – although neither one of them knew that. Life was complicated.

"Hush up," I whispered. "If we've got the key, we're not B-ing. We're only E-ing. You a chicken? You were in the Army, for heaven's sake. You kicked asses in Desert Storm."

"But only the asses of my amigas. I never shot at the enemy. You know I am a peace hippie now."

"Stop worrying. I don't believe in lying most of the time. If we get caught, we'll say we're watering Grace's plants while she's on vacation and we'll water one."

"At two in the morning?" A fine spray of spit landed on my ear.

We scanned the back yard and its overgrown boxwood hedges, laurels and azalea bushes. In the gentle breeze, the bare limbs of a white oak waved witchlike branches against the night sky. Where was the shrieking wind, a hooting owl or a trilling nightingale when one needed audio cover?

Step by creaky step, we inched up to the back door. The key eased into the lock despite the rust, but the door screeched open like a scalded cat. We collapsed onto the linoleum but forgot and slammed the door. Sounded like a sonic boom. I'd have hyperventilated if I'd had the time.

"Got the light?" I gibbered, in an advanced state of arrhythmia.

A searchlight the size of Texas revealed harvest gold kitchen appliances.

"Jesus Maria," Chica cried as she switched it off.

"That thing's like the Hatteras Lighthouse. Everyone in Orange County'll know we're here."

She poked me with a gloved finger and shoved the penlight in my hand.

"It's all I could find, amiga. The good one is in a box."

Along with the gun, most likely.

With one sorry-ass stripe of illumination, we moved through the rambling wooden house like a point guard covering his opponent during a fast break. Although Grace hadn't been gone that long, the house smelled musty. Under the essence of mothballs, ancient carpet, collard greens, Blue Emu ointment, decrepit dog, and embedded cigarette smoke, I got a whiff of Randy's British Sterling cologne. I'd loved nuzzling his neck when he wore it. I shook my head to clear the thought and became aware of another fragrance, strong and feminine, that wasn't native to the house.

"Hurry," Chica hissed. "It's bad what we do. I have an honorable discharge from the U.S. Army, you know.

Breathe in and musn't forget to breathe out.

We stole into Randy's room at the top of the stairs. The scent of perfume almost knocked me over. I sniffed at a pillow from the rumpled double bed. Chanel No. 5. Hmph.

I threw the pillow. Randy was always randy.

A bit of moonglow through the window revealed an open suitcase on tangled sheets and, to my surprise, Dare's white crib still standing in the corner.

Chica saw it, too. "You sure this is Randy's room?" she said.

My throat closed. I sat down heavily on a corner of my former marriage bed. The crib looked lonely. Grace had rescued it from the attic and slapped on a coat of paint after I'd married Randy in December 1994. Dare had just turned two. Although this was no time to wax nostalgic, the moment claimed me. I patted the bedspread, Nana Blanche's patchwork quilt. Mother had given it to me for my hope chest. I'd forgotten to take it when I moved out of Grace's house.

"Bridget. Hóla." Chica rapped my head with her knuckles. She pointed at the laptop on the desk beneath the window.

Nothing like a possible clue to stir the blood. Besides, Randy was gone, but our daughter wasn't. I popped the silver lid on the laptop and thumbed it on. Banking on Randy being too lazy to invent passwords, I tapped the enter key when the system requested one and the desktop appeared. I right-clicked on start and double-clicked on the browser icon to examine his files.

I couldn't find any files or folder names for bank statements. I assumed those were on his bank's website, and I didn't know that information.

I opened a folder titled "Dare." Inside was a document

called "Miscellaneous Feb. 26," which was less than two days ago, and an Excel file called "Savings." He'd last opened this one on the first of February.

The Miscellaneous document was a to-do list.

1. Tell Dare
2. Get Bridget on board. Also, Richard, Sarah. Get Mom's help
3. Talk to Malcolm
4. Check on buying condo here. Not Marla Ann
5. Is she really pregnant? Check timing!!!!!!
6. Call Davey
7. Decide about sb's
8. Put Charlotte townhouse on market/sublet?

I opened the Excel file. Randy had created a worksheet titled, Regular Savings for Randall La Russo and Bridget O'Brien La Russo, Custodians for Angela Dare Benedetto. We'd opened this account after we were married to make deposits whenever we could, which wasn't often back then. He'd been a new stockbroker, and I was a stay-at-home mom with dreams of being the next Georgia O'Keeffe. The savings account never really grew much before we separated, and I'd forgotten about it.

Chica peered over my shoulder as I scrolled down the document. For the first twelve years of Dare's life, the savings account grew to a little over four hundred dollars with interest. Randy must have forgotten about it, too, until recently. But in 2005, he'd added a hefty chunk of $100,000???. The question marks were Randy's. By the end of November, the account totaled a whopping $100,556.56.

"Jesus Maria," breathed Chica. "Baby girl is rich."

"Wait."

I scrolled down to the end. It looked like Randy had removed $100,000.00 during December, leaving a total of $556.56.

I began to pace.

"Did he get that much money from Malcolm? What the hell?"

"Malcolm?"

"I think Randy was blackmailing him. They argued about it today … yesterday, whatever. I haven't had time to tell you, but it was ugly. And here's the proof." I stared at the numbers and dates. Hold on. The entries were dated before Randy joined the country club.

"He saves it for Dare?"

"Huh. I bet he was using this account to hide the money. I'm still on the account too. The bastard fixed it so we could both be arrested for money laundering or theft or whatever illegal thing he was working on."

I pawed through Randy's suitcase until I found his appointment book and paged to February. There were four entries for this week.

For Monday, February 27th, "MLJ. $$$," which had to be Malcolm L. Jones.

He'd penciled in B.O.B., Bridget O'Brien, for Tuesday. Hmmm. Guess he ran into me by accident on Monday morning.

Wednesday's entry was a cryptic "Condo - S.V. 2 p.m." Was he referring to a condo in Southern Village, an upscale retail/housing subdivision full of kids and Gen-Xers shopping in boutiques surrounding a village green? Faux Finish had completed a job there a few weeks earlier, a Shakespeare-themed dining room mural of *A Midsummer Night's Dream.*

Below the Southern Village entry, Randy had scribbled "Tickets" and under that "D.D." Had to be the Dean Dome. The men's basketball team had a couple of games there in the next week or so. Maybe he was trying to get tickets.

Some of the appointment book information matched the miscellaneous to-do list and some of it didn't. For instance, I didn't know what "decide about sb's" meant. But there wasn't time to figure it out now.

What to do with these items? I'd left no fingerprints, but what the heck? I stuck the appointment book in my waistband and powered down the laptop, clicked it shut and tucked it under my arm. Problem solved.

"Vámanos," I said.

"I didn't see you steal that stuff."

"That's right."

"Just making sure."

We rearranged the clothing in the suitcase. Chica turned in the doorway when she realized I wasn't following.

"Psst, you say 'vamanos' so hurry up."

"I've been trying to remember something that I can't remember."

"Now it is important?

"It might be. How would I know when I don't know what it is I can't remember?"

Chica crossed her arms.

"Oh, all right. Don't get your panties in a wad," I said.

We headed downstairs. As we got to the bottom, the front doorknob jiggled. I hugged the laptop to my chest and dropped to my hands and knees. Chica crouched beside me.

Someone pushed hard on the door.

"Stun gun," I hissed.

I heard small clicks.

"Uh oh. Battery is dead."

I tugged on her screw-with-me-and-you-die weapon belt. "Why bring it then?"

"It looks hot."

Who says women are shallow and frivolous?

The intruder peered into one of the porch windows. He cast a big silhouette with a hand cupped a hand against the glass, but it was too dark to tell who he was.

Chica opened her mouth and I pinched her lips shut, motioning for her to follow. We scuttled out the kitchen door like crabs chasing the tide.

Five

The next morning, I awoke unable to breathe. Well, duh. Sleeping on one's face is known to make breathing difficult. Especially with wake-up dragon breath. When I tried to move, I couldn't feel my right arm. I'd fallen asleep clutching a pen and my journal, which Chica had obligingly placed on my bedside table the night before. Untangling myself from the covers proved harder than usual as I still wore the breaking-and-entering ensemble. I don't think I'd moved at all. If this had been a movie, I'd have stretched prettily in lacy lingerie.

Using my left arm, I dragged myself upright and shook the hand that was numb from lack of circulation. I opened the journal and scribbled.

Tuesday, February 28, 2006

Randy's room! Seeing it made me want to curl into the fetal position. You'd think Grace would've changed SOMETHING by now. (Note: Find '94 journal and see what I wrote then. Bound to be instructive). The red burlap curtains still hang crooked. I can see Randy now, curtain rod in one hand, beer in the other. We almost peed ourselves laughing. Nana Blanche's quilt still looks good. All those fairy stitches. Mother said she'd made it right after I was born. Wish I'd known her.

Mother says I have her hair and eyes. Nana Blanche would've pitched a fit to see us playing cards on her quilt. She was strait-laced. Back then, I'd wake up early and watch Dare sleeping between me and Randy. Heaven didn't last, though. Randy rarely showed interest in her and, at times, seemed to resent her. Was it jealousy because Marcus doted so on being Dare's "father?" And, by golly, I made sure he believed it until the day he died, because he deserved it. Was I wrong about Randy's feelings back then? Honey says men can often be "afraid" of babies and connect more with older children.

I closed the journal. Nana Blanche stared at me from her sepia wedding photo on my dresser. They never smiled in pictures in those days, so it looked like she was gazing at me in disapproval.

Just outside the French doors, a spider web waved in the morning breeze, spun across the railings of the tiny Juliet balcony. It was the architectural feature that had clinched my decision to move in with Chica, who, by the way, would knock the spider and web to kingdom come if she knew about them. Bugs freaked her out.

Mesmerized by the concentric rings, I almost nodded off for a few forgetful minutes. Just as my head drooped, my eyelids snapped open.

Dare. Murder. Prison. Oh God.

I swung my feet to the floor and faced the door of the secret room. Dare and I had named it this for its arched entryway, niches, octagonal leaded window inside, and because we both believed in fairytales. Inside, the walls were covered with dozens images of Dare. Sketches and quick watercolor studies of her grinned, winked, sobbed and stuck their tongues out. In one drawing, she pumped long legs on a swing; in another, she nosed a rose in Mother's garden. Randy had hit a nerve when he mentioned my unfinished painting of Dare. For years, I'd tried to capture her essence but hadn't gotten close. It's not that the variations on the wall didn't look like Dare. The latest sketch, done after I returned from Italy, stared with the usual teenaged insolence. Hard to get sentimental about a sullen mouth, spiked hair and multi-ple-pierced ears. Combined with the maternal guilt that had been nibbling around my edges at that time, the harsh result seemed inevitable. One day, though. One day, I'd create an image suffused with her soul.

"You wait and see if I don't." I shook a finger at the Dares before locking the spare room with the big, old-fash-ioned key and hanging it on a hook attached to my bedside table.

"Amiga," Chica hollered from downstairs, sounding cranky. "You sleep all day?"

"All right," I shouted back. Before heading toward the bathroom, I pulled Randy's appointment book from the waistband of my jeans and tucked it under my pillow for now.

In the shower, I prayed the hot water would stimulate my brain cells and pinpoint Randy's killer. After all, Nero Wolfe did his detecting without leaving the comfort of his brownstone. I squeezed shampoo into my palm. An indus-trial scrub was just the thing for my crunchy hair and for cogitation on the events last night.

After fleeing the scene of the B and E, as Chica called it, we'd almost run over the paper boy on Randy's street while debating whether the big shadow on the porch had been Malcolm. Not too many men were so big. Even if it was Malcolm, did that make him a murderer? What a pickle. He was our client. We still had tons of work to do at the club, not to mention that I'd known Malcolm for a long time.

But if he killed Randy, I told Chica, I'd expose him in a heartbeat. After trying to dial nine-one-one on my dying cell phone, I briefly thought about calling the police when we got home to tell them about the stranger on Randy's porch.

"You're loco," Chica said when she learned that plan. "The fuzzies will say, 'How do you know?' Jesus Maria. How will you explain the laptop and the appointment book?"

She was right. How in the heck would we know about another burglar unless we were burgling too? Solving crimes was too complicated. Poor Lieutenant Hendricks.

I emerged from the scalding shower clean but no closer to answers. I combed my hair and braided it wet, same as yesterday. My work do, as I called it. The moussed and scrunched shepherdess look that Alessandro had raved about in Italy was for special occasions only. I donned a fresh uniform and socks and my other pair of boots. On my way out, I pocketed my journal.

In the kitchen, Chica hunched over a 2006 horoscope book while the television hummed on the countertop. Her gray-streaked mane sprung in all directions, and there were dark smudges under her eyes. Nothing a good dose of concealer couldn't fix, though. Her feet rested on Big Foot's head under the kitchen table, while Bubba snored beneath a giant white paw.

"I shouldn't go out anymore," Chica announced with a woebegone expression.

"Never mind what that horoscope says. You have to go out. Hendricks thinks we can get back in the club early this afternoon."

I poured a glass of McAllister's sweet tea from a gallon jug in the refrigerator. I liked it cold and straight, no rocks. Artificial sweeteners were also a no-no in this house. Nothing like a sugar high.

"There's still a lot to do, and I have to be in juvenile court tomorrow morning for Dare. Something they call a first appearance. Daddy said he'd let me know today."

"Crap."

"You bring this stuff on yourself, Chica. Read the newspaper horoscope instead. It's only one paragraph and full of crap, as you would say, but at least it doesn't change your life."

She wrinkled her nose in disdain.

"You and Nancy Reagan have made astrology a religion. Not sure how that fits in with the Catholic Church."

"I think Nancy didn't understand it the day Ronnie was shot. Anyway, Señorita Smarty, no paper this morning. It never came."

I dropped into a chair, exhausted, and it was only morning. Being a grown-up wore me out.

"Does that silly book say why you can't go out? Damn thing was probably printed a year ago. How would it know you shouldn't go out on a particular day?"

"It says, 'You must avoid all temptation. If you must leave your sphere of comfort, avoid Sagittarians and situations that reek of compromise.' What is reek of compromise?"

"Means something like don't do what you don't believe in. Don't sacrifice your values."

"I never do this reeking."

"What about breaking and entering?"

"If it's right for you, it's right for me."

"Aw. That's so sweet."

I unplugged my cell phone from the charger, congratulating myself because I'd remembered to plug it in before collapsing into bed. Miracle of miracles, a couple of bars appeared. Maybe the dang thing could be useful after all. I sat down at the table with a pad and pencil determined to list my priorities. "Spring kid from jail" got scribbled down before I even knew it.

I wadded up the sheet and reached for my tea. Maybe

sugar and caffeine would help. Just as I took in a big gulp, a local female news announcer appeared on television.

"And in the local news," she said, as a wide shot of the mob scene in the club parking lot ran under her voice-over. "Chapel Hill police are keeping mum about suspects in its investigation of the murder of Randall La Russo, 36. La Russo, a Chapel Hill native, was found dead at Magnolia Blossom Country Club last night."

Then there was some electronic snow and a shot of my blonde fright locks sticking out from under the fire department blanket as Bubba panted evilly at the camera.

I sucked tea into my lungs and coughed up and down country as Chica cut off the TV and pounded me on the back.

"It is not so bad. Your frizzy hair is on TV only, not your face."

"It wasn't that frizzy," I squeaked, my lungs almost tea-free. "You took care of the laptop?"

"I hid it at a friend's house. She's out of town. I water her plants."

"For real out of town?"

"Absolutamente." Her eyes crinkled at the corners. "You take care, amiga. Where you going this morning?"

"We have got to get to the club this afternoon to work. We may be working really late. Right now, though, I've got errands to run, and I need to swing by my parents' house. Wanna go?"

"Your mama doesn't like me."

"She's just permanently uptight. Like June Cleaver in a snit."

"No. She is like that Martha Stewart lady with nothing to decorate. Very scary." She patted Big Foot's huge head. "I stay for the doggie whisperer. He drives from Greensboro this morning."

Both dogs snapped to attention, wide-eyed as if they'd heard they were going to be put down. Bubba clicked over to my boots, his little bell tinkling. He jumped up and pawed the air for me to pick him up. Hmmm. I never knew if I'd lose a finger or be licked to death. No wonder he and Dare got along. They were just alike. I tucked the furry football into the crook of my arm.

"We should learn the tough love skill set he says. But he must study la familia first."

"Do what?"

"Watch us living with the doggies."

For heaven's sake. The only skill set these dogs cared about was our ability to shovel kibble. I set Bubba in his basket and grabbed the van keys. Better to chase a killer than deal with a bow-wow therapist.

Six

To park on or near the UNC campus challenged one's cunning and stamina. Over the years, the city planners had jury-rigged a system that eliminated twenty parking spaces for each new driver introduced into the area. Cross my heart. Consequently, Franklin Street's parking resembled a nasty game of musical chairs on wheels.

However, this morning I was a woman on a Prozac mission. As I waited with the left-turn signal blinking to pull into a prime spot, a rusty Buick chugged from the other direction and slowed to nab my ten feet of parallel curbside in front of Morehead Planetarium. I laid on the horn. The crone in the Buick slammed on brakes. I zoomed in beside the meter. I read her lips, the syllables ugly and surprisingly graphic for a woman in her age demographic. However, submissive wasn't in my repertoire that day. After she drove off, no doubt putting a curse on my head, I fed the meter and trudged up the sidewalk toward Sutton's Drug Store. A few hundred yards away, thousands of innocent students rushed to classes while I brooded over my self-confessed homicidal offspring.

I dug through my bag for the dog-eared prescription that Honey had given me for depression last year. I'd never filled it. Not that a chemical boost wouldn't have been welcome back then, especially during the dark moods when I first returned from Italy to beg for the love and forgiveness of my family. No, I'd had a more prosaic reason for postponing Prozac. The drug supposedly packed on pounds, a circumstance I was sure would exacerbate my depression. Cripes, my jeans already cut off my circulation when standing. Sitting down was pure torture. Vanity precluded me from going up a size, even if I developed blood clots.

I'd argued with Honey about not becoming a Prozac poster babe.

"Speed without Ephedra is the thing," I said. "You kill lots of birds with one pill – depression, appetite and laziness."

"The operative word is 'kill,' Bridget," she barked. "Was that a Freudian slip?"

Honey's onset of "mean-o-pausal" hot flashes had split her personality. I never knew if Glenda the Good Witch or a grimacing gorgon would be tapping a pencil on my fat file folder when I collapsed into the tweed Barcalounger for a session.

But oh, what a difference a day makes in this life. Instead of obesity, I now feared that insanity would consume me if my numbness of spirit ever lifted. After I left Chica's house, I realized that I could very well lose it if I confronted my mother about her no-show at the police station last night. Fractious encounters with the former Miss Sarah Selwyn followed a certain dead-end pattern. Hence, the urgency to swallow a jagged pill or some placebo-like alternative.

As Sutton's glass door closed behind me, I spotted Pit Bullard and Davey at the lunch counter. Seeing me, Davey rolled up *The Chronicle* he was reading and choked on a mouthful of fried egg sandwich.

"Fancy meeting you two in here," I said in singsong even though anxiety lurked just underneath the surface. I pounded

Davey on the back as he gulped water. "Thought you were awaiting bail in the Orange County Hyatt, Pit." He wore a fresh powder blue suit, wrinkled but clean.

"The Lord works in mysterious ways, young woman," Pit backed off his stool with a coffee cup in his hand. "May I offer you my seat?"

"No, no, sit. I'm only here to fill a prescription." I started toward the pharmacy but turned back, eyeing Davey's newspaper.

"What's up?" I grabbed at the paper that Davey had lowered to his lap. "My ears were burning when I walked in."

"No reason they should be." Davey's hand tightened around the paper. "We were … uh … talking about the D-O-O-K game, huh, Pit?"

"I told you, son, you mustn't count your chickadees before they hatch. There is the little matter of the Virginia game tomorrow night, you know."

"Right, right," Davey agreed.

Even a woman whose life was plummeting into a black hole could recognize a couple of liars when she saw them.

Davey stared hard at me, his jaw working. "Eye bags. No sleep last night?"

"How nice to point that out. And yes, no sleep. I, uh, walked the floor, as they say."

"Excuse us for a second, Pit." Davey took my arm and steered me behind the feminine hygiene shelves.

How embarrassing. I turned him away from facing the products lining the shelves in bright pastel rows.

"What?" I demanded. "And you can un-grip my arm now."

"The hell I can." He bit his lower lip and turned away for a second. "Are you crazy? Where did you two go last night?"

"Who says we went anywhere? I was walking the floor."

"Whose floor?"

"Mine."

"Bullshit."

"If you say so."

He grabbed both of my arms and pulled me up to his fiery blue eyes. Whoa, this was definitely a better sight than the boxes of extra super gigantic tampons. Something fluttered in my nether regions. Must've been a low-level stomach cramp.

"I came back to the house after I dropped you off. Worried. Chica's car was gone and no amount of banging on the door seemed to rouse either of you, whereas the dogs went ballistic." His jaw line relaxed a bit with that revelation.

"Whereas? I know you're a lawyer, but whereas?"

"Don't change the subject."

"I plead the Fifth. Can't explain right now. I've got to see my parents. Besides the cashier's eyes are about to pop out of her head."

Davey grinned in her direction and let me go. The cashier blushed and turned away.

"Will you tell me at lunch?"

"Sure." I most likely wouldn't, but I said it anyway. I rubbed my arms to encourage the blood circulation.

"Well then," he replied, looking somewhat deflated. "OK."

Wish he wouldn't stare at me so. He ought to have a girlfriend by now. But not that Jennifer Jones police person who seemed to be panting for him. She seemed wrong.

"Gotta go," I said. Detecting waited for no man – or woman.

I pulled Davey toward the lunch counter where Pit dozed upright on his stool.

"See you about noon, right?" I pointed across the street at the worn marble bench under the huge Davie Poplar, named in honor of the Revolutionary War General and university founder, William Davie.

"Absolutely," he said before going in search of the restroom.

Men. Couldn't live with 'em. Couldn't live without 'em. Except, of course, I was doing just that at the present time.

I hoofed it up to the pharmacy window. When I handed the ratty prescription slip to the pharmacist's assistant, she squinted at it through her glasses and shoved it back across the counter.

"Can't fill this. Expired."

"I thought I had a year to fill it."

"It's more than a year old. You should've checked the date," she said like she had no time for fools.

I stared at the prescription. "I guess I thought this 'one' was a 'seven.'"

"You could be getting presbyopia," she said. "Your focus mechanism starts to rot, you know. You close to forty? That's when it starts."

"Nowhere near forty. And I can see just fine, thank you. It's the handwriting that's hard to read."

"That's what they all say." She said, disappearing behind the shelves.

"Bitch," I mumbled as I turned on my heel.

Well, shoot. Now what was I going to do? Not that the medication would work immediately. But there's something about starting on a plan that was soothing in itself. In theory, one was trying. Honey had said it would take about three weeks to feel the full effects. Three weeks! I could be carving my wrists by that time.

As Pit hunkered over his coffee, I swung by the counter and grabbed the newspaper Davey had left on his stool. Seeing him returning from the restroom, I waved goodbye. His high-wattage smile almost stopped me in my tracks. What was wrong with me? Surely, this wasn't a new behavior on his part. Maybe he'd whitened his teeth or something. Trouble was, I valued our friendship and didn't want to screw that up. Déjà vu once again. I'd gnawed at this issue years ago when he was Daddy's teaching assistant and wanted to marry me. Back then, I hadn't minded that we'd be paupers. But if poor, I felt I should've been passionately in love. Davey was more like a cousin, a kissin' cousin, but a cousin just the same. Besides, I didn't believe he was in love with me, then or now. My theory was that he wanted to be Daddy's son-in-law because he never knew his own father. He wanted the family he'd never had.

Glad to emerge into the cool sunshine, I plopped onto one of the sidewalk benches lining Franklin Street and opened the paper to the headline, "No Suspect in Murder of Chapel Hill Man."

Amazing what camera equipment could capture these days. The photo with its subtitle of "Local Woman Discovers Ex's Body in Sauna of Country Club" spoke a thousand words with its ominous black sky heralding dark deeds and colored lights streaking over a blood-sniffing mob. The focal point, my powder-blue uniform, matched the front chunk of fire truck in the foreground.

Although I couldn't bear to read the main article, I was sucked in by the cutline, which said, "Bridget O'Brien, local artist, exits Magnolia Blossom Country Club just as the authorities arrive."

My stomach clenched, and sweat popped out on my forehead.

An inner devil whispered, "Oatmeal raisin cookie."

I swear.

When an inner angel didn't argue back, I jogged up the sidewalk to Starbucks. Who needed a pharmaceutical intervention when baked sugar, flour and butter were so close by?

At one of the tables ranged along the brick wall of the

coffee shop, my psychiatrist, Honey Kimball, sipped from a bucket-sized container of coffee. Draped in ample honey-colored layers of clothing, she was working on a crossword puzzle in a tacky movie star magazine, the weak spot in her otherwise intellectual reading interests. She'd once admitted that these gossip rags eased her boredom from the realistic, but dreary, problems of her actual clients. I'd counted myself as one among those humdrum souls in her rolodex until she told me one day that my love life was a soap opera extraordinaire.

If I hadn't been so upset this morning, I would've been comforted seeing her stack of brightly colored Hollywood celebrity glossies.

Honey finished her crossword puzzle and looked up. She spotted me in line.

"Well, ta-da, if it isn't Miss Bridget," she exclaimed in her invigorating Virginia Tidewater accent. She extended her arms in welcome. "Where have you been? You should be mortified, unless I've healed you and everything is perfect."

Ah, Glenda the Good Witch.

I hugged her and sniffed her favorite white chocolate mocha Frappuccino. She felt big and warm, like a comfortable old sofa where I could cry my eyes out and drift off to sleep. I rubbed my cheek on the hooded fleece poncho that smelled like lavender with a pinch of oregano.

"Is that uniform clean? Reeks of paint thinner." She wrinkled her nose. "Which means you're working. A good thing, right? I just got back from a trip last night, but I'm still on vacation, mind."

"Oh yeah, where'd you go?" She could tell I didn't really care and didn't answer at first. She set her cup on the table and folded her hands over her puzzle.

"Why have you not scheduled another joint appointment? You and Dare. Or even one for yourself? How is she, by the way?"

Honey's face swam before my eyes. She finally rose to ease me into the other chair and then sat back down, tilting her gilded head. I examined my hands to avoid the x-ray intuition that always exposed my emotional skeleton.

"Dare is an intelligent, lovely girl. But thirteen is thirteen, you know. Don't be surprised at the roller coaster ride you'll be on for the next few years."

So, she hadn't heard.

I smoothed the newspaper and held it against my chest. "Can't stay, really. A woman's work is never done, you know."

Honey pressed cool fingers on my forehead to check for temperature. She dug a bottle of water out of her bag and handed it to me. I sipped, glad not to have to make one decision that day, even if it was only what to drink.

"No fever," she said. "But are you aware that you're not making sense? I presume you entered this establishment to buy coffee. Perhaps it would behoove you to get some before you leave? You weren't looking for me because even I didn't know I would be here." She eased back in her chair with a raised eyebrow.

"Course I'm making sense," I said. "Working a lot lately is all. Can I make an appointment with you now? I could really use one."

"I don't have my appointment book. I should probably break down and get some fancy hand-held device to run my life, but I refuse to succumb to the evils of technology." She smiled. When I didn't smile back, she crossed her arms and became the gorgon.

"Don't play games with me, Bridget," she snapped. "Something is wrong. Let's be sensible, discuss it like adults. You cannot make erratic appointments. I'm not a fast-therapy joint. Counseling is not like buying a double cheeseburger. Continuity is paramount in crisis situations, and this feels like one to me."

That's the trouble with therapists. Are they friends or what? On the one hand, a shrink should be a friend because a client has told her (or him) just about everything. On the other hand, the shrink can't really be a friend because she must maintain objectivity and control the sessions. Friend or not, because she probably knows more about you than you know yourself, a client better hope she's ethical and doesn't revert to blackmail.

"I've been thinking about dropping your professional services so that we can just be friends," I said.

Honey bit her lip.

"But I don't know if you'd listen to my problems if you weren't being paid."

She laughed.

That seemed to be a good sign, so I stood up.

"I'd like to make a proper appointment. Wouldn't want you to feel like a drive-in window."

"I said I'm taking this week off." But she wasn't angry because she hadn't turned red. She'd once explained that uncontrollable blushing made her face clash with her shades-of-honey wardrobe choices. We all have priorities, I guess.

"This is an emergency appointment. Thanks for being here for me. I've got to go to work now or I'd stay and do coffee. Meanwhile..."

I laid the paper in front of her and pointed to the headline and then the photo.

Honey gazed at the paper for several seconds, her mouth open.

"We have an early court date in the morning that I'd like for you to attend even if it's your vacation. Dare has confessed. Can you be there by 8 a.m.?"

As she reached for me with a stricken look, I turned on my heel and escaped before I could start blubbering like a baby.

Seven

The van crunched over the gravel drive as I approached the country club. With this sound, familiar since my babyhood, came tears that blinded me so that I stomped on the brakes.

Trouble was, I couldn't remember anything negative about Randy. His arrogance yesterday now seemed as sexy as fifteen years ago when he'd stubbornly dodged matrimony. His exasperating immaturity had morphed into a glamorous Peter Pan syndrome, that stupid – but alluring – bad boy thing.

This was ridiculous. What about Marcus? Yeah, Marcus, my first husband who'd loved me enough to marry me and make me a respectable woman. True, he'd been old enough to be my father, which eventually became unreasonable jealousy about my male friends and especially Randy. But Marcus was also kind, even if deadly dull – the prosaic professor, I'd called him. But maybe not. Maybe, it was me. Honey suggested about a million sessions ago that I should cull the soap opera elements in my emotional psyche and grow up.

Was I falling back into that "because you can't have Randy, you love him" ditch I'd wallowed in all those years ago? Scary thought. Talk about regression. I'd scaled life's ladder with the aid of an enthusiastic certified mental health professional, yet I'd slipped down several rungs, it seems.

Daddy once said that the living often sanctified the dead, so, perhaps I'd not dropped too far after all. Could be I was just catching my breath. With the passage of time from this horrific event, proper perspective might be achieved. Whatever. The long-deferred appointment with Honey seemed in order. I relaxed a bit. Angel or demon, Honey played hardball with my emotions for an exorbitant fee, but it usually helped.

I dried my eyes and drove toward the club house. Rolling into a parking spot near the front entrance, I looked up only to be sabotaged by another memory. Thriving pink camellias pruned and trained to climb a wall trellis recalled a late spring day ten years earlier when these same flowers had been immature and lined the curb in pots.

Randy and I had parked here at that time, bringing Dare for a private swimming lesson insisted on by my father. A man had been attaching trellis to the club's left outer wall. A woman had stood among the dwarf camellia pots giving him directions.

"Isn't it kind of late to be planting these?" I'd said. "You'll never get them to grow up that trellis."

"It's late, but they'll make it with proper care," she'd replied. "You can teach anything to climb, you know. Just wait and see."

"Wait 'n' see, Mommy," Dare had echoed, bobbing in Randy's arms. She'd sounded so serious and grownup.

"Okay, punkin, I'll do that." I remember being relieved that she'd stopped crying for her "daddy" (for Marcus). Randy and I had picked her up from him an hour earlier. When Marcus had kissed her goodbye, she'd tuned up, heartbroken. Even though we drove away quickly, Randy had looked mutinous. What did he expect? To the rest of the world,

Marcus was Dare's father. He'd loved her and seen that she wanted for nothing. Randy should've been grateful.

However upset my little daughter felt leaving Marcus that day, Randy had managed to charm her out of her funk by the time we reached the club. Her velvet-brown eyes had danced above pink cheeks, her hair sprouting atop her head, a shiny ponytail of chocolate curl propped up by a bow that matched her yellow polka-dotted bathing suit.

"Kiss me, Randy," she'd demanded grasping his face, a baby empress at three.

"Mighty bold talk." Randy had smooched the tip of her nose. "Where does she come by it?" He and Dare had headed toward the pool complex.

"I wonder," I'd whispered, bursting with the pride and happiness characteristic of the early days of my second marriage. After stroking the dark green leaves of a young camellia plant, I had to run to catch up with my little family.

Today, a decade later, those same camellias climbed the trellis just like the woman had promised, thick and vibrant. For me though, their blushing winter glory proclaimed a different season in a different life. My head drooped, and I gripped the steering wheel so hard my wrists like to have snapped.

Someone tapped on my window. Long Johnson, the club's assistant manager, pressed his face against the glass.

"You okay?" he asked, looking concerned.

I opened the door as he stepped back. "Sorry, just remembering stuff." I jumped to the ground. "I need to drop off some supplies in case Chica comes over before I get back with the van."

"I'm so sorry about your… about Mr. La Russo," he said.

Crikey, did everyone know everyone else's business in this place? I'd never told Long about my relationship with Randy.

"Where's, uh, Miss DeMoya? I hope everything is all right," he said.

Although Long burned for Chica, he was probably suffering in vain. She maintained a friendly distance, brushing him off as "cute but short, amiga. I like my hombres big."

"She's home, exhausted. A really bad night, you know. But she'll be around later."

Long and I became friends after I returned from Italy and met him when I was having dinner at the club with my parents. He often pestered me with questions about Rome because he worshipped the movie *Gladiator* and was dying to explore the Colosseum.

"I don't know if you realize it, but Randy and I have been … were … divorced a long time ago. I saw him yesterday for the first time in five years and then …." My throat tightened.

"Terrible business. Terrible." Long patted my arm. "The police were here earlier. That lieutenant, the one doing Columbo in a trench coat, just left. He questioned me, but I didn't have much to say because I was off yesterday. He talked to Hermann, too, even though he wasn't here when … well, when it must've happened.

"The lieutenant laughed when I introduced myself and tried to hide it when he wrote down my name." Long scowled, poor guy.

He scowled a lot because he's spent so many years explaining his first name. Long says his first name means "dragon" in Chinese. His father, an African-American army veteran from Durham, met and married his mother while on leave in Taiwan during the Vietnam War. When Mrs. Johnson wanted to name their baby son Dragon, in English, after the Chinese year in which he was born, Mr. Johnson pitched a conniption fit until he learned the Chinese word for dragon. An unrepentant practical joker, he thought "Long Johnson" sounded funny as hell. His wife, who could barely speak English then, didn't know that "johnson" was slang for penis. The upshot? Long scowled a lot, especially when first meeting people.

I opened the back doors of the van and hauled out a box filled with odds and ends and paint cans.

"If you can get the other box," I said, "we'll put these inside with our other supplies. Did you have to move any of our stuff for the police?"

"No, but they searched all the boxes and got that awful fingerprint dust all over everything." He shivered in fastidiousness. Long embodied cleanliness in his personal habits and surroundings. Woe to the employee who left dust on the furniture or leaves on the carpet during his watch.

He fluffed his tall buzz cut of salt-and-pepper hair, which added critical height to his five-foot-three-inch frame, before reaching for the box. I bumped the van doors shut with my hip.

"You sure you won't mess up your clothes?" I eyed the smart pin-stripes, snowy shirt, and gray tie. If I'd spent as much time in front of a mirror as he did, I'd have been in Hollywood by now.

"I'm not fussy about that kind of thing," he replied with a bleached-tooth smile of denial.

"Uh-huh, right."

I labored up the short wheelchair access ramp and punched the chrome automatic door opener installed on the handrail. As the door slowly swung open, an older man and younger woman, oblivious to their surroundings, faced off on the threshold.

"I was at the mall after I left the driving range yesterday afternoon," said the tall, well-endowed redhead in a breathy Marilyn Monroe voice. This had to be Muffin, Mr. Ruffin's new trophy wife Mother had mentioned yesterday.

"Doesn't that fancy cell phone work in the mall?" Mr. Ruffin asked of his spouse.

"Sometimes there's a signal, sometimes not," she said with a sigh, as if the gods were against her and she needed Mr. Ruffin's protection. "Why should I fib, Mikey, honey?"

Gag.

He'd been "Mr. Ruffin" to me for most of my life until insisting a couple of years ago that I call him Mike. But I was having a hard time with it. One thing I was certain of though, he wasn't, and never would be, a "Mikey."

"You're just cranky because we can't get into the locker room. When did you leave those papers in there anyway?" Muffin asked.

"Yesterday," he replied. "They weren't that important. I didn't have time to deal with them last night before the Raleigh meeting."

The Ruffins finally turned and realized they had an audience.

"Little Miss Bridget," he exclaimed after an awkward pause. "A business woman now, I hear." He took his wife's arm and pulled her next to him. I caught a whiff of Chanel No. 5 and my hackles rose.

"I used to pull Bridget's pigtails," he said.

Everyone looked embarrassed for a couple of seconds; my hair was still in braids thirty years later.

"Yes, well, Bridget," Mr. Ruffin harrumphed, "Don't think you've met my wife, Margaret Mary." He put our two hands together as if we were exchanging vows. "It's Margaret Muffin, though, right, hon? Her daddy declared she was his Muffin the minute he saw her in the hospital. He owned a string of bakeries."

Probably her daddy was younger than Mr. Ruffin.

Margaret Mary "Muffin" Ruffin shot me a cool glance, a tough customer camouflaged with perfect makeup and flawless skin. She also wore the finest of LPGA golf apparel under a sporty mink vest. No wonder Marla Ann had seen green. To top it off, she smelled like Randy's perfume-infused pillow.

"You can call on us for anything, you know," Muffin said with the sincerity of a crocodile. "I'd come to know Randy well. We are absolutely devastated."

Mr. Ruffin sucked in a breath and gave her a calculating look.

"Anything you need, Bridget, you name it. Randy was like my son," Mr. Ruffin finally said, turning back to me after glowering at Muffin.

"Really? You two hadn't spoken for weeks if I recall correctly. Until yesterday," she said politely with a tinge of sarcasm.

"My darling girl," he said to his wife. "Randy and I are not, or rather we were not, doing business anymore."

Here was life imitating prime-time soap opera art.

"You saw him yesterday?" I asked.

"Only briefly in passing," Mr. Ruffin said. "We spoke a bit about the basketball game on Saturday."

Muffin pursed her lips and turned back to me.

"I thought perhaps a deli tray from Dean & DeLuca would have been appropriate for your family whenever you have a service," Muffin said. "But Mikey says there isn't one in this godforsaken town."

"And where might you be from?" I inquired with Mother's pointed delivery. Considering my seething emotions, this was an Emmy-winning performance. I balanced my box on the handrail, ready to roll up my hypothetical sleeves, if necessary.

"Born and raised in Charlotte. The Eastover neighborhood actually," she said with a sniff and glance down her nose at Long. "But I went to Duke. Tri-Delt. What about you?" She tucked a strand of hair behind her ear, revealing an odd-shaped purplish mark on her neck.

Please tell me that wasn't a hickey.

"Unluckily for me, I went to school here at godforsaken Carolina," I drawled, wondering if I could drop the box on her designer shoes and call it an accident. "And speaking of godforsaken …."

Long nudged me just in time.

"Mr. Ruffin, can I be of service to you and your lovely wife? Is there anything you need?" he asked.

I felt like slapping Long's jaws.

"No thanks, Long. We've gotta run. Take care, Bridget," Mr. Ruffin said as he and Muffin headed for the parking lot.

"Yes, do," Muffin called without a backward glance.

"Why'd you stop me?" I poked Long as the Ruffins climbed into their fine black Mercedes roadster.

"Because I'm your friend," he said. "And there's work to do. You're not a member anymore, remember? I want you to keep your contract with us, and there'll be more work in the future as long as you don't get into it with the members."

Hmph. I was more concerned about her possible illicit relationships than with her opinion of my alma mater.

At the top of the steps leading to the ballroom, we placed the heavy boxes on the carpet for a breather. Long nodded toward the men's locker room door where the yellow police tape was rolled up on the floor.

"They released the room to us this morning. Hermann is coping with the mess now… I mean … I didn't mean … oh Lord," he stammered. "I knew he would make sure everything was in order, so I asked him to supervise it."

Hermann opened the door from inside the men's locker room, pushing a bucket and mop ahead of him. His glasses were atop longish gray-blonde hair that was pulled into a neat ponytail, his aging face still handsome. Pilar said he looked a lot like his grandfather, who'd emigrated to Argentina from Germany after World War II.

Hermann paused for a moment before peeling off his rubber gloves. He approached slowly and took my hand. I swallowed another annoying knot of tears.

"May I say that we truly regret your loss, Miss O'Brien?" He spoke English like BBC programming tinged with the faintest Spanish rolling of the 'R.' If you need anything, you ring me or Pilar straightaway."

Of course. Pilar. I mentally kicked myself for not thinking of her sooner with regard to Dare's mental state. In her position as co-chairwoman for UNC's Habitat for Humanity program, I saw her often. She had contacted Faux Finish to work on the latest house project. Besides being Dare's former babysitter, she supervised her on projects and fundraisers whenever possible, and the child adored her. Maybe she could help me navigate the stormy waters of an adolescent mind. Waiting for a chance meeting with her was out of the question.

"Oh yes, Hermann, yes, Pilar could help me so much! I need to speak to her today. What's she doing right now?"

"Unfortunately, she felt poorly last night and wouldn't let me stop at the chemist's." He dropped my hand and, putting both of his behind his back, gazed at the carpet.

"Think she'd mind if I called? I'm a basket case about Dare. I've got to find out if she's talked to her lately or …."

Sometimes I hated being a woman. Tears sat in ambush and erupted at the most inopportune times.

"Right," he said. "But she might not pick up. A bit knackered and run down is my call, although she ate a big bag of crisps last night. And she spends too much time on her studies, as her marks prove." His usual glowing pride was relatively low-key, but I put that down to my current circumstances.

"I hope Dare will be all right," he said. "I'd forgot that

Mr. La Russo was her stepfather all those years ago. She was barely out of nappies then."

I came all over goose bumps.

"Miss O'Brien is in a hurry," Long said, seeing my face crumple.

"I didn't mean to ...." Hermann said.

"No, no. Please don't worry," I said. "Tell Pilar I'll call her."

"Pilar is like her father," said Long, the diplomat. "They both have a strong work ethic. I didn't expect you to clean the locker room yourself, Hermann. I just wanted you to make sure it was done right."

"Best to handle some jobs one's self," Hermann said. "Especially on your own patch."

Long checked his watch. "I'm not sure when Malcolm is coming in, and I've got paperwork piled a mile high on my desk."

"If you will excuse me, I've got to find that git ... pardon me, Miss O'Brien...I mean Virgil, for a heart to heart," Hermann said.

"The guy who chews tobacco?" I asked.

"Virgil Spoon," Hermann said. "You've met him? I hope he hasn't done something dodgy, but I wouldn't put it past him."

"No. I've seen him with the weed whacker and wondered, is all." No need to mention that he'd been at the police station. I didn't want to get him in trouble just because he looked like a serial killer.

"Did he work any last night?" I said. For Dare's sake, I was leaving no stone unturned in the suspect pool.

"No, he wasn't scheduled to," said Long. "The police questioned him. He was working at a Habitat house. Same one Pilar is helping with, if I'm not mistaken." He frowned at Hermann. "Didn't you warn Virgil about that damned chewing tobacco during work hours? Disgusting habit."

Long's cell phone rang, and he stepped away to take the call.

"I live without one of those phones myself," Hermann said. "Do you have Pilar's mobile number?" He used the long 'I' when pronouncing 'mobile.' That thing is never out of her sight." A fond smile lifted the corners of his mouth. "Our young folk are spoiled these days."

"You got that right." I pulled my phone out of my pocket. No bars. I held it in the air and one appeared, as if doing me a favor. I wanted to stomp on the whole gizmo. "I'm pretty sure I have it in my address book, but my phone is dead. My parents have the number though, and I'm going over there now. Besides, all I have to write with are these things and no ink." I indicated the turkey feather piled atop the other paraphernalia in the box.

"Hermann, please take these boxes to the ballroom," Long said, hurrying back from his call. "That was Malcolm. He'll be in this afternoon. He wants to have a short employee meeting with us at about six."

"Bridget. I mean Miss O'Brien, sorry," said Long. "Are you coming back this afternoon for sure? And Miss DeMoya too? In spite of all that's happened, everything has to be shipshape for that wedding reception." He rolled his eyes. "Never know when the designer brigade is going to show up, or even worse, the bride-to-be."

"Please call me Bridget. Like you said earlier, I'm working here, too. Don't worry about little Miss Alexandra. She's probably not all that bad even if her mama is the mayor. Being a new bride is pretty nerve-wracking. Been there, done that."

"I hope you're right," he said.

"Thanks for all your kind words. Both of you. And Hermann, please let Pilar know I'm trying to get in touch with her."

"Maybe she's on the mend," Hermann said, not altogether convincingly.

"Chica and I'll be back later. I'm just not sure when."

I descended the steps, pausing to pat my pockets for the van keys.

"Don't beat around the bush with Virgil, Hermann," Long said in a low voice before the two men disappeared inside the club.

Eight

As I turned the corner onto Rosemary Street, the faded blue house appeared like a glimpse of morning sky through the wooded lots. I parked the van at the curb. My blood pressure percolated as I watched for Mother to walk toward me down the brick sidewalk, checked for her face at the windows. She should be on the lookout for me.

"What, can't you read my mind? You didn't know I was coming?" I said to the closed door and empty panes of glass. We are always children with our mothers.

Is this what Dare was thinking, too? Being caught in the middle was an uncomfortable conundrum. I left the van and headed for the peace of my mother's backyard Eden. A control freak in most things, Mother had loosed her passion on this little patch of God's country as had my namesake, St. Brigid of Ireland, in hers.

To delay confronting Mother about her no-show at the police station, I wandered to the live oak rope swing, asway in a gentle morning breeze. Daddy was fond of saying he'd rigged it when I was knee-high to a grasshopper. I wiggled onto the seat, which felt smaller. Maybe wood shrank.

Daddy had put me on the swing for the first time and

pointed to the limb holding the ropes, its branches waving at the sky like pointed fingers.

"That branch prays for his angel," he said, kissing the top of my head, "so you will be safe."

My mother, up to her green thumbs in red clay and potting soil, had glanced up gimlet-eyed. "For pity's sake, Richard, you're too sentimental for your own good. Don't push that child too high or she'll break her neck."

She was always the practical one.

Deciding I'd reminisced enough, I wiggled off of the swing. En route to the house, I paused before a small stone fountain rimmed with green moss and banked by Christmas ferns. After one Hail Mary and Our Father for Dare, I marched up the slate path to the back door.

I knocked, but the door was already open and swung into the kitchen. I hesitated and peered into the room.

"Daddy?" My voice pinged off of marble, granite and hardwood.

The grandfather clock in the foyer tolled the Westminster chimes and then gonged eleven times. The quiet gripped my gut.

"Hey, y'all left the door open," I called half-heartedly.

The faucet dripped in Mother's prized copper sink. Crockery broke the greasy surface of dishwater like the humps of a sea serpent.

"Hello? It's me." They could probably hear me in Durham County. "For heaven's sake!" But I couldn't help my concern. Standing dishwater in Mother's usually neat kitchen did not equate.

The ceiling fan rotated slowly over the island stacked with an *Architectural Digest,* blue exam books and the front section of the newspaper. Coffee stained my photo on page one. Mail order catalogs teetered beside bowls of hardened pasta, goblets with red wine dregs and a glass of sour milk.

My parents had to have been murdered in their beds – or no, murdered before bedtime – because the Sarah Selwyn O'Brien I'd known for three-and-a-half decades would not have retired to the boudoir with her kitchen in this state.

I tiptoed to the swinging door that led to the dining room and waited, preparing to poke my head through. Someone on the other side banged the door open, smacking me on the forehead.

"Shit." I backed into the carved ram's head decorating one end of the island. "Damn." I rubbed my fanny.

"What in the world?" Mother declared as she burst into the room. "Why in heaven would you be skulking behind the door, Bridget?"

"I thought you were a crazed killer?"

"Come here." She laid a cool hand on my forehead. In one smooth movement, she steered me to a stool, wrapped ice in a dishtowel and held it to the bump.

"So, it was you screaming like a fishwife down here."

As I grabbed the icepack, I finally looked at Mother – and gaped. I guess this was my mother. But no, it couldn't be. My mother dressed to the nines to pick up the morning paper in the front yard. She negotiated her garden, her bridge, her charity work and her family twenty-four hours a day with nary a fair hair out of place. Her pearls glowed with creamy perfection; her twin sets whispered of the finest cashmere.

But the woman standing before me possessed Medusa-like locks. Daddy's favorite-but-holey Carolina t-shirt and faded sweat pants drooped on her slim frame. Earth-stained tennis shoes adorned her feet. If Mother's Chi Omega sisters could see her now, they'd recoil in prune-lipped horror.

"Close your mouth, dear," she said.

I tried to and couldn't.

"If I didn't know better, I'd swear that you didn't have

the sense God gave a goat. Surely you didn't sustain a concussion from one little tap on the head."

This sounded bitchily normal.

"By the way, the police were here earlier," she added.

"What for?"

"They searched your room … Dare's, rather. He asked me about her movements yesterday. Was it only yesterday?"

"Who did?"

"A Lieutenant Hendricks." She patted her frightening hair, an encouraging feminine gesture. Vanity generally signaled that all was well among the women on Mother's side of the family.

"A bit Columbo-ish for my taste, all huddled in that trench coat. It could use a good dry-cleaning."

"It's his wardrobe signature. I guess he had a warrant?"

"Honestly, Bridget, you watch too much crime television. I didn't ask and he didn't say. It would have been rude."

"Bet he had one. Did they take anything? God, Mother, did it ever occur to you that … well, that there might be something that we should … um …."

"What? Hide? Burn? Eat?"

I just looked at her.

"Yes, it did occur to me."

My throat felt dry.

"Don't gawp, dear, makes you look simple-minded. Anyway, he and another policeman asked if she had a diary. I told them there was a locked one on her desk next to her computer. They didn't find it, but I still gave them a piece of my mind. Such bad taste to go through one's personal possessions."

Mother waxing insufferable was another good sign.

Clawing through the disorder on the kitchen island, she found her brown Coach handbag. She draped it on her arm like Queen Elizabeth at a ribbon-cutting and stood with one ratty shoe diagonal to the other.

Sweat sprung out on my forehead for the second time that morning, despite the ice still cooling the bump on my head.

"Daddy?" I shouted through the ceiling.

"He has office hours this morning." She pulled her keys from her purse and clicked her tongue at my forgetfulness. "It's Tuesday."

"I knew that," I said, even though I'd clean forgotten about it.

Mother pushed past me.

"The back door was wide open when I got here," I said. "That's why I hollered. I thought y'all were lying dead upstairs."

"Of all the foolish notions."

"Okay. Right." I tamped down my anxiety. "Then do you have Pilar's phone number around here somewhere?"

She pointed to the rolodex next to the phone on the countertop.

"She's a sweet child. Pilar," said my mother, "despite her poor father."

"What do you mean by that?" I jotted down the number on a scrap of paper and clapped my cell phone shut to hold it. Maybe it was good for something after all.

"Nothing, nothing. He's just a parent, worrying about his child like the rest of us." She sighed knowingly, as if I were one of her women friends instead of her daughter. "How sharper than a serpent's tooth it is to have a thankless child."

I swept a game-show bimbette arm in the air to indicate the filthy kitchen despite Mother's recital of King Lear's rant at his daughter Cordelia.

"Look at this pig sty, Mother. This is so not you." Better to incur anger than witness another ill-thought-out, lackluster delivery of the bard's dialog. "Looks like trashy folks live here." I steeled myself for a severe reprimand.

Mother ran a vacant eye over the room. "Well then, clean it up, dear."

The former fraternity sweetheart was now a zombie. My mother had gone missing.

"I must run," she said.

In that ensemble? She had to be ill.

"Don't go anywhere. You're not well." I reached for her forehead this time, and she drew back as if I were the devil. I fingered the lump on my head. Could be I was unconscious and having a nightmare.

I watched that god-awful t-shirt scuttle out the door and ran out of the house in time to see her gun the Volvo down the driveway. I could've kicked myself because I'd forgotten to grill her about her no-show last night at the police station. Probably a good thing though, what with this first glimpse of her dark side. Then, I got mad again.

"So, what exactly is a fishwife?" I yelled in frustration as the car zipped around the corner. A passing jogger took one look at me and sprinted to the other side of the street.

Ah well, Mother's attendance at the hearing was out of the question. Too embarrassing for her. At this point, functioning normally there was going to be hard enough for me, much less my mother.

I trudged back inside the house to call my father. He didn't answer his office phone, so I left a message describing Mother's behavior, how she'd driven off to God knows where, and how he'd better do something about it.

I forgot about making Davey's sandwiches and trotted upstairs to Dare's bedroom to search, although I wasn't sure for what.

My old sleigh bed still stood in the corner next to the window that faced Mother's garden. Dare's make-up, lip gloss, jewelry box and a prescription bottle for her acne medicine sat on Nana Blanche's polished vanity table.

Two framed pictures decorated the chest of drawers: a photo of Marcus and me blowing out Dare's first birthday candle as she smeared pink icing on my face, and a watercolor of Bubba that I'd done at her request.

On the bedside table, a snapshot of Dare and Marcus that I'd never seen took pride of place. She stood with him on the steps of Ackland Art Museum. Judging from her long hair, it had been taken last summer before Marcus's final illness, while I had dallied in Italy. Gauntness and a gray goatee attested to his struggle with congestive heart failure. Despite his pallor, he was grinning like a boy as Dare stood on tiptoe to kiss his cheek.

Shifting clothing in one of the drawers, I found Dare's cell phone cord. If only she'd not dropped her cell… I slammed the drawer shut. There was no time to reflect on what might have been. Who could plan these things? Nothing in the other drawers or her closet gave up any secrets.

I gazed about the room. How the child had convinced my traditional mother to allow the celebrity décor and let her paint three walls turquoise and one green was beyond me. Obviously, she inherited Randy's powers of persuasion.

Like my mother (until today, that is), Dare always kept her things immaculate, a sure sign that genes skipped generations. Her perfectly aligned posters surrounded me – Eminem, Fifty Cent, Tolkien's King Aragorn and Al Pacino's *Scarface*, of all things. A life-sized cardboard Captain Jack Sparrow smirked from a corner. The adolescent milestones reassured me until I recalled the stone-faced girl at the police station.

I slid the bed away from the wall and pried up two loose boards. Several ancient shoeboxes crowded the shallow space beneath the floor. I'd been storing – okay, hiding – my journals here since girlhood.

I lifted a volume into the light and read a random entry.

Saturday, May 22, 1993

Wrightsville Beach. Friday, we began studying frescoes at the artist's colony. Not on our backs like poor Michelangelo at least. But I got antsy and left early to drive back to Chapel Hill. Got home about five. My stuff was ransacked. Drawers, closets, boxes in the attic, books all turned inside out. I panicked and called my parents, thinking kidnapping and murder, but Marcus and Dare were there. He mumbled a piddling apology for the mess, said he was looking for our marriage license. Not expecting you home until tomorrow, he said. Right. I asked what he was really looking for. He got mad. We had a good old scream. Your journals, he yelled. You write in them all the time and never let me see. About that time, Dare started crying and we called a truce. He's a middle-aged professor, for heaven's sake. What if he'd found the things I'd written about not loving him, about Randy being Dare's father? I'll have to put my journals somewhere else. How can he not trust Randy? I've not seen him since before Dare was born. Marcus said he hates that I'm so young. I laughed in his face. Bad move, but I was so angry. I told him that many senior citizens dye their hair. He slapped me so hard my teeth hurt. Then he started to cry, hanging onto my waist. He said Randy had been calling. Marcus demanded to see my journals. I told him I burned most of them after I married him. God, the guilt, and I haven't even done anything.

I tucked the journal back into its hidey hole and repositioned the bed; I was breathless among the dust motes as if I'd just run around the block. Marcus grinned at me from the bedside photo. I turned the picture face down and ran down to the kitchen where I tried to call Pilar on a real telephone. No answer. She was most likely in class.

I stopped at the refrigerator, recalling that Davey would not get the sandwiches he anticipated. As my father's starving teaching assistant, he had lollygagged around the house so much he became smitten with my bologna specialties. But just because there wouldn't be an entrée didn't mean we couldn't have dessert. I foraged in the freezer for the oatmeal raisin cookies that Mother baked for me every week. Seemed the least I could offer Davey and, most of all, myself. However, nary cookie was in sight among the neatly stacked contents. Considering the current family crisis and my mother becoming a frenzied bag lady, the lack was understandable but unfortunate. I needed her cookies now more than ever.

Nine

I plonked onto the bench under the Davie Poplar. In this peaceful place, I often mulled over my problems. Today, I had lots to go on about. Who killed Randy? Can I fix things for Dare? What's wrong with Mother? What's with my marital track record? Will lightning strike at the hearing?

But the lightning-struck poplar only waved its branches in the cool breeze.

My grandfather – PopPop – had formally introduced me to the one-hundred-foot tree after I'd run home tearful from my first brutal day of kindergarten. He'd taken my hand for the short walk to campus from my parent's house. PopPop's crinkly blue eyes filled as he gazed upward.

"There is a legend about this tree," he said. "A committee was headed by Gen. William Davie to find a site for the state university. After a long day of searching, committee members sat down to rest on the grass under a giant tulip poplar. They lunched and 'regaled themselves with exhilarating beverages,' according to Archibald Henderson's 1949 book, The Campus of the First State University. That was when the committee members decided that 'no more beautiful or suitable spot could be found' for the university. And the Davie Poplar became a symbol of lore."

I'd loved the Davie Poplar since that day with PopPop. It marked my special spot on campus, a link to the past that sometimes seemed to ease the way to my future.

I stood and brushed the seat of my pants as Davey stepped over the low stone wall that ran along Franklin Street and separated the main campus from town. He strolled uphill over the sparse winter grass.

"So," he said when he stopped before me, "tell me what you and Chica did last night. Omit no details."

"Hello, good to see you again." I motioned that we head toward town. "Is this a deposition?"

"You realize this is not a situation comedy, don't you, Bridget? Your daughter is in detention through a combination of teenage drama and a wild imagination, I hope. But then instead of sitting tight and letting the police do their work, you and Chica rampage around in the dead of night like Lucy and Ethel. At the very least, to stir up trouble. At the very worst, to get yourselves killed. And last, what happened to your head? Oh, wait. You're going to tell me you ran into a door, right?"

"Great off-the-cuff delivery. You'll make a good lawyer someday."

"It's a learned skill set," he said. "But can we please be serious for a moment?"

"Serious is all there is lately. OK, so pay attention. Number one. My mother battered me, swear to God. She used a door. This also explains why there are no sandwiches. Number two. As to my rampaging in the dead of night, remember those lines you once quoted from that old Scottish ballad? 'Did you ever hear of a loyal Scot, who was never concerned in any plot?'"

"You're not a Scot, and I don't see what that's got to do with the price of kilts," he said.

"I beg your pardon. My ancestors came in the Scots-Irish

migration to North Carolina too, Davey McKenzie. The McCords. I'm also loyal. That makes me a loyal Scot, as is my child in that Orange County kid prison. I don't care if you're my friend or lawyer, you won't stop me from trying my best to get her out." I punched his shoulder, ready to take on Scots, Italians, the Russian mafia or anything that got in my way.

He grinned. Hell, he laughed.

Bastard.

"What's so damn funny?"

"You sound so tough. You're afraid to climb ladders and scared of your gun. You're the queen of vertigo and get sick faster than anyone I've ever seen. Do you imagine the killer will take your hand and surrender happily?"

As we walked, we dodged a lunchtime stream of students and sat on the wall in front of the Methodist church.

"Oh, shut up."

"I will not."

"I'm not the wimp you make me out to be," I said. "But this hearing thing is freaking me out. Is the district attorney like that mean D.A. in the old Perry Mason TV shows?"

"He's not bad. Went to Duke, though. Don't worry, you'll do fine. This a first appearance and detention hearing, so we should be in and out fairly quickly. The judge will check that she is represented and that a guardian was present during the interrogation and that's about it. He will also make sure she understands the charges against her. But I doubt she will be released back into your parent's custody because of the seriousness of the charge. Most likely, she will remain in detention until trial or until the police find a better suspect."

"You mean until they find the killer."

"That's what I meant."

He really was a poor liar, a bad thing for a lawyer, to my notion.

"What is it with you guys? Why can't you just say what you mean instead of trying to confuse the issue?"

He ignored my questions.

"Don't practice a speech for the hearing," he said. "You can speak in her defense, but I want it short, sweet and genuine. Richard will be there, and he's a dream witness. Silver-haired, upstanding, honest, articulate, intelligent without being pompous. I suppose your mother isn't coming?"

"Duh."

"That's OK. Don't push her."

"As if I could."

"So, tell me about last night."

After I recounted my activities with Chica and most of what we discovered, Davey closed his eyes.

"Oh, for Pete's sake. It was just a teensy infringement that nobody saw."

"Teensy? Breaking and entering? Do you know the meaning of burglary? That's when you break in and take something that doesn't belong to you. We're talking possible jail time here."

"You're just trying to scare me. A first offender probably wouldn't go straight to jail."

"Yes, you would. Then you might get probation and community service."

"Besides, it wasn't breaking. Only entering. I had a key. It's not my fault no one was at home. I bet it's not burglary if the house belongs to your child's grandmother."

Oh no. Will he notice the slip of my idiot tongue?

"You mean her step-grandmother, don't you? Grace hasn't been that for years, and it's not a particularly close relationship," he said, still a touch resentful of anything to do with my past husbands.

"Uh, yeah, I forgot."

"Are you really this naïve about the consequences of breaking the law at your age?"

"You worry too much."

"Of course, you won't have to go to prison if the real killer murders you."

"Well, there is that," I said. Mister Optimistic rides again. What did he mean, at my age? He was three years older.

"Now that you're up on my dangerous escapade, can we go?" I rose and started toward the curb.

He yanked me back down.

"Don't change the subject. Stealing that laptop comes under the category of throwing a monkey wrench into the investigation. Something the police frown upon."

"Someone's got to do something. It wasn't stealing. Not really. It belonged to one of my husbands. More like borrowing. What do you think about that $100,000 that disappeared? Maybe it's in the Caymans."

"You've been watching too many spy movies."

"Whatever."

"I have no idea where the money came from or where it went or even if it ever was, Randy being Randy. It might not be relevant at all. I'd have to see that list. You didn't borrow anything else of his, did you?" Davey's chin was as fixed as that of the Davie Poplar's roots.

During the protracted silence that followed, several people got off the bus just a few yards away from where we sat, including Hermann. I thought he saw me, and I raised my hand to wave, but he turned in the opposite direction. He looked a bit distracted.

"Don't get all mad," I said. "I'll figure a way to get it back in the house or give it to his mother or something. Have the police located her?"

"No luck so far," he said. "Turns out she doesn't have a cell phone, and the only person who might know her whereabouts is Randy. So say the neighbors. And I don't want you breaking into the house again."

We needed a change of subject. I pointed across the street.

"Let's go bug Marla Ann right now as we're so close to her office."

"You must be kidding. Is that why we're here?"

It was, but I didn't want him to think I'd manipulated him.

"If Randy's notes are correct, someone is pregnant," I said. "Maybe I can tell if it's her. I wasn't looking for the signs when I saw her yesterday."

"Now I know what Dr. Watson must have felt trailing after Holmes. If you plan to ask Marla Ann if she's with child, you can do it alone. I've got to call Greg and see if there's anything new about the cause of death."

"You mean the autopsy?" My world tilted at the picture conjured up by that word, and I started to sink backward.

"Yeah, you're a real tough lady." Davey yanked me back to a sitting position. "I think I just made my point about your hang-ups and inner ear troubles, but I won't rub it in."

I covered my face with my hands. He put an arm around me and for a few seconds I was sheltered and warm.

"I just need sleep. I'm good now." I shook him off. "I notice you call him Greg. Are you close friends?"

"We met when he arrested a client a few years back. No big mystery, I assure you."

"Knowing him can't hurt, though."

We crossed the street and descended a staircase into Amber Alley, a grimy, tiled walkway between Franklin and Rosemary Streets. Famous in Chapel Hill as the location of the Rathskeller restaurant, or "Rat." Marla Ann's business, Furr Realty, was next door.

"I'll only go in for a minute," he said. "I don't figure her for a hammer-wielding maniac. And please don't say what you're going to say."

"Hell hath no fury like a woman scorned," I said anyway. "She could be pregnant with Randy's baby, God forbid. A woman's hormones are hell during a time like that. Come on, don't leave me alone with a potential murderess. This is your chance to keep me safe while I – what did you call it?—rampage and stir up trouble?"

As Davey pushed the office door open, a set of tiny silver wind chimes tinkled.

Marla Ann's domain smelled like the Rat's Gambler platter, pounded steak smothered with onions and a baked potato served on a sizzling griddle, which was not surprising given its proximity to the restaurant. But the office's interior design was pure bordello, black and violent pink, reminiscent of seedy lingerie shops.

The woman could cozy up to plastic surgeons and cruise around in a posh ride all she liked, but her work environment revealed a former country school bus driver with new cash.

There was no one at the receptionist's desk, but Marla Ann's office door opened and her chest, mashed by red cashmere, appeared first. A short, black floaty shirt and hooker stilettos followed a split second later.

"Look at what the cat drug in," she drawled, displaying the regional variant of the word "dragged." My mother would have been appalled. Still, this was Marla Ann and one had to make exceptions.

"Long time, no see," Davey said, mewling like a newborn kitten, his eloquence throttled by the sweater.

It was impossible to check for a telltale belly pooch beneath the pleats. Marla Ann glowed, but that could be her irritating perkiness instead of Randy-induced motherhood.

"Can I help y'all?" She eyed us for a moment. "Omigod. Omigod." She and her short skirt jumped up and down separately, causing Davey's head to bob like a puppet's.

"Y'all are gonna cohabit like rabbits, aren't you?" she

squealed in the couplet-speak she'd perfected by her sophomore year.

"Settin' up housekeepin'? That buddy-buddy thing in college was hooey, Davey McKenzie, and you know it. You always had the hots for Bridget." She rubbed her hands together. "I got the perfect nest for you two. It's adorable. Cute as a bug in a rug."

I looked heavenward.

"And there once was a man from Nantucket," I said under my breath.

"Say what, Bridget? I've got a condo y'all'll love. Like in a middle-ages village. I remember you droolin' over that Ideals of the King freshman year."

Davey, the former history/English lit major, turned pale at her mangling of Tennyson's title.

"I'm all cohabited out, Marla Ann." I patted Davey's arm. "No offense."

"None taken. I think," he replied, his color returning.

"We're not here to shop for a house," I said to Marla Ann.

The air whooshed from the room. Marla Ann's shoulders sagged.

"S'pose I'm just a romantic at heart." She motioned toward her desk while eyeing my grubby hiking boots. "Um, why dontcha get a load off your feet?"

We all stared at each other for several awkward seconds, Marla Ann from behind her desk and Davey and me in client chairs. Either Marla Ann didn't know about Randy's death, or maybe she was the one who'd bashed him to beyond. I hesitated to introduce the subject. I gave Davey a big, blue-eyed pleading look and then waggled my eyebrows, a ploy that always worked with my father.

Davey pulled out his cell phone. "I'm still trying to get

basketball tickets for Saturday, so I'll leave you ladies to it. I'll be outside, Bridget."

Probably lying about tickets just to escape. Coward.

Before fleeing, he winked at my evil squint and hugged Marla Ann goodbye, which was totally uncalled for, in my opinion.

She started to cry, mopping up mascara-laden tears with a tissue. After blowing her nose, she raised bloodshot eyes to frown over my head.

I swiveled in my chair. What looked to be a student with long brown hair and a book bag hooked on one shoulder stood in the doorway. She swayed to music that even we could hear blasting from iPod earbuds, while texting madly on her cell phone.

"Omigod, Bridget," said Marla Ann, ignoring the young multi-tasker, "I loved that blasted Randy, even if he was an asshole." She dug through a bulging cosmetics bag. "They got a suspect yet?"

Typical of Marla Ann to forget that I had once loved Randy, too.

"It's been all over the news," I said. "How have you not seen it?"

"TV is broke. As for the paper, I only check the real estate section."

The woman was fibbing, but I didn't know why at this point. I wasn't about tell her what I knew, which seemed like precious little anyway. I wouldn't reveal Dare's possible role in this tragedy, because if Marla Ann got catty about it, I'd have to rip out her tongue.

"But you know what happened, don't you?" I whispered.

Her eyes narrowed. "What's that s'posed to mean?"

"The police haven't gotten up with you? You were at the club yesterday. Didn't you sign in?"

"No one does that anymore," she said.

"So I've heard."

"Maybe they called my cell phone. It's broke again. Piece of shit. Cost me more'n three hundred dollars. Every realtor I know has got Bluetooth or a Blackberry. But I ain't gonna tie myself up to all that techno crap like Miss Too-Busy-To-Come-To-Work over yonder." She eyed the girl still waiting in the doorway. "Speakin' of crap, that's how I felt this mornin'. Wonder if the police came by here? I was … uh … late."

"You were ill?" Maybe it was morning sickness.

Marla Ann shrugged and glared at the girl. "Crap, Tiffany, where you been all day?" she yelled suddenly, almost blasting me off my chair.

"Like I'm supposed to start at one today," Tiffany said, pulling out an earbud. "The phone's blinking. Want me to write the messages down or do you want to listen to them yourself?"

"What else you been hired for, girl? Write 'em down. We ain't got all day around here."

"Yes, ma'am." Tiffany saluted Marla Ann military style and marched lockstep to her desk.

"Kids don't have no respect anymore. Gets on my last nerve," Marla Ann said. "And lose the ma'am bit, Tiff. I ain't that old, for cryin' out loud. Unless you want me to get arthritis when it's time to sign your paycheck." She zipped up the cosmetics bag. "I'm just too wore out to do eyeliner all over again."

For which we can all be thankful.

"When did you leave the club yesterday?" All of the interrogating officers I'd seen on true crime TV said it was a good idea to catch your suspect off guard.

"You Columbus or somethin'?" Marla Ann said with all the aplomb of a repeat offender.

"Columbo. And cut me some slack here. I'm the one who found him, for heaven's sake."

She stared at me.

"Just answer the question, Marla Ann. Consider it practice for the police."

"No call to be rude, Bridget. If you gotta know, I did the treadmill then hit the salad bar. Love those sweet raisin biscuits the club makes." She examined her red acrylic nails. "Left about two."

"They're not saying exactly when Randy died. I found him after seven," I said. "I guess you came back to the office yesterday after the salad?"

"I guess I did," she replied, sarcastic and looking up and to the left, which, Chica once explained, was the sign of a liar. "I…I diddled some contracts 'til about six-thirty."

Bet she was diddling more than contracts.

We locked eyes for the Who-Blinks-First thing.

I lost, as spontaneous contests of will was not one of my strengths. Marla Ann had always been the one with killer street sense.

"I got a house to show near South Pointe Mall, sweetie," Marla Ann checked her watch, "in, oh my, thirty minutes. Been real fine chattin' though. Don't let the door hit you in the ass on your way out."

Hmph. I sashayed to the door for her benefit. She might have big knockers, but I had a great butt, if a tad on the wide side.

"I'll let you know if I hear anything," I said.

Like hell I would.

"Hey, wait a sec. You ain't the only one with questions, you know. What all were you doin' when Randy up and died?"

"Painting in the ballroom."

"Alone?"

"What's your point?" I clutched the doorknob.

"Bet you're a prime suspect." Her capped teeth shone like a row of Chiclets gum. "Bein' on the premises and all."

"Not the only one, though," I said, slamming her office door as her phone rang.

In the reception room, Tiffany, reinvolved with her iPod, wasn't paying attention.

"Mind if I sit in here and make a quick phone call?" I said in her face.

"What?" She freed up one ear to communicate with the outside world and fanned a handful of small pink forms in the air.

"I'm like so done with these. Miz Furr is obsessed with messages, you know. Most of these called yesterday afternoon anyway. Go figure why she was like having a cow today."

"She's had a shock is all. Did she miss something important? I, um, called too, but when I got the machine, I hung up."

Another lie couldn't hurt.

"You a friend or client?"

"We go way back," I said.

"Well, she left ages before lunch yesterday," Tiffany said. "She didn't, like, call me until about four and I missed Oprah. I go, 'What's wrong?' She goes, 'I'm sick and won't be back in today.'"

I might be a fairly decent fibber, but Marla Ann was a pro.

"I need to go to the bathroom," she said, jerking her chin at Marla Ann's door. "But she's like P.M.S.-ing or having a hot flash. She'll totally lose it if she comes out and I'm not sitting here like some O.C.D. secretary."

"She worries about losing commissions, I expect." I tapped random numbers on my phone's keypad as if making a call. "You run on. I'll cover for you." One of the office lines lit up. "Besides, she just got on the phone."

Tiffany hurried to bathroom.

Marla Ann's client-schmoozing commentary was audible

through the closed door, so I riffled through the messages Tiffany left on the desk.

Randy had called at 12:15 p.m. yesterday but left no message. I shoved that slip into my pocket. Wouldn't do Marla Ann any good now anyway, or the police for that matter, at least until phone records were checked. The last message in the stack showed that Hendricks had called this morning.

Tiffany, earbuds still in, hip-hopped back to her desk.

"I'm, like, so into Eminem," she said. She spotted the messages and pouted. "Guess I'll go give her these."

"Good luck!" I pulled out one of her earbuds. "Try not to obsess too much, Tiff. Marla Ann used to do that and look what it's done to her."

Tiffany's eyes bulged as I opened the door into Amber Alley and headed back up the steps to Franklin Street.

Leaning against a street lamp, Davey cradled two bags in his arms.

"Food?"

"Yeah. Sutton's," he said. "Two fried bologna sandwiches and sweet teas to go." He held up a cellophane-wrapped, store-bought oatmeal raisin cookies.

I backed away in horror.

"Your mama spoiled you. Never mind, I'll eat them." He lured me down the sidewalk by waving a sandwich in my face.

"You really know the way to a girl's heart."

"How did it go with Marla Ann?"

"I couldn't tell if she was pregnant, but I do know that she lied about where she was yesterday. And she lied about having lunch at the club. There is no salad bar on Mondays when the club is closed."

"I told Greg I'd be at the station around one," he said. "Let's go, and we'll give your Marla Ann story the attention it deserves on the way over."

Ten

Hendricks sat behind his desk with pen and notepad poised.

"Tell him." Davey nodded at me in encouragement.

I hated tattletalers, but....

"Marla Ann told me she was in her office all of yesterday afternoon. Her receptionist says she wasn't, and I don't think the girl is lying."

Hendricks made a notation on the pad.

"You mentioned Miz Furr last night, but she wasn't on the club sign-in sheet and no one we got up with so far remembers seeing her."

"I saw her. Did my mother tell you about it this morning? She saw Marla Ann yesterday, too. I hope you forgive Mother if she seems a bit off. She's worried about Dare."

"Uh huh." He looked down at his notepad.

In the embarrassing moment, I studied his political science degree from Carolina, which hung on the wall behind his desk. Various certificates of achievement within the police force were arranged around a grip-and-grin photo of him and former UNC basketball coach Dean Smith. At least the lieutenant was a Tar Heel.

"She hasn't been herself since all this happened," I said.

"This morning, she … well, she was odd." Unhinged, more like.

Hendricks raised his hand.

"No call to explain," he said. "Folks deal with things in different ways."

"No kidding," Davey said with a piercing gaze in my direction.

"If you run on by later after Daddy gets home, she might be better then," I said, although this didn't seem likely.

"You happen to know where your mama was late Monday afternoon?" Hendricks said.

I froze.

"I believe she was at home," Davey said, and I breathed again.

"Good, good." Hendricks nodded. "Now, what's all this about Miz Furr?"

"I … uh … we got to talking. She was all torn up about her breakup with Randy. Supposedly, she threatened to kill him and herself recently. According to his mother anyway."

"You talked to his mama?" He turned to a fresh page on his notepad.

"No, but my mother did at the beauty shop a couple of weeks ago."

His face fell.

"Speaking of mamas. We haven't had a bit of luck locating Miz La Russo. We need to talk to her."

"Randy said she went down to the Daytona for the race a couple of weeks ago," I said. "Something she does almost every year. Mother saw her right before she left and said that Grace was probably going to drive her truck camper and rough it in a campground. I like Grace and all, but the woman is tight as a tick and refuses to stay in a motel."

"I doubt there was any mention in a newspaper down there," Davey said.

Newspaper. Ugh. Reminded me of Hall Hooper. Nausea roiled inside me at the thought of him lapping up scandal at Dare's hearing in the morning. A thirteen-year-old murder suspect was just what the local paparazzi ordered, much better copy than the revenge of an ex-wife or former lover.

"Wait a second," I exclaimed. "Grace's cousin lived off some highway in central Florida years ago. She put me and Randy up once when we took Dare to DisneyWorld. Grace usually got together with her during race week. They both grew up in Shelby."

"Her name?" The lieutenant's brow lightened a bit.

"They had the same name." I rubbed my forehead as a fatigue headache pulsed over my right eye. "Only in reverse. Grace's name is Grace Claire. Her cousin is Claire Grace. They were born a couple of months apart. Both were named after their paternal grandmother. Randy called her 'Aunt Claire Grace' even though she was actually his first cousin once removed."

Davey stared at me with concern and then left the room.

"Last name?" Hendricks sounded hopeful.

"Sorry. No. Wait. Okay. Baucom. Randy's mother's father and Claire Grace's father were brothers," I said.

The lieutenant scribbled on his notepad.

Davey reentered the office with a Diet Pepsi. He popped the tab and pulled an Excedrin bottle from his pocket.

"Take two and drink this. Believe me, it will help."

My own knight on a white horse bearing drugs and caffeine. Weariness and gratitude almost made me cry. I took a slug of soda with the pills and held the cold can against my hot forehead.

"I don't reckon you recall your mother-in-law's cousin's married name, do you?" said the lieutenant.

"She never married. Didn't I say that? Sorry. Grace said that Aunt Claire Grace was the eldest of the Three Ugly

Sisters, as they were known in the family, and couldn't find a husband."

"Kinda cold," Hendricks said.

"Don't tell me that you actually followed that?" Davey asked.

"Well, sure, didn't you?" Hendricks replied.

Davey shook his head in disbelief.

"What?" I pointed at Hendricks. "He gets it."

"Will y'all excuse me?" Hendricks rose from his chair. "I'm gonna get someone on this right now. See if we can't find this Aunt Claire Grace Baucom so's she can help us locate Miz La Russo."

I got to my feet. Davey waved me out of the office saying he'd find a ride to his car. "And don't be late for the hearing," he added.

"I'll be there. It's not as if I'll be able to sleep, you know."

As I hurried through the hall, I tried to call Pilar again with no luck. Maybe I'd just run over to her father's house if she wasn't feeling well. Banging out the front door of the station, I almost tripped over Hooper, scrambling to retrieve papers scattered on the sidewalk.

"Hoped we might run into each other," he said with a nasty grin, nodding at my van. "So to speak."

"Ha ha."

"About that picture of you in *The Chronicle,*" he said, stuffing papers in his messenger bag. "Our photographer happened to mosey on by as the drama was unfolding."

"Funny thing about me," I said. "I like to powder my nose before getting crucified by implication on the front page of my hometown paper."

"Implication isn't accusation, although I was tempted to say a bit more in the copy." He flicked on a voice-activated tape recorder and pointed it at me.

"Would you care to comment?"

I tried to slip past him and, oops, bumped into him instead. The tape recorder clattered to the ground and hopefully got crushed when I tripped on it with a clumsy boot.

I climbed into the van and rolled down the window.

"Sorry about that, but I remember the shenanigans that got you kicked off *The Daily Tar Heel.* Guess you found out that college papers tend toward the ethical in their reporting, unlike the grown-up media these days."

"I was a kid then," he said with a smirk.

"And now you're an adult?"

"Just remember," he said as if I hadn't spoken, "the truth shall set you free."

I could set the clever dude free for good if I flattened him with the van, but, lucky for all of us, my cell phone rang. Chica, with a nudge from the Almighty, had probably kept me from justifiable homicide.

"There was a lot I didn't say in that story this morning," said Hooper, Ace Reporter. "By the way, see you at the courthouse tomorrow."

I caught my breath. We stared at each other, and he blinked first.

I pressed the talk key on my phone, hardly aware of my surroundings as Hooper snagged the tape recorder and strolled through the front door of the station.

"Come home," Chica shrilled. "All hell breaks loose here." I held the phone away to preserve my eardrum. "Bubba bit the doggy man. Big Foot is humpy-humping his leg. Your father is drinking mojitos. ¡Andale, arriba!"

Guess I'd run by Hermann and Pilar's house later.

Eleven

Chica's living room, usually as neat as a magazine layout, resembled post-tornado news footage.

Torn paper and dog toys littered the floor. Bubba's teeth clicked like castanets as he jumped up and down snapping at a storm of drifting feathers from a burst pillow. Chica tugged to no avail on Big Foot's leash. I ran to help her pull the lovelorn Samoyed off the dog whisperer's right shank as the old man hollered for all he was worth.

My daddy, who only drank on rare occasions, was nursing a twelve-ounce mojito, for heaven's sake. He sprawled spider-like in one of the yellow ochre wing chairs by the fireplace, and chuckled as I lost my balance and fell at his feet.

Cripes, it wasn't even dark yet, and he seemed a tad tipsy.

"What are you doing here?" I asked as I jumped up and grabbed the drink out of his hand, spilling it on the carpet.

"This whispering phenomenon beats all. This fella hasn't the hang of it, though," he said in a soggy chuckle. "Horses, dogs. Are kitty cats next?"

"Señor Leipzig will make our doggies good companions," Chica said, trying to smooth Mr. Leipzig's pant leg.

"It's obvious you two need a firm hand with these creatures," Leipzig said with a stab at dignity.

At eighty bucks an hour, I bet he thought he could help us.

"I'm Bridget." I shook his damp hand. "Sorry about Big Foot here. He's got hormonal issues. A bitch is in heat a couple of houses down."

"You young ladies will ruin them." He replastered the four sweaty strands of gray hair that had unwound and were hanging the wrong way on his head. "These canines are out-of-control juvenile delinquents. Most distressing. They must be taught there are consequences to certain actions. In their present state, they cannot contribute to the family unit. They were meant to be our best friends. Helpful and protective."

Pompous old goat. Dissing my dog was my job.

"They're not joining the Peace Corps," I said.

Daddy snorted.

Bubba, weary of playing snag-the-feather, growled.

Leipzig ran out of the room with Bubba close on his heels.

"Don't run," I yelled. "They love to chase."

He circled back into the room and ran to a corner. Bubba followed, nosed under Leipzig's trouser leg and latched onto a chunk of bony ankle.

"Eeee-ow," the dog whisperer cried, dancing a one-legged jig to shake Bubba loose.

I pried Bubba's jaw open and lodged him in the crook of my elbow.

"Looks like Bubba's got the protective thing down pat," I said. "I don't know what you tried to teach them today but, by the look of this room, we were better off before you showed up."

"Hear hear." Daddy raised his glass.

"It's not Señor Leipzig's fault," said Chica, as the man disappeared in search of a bathroom. She sank exhausted into the yellow chair facing my father. "The doggies ate some of your purple energy pills."

No wonder they went ballistic.

"You take care of the papa," she said. "I will pay the doggy man."

***

Thirty minutes later, I stopped pacing in the kitchen long enough to place a mug of coffee, glass of water and two aspirins on the table in front of my father.

"You probably have a headache," I said. "I hope you didn't have office hours this afternoon. I still don't know why you're here at all."

"I wanted to talk to you about the hearing in the morning. Then Chica mentioned mojitos. I only drank part of one. Pretty potent stuff."

"Not your fault; she makes them strong."

I peeked through the dining room.

"She didn't drink any though, did she?" I said. "I didn't even know we had rum in the house."

"No, no. She drank some water. If she relapsed because of me, I'd never forgive myself."

"You sure it was water?"

"Unless that freezer door dispenses vodka."

I pulled a chair around in front of him. "Tell me what happened last night. How was Dare after you left the station?"

"Mrs. Breedlove was very kind, bless her heart. She saw Dare through the intake process while I waited. Then she gave me a ride back to my car." He swallowed the aspirin with some water.

"God, you sound like you know prison jargon. But how's all this going to affect Dare? She has no idea what she's gotten herself into. I know she doesn't."

Daddy didn't answer.

"She didn't do it."

He just looked at me.

"She didn't!"

"What makes you say that?" he said, making creepy crawlies race along my spine.

"She couldn't have. She was at home with you and mother yesterday afternoon. I never saw her at the club even though they found her phone there later. I'm so confused. I don't know who was where at this point."

He shook his head.

"I came home to grab a sandwich about two o'clock. Your mother's bridge tables were going full steam then. As I'm *persona non grata* on these afternoons, I high-tailed it back to campus at about two-thirty."

"Didn't you see Dare when you were at home?"

"No, but I assumed she was at school or the club or maybe even upstairs. I think the bridge tables broke up early, because I called home just before five and got no answer, although they might just have ignored the ringing. Late last night, your mother told me that Dare went to the club to exercise and then played tennis with Ellie. She says she called the Weathersbees at dark looking for Dare, but Ellie's mother hadn't seen Dare all day." He grimaced after sipping the cold coffee.

"That doesn't mean the girls weren't doing what they said they were doing."

"Ellie's mother said the same thing. That as both girls are trying out for the tennis team, they were probably practicing at the park."

"Dare has an amazing forehand."

He gave me a pitying look.

"Anyway, your mother says the child came home way past dark, which I don't approve of, by the way, and then she went straight up to her room."

"From where she called nine-one-one, I presume. But back up. Did you tell the police all this?"

He shook his head.

"Didn't they ask you where she was?"

"I told Lieutenant Hendricks that I couldn't swear where she was in the afternoon, but I thought she was at home. I believed it at the time, and I haven't volunteered any information since then."

"Good."

A car started up outside.

"And so ends the chapter of the dog whisperer," I muttered.

The dogs trotted into the kitchen looking smug. They nosed in their empty bowls before settling onto the floor in their favorite patch of sunshine. Clever buggers had saved us a fortune in dog therapy.

"I'll pick you up at 7:15 a.m. for the hearing. Davey will meet us there."

"Honey will be there, too."

Daddy rose. The dogs pattered over to him to have their heads scratched. "I'd better run on home, Sugar."

"Maybe I should drive you."

"I'm fine now. Just a slight headache, which I deserve." He smiled a little. "Your mother doesn't feel well. I left her napping."

"Doesn't feel well? Talk about understatement, Daddy. Are you in denial? She was raving this morning."

"This will pass," he said. "It always does."

"She's been like this before?"

"The last time was right after you left for Italy," he said almost to himself.

Guilt again reared its ugly head. I had news for old Mr. Leipzig – consequences were a real pain in the ass, for people as well as dogs.

"Deeds are like boomerangs," he said. "They tend to come back at you."

"Then things will never be right for me."

"Don't beat yourself up. Our family history shows this is not the case. You've turned your life around. That's what's important to your mother and me."

I walked him to his car.

"But shouldn't Mother see someone, you know, professional?"

"She already does, in a way."

I was too tired to ask him what he meant.

The doorbell chimed. Bubba and Big Foot barked en route from the kitchen.

Snuffling, I opened my eyes from my position face down on the living room sofa. Blue cornflowers on a yellow background blurred as I raised my head to look around. Chica had cleaned the living room; all was neat and tidy with no evidence of a dog whispering incident. I dragged myself up and tottered to the front door.

"Hey, Wild Kingdom," I hollered at the dogs leaping in the foyer, "Hit the road." They hushed but stood at my feet, vibrating fit to be tied. I checked my watch. I'd dozed for about thirty minutes – not long enough to feel refreshed but plenty of time to incubate a raging headache.

I peered through the peephole.

Yikes, it was Malcolm. Shouldn't he be managing at the club tonight?

He looked even bigger on the porch than he did in the club ballroom.

"Just a minute," I shouted at the peephole. I ran to the stairs and called in a loud whisper, "Chica, you up there?"

She appeared on the landing, looking peeved. Her hair dripped with water as she tied the belt of a terrycloth robe.

"Dios mio, I am very undressed."

"Just come down here, please."

The doorbell chimed again.

Bubba lifted his little snoot and howled. Big Foot followed suit.

Malcolm coughed on the other side of the door.

"Grrrrrrr!" I raised my arms and stomped my feet like a grizzly bear. Bubba nipped the toe of my boot before fleeing the foyer. Big Foot, a tad slow on the uptake, plodded after him.

Chica shook her head as she descended the staircase. "Do not shoosh the doggies barking at strangers."

"Forget the dogs." I hissed, pointing at the door. "That's Malcolm."

"Ah. Good thing. We find out if we can work today." She grabbed the doorknob.

"What if he's the killer?" I said.

"Crap," she said, pausing.

"We will find out, no matter." She yanked open the door. "Hey! Boss Man."

***

Malcolm's huge frame wobbled on Chica's antique harp-backed kitchen chair. We laid out three of the dwindling supply of oatmeal raisin cookies from the freezer and a pitcher of sweet tea like the good hostesses we were, even if our guest might be a bludgeoner. Bubba and Big Foot, bored with sniffing Malcolm's cuffs and crotch, respectively, flopped onto the floor under the table.

Malcolm put a dishpan-sized hand in his windbreaker pocket and removed a newspaper clipping.

"From the Durham paper. You can look at it later," he said.

I glanced at the headline – CHAPEL HILL WOMAN FINDS BODY OF EX IN COUNTRY CLUB SPA.

"You know we're going to kill you in the game on Saturday night, right?" Malcolm made a pistol with his thumb and index finger. "Bang."

If he was trying to scare me, he was doing a damned good job. Probably, though, he was trying to break the ice.

"I hate Cameron Indoor Stadium and the Cameron Crazies," I said.

Rule Number One in my new list of survival skills: Make sure killers underestimate you.

"It's a crappy basketball venue." I warmed up to my rant. "There's never any air circulating. Yeah. And hey, what about those maniac Duke students painted blue? Half the time, they're almost on the playing floor. It's just wrong."

Malcolm cocked an eyebrow and nodded as if, on my soapbox, I'd confirmed his opinion that Bridget didn't have a whole lot of sense.

Of course, if he wasn't the killer, then maybe he was right.

Chica shook her head as if we were both stupid.

"Always the basketball in Chapel Hill," she moaned. "You need to get a life."

Randy's lifeless face appeared unbidden in my mind's eye.

Chica saw my stricken expression and grabbed my hand. "So sorry. I forgot."

"It's OK." I said. "You're right. It's usually all about basketball this time of year."

If only it were.

Malcolm sipped his tea and then stood, scraping the chair on the floor.

"I came by to say you could work in the ballroom this afternoon. You need to get cracking, though. Time's running out, and there is still a lot to do." He looked down at me. "But only if you're ready to work. I'll understand if that's not the case, but then we'll need to make other arrangements."

"It's better if I keep busy," I said. "We'll be there later, but I've got an errand to run before I come in tomorrow morning. Chica will be in early," I said, deciding not to mention Dare's hearing.

"It's the best thing to work sometimes, yes?" Chica added.

"I didn't realize until yesterday that you and Randy knew each other so well," I said to Malcolm.

He studied me for a few seconds. "I make it my business to know all of the members as much as possible."

"I will dress for work, OK?" Chica ignored my glare and hurried from the room.

"Bridget, I –," Malcolm said.

"Where were you last night?" I leaned toward him with my palms on the table. "You left me alone in that clubhouse."

"I told you before I left that I had a family emergency," he said.

"You didn't tell me a thing."

"I did so. At about 5:30. It was getting dark."

"I don't remember that, and I don't have Alzheimer's yet."

"You had your back to me. Dancing. Kind of funny, actually." But he didn't look amused with his brows drawn together like black thunderclouds.

"Dancing?"

"Around one of your supply crates or something," he said. "It was dark in that corner of the ballroom. Not any dance I'd ever seen, that's for sure."

"Oh that," I muttered, as I recalled my "Safety Dance" break in the ballroom. Sheesh, take a breather and your world goes to pieces. "I was probably, er, just stretching my legs for a minute. You know, being stiff after painting for so long."

"I shouted, so I figured you heard me," he said. "You flung your arm like you were waving goodbye."

"But, well, what about you and Randy?"

"What do you mean 'you and Randy'?" He crossed his massive arms.

Suddenly, my five-foot eight-inches seemed kind of puny. I gulped some tea. The cool sweet liquid rolled golden down my throat.

"I heard you arguing. About money or something." I tried not to remember the big shadow on the front porch of Randy's home.

He stared at me and laughed like a goblin.

The hairs stood up on the back of my neck, and jingling doggie tags told me two canine heads had popped up at my feet.

"Aw, come on," he said. "About money? Yeah. The man is habitually late in everything he does … did … but I bet you already know that about him. He was late with his dues and didn't like hearing about it."

That's not how I remembered the conversation between the two of them. Was it only yesterday? It felt like a lifetime ago.

"By the way," Malcolm said pulling keys from his pocket. "How's your daughter?"

The doorbell chimed, and the dogs took off barking.

"What?" I pretended not to hear over the bedlam.

"Little Miss Dare," he said. "How's she doing? Mr. La Russo was her daddy, I mean her stepdaddy. Same thing really, I suppose."

"What do you mean by that?"

"He seemed worried about her. Yesterday, you know. So, I kind of wondered. She must be upset, poor thing."

"Randy was worried about her?" I'd not heard this part of the conversation during my eavesdropping outside his office door.

"Said he hadn't done right by her. That he wanted to make sure she never wanted for anything," he said. "Right before I left yesterday, I was thinking about what a lucky girl she was to have folks who cared about her so much, when suddenly I saw her running out the door."

Dare. He'd seen Dare at the club yesterday.

Someone was leaning on the damned doorbell.

"Running?" I said with numb lips.

"Out the door that opens onto the putting green." He studied me like a cat does its prey, laser-focused.

"Did you tell the police that you saw her?" This would've been a good time to crack my knuckles, but Dare, who was so good at it, had never shown me how.

"Tell you the truth, I probably wouldn't have remembered it," he said, "except he asked me specifically."

"Lieutenant Hendricks?" I tried to sound calm.

"Yep." He glanced at his watch. "Look, we can talk later." He stood and reached the kitchen door in two giant strides. "I'm going back to the club now. I've got some business to attend to."

Maybe "adjusting" club records to ensure that nothing Randy had mentioned in their little "talk" I'd overheard was incriminating.

Couldn't let a D-O-O-K graduate get the best of me in the unmapped landscape of murder.

"You seem to be in a big hurry today, too," I said.

"Hermann's in my car. I think something is wrong with Pilar's, and I'm giving him a ride home." He frowned at me for a second. "Wait a minute, what did you mean 'today, too'?"

"I was referring to that family emergency that you rushed off to yesterday. I hope it wasn't serious," I said, as opened the back door.

"Family emergency?" He turned in surprise, and we locked eyeballs.

The doorbell rang once, twice, three times. The dogs

went berserk in the foyer. And to think that only yesterday I'd loved those blasted chimes.

"Jesus Maria," shouted Chica as she pounded down the stairs. "It's a crazy house."

"The family emergency," I said, "the one you left the club for last night?"

"Oh, that one," he said as if family emergencies happened daily. "Turned out to be nothing."

"That's good," I replied. "I'd hate to think you were driving around in the wee hours stressing out over it."

Good grief, shut up, Bridget.

Malcolm slammed out the door, which I locked and sagged against.

"Where's that sorry bitch?" Marla Ann demanded from the front of the house. High heels clattered toward the kitchen.

"Don't run, Marla Ann," I yelled, "the dogs will chase you."

She ignored me.

Great. Just what I needed. A hysterical realtor/slut-cum-possible-killer barging in on me.

I inhaled deeply before she could suck all of the air out of the room.

"Get away from me," Marla Ann cried as Bubba yelped in pain and Big Foot growled. "Oh no, not my Jimmy Choos!"

"It's the woman with big cha chas," Chica yelled.

Two females and two dogs clattered into the kitchen. Marla Ann stuck a high-heeled shoe in my face. Tiny perforations that matched Bubba's needle-like dentition decorated the toe. I'd seen them enough in my own footwear. Chica, who'd managed to get dressed despite all of the chaos, seethed as she cradled Bubba against her uniform.

"She smacked Dare's doggy," she said.

Marla Ann rammed the shoe back onto her foot and

faced Chica, glaring down from stiletto height and across the vast acreage above her thorax.

Chica raised her pointed chin, her hair roiling in a black-and-gray tsunami about her head.

"Remove your zapatos," she demanded.

"What?" Marla Ann said.

"Your shoes," Chica said. "Take off the shoes. You are not so tall then."

"Chica fought in the Persian Gulf," I said.

Marla Ann's shoulders slumped. She plonked into a chair.

"Hell's bells, Bridget, I came here to find out why you told the police I could've murdered Randy. I didn't come here to fight with someone who can't even speak American."

"You are deaf? I am American, and I speak it." Chica set Bubba on the floor. She did some convoluted arm circles and assumed a kickboxing stance. "You understand this?"

"Jesus Christ," Marla Ann said. She laughed, and then began to cry. "I just got grilled by that ol' cop who thinks he's Columbus."

Bubba eyed her, tilted his head in curiosity.

"Damned dog," said Marla Ann. "Here li'l poochy. I surely didn't mean nothin'. Looks like a football, don't he?" She waggled her fingers at him.

He stuck his snout in the air and clicked out of the room.

"Story of my life," she said.

I handed her a paper towel, which she pressed to her streaming eyes.

"Sorry you're upset," I said, "but I can't talk right now. We've got to go. Tons of work to do at the club."

"Well, excuse me," she said. She crossed her arms over her breasts, but then they almost reached her chin. She crossed them below her breasts, but that didn't suit either. Finally, she dropped them to her sides. "Oh law, Bridget. I came by to give you what for. I no more'n killed Randy than pigs fly." She blew her nose.

"If you're not guilty, what's the problem?" I said. "Look at me. I'm not worried."

I'd become an excellent liar.

"I will finish my hair, and we will leave. OK?" said Chica, backing out of the kitchen, her eye on Marla Ann.

"Your business partner is definitely havin' a hair emergency." Marla Ann spotted the news article on the table. "What's this?" she asked, going for it. But I beat her to it.

"Nothing," I shoved it into my pocket.

"Chrissake," she said and stood up. The Lord only knew where she got the strength to hold her shoulders back.

I walked her to the front door. She peeked into the living room.

"Classy," she said. "Dontcha just love yellow? You must be mintin' money with that old paintbrush."

"It's Chica's house," I said.

"Woo hoo," she cried. "That means you need to move. Tell you what. When you're ready to buy, call me, hear?"

"Didn't we have this discussion earlier?"

"That was for you and Davey. But obviously, you need your own place."

A realtor would never go gently into that good night as long as there was a commission to be had.

"Chica," I shouted, heading back to the kitchen. "Let's go before someone else shows up, God forbid."

I pulled the article from my pocket. Great. Another bad angle of me standing in front of the club looking like a cross between a homeless person and a paintball warrior. At least the photo was smaller than the one in *The Chronicle.*

I stood at the kitchen sink and skimmed the text. Nothing new in it. Just the usual what, where, when and probably how, but not who or why. This made sense because I didn't know this stuff either.

I grabbed the kitchen phone and dialed Pilar's number again. Even if she wasn't back from class, Hermann would probably know where she was. The phone rang and rang. I left a message. A glance through the window revealed a forlorn patch of brown grass within a perimeter of leafless trees and overgrown bushes. Chica loved interior decorating but scorned yard work.

"The little bugs eat at me," she'd complained. "So, the garden goes to crap."

When I first took up residence, I'd promised to try a little landscaping.

"Maybe I inherited my mother's green thumb," I'd said full of optimism.

Tonight, however, optimism wasn't in my repertoire. I spiked the Durham news article with the household receipts on the counter. As I turned away, movement by the giant camellia bushes at the back of the yard caught my eye.

What the hell?

Balanced on a high rung of Chica's six-foot wooden ladder was my mother, her dark blonde bob restored. Her elbows flapped in and out as she attacked the overgrown shrubbery with hedge clippers.

I headed for the back door.

Chica grabbed my coveralls from behind.

"Let go," I swatted at her hand. "Mother's out there. She's supposedly taking a nap. Daddy's probably had a heart attack by now wondering where she is."

"No, amiga, no," Chica whirled me around; she was good at slinging things twice her size as if they were rag dolls. She shoved me into a chair. "She is fine."

"I'm calling Daddy." I sprang up. She pushed me down.

"It's OK. I called your papa and told him she was here. She left a note for him."

"Right."

"It's fine. Fine. She trims bushes, and we go to work."

"But how'll she get home? We can't just leave. She's off her freaking rocker." Tears threatened for the hundredth time in less than twenty-four hours, and my nose got stuffy.

"She came before the doggie man left and parked down the street. OK? Yes? Say yes," she demanded.

"Yes," I said. "But …"

"The mama, she cannot fix your life. You get me? So, she fixes your garden." Chica looked out the window and chuckled. "Let her."

"What's so funny?"

"When she fixes your garden, she fixes mine."

"Just goes to show that astrology stuff is crap." I said, determined to show her that I knew a thing or two. "She's doing something good for you even though she's a Sagittarian."

Chica's mouth popped open.

"We leave now," she cried. "I shouldn't be close to those people today. ¡Vámanos!"

Mother set the clippers on top of the camellia bush and stretched her lower back. She'd shed the scary T-shirt of the morning. Now, she wore starched khakis, a white turtleneck and a kelly green sweatshirt with white lettering on the back, a birthday present from me years ago. I couldn't read the quote from that distance, but I knew what it said.

"Nothing is more the child of art than a garden."—Sir Walter Scott.

Chica dragged me through the house with the dogs at our heels. She banged the door in their faces. After a few seconds, we heard Bubba's muffled yowling.

Chica shoved me into the passenger seat of the van and pelted around to the driver's side.

"What if she falls off the ladder?" I whined.

As we rocketed into the street, she cranked up the volume

on what she called "the van's song," the 1975 hit, "Chevy Van" by Sammy Johns. Her falsetto would have made a bat cringe. Not to mention her massacre of the lyrics. "She made love in my Chevy van, and it's OK to me."

I recalled Dare singing along with her once and swallowed the lump that rose in my throat. This was no time for memories.

I settled in for the ride. When Chica's blood was up, I stayed out of her way.

Twelve

"Imagine Daniel Boone leading an expedition into Kentucky from this very spot," said my father as Honey and I rushed him through the door behind the judge's bench. It was Wednesday morning, March 1st, and juvenile court in Hillsborough, North Carolina, was packed.

"Not now, Daddy, please." I snapped, still tearful after hugging Dare in the hallway earlier and getting no response. What's more, Chica and I had worked most of the night at the club, and I had not slept a wink afterward.

"And they marched away solemnly," Daddy continued in a faraway voice, "as if going to the ends of the world."

"Your father is nervous. This is his way of coping," Honey whispered. "He's quoting from that big stone memorial outside. He learned it so quickly. Amazing under the circumstances and at his age."

"I'm not into coonskin caps today," I said.

Honey laughed. "A historical *faux pas*, darling, according to your dad. I said we'd get him a coonskin cap like Daniel Boone's and he said 'codswallop.' Do you not think that's a great word? Anyway, he says Daniel wouldn't have worn a coonskin cap. It would've been a wide-brimmed hunting hat."

Honey took my elbow, as we dodged milling court minions. The three of us sat up straight on the pew-like front row of the spectator section as if we were the descendants of a church's founding family.

"I just can't do Daddy's quoting game today either."

My father could quote 'til the cows came home, wresting factoids from the Bible, historical chronicles, important people, poetry, movies and *The Andy Griffith Show*. I would identify or cap the quotes, which didn't happen often, or he would explain their source, which happened a lot. He'd initiated Dare into this tradition during her Mother Goose days.

I kissed his cheek. "Sorry, Daddy, I didn't mean to be ugly."

"I know, sugar. By the way, isn't that Hooper back there?"

I looked behind me and squinted. "Yes."

I'd argued with Davey when he told me to sit up front but saw the wisdom of the suggestion when I spotted *The Chronicle*'s ace twitchy nose several rows back. The court reserved the first rows on both sides of the aisle for victims, families and witnesses.

"Thank goodness, Tomahawk Theimer is hearing our case first. A good man." Daddy whispered. "A Demon Deacon, you know. Law review at Wake Forest."

"Tomahawk?" Honey said. "That doesn't sound good."

"We played in the same flight once in a tournament at Finley Golf Course," Daddy explained. "He doesn't swing his club, he chops it as if he's using a tomahawk. He's taken a bait of teasing since then. He's a mite sensitive about the nickname though, so mum's the word."

Honey giggled, but I failed to find anything humorous at the moment. Despite the cold, dry weather, my skin felt clammy. Time dragged excruciatingly toward 9 o'clock.

I tugged at the tight, black "businesswoman" dress I'd

found in the back of my closet. It had been loose last year. Probably it had shrunk in the dark.

Honey, on the other hand, was awash in textiles, her hair tucked into a wooly dark beret and her body hidden by a huge tomato-red cape. She removed it and rolled it into a ball to reveal a black jumper over a high-necked white blouse with black hose and shoes. The hideous cape was bad enough, but I had expected her next layers to be in shades of gold. Honey's flaxen ensembles were as reliable as church vestments, and this departure into black and red was discombobulating.

I fingered the hem of her jumper. "Did you run out of your regular honey-colored clothes?"

"Just a hunch I had." She gave me a conspiratorial wink, as she pulled yet another celebrity magazine out of her bag and started to flick through it. "Never you mind."

I slid down on the bench and studied the six brass chandeliers instead, checking for spider webs by the sunlight slanting through the tall formal windows lining the walls. As a child, I'd done this in Mother's Episcopal church. The sanctuary had had this same quality of light and, as Mother was a bear on fidgeting, counting cobwebs kept me still. But so far today I hadn't found one spider spinning a web.

As I scanned the historical wall murals, Davey entered the courtroom, all lawyer-y in a charcoal suit and light blue tie. He stood behind the defense table. When my daughter appeared a few seconds later with Mrs. Breedlove, all sound ceased in the courtroom.

Dare took two steps into the room and froze, a yearling sensing danger. Her dark eyes searched the crowd. With her hair smooth and unspiked, she resembled a young Audrey Hepburn in the white turtleneck, black skirt, black vest and tights I'd sent to her for this court appearance.

I stood slowly, seeing my child through a focused tunnel of light, and nodded encouragement. Her shoulders dropped, and her chin lifted a fraction. Mrs. Breedlove, plump and efficient in gray wool, led her to the chair next to Davey's. He motioned us to move inside the railing.

"Does he want us up there?" asked my father in a rare moment of confusion.

"You two go on," said Honey. "You must've misunderstood where he wanted you to sit."

I hurried through the gate and sat next to Dare. Mrs. Breedlove and Daddy took their seats beside me. Davey smiled briefly at us.

The first part of the hearing zoomed by with the blurry speed of a microfiche reel.

"All rise," intoned the bailiff just as his predecessors had done in that very spot since the middle of the nineteenth century.

"Oh yes, oh yes, oh yes," the bailiff continued as the black-robed judge swept up to the bench and took his seat. "The Honorable Court for the State of North Carolina, County of Orange is now open and sitting for the dispatch of its business. Judge Robert H. Theimer is now presiding. Please be seated."

Judge Theimer glanced over his Ben Franklin glasses at some papers before eyeing each attorney briefly.

"Good morning, counsel," he said, in a booming voice.

"Good morning, Your Honor," said Thomas Chatsworth, the portly district attorney, whose most distinctive characteristic appeared to be his bushy gray eyebrows.

"Good morning, Your Honor," said Davey, who would again be my Scottish highlander if he did well today.

"Mr. Chatsworth, please proceed," said the judge.

The district attorney's caterpillar brows waggled as he stood.

"Your Honor, we are here today to determine if there is probable cause to try this young lady, Miss Dare Benedetto, who is thirteen-and-a-half years old. She has been charged with the murder of her former stepfather, Randall La Russo, on the night of Monday, February twenty-seventh. She has confessed to this crime and is currently detained in the Orange County Youth Home. Due to the serious nature of the crime, I request that she be tried as an adult."

As Chatsworth took his seat, Judge Theimer turned to Davey, who stood up.

"Mr. McKenzie?"

"Your Honor, as you can imagine, this crime has caused great distress in the community, especially to the victim's family as well as that of the child. Miss Benedetto's mother and grandparents are well respected members of the Chapel Hill community. Her father, Marcus Benedetto, is deceased. They want to do what is best for their child under these circumstances. Also, Your Honor, she has a clean record. I do not believe that transferring a minor this young to adult court would be in anyone's best interests."

"Well, Mr. McKenzie, perhaps not, although this was a brutal crime for any age, and in that regard, I have to consider the victim and his family, too. However, I might concur with your view regarding a waiver depending upon the particulars of the crime. Before I can make a disposition in the case, however, the child would need to be assessed clinically by court-appointed evaluators or ones agreed upon by both sides."

I shook my head and pulled my dress down over my knees, wondering if these folks talked in such long, boring sentences outside of court.

As Davey sat down, Dare began to tremble. I ached to put my arm around her but was strangely afraid to move. I also knew she might shrug me off and I didn't want to embarrass her.

Then Mr. Eyebrows Chatsworth stood and said that Dare

should be maintained in secure custody while she was being evaluated due to the seriousness of the felony.

What a cranky old goat. I wiggled in my chair, dying to stand up and declare that my daughter was not violent – although I had sometimes been known to be – had not committed this crime and shouldn't be locked up like a rogue lion escaped from the zoo. But of course I didn't. I'm not good at gauging consequences and thought I might just screw things up royally. So, I bit my lip and sat on my hands instead.

When the judge told Dare to stand, the microfiche reeling in my head slowed to threatening clarity.

"Do you know why you are here, Dare?" the judge asked, reminding me of the kind uncle who'd teased us kids at Thanksgiving tables long ago.

"Yessir." Dare's response was barely audible.

"Do you understand that you have been charged with murder and the serious nature of these charges?"

Dare hesitated.

I clicked my heels together like Dorothy in her ruby slippers and wished we were any place but here.

"Yessir."

Judge Theimer leaned forward, his hands clasped in front of him.

"Have you been advised of your rights?"

"At the police station. Yessir." She reached a hand out for me, and I was so surprised I almost didn't take it.

"Mr. McKenzie is your legal counsel?"

"Like is that the same as a lawyer?"

"It sure is," he replied with a slight smile before turning to me and my father. "As her legal guardians, would you like to say anything?"

Davey nodded at us, and we stood beside Dare.

Daddy spoke first.

"Yes, I'm Richard O'Brien, your honor, her grandfather.

I believe we met once at Finley." Then, to my horror, Daddy did a discreet tomahawk chop.

Judge Theimer turned pink. "Ahem, yes, I seem to remember you."

I pinched Daddy's arm. So much for the judge's sensitivity.

"I'm also her legal guardian," continued Daddy when the floor didn't open up to swallow us, "as is her mother, my daughter, Bridget. Dare lost her father last year."

"Yes, I see," the judge said, consulting his notes and doing the furrowed-brow judge thing. "Thank you both for coming."

Paper rustling and recorder buttons popping were the only sounds in the courtroom for what seemed like forever. Sneezes or hacking coughs would've come in handy just then. Where was pestilence when it was needed?

Daddy nudged me, and I stood up straight and looked the judge in the eye.

"I just want to say, Your Honor, that my daughter has always been a good child and a good student, trying out for the tennis team and making good grades. A good citizen too. She helps out with Habitat houses."

More paper rustling and button popping.

"But this terrible thing that happened to my ex-husband, Mr. La Russo. There hasn't been enough time to get it all figured out, you know? I mean, she's growing up too fast and I … in the last year … well, she's grown up faster than I have, if the truth be known. I should have been a better mother. I … um … she's never been in trouble before and…." I started to choke up. "I didn't do this too well."

"You did just fine," said the judge.

Dare squeezed one hand and Daddy the other.

"Thank you for understanding," I squeaked before sitting back down.

The judge squinted at some papers.

"Mrs. Breedlove," he said, looking down at her and smiling. "What can you add to this discussion?"

She stood up with a notebook and pen in hand.

"Dare Benedetto came to us in the wee hours of Tuesday morning after ... the incident. She has been most cooperative since then. Very quiet though, Your Honor, which I think is not unusual considering the circumstances."

The judge nodded. "Thank you. Miss Benedetto should remain under your supervision there until the preliminary hearing next week. Let's see about scheduling some psychological assessments as soon as possible, too."

"Yessir," she replied, jotting in her notebook. She sat down.

"Your Honor," said D.A. Chatsworth. He stood and tweaked one of his eyebrows. "I just wanted to add that I've spoken with the investigating officer. He's told me that the criminal investigation is ongoing."

The judge thought about this for several seconds as if he was about to utter something sarcastic, and then thought better of it.

"Dismissed until next Wednesday at 10 a.m," said Judge Theimer. He pounded his gavel, stood up and left the courtroom.

Dare, drained of color but ramrod straight, clung to me but wouldn't look in my eyes. After a moment, we exited through the same door we'd entered.

As we waited to go out the back way, I glanced into the courtroom but couldn't find Hooper in the media crush to get outside and confront Dare as she left the premises.

"You were good back there," Davey whispered and kissed my cheek. "Honey and I will bring the car around." He was gone before I could reply.

"Granddad," Dare whispered on tiptoe as she hugged my father goodbye. "Do they think I'm like … crazy?"

"No, sugar pie, it's just standard procedure. This happens

to … everyone in your situation. Think of these tests just like you do the basketball quizzes I give you. For example, should Coach allow or deny the wing pass?"

Dare lit up. "You mean like the pass from the point guard to the wing player?"

"See there?" he exclaimed. "You'll ace any old test of theirs."

The dear, dear man. I buried my face in his shoulder and closed my eyes for a blissful second.

Then the microfiche reel mercifully sped back up, and the whisking began. Everyone seemed to scatter. Mrs. Breedlove whisked out the door with her arm around Dare, who was holding my father's big all-weather coat like a canopy over her head and torso. Only her hose and black flats were visible. I was delayed by some courthouse employees and lost track of Daddy. When I finally exited, I spotted a blur of red cape and black beret in a far corner of the parking lot and realized that Honey and Davey were headed toward his Jeep. I bumped into a maelstrom of microphones and cameras and rude strangers bellowing questions at Mrs. Breedlove and Dare up ahead, but I couldn't see her under the coat.

"Why did you do it, Dare?"

"Dare, look this way!"

"Bridget, can you explain any of this?"

And worst of all.

"Did your stepfather do something to you, Dare?"

I couldn't tell who said that, but I picked Hooper out of the crowd and he appeared to be shaking his head in disgust at the question. Maybe he did have some redeeming qualities.

Mrs. Breedlove stopped dead and shoved Dare at me before she turned and clumped back toward the courthouse.

"Wha…?" I cried to Mrs. Breedlove. "Wait a minute, aren't you coming with us?"

"Shut up," Dare said in a throaty voice as if she was coming down with a cold. She steered me forward. "Come on."

This was not the time or place to handle a teenager's backtalk; and besides, nothing could shock me anymore.

Daddy pulled up just in time for Dare and me to bundle into the back seat. As my father edged the car through the throng with gentlemanly toots to the horn, I peeked under the big overcoat to find Honey grinning at me instead of Dare.

"Dontcha just love it?" Honey trilled with sparkling eyes.

I stopped breathing for a minute.

"Well then, who was that with Davey … oh my God." I started to blubber, which even my shrink hadn't expected. "So that was Dare under the red cape?" How had Honey and Dare switched places with no one the wiser?

"What's the matter, sugar?" Daddy said. "Everything's all right. Our little decoy plan worked. Dare is with Davey."

I pointed to Honey's feet. "I didn't even realize those weren't Dare's shoes."

"I'm not surprised. You're a zombie today, so don't fret over it. Sometimes we see what we expect to see. We were counting on it with the press."

"How'd you come up with this idea?" I said, recalling now that she and Dare had both worn similarly configured black-and-white clothing.

Honey pulled one of her Hollywood entertainment magazines from her bag and waved it at me. On the cover, a young woman unrecognizable because of the big coat pulled over her head was running through a lane of photographers.

"Britney Spears," Honey said triumphantly.

Maybe trashy mags weren't so bad after all.

Despite everything, I laughed at her ingenuity until my asthma kicked in and I pumped my inhaler a couple of times to calm myself. When I could breathe easily again, I forced myself to think about completing the work at the club, at least for the next few hours and until the next hearing.

Thirteen

Bless her heart, my business partner was slaving away in the ballroom by the time I arrived at Magnolia Blossom Country Club, near lunchtime. I fell into the rhythm, and we worked steadily despite the assistant manager's amorous attentions toward Chica.

Long Johnson said he was "steadying" the ladder – the tall scary one instead of the stable rolling one – or Chica, who was gilding cherubs at warp speed. The gold leaf flakes sprinkling onto Long's suit attested to his zealous concern for Chica's welfare and his rapture with the upward view. Obscured by safety lenses, Chica's eyes had to be rolling in exasperation at all this solicitousness, because only a couple of days remained to complete the work.

"I do not fear heights like Bridget, Señor Johnson," Chica scolded mildly as she pointed at me. "Do not shake the ladder, please." But she couldn't be too mean to Long. After all, no sane single woman kicked a worshipful man to the curb when there were so few of them about.

"Please call me Long, Miss Chica."

Chica raised the safety glasses and gave him her sweetest smile. "Señor Malcolm is your friend, no?"

He should have been suspicious of this question, but he was in lust.

"Good enough," he said. "Why?"

"Nada, nada. I am sad for his family is all. He frowns a lot since last Monday night, yes? You know, the emergency?"

I hiney-swiveled back to marbleizing. Didn't want to be obnoxious in my eavesdropping even if I was befuddled by lack of sleep. Chica was doing a pretty good job interrogating Long.

He basked in her confiding tone. "He hasn't said anything about it to me."

"We worry for you and the people in the club."

"All of us?" He looked hopeful and mounted another rung. More gold flakes floated down.

"Nice of you to be worried about him, but I don't think there was a family emergency. He would've said something. Besides his son lives in D.C., and he's separated from his wife. Whatever the emergency was, I doubt it concerned them."

"Bridget was very scared that night of the murder."

"And no wonder. I wish I'd been here."

"I am sure."

I sure wondered what Malcolm was into that night, if not a family emergency. I squelched the thought and turned back to the panel. Only a few more to go, plus Malcolm wanted us to touch-up paint in a couple of other rooms. Although my concentration and speed were way off kilter, and we'd be hard-pressed to finish all of the work by Saturday morning, it wouldn't do to carry on about it. Chica would help me finish the panels when she completed the medallions, if adhesive fumes or Long shaking the ladder didn't kill her first. At least she hadn't made me practice ladder therapy today.

I slid away from the wall and stretched out full length on the floor, my hands beneath my head. For about five seconds, I contemplated doing abdominal crunches. But the grueling hours of faux finishing had my knees, shoulders and eyeballs burning, so I squelched that thought, too.

Maybe Malcolm never left the club the night Randy died.

A pulse drummed in my right temple at this thought. I sat straight up, gasping for air. I dug for my inhaler.

Seeing my distress, Long leaped off the ladder, which shook violently. Chica dropped the adhesive brush.

"Jesus Maria and José," she cried.

"You OK?" Long knelt beside me.

I pumped the inhaler and gradually began to breathe easier.

"She does not sleep much," Chica said with an amazing lack of sympathy. "Señor, you lost my glue brush for me." She glared at me. "Ask when is his birthday, amiga." She pounded her fist on her chest. "I have bad feeling here."

"December sixth," Long replied with wide eyes. "Why? Got me a present already?"

"Dios Mio," Chica moaned. "Enough! You see? The astrology?" She clattered down the ladder and marched to the powder room, mumbling in Spanish.

Long hefted me to my feet. Poor guy, I had him beat by five inches in height and who knew how much weight. I steered him through the front door to the driveway.

"Is she mad at me?" He pulled away like a rebellious child.

"Not about anything important." I brushed gold flakes from his shoulders, but they settled back in the same places.

"Say what?"

"Astrology. She's a believer, and you're Sagittarius. I'll explain later. For now, I think you should repair your suit and hair," I said.

"That bad?" he cried, vanity overriding hormones. He high-tailed it into the club as Muffin wheeled up abruptly in her black Mercedes SLR.

She lowered the passenger window and leaned out to

look at me. A mega blast of beach music, "Miss Grace" by the Times, filled the air.

Crap. Randy loved that song, declaring it the best shagging song ever (the dance kind of shagging, not the British slang for fornication). We'd learned to shag together at Myrtle Beach. Nothing like being young and barefoot, shuffling in golden sand.

"Isn't that the best shagging song ever?" cried Muffin, bursting through my reverie. She reeked of Chanel, rum and disloyalty. Tears streaked her face, the mascara come and gone. She blew her nose, blinking like a daytime soap opera starlet.

I fought the urge to tear her red hair out by its mousy roots.

"Gotta go back inside," I muttered, discretion being the better part of cowardice.

"Bridget, wait." Muffin lurched from the car and tottered to where I stood. "Have you seen Mikey by any chance?"

I eyed her from head to toe.

Her slacks were wrinkled, and her cashmere sweater was inside out. Her red mane stuck out in odd humps from unsmoothed teasing.

"Are you deaf?" she snapped, blowing booze-cooties in my face.

"Junior League teach you these manners?" I huffed. I forget my mother's Southern-lady drill when sleep-deprived and goaded by people named after baked goods.

Muffin stiffened in anger and then began to boo-hoo on my shoulder. Great. A crying jag by a gold-digging tart that I suspected could have been shagging my dead ex-husband – and I didn't mean dancing in the sand.

With Muffin draped all over me, we stumbled against her car. It started to roll, which was what cars do when they're left running in the wrong gear on a slanted driveway.

I shoved her into a large shrubbery and raced to the driver's door. I jerked it open, but the dip in the driveway defeated my nonexistent leaping-into-a-rolling-car skill set. I two-stepped beside the Mercedes, whimpering as it headed toward hunched, arthritic Dudley Floyd, who was shuffling to his Oldsmobile.

"Dudley," I screamed.

Big as his ears were, he still didn't hear me and continued to perambulate at a fractional pace, which would've been fine if a drunken bimbo's runaway vehicle wasn't fixing to mow him down.

"Help," screeched Muffin in her best Duke Tri-Delt bellow. "My car will be ruined. I'm gonna barf. Bridget, do something."

I made a mental note not to ever go snow skiing with Muffin because, rich sorority girl or not, her screechy voice could cause an avalanche.

Why had Dudley parked near the road instead of in his usual handicapped space near the front door? With winged feet, which I only sprout in life-or-death emergencies, I pounded past the Mercedes and snatched Dudley's chicken wing arm, plucking him from harm's way just in time.

That's when Andrew Holly shot through the laurel hedge bordering the parking lot. He must've been caddying at the first tee and heard Muffin's baboon-like shrieks.

"Got it, Miz O'Brien," he yelled, sprinting for the Mercedes. He jumped in and took control before it reached the street. He finally eased it into an empty parking space.

As Dudley and I arrived at the Olds, Andrew trotted over and handed me Muffin's car keys.

"Please call me Bridget," I replied, my hands shaking.

"Yes, ma'am, Miz Bridget," he said, probably thinking I had delirium tremens before vanishing back through the hedge like Peter Rabbit.

Dudley wedged himself beneath his steering wheel. I marveled at the volume of hair growing from his nose and ears instead of his head. Bless his heart, he would never know that I'd saved him from becoming a road pizza.

I trudged back to Muffin, who sprawled on the gravel.

"Come on. Let's go inside and find your Mikey." I grabbed the hand with the biggest diamond ring and pulled her to her feet. "Then you can go home and try on those shoes or whatever you bought at the mall the afternoon Randy died."

"What shoes?" A cigarette dangled from her lips like a truck-stop floozy as we entered the foyer.

"Didn't you buy something after you left the club that day? You told your husband you went to the mall. About four o'clock or so?"

"The police came and talked to us today. Someone blabbed and said we were at the club yesterday. Well, someone in the golf shop or the dining room, I guess. I know I didn't sign in."

She fumbled inside the front of her sweater and pulled out a gold necklace. She frowned at it.

"Bastard S.O.B.," she cried. She tore the chain from her neck and threw it on the ground. "He laughed when I tried to give it to him. Said it was over. That I should get my money back because Saint Christopher wasn't in the travel business anymore. Fuck him."

She clapped her hands, as if applauding this pronouncement, and then dry-heaved. I almost pushed her back on the ground. It didn't seem right that this nutcase was on the loose while my daughter was locked up.

Nothing coherent seemed to be forthcoming from Little Miss Muffin despite PopPop's sage advice to me once when he'd discovered me sneaking into the house after a keg party. Assisting me up the stairs, he told me to "hush up" as I tried to make excuses.

"If you're going to drink, young lady," he said, "you'd better learn how to handle it and keep your trap shut. What you think when you're sober comes out when you're drunk." He'd patted my cheek. "Nighty-night now."

In Muffin's case, there didn't appear to be much thinking going on even in her sober moments. I got her inside the main door.

"Mr. Ruffin probably didn't mean what he said about St. Christopher," I said even though I'd also read the same thing somewhere. "I'll run outside and get the medal. You can give it to him later. We'll find him so y'all can go on home."

"He stopped drinking, you know," she said. "Hasn't taken a drink in ages." She collapsed on a loveseat in the foyer.

"That's nice."

"Told me I should stop drinking, too. That's, like, so God damn random. When I first got married, you know, he told me that all grownups at this club start drinking at five o'clock every afternoon. Like it's the law or something, he said." She hiccupped as her head lolled on the cushions.

I went outside to retrieve the medal.

The chain coiled in my palm like a shining snake. I turned the medal over. The engraved script read "M.M.R. to R.R.L." Margaret Mary Ruffin to Randall Richard La Russo? My fist closed over the necklace. The bastard S.O.B. Muffin had been cussing out had been Randy, not her loving hubby "Mikey." My suspicions had been correct.

Right on cue, Mr. Ruffin banged out the front door with his bedraggled arm-candy in tow. At least I wouldn't have to hunt him down in the men's card room. I'd had enough of that place.

"Talk to you later," I murmured to Muffin as they passed. I managed to drop the medal in her slacks pocket unbeknownst to either of them.

She stared hollow-eyed, but Mr. Ruffin glowered at me.

Probably nothing personal. Probably just a bad case of acid reflux or spousal pain in the butt.

***

The ballroom was empty when I returned. Chica must have gathered our faux finish impedimenta and stored it in a corner with the boxes of paint and supply crates. My dreaded nemesis, the scary ladder, lay folded and neutralized on the floor next to the wall. Someone had turned on the lights. Ten medallions were finished and looked lovely. Ten chandeliers were uncovered and the crystals were sparkling. There was only one left to do, thank goodness. I got dizzy gazing straight up and staggered backward into the ample belly of Pit Bullard.

"You all right, girlie?" He clutched my upper arms and gently turned me to face him. "You look kinda green."

"I'm not the only one, Pit," I laid my head on his shoulder and smelled his apple pipe tobacco and man sweat. There was something soothing about the combination. I would have lingered there with him patting my shoulder if a slamming door nearby hadn't jerked me up short. Another slamming door that made my heart race. What were the odds? It was fast becoming a phenomenon to rival my fear of ladders.

"What the hell?" said Pit. He sucked in his belly and put me to one side with surprising muscle for a ranting old holy roller.

"Man, you really think you're somethin'," a man slurred in the rural accents of redneck America, somewhere nearby but out of sight. "Sent your Guantanamo messenger boy first, so's you wouldn't have to mess your hands. Then along comes the Chinaman."

"Good old Virgil Spoon," muttered Pit, crossing the ballroom. "And schnockered to boot."

We peered around the set of French doors.

Malcolm, Hermann and Virgil faced each other in the corridor.

Malcolm stood tall, dark and forbidding. Hermann seemed pretty calm what with being called a Guantanamo messenger boy. And then came Virgil, a banty rooster with a jutting chin, closed fists and curled lip.

"I regret this, Mr. Jones," Hermann said. "The tosser would not listen to me or to Mr. Johnson. I told him he was redundant and to vacate the premises." He turned to Virgil. "Guantanamo is an American military base in Cuba. I am from Argentina. You should take care what you say. It would behoove you to learn political correctness."

"Be-what me? Argentina, Gitmo, same difference. All down around with the Communists and drug dealers somewheres, ain't they?"

Virgil sounded so confident in his ignorance that I clapped my hand over my mouth to keep from hooting.

"Thank you, Hermann," Malcolm said. "We can continue our talk later."

Hermann hesitated. He looked as if he had plenty more to say, but he must've thought better of it because he walked away.

Virgil spotted me and Pit watching the exchange. His chin rose, and he began to strut back and forth.

"So, Mr. Malcolm Jones. Fine car out there in the best parkin' space. Fine suit. Fine job. Betcha you can even tap dance."

"Do something," I whispered to Pit.

"I've had about enough of this," roared Malcolm with the force of a category five hurricane. "You didn't bother to show up or call in yesterday. And now you dare to barge into my office. Hermann and I were in the middle of an important meeting. What part of our dismissal policy don't you understand, Virgil? I'm sure it was explained it to you."

"I'se sick yesterday. Can't a body be sick anymore?"

"Trouble in paradise?" An unexpected tap on my arm almost sent me sailing over Pit's shoulder.

I looked into the bold green stare of Hall Hooper.

"No black sumbitch gonna talk to me like this," said Virgil. "Ain't gonna fire me neither 'cause I quit." He spit a plug of chewing tobacco at the nearest wall. We all watched it slide to the carpet.

"Go on home, Virgil," Malcolm said. "You're drunk. I'll send your final paycheck by the end of the week. I don't have time for this right now." He backed into his office, slamming and locking the door.

"Uppity bastard," shouted Virgil. He drop-kicked the door and hit it with his fists. "Cain't do this to me. Just see if you ain't sorry." Virgil stood before the closed door, his jaw twitching.

Pit moseyed up to him.

"Son, when one door closes, another opens. No pun intended. Remember this, happy are those who do not follow the advice of the wicked, or take the path that sinners tread."

"Shut it, you old coot," Virgil said. "Who asked you anyways?" He loped off and banged through a rear door.

"You okay, Miss Bridget?" Pit said.

"You sure know your Psalms," I replied.

"And behold our own Jimmy Olsen, the prodigal reporter," Pit added with a wink in Hooper's direction. "Take care of that nose for news and those big ears, son. Sometimes curiosity can turn you into a pillar of salt."

"That happens, Pit, just cart me to the woods and let the deer lick me," replied Hooper.

"Wait," I said as Pit headed toward the door Virgil went through. "Don't go out there. He's bound to be a mean drunk."

"That he is," Pit said. "But I've known him ever since his

diaper dragged the ground. He needn't fear me nor I him." He shuffled out the door.

"What are you doing here anyway?" I asked Hooper.

"I'm a news hound," he said with an annoying grin full of bleached teeth. "And lately it seems like this place is where the fox is hiding." He leaned against a doorjamb as casual as if he had all the time in the world. But he twirled a pen constantly between his fingers and kept biting his bottom lip. Even his nose appeared to be twitching.

"Hound is right," I said. "You sniffing at a story?"

"Can you blame me? Feel like I've hit the jackpot again tonight. Got a quarrelsome redneck high school dropout, who probably owns a white sheet and pointy hat, cussing out his boss, a black, former Duke benchwarmer several rungs above him on the social ladder. What a recipe for disaster."

Disaster for the average schmuck was manna from heaven for a reporter. So, why was I talking to one who not only wrote in bad taste but also talked a blue streak?

Chica and Long strolled into the ballroom. Although it was another moonless night, some heavenly light seemed to be reflected in Long's eyes.

"Better go in there and check Malcolm. In his office," I said to Long. "He and Virgil almost had it out a minute ago."

"Good Lord," he said. He looked at Chica one last time and blushed before hurrying away.

"It is late, amiga," said Chica as she studied the boxes in the corner. "Vámanos."

"Guess we're heading out," I said to Hooper. "Catch you later. Like next year maybe."

Chica dug through the boxes.

"What're you looking for?" I asked.

She stood with her hands on hips, surveying the supplies. "I will wait in the van for you." She left the ballroom.

"Here's your chance," I said to Hooper. "Malcolm is ripe

for the picking, I bet. No telling what you could misquote for your next story."

"My my, we are cynical. Actually, I've been keeping an eye out for that van of yours," Hooper said. "The person I really came looking for tonight is you."

"No comment," I said. I'd always wanted to say that to a nosy reporter, although a murder investigation with me in it wasn't the scenario I'd envisioned.

"Now that surprises me," Hooper said, stowing his pen in his jacket pocket.

"Why?" Mental head slap. Why'd I ask that? I'd hate the answer. Maybe inhaling craft glue had killed off some of my little gray cells.

"I was sure you'd want it plastered on the record that your daughter had nothing to do with Mr. La Russo's murder." He crossed his arms and scrutinized me.

I smiled and bit down on the inside of my cheek. How lucky for both of us that the dead-blow hammer wasn't available.

"My daughter had nothing whatsoever to do with it." A smile was now impossible. "I have to go. Good luck at digging up dirt. You're good at it."

Hooper grabbed my arm.

"Wait. I'm not out to get you or your daughter," he said. "I'm only trying to make a living. That's why I wanted to talk to you."

I eyed his hand. He dropped my arm.

"So, tell me what you know so far," I said.

"Tell you the truth, I'm not exactly sure that you didn't do it," he replied, looking at me in such a way that I had to remind myself I was innocent.

"See there," he said, "You looked up and down and to the left. I read somewhere that people who do that when you're talking to them are probably lying."

Looks like we'd read the same thing, but I wasn't about to agree with him.

"That just goes to show that you read crap," I said.

Hooper laughed. "I've got the old instinct, you know?"

Arrogant so-and-so.

"And I don't think you did it."

Maybe not so arrogant after all.

"And why's that? Did I sprout wings or something?"

"It was that picture." He chuckled and shook his head.

"Picture?"

"Of you in front of the club looking cute and scared, a deer in the headlights," he said.

"The scared part was right."

"Okay, I'll tell you this much," he said and lowered his voice. "The victim died at about 5:30 p.m."

"How do you know that?" I whispered. The ballroom felt like a fishbowl.

"I never reveal a source," he said.

"You've been watching too much TV."

"Maybe," he said. "The coroner's preliminary examination at the scene, which, of course, was here, indicated severe intracranial bleeding from blunt force trauma to the head. This will most likely be supported by the autopsy, according to my source. Nothing official yet. The murder weapon was probably the little ol' hammer left conveniently near the body."

"And?" I donned the impassive face I'd learned from my mother.

"And it appears that you own one of those. Missing a big orange one, maybe?"

"So do a lot of folks who shop at The Home Depot. So, he died from bleeding in his brain?"

"Well, yes, indirectly. He had two depressed compound skull fractures with external lacerations. The intracranial bleeding would cause pressure in the skull, which, in turn, would cause brain stem herniation or compression. This would result in him losing consciousness and, eventually, it would shut down his respiration."

He just had to show off his medical expertise.

To keep from screaming at this horrific vision, I pretended we were chatting about an episode of *C.S.I.: Miami.* But pain must have leaked to my eyes because Hooper took my wrist in his sweaty palm.

"If it's any consolation, he never knew what hit him. Literally."

"I was afraid he'd bled to death. And suffered. There was this blood and…"

Hooper licked his lips.

"You want more stories, don't you?" I said. "Big ones? And you don't give a fig who you destroy to get them?"

Shut up, Bridget.

"Is there something to hide?" he said. "About your daughter's relationship with her stepfather, for instance?"

My bronchial tubes began shutting down, but I was not about to let him see that I knew that he might be on a track I refused to let him follow. I imagined he was thinking of some improper sexual deviance.

"Randy and Dare hadn't seen each other in years. You're way off base there."

In my mind's eye, I could see Dare's hands gripping a ragged bunch of flowers. After I'd returned from Italy, we'd picked blooms from my mother's fragrant Fortune's Osmanthus bushes and drove to place them on her father's grave. Dare had run her fingers over the gold lettering on the plaque – In Loving Memory, Marcus A. Benedetto, 1950-2005.

"I don't get why you left me to go to Italy," she'd said.

She'd been crying; I'd been crying. We were a mess.

"But I didn't," I'd said. "Leave you, I mean. I was trying

to leave me." Boy, that sounded lame, but I plowed on, trying to take on her hurt and the guilt she shouldn't have had to carry on her slender shoulders. "I was miserable because I felt like a bad mother, even though you were the best thing in my life."

"But you so left anyway," she'd said in my mother's uncomfortable tone.

"I was wrong. I admit it. But I thought it would be better for you to stay here, not take you away from your safe world and Marcus. You and I should have gone to Italy together. I know that now. But I felt claustrophobic, smothered. Worst of all, I knew I'd done it to myself. It was me, not you."

She'd turned her back to me.

"Not you, sweetheart." I reached for her arm and tried to turn her around but she shook herself loose.

"Mom, I heard you," she'd said, refusing to look at me.

But had she gotten it? How could she have, being so young? I scarcely understood it myself despite Honey's eye-opening sessions.

"Hello?" Hooper's nagging voice echoed from a distance. "You all right?"

I blinked. Oh yeah, here I was back with his obnoxious insinuation about Dare and Randy.

"You zone out a lot?" he asked.

Lately I had.

"You can control the dissemination of information, you know. You've just got to trust me," he said, trying on boyish for size.

"I suppose I am protecting someone." To pierce that pose, I gazed at him as if helpless and lost.

His eyes gleamed with a reporter's zeal.

Hmph, I thought so.

"I found Randy's body," I said. "That's all. You want the story? Here it is. We divorced a long time ago. The day he died was the first time I'd seen him in five years. I'm not a club member, just a member's grown daughter. I'm working on a job here. It was a chance meeting with Randy and was as friendly as these things are. Neither Dare nor I have had diddly squat to do with him in forever. The next time I saw him, he was … in the steam room. End of story. Boring copy really."

"On the contrary," he replied, "not boring at all because I don't think you're being truthful."

A reporter talking about truth?

"I've done this for a long time," he added. "I know a rat when I smell one."

I sniffed in his direction.

"Now that you mention it, so do I."

He flinched as I rushed away with my head high, but my breath coming in gasps.

Fourteen

"Relax," Chica said, glancing at me as she drove home.

"Easy for you to say," I said, lowering the window for fresh air. "You can breathe, but I'm dying." I'd sucked on my inhaler since escaping that pinhead Hooper at the club, but my chest was still tight.

"Breathe like Alessandro said to do."

Breathe in, breathe out. Four breaths later, my little bronchial trees were refreshed, but then I started to sniffle.

"Hopper does not cry for you, amiga," Chica said.

"Hooper." I corrected her as I mopped my face on my sleeve. "What if the slime bucket writes something nasty about Dare?"

Chica tsk-tsked, which somehow sounded Spanish when she did it.

"Slow down. Where are we headed anyway, going so fast? I thought we were going home."

"We are making the fast break like our Tar Heels do on the court, to score some food. I am an excellent driver. You know I drove the Big Tank in the desert. Compared to that, the sky van is a piece of pie."

"Cake." I said. "No wonder that war ended so fast with you driving around." She swerved into the drive-thru lane of the Sunrise Biscuit Kitchen where we always got melt-in-your mouth, homemade biscuits the size of basketballs. We called them the "slam-dunk" calories.

"Oh, now I get it," I said. "We're going to O.D. on carbs and fat."

"Yes. We must get food to stay strong for the emergencies ahead. This whole week is an emergency. You will order while I hunt for the gun."

"Is that what you were doing when you left me talking to Hooper?"

"Yes. We need to find it and know it is safe. Too much scary crappiness these days," she said.

She crawled into the back of the van, and I scooted into her seat just as the biscuit lady asked what we would like to order.

After grabbing two fried chicken biscuits and two sweet teas, we drove into one of Sunrise Biscuit's parking spaces. Might as well overdose while the food was hot.

"Come eat before it gets cold," I said.

I heard some fine Spanish cussing from the bowels of the van and saw Chica's hind-end rear up amid Faux Finish's paraphernalia.

"Hijo de perro," she shrieked, chucking a paintbrush over her shoulder and whacking me in the same spot where Mother had nailed me with the door yesterday.

"Son of a bitch is right," I cried almost strangling on a big bite of chicken biscuit. I coughed and said, "If you kill me, you'll have to finish the club job alone."

"La pistola is bye bye, adiós."

"Didn't we decide it must be in the van?"

"Yes. But no gun is here. And I checked the boxes in the club when you do handsy-pantsy with Hopper just now."

"It's Hooper, and that's just plain gross. I'd rather have

my gums scraped than hanky-panky with him. Where are the puppy toys? You said you put it in that box."

"Mistake. Toys are here but no gun."

"You sure?"

"Sure."

"Move over, I'll look."

She crawled up front, snagged a biscuit and gulped some tea. I knelt in the back, digging through our stuff.

With a killer on the loose in the area, we wanted the gun front and center, even though it could be disastrous if I ever needed to use it for more than a paper weight.

Chica had once said that, in a confrontation, "You shoot to kill," when I'd said that blowing off a toe might stop someone.

"Crazy hombres on drugs don't stop, amiga, for a shot toe. And if you shoot a toe only, he would go loco."

I was counting on Chica chucking her current aversion to guns to handle any bad situation that might arise anyway, sort of like riding a bike after you hadn't done it for a while. I wasn't planning to become a gunslinger myself.

"We don't have a permit to carry concealed," I hollered from the depths of a big plastic leaf bag full of junk. "We could be in big trouble."

"It's not concealed. It's gone," she said, cranking the engine.

"Don't start the engine yet," I said. "I'll get car sick back here. I'll be done in a minute."

Chica turned up the radio in time for top-of-the-hour news.

"Police continue to investigate the murder of Chapel Hill native Randall La Russo whose body was discovered on the premises of Magnolia Blossom Country Club this week. According to a police department spokesperson, La Russo, who had lived in Charlotte for several years, had recently joined the private club located on Magnolia Blossom Lane in Chapel Hill. Police stated that although a minor has been arrested in connection with the case, other arrests could be imminent.

"Meanwhile, in sports, men's Tar Heel basketball coach Roy Williams says he is looking forward to tonight's game with the Virginia Cavaliers following the team's big win over the Maryland Terrapins last Sunday."

Chica cut off the radio. "It's crap," she said.

"They said other arrests are imminent."

"¿Qué?" Her Spanglish would be the death of me yet.

"They might arrest someone else soon," I muttered. "It's like a landfill in here. Hijo de perro." I sneezed through floating dust and hurled an empty box out the back doors just in time to see Lieutenant Hendricks at Chica's window.

"Dios mio," Chica cried in his face, "you scared me."

He saw the discarded box and laughed. "Y'all are littering here."

"I forgot where I was," I said. "We're going to pick it up."

"I mostly flunked high school Spanish," Hendricks said, shifting a toothpick to the other side of his mouth. "But I do believe I heard you say something about a dog. Perro, right?"

If timing was everything, mine was off again. Good thing he didn't understand the whole phrase.

"What're y'all doing? Whoa, that biscuit smells good. I happened to see your colorful van as I was passing and got hungry for a biscuit all of a sudden."

"¡Adiós a la pistola!" Chica said in what was rapid Spanish even for her.

"Huh?" Hendricks said. "Got the adiós part."

"She said goodbye in Cuban, that's all." I'd lied so much lately, I fully expected to dangle in Dante's fifth circle of hell through all eternity.

"Cuban is right," Chica said under her breath.

Hendricks raised an eyebrow and stared at me as if I'd lost it, which, of course, I had. As for Chica, she was way beyond his comprehension.

"I'm glad you wanted a biscuit because I wanted to speak with you on a matter of concern," I said in a tone modulated to show my sanity and good sense. "It's about that scuzzbag reporter Hooper."

"Most reporters are like an infestation of fleas," he said. "Once they dig in, they're hard to root out without first you kill the blamed dog. If I were you, I would just ignore him."

"I say she should kill him," Chica said.

He raised his eyebrows.

"You didn't tell Hooper anything about Dare, did you?" I asked. "He seems to know a lot of details about how Randy died, and none of that information has been released yet."

"Lord, no. We don't tell the press anything if we can help it. Especially about juvies. But reporters have their ways of finding things out. You know, cultivating sources and such like. It's their job."

"We need to get home to our dogs. Then, I'm going to my parents' house to watch the Virginia game with them. We're all so upset, I'm hoping the game de-stresses them at least a little bit."

He checked his watch. "I've got a bait of paperwork on my desk, and I'll be burning the midnight oil. With the game on the radio in the background, of course. Would it be too late to come after the game? If y'all have decent coffee, I'll kiss your feet."

"And Señora Hendricks?" Chica asked, eyes big and innocent. "She will wait up for you?"

"Ain't no Missus Hendricks anymore," he said, blushing. "Being a cop's wife didn't suit her."

"I might even have a couple of Mother's oatmeal raisin

cookies in my freezer," I said. If I couldn't beat 'em, I could at least bribe 'em.

"See you later, then." Hendricks said. He winked at Chica and slapped the driver's side door.

"I can't believe how many men you're picking up while my life has become an episode for crime television," I said as we exited the parking lot.

"You, you, always you," she said with a weary sigh. "I like to play is all."

As we drove through the quiet streets, my mind shifted like a kaleidoscope of names, faces and alibis, or the lack of them. Terrified that in my fatigue I might blurt out something to Hendricks that could possibly hurt Dare, I closed my eyes and tried to relax.

"You doing meditation?" Chica tapped me on the arm.

"Trying to."

I gave her the capsule version of Virgil's argument with Malcolm and the episode with Muffin, the St. Christopher's medal and Randy's favorite shagging song.

"Poor Bridget. Close your eyes. Forget about Hopper, Virgil and the bad Mrs. Muffin in Randy's bed." She patted my forehead and chanted, "Om. Om Mani Padme Hum."

"You're kidding, I can't say that stuff. And it's Hooper not Hopper. How many times do I have to tell you?"

"It's OK. Hooper then. This is more important. The astrology lady showed me. Is from Tibet. Close your eyes again. Do it."

"OK, but you keep yours open," I said. "Om. Om Mani Padme Hum." Talk about idiotic. "What does that mean, anyway?"

"A mantra. You are a dummy or something?"

"Om. Om Mani Padme Hum," I said. Not bad. Not Gregorian, but not bad.

Chica joined in, and we notched up the volume.

"Om. Om Mani Padme Hum. Om. Om Mani Padme Hum. Om. Om Mani Padme Hum. Om. Om Mani Padme Hum."

We pulled into the driveway, windows closed now, and screamed, "OM. OM MANI PADME HUM."

Relaxation? Who knows? But it sure felt good.

Bubba and Big Foot barked inside the house, dog antennae alert to the bizarre sound of their masters in manic unison.

Fifteen

Despite the Tibetan meditation with Chica in the van, or maybe because of it, I was not relaxed when I pulled up in front of my parents' house. I missed Dare terribly. This should have been a family occasion instead of the day of a juvenile first appearance. Feeling numb, I almost didn't get out of the van, but Daddy was expecting me and that was that.

The glowing windows on Rosemary Street meant that every television in every house – including mine – was already tuned into Carolina basketball. Daddy always said that "one wouldn't want to miss any of the sports commentary if one had to move about the house." A Tar Heel win over Virginia tonight would make six straight victories and pay back the heartbreaking loss to the Cavaliers in January. It would also get us ready for the Duke game this Saturday, March 4.

It seemed surreal that Randy had been dead for two days and my daughter arrested for his murder. Although my soul was aching, I dug deep for some positive emotion; otherwise, as Chica had been carping, "your karma will go to the toilet."

Huffing up the driveway in the brisk night air, I caught a whiff of Daddy's special hot-air popcorn slathered in garlic butter. Rubbery shoe squeaks on wood and the halftime horn greeted me at maximum volume as I opened the kitchen door. Mother only permitted excessive broadcast noise for Carolina games.

This sensory chaos that also included Daddy's fervent pacing and Mother's unseemly, but endearing, epithets in front of the TV was usually soothing. But tonight the vision of my changeling offspring locked up instead of cheering in her special blue chair roiled inside of me.

I axed this line of thought immediately. I would not ruin my parents' two-hour basketball escape from reality. Picturing my father's shadowed face in recent days and Mother's odd panic, I yanked the freezer open to commune with food.

Still no oatmeal raisin cookies? For heaven's sake, what had Mother been doing lately? She'd tidied the kitchen, at least. She might be a bit whacked out, but that was beside the point. The state I was in required my favorite comfort food.

I breathed in and out and then hurried to the den as Woody Durham's radio show echoed down the hall. Daddy had some of the TVs muted so he could listen to the man who'd announced Carolina games on WCHL radio since the flood. Woody almost sounded objective about Carolina's 49 to 24 halftime lead over Virginia. But Daddy's scholarly voice had taken on the zeal of a frat boy as he lauded the rebounding skills of the senior forward, David Noel.

"Yes sir," I heard Davey add, matching Daddy's intensity. "It's so sweet. Nineteen points already and Senior Night at the Dean Dome. Couldn't ask for more."

Davey? What was he doing here?

"Don't you Confederates knock on wood when you make statements like that?" said a Yankee voice that sounded like Officer Jennifer Jones.

What was she doing here?

I paused to compose my features and then clumped into the room. Davey, thigh to thigh with Jennifer Jones on the sofa, leapt to his feet.

Officer Jones was still in uniform. Davey's navy pin-striped coat lay on the back of the sofa. His snowy, cotton buttoned-down shirt was open at the neck. A fine-looking law-and-order couple.

I crossed my arms over a catsup stain on my rumpled Faux Finish coveralls. The plan to freshen up for Mother's sake had come to naught.

Davey turned the alizarin crimson of my acrylic paint colors, or, as is usually said in these parts, red as a beet.

"We were worried about you, sugar." Daddy pulled up short in his worn carpet groove and covered the distance between us in three giant steps. "You missed an astonishing first half."

I clung to him as he patted my shoulder.

"You remember Officer Jones?"

Jennifer rose quickly despite her tight police britches.

"No, no, don't get up," I said.

She did anyway and grabbed my hands.

"How are you doing, Mrs. O'Brien?" Her eyes were full of pity.

Hmph. I forced my lips to rise at the corners. "I'm fine, and that's Miss O'Brien."

She gave Davey a rueful shake of the head as if to say "poor thing."

"I'm surprised you're interested in the game," I said, a little bit catty. Well, a lot catty actually. "Not from around here, are you?"

"New Jersey originally, but I went to Carolina."

"Really?" I said politely.

"In Columbia," she added under her breath.

"Oh, you mean South Carolina?" I crowed.

Davey looked pained, so I pointed to the reading glasses and stack of magazines on the opposite end of the sofa.

"Where's Mother?"

"Stepped out for a minute," Daddy said.

He stared at Dare's chair, and his shoulders sagged. I clutched his arm, but he recovered quickly.

"I think my wife's just tired," he said to Jennifer, as if she needed an explanation.

That was a lie, though. Mother never got tired when we were winning big. She loved the games when she could relax, and agonized over the exciting, close ones. Full of good cheer during what she termed the "fun" games, she and Daddy would regale me and Dare with stories about the basketball players she dated in the Sixties.

"Of course, this was before your grandfather showed up to ruin my life," she'd say to tease us.

Daddy would wait for us to beg for the "sorry" player's name, which we always did for his sake.

"No one remembers his name," he'd boast. "Some benchwarmer who saw a minute of playing time per season. Never even broke a sweat."

Mother would feign huffiness, and Dare was always so tickled.

The memory washed me in pain.

"I'll go get Mother," I said, fighting the unwelcome nostalgia. "The game's about to start."

As I left, I glanced at Davey being mashed into the corner of the sofa by Jennifer.

Davey caught up with me in the hall. "Where's the fire?"

"Do you or your date need anything? A pillow? A blanket?" I asked.

"Ha ha, and she's not my date."

"Could've fooled me."

"What's the matter with you?"

"Nothing." I faked yet another smile. "I'm upset about Mother."

"You're jealous, aren't you?" he said, pleased.

"You wish."

"Jennifer saw me on Franklin Street when I was on my way over and offered a ride. I couldn't be rude and not ask her in when we got here. Besides, your dad likes folks around during a game."

"Right." I chewed on that and my lip for a few seconds.

"What are you thinking? I don't like it when you do that," he said.

"You reckon she'd talk about the case with you?"

"Ah." He flashed excellent dentition at me. "You'd pimp me out for information?"

I shoved him away. "Go do some sweet talking. Always knew you were good for something, even if only to charm Yankee girls off bushes. None of my business whose badge you mess with. I couldn't care less, so there."

He kissed me hard on the mouth.

"You talk too much," he said, coming up for air. This was a ridiculous comment as I couldn't say a thing for several seconds after he was gone.

"That boy has the hots for you," Mother said behind me. "Always has had."

"I wish you'd stop sneaking up on me," I said. "Where did you get "the hots" from? You've been reading too much *Cosmopolitan*. It's bad for you."

"Dare told me."

"I don't believe it."

"She's quite bright, you know. Too bright. Too much like ..."

She slipped past me, but I followed her into the den.

"Are you feeling better now, honey?" Daddy asked, his forehead creased with worry as he stalked over to her.

Mother took in the empty popcorn bowls and the iced tea dregs in the big plastic Carolina cups.

"What are you thinking, Richard? No one has a thing to eat or drink, and the second period is about to start."

All eyes slid to the television. The players on both ends of the court were taking practice shots. Then the program cut to quick clips of students on the UNC campus and the rich avuncular voiceover of Carolina alumnus, Charles Kuralt.

"What is it that binds us to this place as to no other?" he said. "It is not the well or the bell or the stone walls, or the crisp October nights or the memory of dogwoods blooming. No, our love for this place is based on the fact that it is as it was meant to be – the university of the people."

Tears filled Mother's eyes, and she fled the room. My father and I stared at each other, stricken. Davey and Jennifer rose awkwardly.

"I'll handle it, Daddy."

I found my mother upstairs on Dare's bed watching as the second half began.

"What's going on, Mother?"

I pulled off my boots and sat on the edge of the bed.

"It's called a basketball game, dear." She gave me a pitying look. There seemed to be a run on those looks tonight.

"Why don't you rest?" I said. "It's late." I toed the pale blue afghan that Nana Blanche had made for her freshman year.

"You think I'm crazy, don't you?" she said.

"Why would I think that?" My voice rose involuntarily. "You're the most uncrazy person I know."

Well, she had been until last week.

"You always squeak when you lie, Bridget."

"See there?" I said. "You don't sound a bit crazy."

She unbraided my hair and shook it loose, combing it with her fingers. Ordinarily, I loved such rare attention from her, but tonight it raised goose bumps.

"You've got the most beautiful hair. Just like your grandmother's."

"Can I ask you something?" I said.

"Of course."

"Where were you the other day? Late Monday afternoon?

"Playing bridge, I expect. Why?"

"Daddy says the tables broke up early. You weren't here when he got home."

"What difference does that make?"

Then she rolled to the other side of the bed and stood up, her face a mask of anger with flashing blue eyes. "Are you insinuating something?"

"Just getting the afternoon straight in my mind. So, where were you?"

"I can't remember."

"Were you at the store or maybe the mall?" I was trying to be helpful and hopeful at the same time.

The crowd roared on television, and we both turned to see Number 50 stuff one despite being guarded by three Virginia players.

"Don't you just love that boy from Missouri? Tyler Hansbrough? He plays so hard. Such a good work ethic, they say."

"Mother, were you or were you not here when Dare got home from the club that day, probably between five and six."

"I want to watch television, Bridget. This is my kind of game. Please extend my apologies to Davey and Jennifer. She seems quite taken with him, by the way." She arched an eyebrow at me. "Don't frown, your face will grow that way. I'm going to rest as you suggested."

Cunning woman, but I hoped I'd learned from the expert.

I spread the afghan over her legs.

"What did she say to you?"

"Who, dear?"

"You know perfectly well. Dare. When she got back from the club on Monday night, what did she say?"

"Nothing. She didn't feel well. I made her change out of her sweaty clothes after we got in so I could launder them."

"What do you mean 'after we got in'?"

"Look at that Reyshawn Terry," she said, shoving me none too gently out of her line of vision. "He's having a fabulous year. I bet his mother is pleased as punch. He's from Winston-Salem, you know."

"Mother, did you and Dare go somewhere together?"

She smiled again, and my neck prickled.

"When I got back from … an errand, I couldn't find her. Then I remembered that she could have gone to the club after tennis practice, so I walked over there. I was worried."

"About what?" I circled the room, picking up objects and putting them down, examining my daughter's knickknacks without really seeing them.

"I knew Randy might be there. Grace told me not long ago that he might come back here to live."

"Why didn't you say something to me about that?" I stopped in front of the TV.

"Don't give me that look, young lady. You're still my child. I didn't tell you because I hoped Grace was wrong. She's so feather-headed sometimes. And Randy was bad to say what you wanted to hear and then not follow through on it. Anyway, on Monday, I decided to find out why, if I could, and make sure that Dare didn't run into him."

"What difference would that have made?" I went to the window but saw only my pale reflection beneath a sliver of moon.

"I'm not a fool, Bridget. About anything."

This was, of course, something I'd never questioned. I kept staring through the window. Finally, fearing a remark about my rude back, I turned to face the blue and green walls. Dare's posters seemed to whisper her name as if wondering why the old folks were in her space.

"Did you see him?" I asked.

"Yes," she said, dropping her gaze after a long minute

filled with the banal chatter on television. "He laughed at me. Oh, not in a rude way, mind. He's the king of passive aggressive. Part of his charm, I suppose."

We turned back to the safe territory of the basketball game as Quentin Thomas ran the point again for another basket.

"He's doing great tonight," I said.

"Come on, boys," she reprimanded the team, "gentlemen don't run up the score."

"I thought you liked a big lead."

"It's a gray area."

"For heaven's sake, we're going to win. Tell me what Randy said." I paused. "It's just a game, after all." Me trying to be an adult again.

She slammed me with those blue eyes.

"It's never just a game, is it?"

The possible depths of this question held me in speechless thrall. Maybe the years of blonde hair color applied to camouflage her gray hadn't penetrated to her brain after all.

"It was kind of peculiar, really," she added. "He said that no one was going to stop him. That you knew he was right. 'She'll just have to live with it,' he said. He never explained what 'it' was. Then he turned his back on me and strolled into the men's locker room as rude as you please. Grace spoiled that boy rotten."

"Tell me you didn't follow him into the locker room."

She picked at yarn in the afghan.

"Does that sound like something I would do, dear?"

Game broadcasts reverberated from five different TVs in the house, even to the extent that there seemed to be an echo coming from the whole neighborhood and the whole city beyond the windows. Inside the blue residence, the different cable feeds were not in synch, so we heard a cheer from

Daddy and then saw Noel reach a career-high of 26 points about four seconds later.

"I looked for you when I was there," Mother said.

"You and Dare walked home? Did anyone see you? Why didn't you tell this to the police?"

"I couldn't find Dare then, so I came home alone, thinking I'd find her here. Why should I tell the police anything?"

"To show that she couldn't have done it?"

She shook her head and blinked at the television screen. "Leave me alone, Bridget. Go tend to your daddy and his guests."

"I'll stay, if that's OK with you."

We watched the rest of the game, pretending it was the only thing going on in the bedroom and in the world, for that matter. This wasn't so hard considering my family had been doing it for real ever since I could remember. Our faked politeness was killing me by the time the final buzzer sounded. As it was, the Tar Heels trounced the Cavaliers 99-54.

I took up the gauntlet.

"So, you went back the club, Mother?"

She clicked the television off with the remote control.

"I went back to the club and found her then. She was in the hallway looking like she was in shock. Then I saw this on the floor and took it."

She reached under the bed and pulled out a black cell phone connected to its charger.

"That's her cell," I cried, ripping it and the charger from the wall socket behind the bed. "How'd you get it from the police?"

She ignored my question.

"Of course I thought it was her phone. It's a flashy little thing," she continued, "and I wasn't about to leave it there. That cord with it was in her dresser drawer. I'm not a bit surprised that his taste ran to the juvenile."

Her bland self-control was defeated by a mischievous glint in her eye, reminiscent of the freaky behavior of Tuesday morning.

"Whose taste? What're you talking about?" I gazed at the slick little phone in my hand.

"Randy's, of course," she said. "That's his phone. The police have Dare's."

Daddy's voice floated up from downstairs where he was exchanging overly hearty goodbyes with Davey and Jennifer. They must have been glad to escape the strained vibes zigzagging through the house that evening.

Mother pointed at Randy's phone, saying I could take it as long as I did "the right thing with it." An ensuing one-way conversation failed to reveal what that might be, so I left with a half hug for her and a flying kiss for Daddy.

I drove home, rehashing little issues such as right and wrong, heaven and hell and life in an orange jail ensemble. Through all that, the digital image of Dare's phone number as the last call on Randy's phone the night he died branded itself into my retinas. Then I turned off the phone and removed the SIM card.

Sixteen

Thoughts of my family visiting me in prison for obstruction of justice were dancing through my head when I pulled into the driveway close to midnight. Chica flitted out the door with the leashed dogs and trotted by Hendricks who was climbing out of his car.

"Adiós," he called after Chica. "Careful out yonder now. Should I go with you?"

"It's OK," she said. "Big Foot scares everybody."

"I bet."

"She won't go far," I said to him as I locked the van. "I'll get the coffee and be right out if you don't mind keeping an eye on things out here." I scampered into the house.

Back outside I handed him a mug of steaming coffee and a napkin-wrapped cookie. "If I recall, you like it black. So, how about that Virginia game?"

"Heard it at my desk," he said, snug in his trench coat and gloves. He sipped his coffee thoughtfully.

"I'm wondering if you found out anything important about this case seeing as how you've been playing detective all week," he said after a long silence.

"Maybe."

"Ever hear the expression town-and-gown?" he asked.

"Daddy explained it to me once."

"What you come to find out in a place like this, a village that grew up around the college, so to speak, is that you've got two perspectives. Even these days." He dunked his cookie in the coffee and bit into it.

"I think I see what you mean," I said.

"I'm sorta between a rock and a hard place when it comes to the club," he said. "A friend sponsored me for membership there several years back. We still play golf if I get a chance when he's in town."

"Change your mind about joining?"

"Got blackballed actually," he said. "Years ago. Then my friend transferred to California, so it was no big deal. Too expensive anyway. Reckon someone there didn't think I'd fit in."

"Ridiculous," I said. "Although some members do tend to have a high opinion of themselves. There's more new money out there than you can shake a stick at, and they're usually the snootiest. I wonder if Daddy knows about that. He wouldn't blackball for a reason like that."

"Yeah, well. He's bound to have heard something. Anyway, like I said, saved me a ton of money in the long run. Work all the time anyway. But that's all water under the bridge now. Thing is, I can interrogate folks out there all I want and not get a straight answer. But someone on the inside, like you, can talk casual-like, know what I mean?"

"At least you must think I didn't do it."

"Not necessarily, but that don't mean what you learn won't be useful."

Of all the nerve. He wanted me to do his dirty work for him.

"Davey thinks the world of you and your family," he said, "and I think a heap of his opinion most of the time. That's not to say that an upstanding family ain't hiding a body or two in the basement."

"My mother wouldn't hear of anything so unseemly in her basement. She'd put it under the forsythia bushes." I laughed until I thought of poor Randy.

"Also, I gotta keep in mind that Davey's a tad sweet on you," he added.

My cheeks burned.

"You're mistaken if you think I'm playing at detective," I said. "I'm serious as a heart attack. This is my baby girl we're talking about. I want her out of that place. Untainted. You know she didn't do it, don't you?"

"I know most of you folks don't think so," he said.

"Lots of other people have motives," I cried. "Dare doesn't have one."

"Don't she? She must think she does to up and confess like she did."

Hendricks pulled a pack of Juicy Fruit from his pocket and extended it my way. I took a stick and rolled it up in my mouth despite my mother's warning that women smacking gum resembled cows chewing cud.

We sat down on the top step.

"Dare's a drama queen," I said. "An eighth grader. A child becoming a woman. This past year has been hard for her and I consider a lot of it my fault."

"Why's that?" he asked. "Why doesn't she live with you?"

Lord, did he have all night?

"Hasn't Davey filled you in? I thought you were good friends."

"He's put me in the picture on some of it, without breaching his client's confidence, of course," he said. "About how Dare's daddy died last summer while you were having a nervous breakdown with some Italian boy."

Well, crap, Davey, thanks a lot.

"Alessandro's thirty, he's not a boy." He was twenty-seven, but I rounded upward.

I chewed my gum so hard that I bit my tongue, which seemed to happen a lot. I attributed it to misaligned teeth instead of a symbolic recurrence.

"I'm having a heckuva time figuring out why the child would wanna bust her stepdaddy's head open like that."

"How can I make you see she didn't do it," I said, quickly blocking the memory of Randy on the steam room floor. "Randy hasn't been her stepfather for years, and they weren't close when he was. He didn't really like kids and didn't seem to take much interest in her. That never changed."

I crossed my fingers behind my back. Another lie, as one of the last things Randy had said recently was that he wanted to get close to her. I fought the urge to drop to my knees. Bless me, Father, for I have sinned … again.

Footsteps and eight paws padded up the driveway in the darkness. Chica and the dogs breathed clouds into the cool night air.

"The orange gato and the tree again," Chica said, unhooking the leashes.

"Chica means that the dogs have treed the orange cat," I said. "It's what they live for."

The dogs flew up the steps. I cracked the door open, and they scrabbled over the hardwoods to their water bowls, or in Big Foot's case, the open toilet.

"So, you have questions, you ask me," Chica said, crossing her arms as she stood in the driveway.

"Here's a good one," Hendricks said. "Who do y'all really think did it, present company included?"

Chica held up a left fist and got so up close and personal to Hendricks that his coffee cup paused in midair.

"Uno is Malcolm." Up popped her left thumb.

"Dos." She pointed her index finger. "Marla Ann with the big cha chas."

She wiggled the middle finger suggestively and pulled up

her ring finger. "Tres y cuatro, the Muffin woman and Señor Ruffin. Muffin, she shag-shags with Randy. Mr. Ruffin, he finds out."

"She had me at uno," Hendricks said to me, chuckling so hard his coffee slopped from the mug.

Chica stuck out her pinky finger and second thumb. "Cinco y seis are Virgil, a redneck hombre, and Hermann. I do not know yet why they might do it, but I will think of something. Hermann is a nice man, but his waters run deep."

"She means still waters," I added helpfully.

Hendricks laughed until he had to wipe tears of mirth from his eyes.

"Not funny," Chica cried. "No. It is the suspects. Maybe more though. Maybe a stranger did it."

"One thing about Chica," I added, "she gets down to the nitty gritty. Could be she's right about it being a stranger. There could very well be someone from Randy's Charlotte life that we know nothing about."

"Well, he wasn't robbed. Course that doesn't mean that's not how it started. We are still checking into Charlotte. So far, nothing," he said. "But good going, ladies. Looks like I may have to pay y'all under the table for all this fine information."

"Have you found Grace La Russo yet?" I said. "She could fill in gaps, I suppose, even though Randy never confided in her when we were together. That could've changed."

Hendricks stuffed his napkin in the empty cup and handed it to Chica.

"Nope, no sign of her. Does she stay a long time on these NASCAR trips?"

"You might want to ask her next door neighbor," I said. "An old gentleman called Dudley Floyd. He's a club member, too. Looks like George Burns without the toupee. He's been sweet on Grace forever, and they talk a lot."

"Will you two be working at the club in the morning?"

"Yes," Chica said. "Muy temprano. Early."

"As early as possible," I amended.

"Might see y'all there then," he said.

"Don't forget what I said about the argument that Randy and Malcolm had."

"I haven't."

"Do you know who the last person was to see Randy? Besides his killer, I mean?" A list of my family members floated in front of my eyes.

"I'm checking some things out," said Mister Mysterious.

"Oh ho. I'm supposed to tell you everything and get nothing in return?"

"Something like that."

He was still smiling when he drove away.

Chica and I locked up the house and climbed the stairs.

"Thanks for not naming one of the suspects," I said at the landing.

"I forgot one?" she said. "No way, José."

"Hendricks is no fool, despite his country boy act," I said. "She's on his list, too, I bet."

"You mean …."

"My mother."

Seventeen

My first thought on waking at daybreak on Thursday morning was of Dare in the youth home. What must she be doing and feeling? Although Daddy planned to see her during visiting hours today, he told me, as gently as he could, that she'd made him promise not to bring me along. My feelings were hurt, but I didn't fuss. He didn't say if my mother was going, but I doubted it. Poor Daddy, surrounded by volatile females.

I closed my eyes and gabbled a couple of Hail Marys, hoping for clarity, but afterward was still so clueless and depressed I almost pulled the covers over my head. However, there wasn't a better person to handle Dare's situation than my father, so I took heart.

Peeking out the window, the pink dawn anchored by blue sky for the dedication of Habitat for Humanity's latest blitz build house seemed like a good omen. So, I finally rolled out of bed confident that Pilar, as co-chairwoman of UNC's program, would be at the ceremony and I'd be able to quiz her about Dare's recent state of mind.

On my way to the kitchen, I got the newspaper off of the front porch, which turned out to be a stupid plan when I saw the page one headline.

CHAPEL HILL TEEN MURDER SUSPECT IN CUSTODY

Chapel Hill police have arrested a 13-year-old middle school student in connection with the murder of Randall La Russo, a Chapel Hill native and 1992 graduate of UNC.

Authorities said the teen was arrested on Tuesday about 1 a.m. after being taken into custody, and later transferred to the Orange County Regional Juvenile Detention Center.

The first appearance and detention hearing in Orange County Juvenile Court yesterday will be continued next week when it is expected that the date for the probable cause hearing will be set. It will then be determined if the minor will be tried as a juvenile or an adult, although the latter seems unlikely given the child's age.

According to Lt. Greg Hendricks of the Chapel Hill Police Department, the suspect's age hampers the investigation.

"We can't determine the exact sequence of events at the crime scene in the usual way because of the extreme youth of the suspect," he said. "If the accused was 16, information could be given to the public that would help in our investigation. However, by law, we cannot release the name or photo of the suspect to the public at this time."

North Carolina is one of the few states using a cutoff age of 16 at this time. Several states use the cutoff age of 18. If the 13-year-old is tried as an adult, the case would go to Superior Court, at which time the name of the accused would be part of the public record.

Bridget O'Brien, La Russo's ex-wife, discovered the body early Monday evening. Although she remains a person of interest, according to police, she has not been charged with any crime. Police are not releasing cause of death at this time. La Russo, 36, was a UNC Chapel Hill graduate and an account executive at Austin, Crowe Securities in Charlotte, N.C.

What a way to start the day.

I dragged myself back upstairs and rousted Chica from mid-snore. She shot me the evil eye before rising. By that time, the dogs were clamoring downstairs for food and exercise. Chica took them for a walk while I rolled up the newspaper and stuffed it in the kitchen trash can.

Before leaving the house, we stood over the dogs as they snoozed with their paws twitching on the kitchen floor. Even asleep, Bubba was baring his teeth.

"He's Super Weenie Dog in la-la land," I said, "getting ready to attack."

"Big Foot thinks he is the first in the Idiot Race."

She meant the Iditarod Great Sled Race, but I kept mum because she was scowling into the blue plastic Carolina cup I'd handed to her.

"Cold tea? You crazy? I need hot."

"For heaven's sake, we'll do a latte run before the club. But I want to swing by the Blitz House right now. Habitat waits for no man or woman."

We cruised past the new 1,100-square-foot brown bungalow with cream shutters, perched on a slight hill like a giant chocolate truffle trimmed in vanilla. Dozens of volunteers, including some of UNC's men's basketball team and a cluster of octogenarians in Sergeant Pepper-type jackets milled about. The main part of the house had been built in five days during two long weekends by most of these people and professional homebuilders as part of Habitat for Humanity's National Home Builders Blitz program.

Chica parked in a nearby vacant lot already packed with cars. On the crowded front porch, the new homeowner, a long-time Orange County employee, chatted and shook hands as her young daughter and twin boy toddlers clutched balloons on strings.

As a partner of the Habitat program, the woman had received a zero-interest mortgage and low closing costs in return for helping to construct this house and agreeing to help build future Habitat homes. Churches, businesses and clubs donated time and money in the cause.

Dare had helped landscape this project. Her excitement when Pilar scooped her up for the task a few weeks earlier had convinced me to get involved. In the family room of the new home, I'd used the tromp l'œil technique to create the illusion of a window with a scenic view of the university's bell tower above the treetops. Not to be outdone, Chica had applied stipple brush and tinted joint compound to give the bathroom walls a fossil rock texture.

This morning, Chica stooped to the sidewalk in front of the house to pat the purple and yellow pansies and red tulips Dare had planted. At the time, my daughter had called them by their Latin names – violas and tulipias. One always gleaned some useful tidbits when living with my mother.

"La niña is a good worker," Chica said, brushing her hands off and admiring Dare's handiwork.

Although much of the yard was unfinished due to cold weather, these flowers were thriving – and would continue to do so unless plunderers like that TV reporter and camera crew right in front of me didn't watch their steps.

"Hey, Sound-byte Man," I said to the spiffed-up young guy trampling the border and waving a microphone. The little snot rolled his eyes, annoyed, but this was my daughter's labor he was crushing.

"Look at you. Stomping around in a flowerbed. This isn't the parking lot at Wal-Mart, you know." I pointed to his loafer about to crush some pansies.

The reporter looked down, most likely for the first time, before lifting his foot. "Sorry about that." He gave my blue-collar appearance the once-over and then sneered ever so slightly, adding, "Ma'am."

Oh, that punch to the solar plexus – that nasty "M" word. Often, this polite Southern mark of respect has no reference to age. Today though, the young man had pushed the old lady button and given it the extra kick of a class put-down.

Maybe I was too sensitive. This being on the wrong side of thirty-five had raised my terror-of-middle-age hackles to new heights.

"Chill, Bridget," Chica muttered. "Flowers grow back."

True. It could've been worse. The media moron might've been the dreaded Hooper, and it was too early in the day to deal with him.

The TV crew fled into the crowd as the local officials worked their grip-and-grins amid the unrelenting click and whir of cameras. Chapel Hill's mayor, handsome, auburn-haired Elizabeth Holroyd, stepped to the railing and "a-hemed" twice with the authority accorded to women of a certain size, age and demeanor. She couldn't have impressed the gathering more if she'd been the chariot-mounted Boudicca leading the Celtic tribes against the Romans.

A hush descended, and reporters pointed their microphones and recording devices at the mayor, who clasped the now-weeping mother with one arm and swept the other in a grand gesture that included the house and festivities.

"See … what can be done … with a little help from your friends?" she boomed, pointing to the oldsters standing nearby in ragged formation and wielding band instruments.

On cue, the coats of many colors band wheezed into an off-key rendition of the Beatles tune from the album *Sgt. Pepper's Lonely Hearts Club Band.*

The mayor warbled the wrong lyrics. "What would you do if I sang the wrong tune? Would you get up and run out on me?"

Oh well, her spirit was in it.

Thunderous applause and woo-hooing ensued, and then the audience joined in. Light blue, helium-filled balloons rose into the air from huge plastic bags. After the song ended, the noise dropped a decibel or two and a Baptist preacher uttered a rousing prayer. After the "amens," a city councilman took up the gauntlet, extolling the virtues of the Habitat program by beginning a slow roll call of volunteers and benefactors.

"Miz Terry Gaar, please raise your hand," he said, pointing to a slender, dark-haired woman who waved, embarrassed. "There she is. This li'l lady was the muscle, literally, behind the framing. Put some of the men to shame. An inspiration to us all. All y'all don't wander off now because these names aren't in alphabetical order, and I've got quite a list here."

"Vàmanos. This will take all day," Chica whined

"You're right." I dreaded Dare's name being called.

Chica sniffed the air, now warming up with the sunshine. "Donuts."

She headed toward two canopied tables set up near the house. One held Habitat for Humanity pamphlets and T-shirts; the other was stacked with green-and-white Krispy Kreme donut boxes. A substantial woman with bushy orange hair and scary dark roots presided. She chose two donuts from different boxes and ate them in four chomps, no doubt making sure the delivery was fresh.

"Not for us," I said. "We're trying to be good." As my taste buds began to pulsate, I shoved Chica past the tables. "See Pilar anywhere?"

"No, but Jesus Maria …," Chica pointed back at the porch.

Standing beside the mayor was Marla Ann, red lips writhing above white teeth as she pumped the hands of politicking male officials.

"Ugh, probably drumming up trade. Her realty company donated money to this project," I said just as I spotted Pilar's golden hair in the sunlight. She and a young man in a leather jacket were heading to the parking lot.

"Pilar, wait," I called.

She whispered to her companion, who threw me an annoyed glance but continued to shamble on. He climbed into the driver's seat of Pilar's car and slammed the door.

I couldn't put my finger on why Pilar looked different. The dark circles under her eyes? Was her face a bit swollen?

"Miz O'Brien." She smiled despite her obvious fatigue. "What's happening?" A bad attempt at perky.

When I hesitated, she must have recalled that my life had gone from chicken salad to chicken shit recently because her face immediately creased in concern.

"Sorry, sorry. I'm so lame sometimes. Been out of it, you know? I've had the flu. How's Dare doing, poor baby? They treating her right in that place?" She hugged me briefly.

Her sympathy unplugged my tear ducts, and I clung to her petite frame.

"Oh God, do you have a minute? I've told you to call me Bridget."

Tears filled her eyes.

"I can't believe what happened to Randy. I mean Mr. La Russo. He took me to lunch just the other day."

"He did?"

"Yes. And I need to tell you something important about that. I've seen a lot of him lately. But it's not like you might think."

Good Lord, he hadn't been coming on to her, had he? She might not think that but it would have been just like him. However, I had more important fish to fry at this point.

We walked to some nearby trees while Chica, my Cuban entourage, had my back.

"We can discuss Randy later. I've been trying to reach you ever since, you know. But your father told me you've been sick and I hated to bother you." My voice wavered with emotion. I mopped my face with a clean Faux Finish rag and gulped myself calm. "Didn't mean to go all teary-eyed, but I'm so worried about Dare."

She turned away, studying the ground. I stooped to peer into her face, which was a faint cadmium green, and managed to grab her just as she leaned over to dry-heave.

"You okay?" I glanced at the shrinking number of donut boxes. Probably a glazed one wasn't a good idea. The woman selling them was angrily shaking a donut at a man half her size. Good Lord, was that Virgil Spoon? He spit a stream of tobacco juice at the woman's feet and slunk off.

"I'm fine," Pilar said, coughing and then sneezing. "It's flu, I think. I just need to get back to bed. But I didn't want to miss this morning here at the house."

A horn sounded, and Pilar's male friend glared at us as he started the car.

"Your boyfriend?"

"I can't talk right now." Pilar pressed a tissue to her reddened nose." But don't you worry about Dare. Someone's just made a horrible mistake."

A bit of color returned to her face, and she straightened up. "That's what you're wondering probably. What's up with that confession anyway? Daddy told me everything, and I've read some other stuff in the paper."

"You read about the confession in the paper?"

Pilar's boyfriend blew the horn twice, attracting several stares.

"No, it's just the word around the club. But are they right? Did she confess? Like I know I shouldn't be asking, but here's the thing. There's no way she did this. I know her. She's just a kid, and a good one, too. I have to go, though." She clutched her stomach and cast an apprehensive look at the crowd surrounding the house.

"Are you saying you know she didn't do it?"

"I don't know. It's a figure of speech. I mean like, I couldn't know really, could I?"

"You were at the club that day to drop off your father.

But what about later? You might've seen her leave or something."

"No, it was Monday. I dropped Daddy off because his car has been in the shop for a while. I think they let him use the club truck because I was like home sick and writing a paper for class, and I think he had an appointment."

"Sure." I swallowed the knot in my throat. "Sorry to nag you, but I thought you'd know why she would say something like this. You've talked to her? Girl talk? She couldn't have anything to do with this, right?"

Pilar stroked my shoulder as if I were Bubba in a lather.

"It'll be fine, I promise. I'll call you if I think of...," She froze.

"Amiga," Chica warned over her shoulder, and I followed her gaze.

The sun glinted off Hermann's glasses as, stony-faced, he climbed out of the club's pickup across the street. He scanned the crowd and then spotted us.

Pilar ran to her car with a frantic wave back in my direction.

"I will call you," she said out of the passenger window before she and her friend sped off.

A cloud passed over the sun, but the resultant chill felt like more than the weather.

"Hermann?" I said, approaching him with Chica. "Everything all right?"

Chica nudged me and nodded toward the parking lot. Virgil, with a wary eye on Hermann, was sneaking into a scarred and faded red pickup.

"I wanted a chat with my daughter," Hermann said lightly, but he seemed embarrassed. "I knew she'd be here and saw her car in the car park. She was probably late for her classes." He gazed down the street, his jaw working.

Chica and I exchanged raised eyebrows.

"Yes, we also must hurry." Chica dragged me toward the van, waving at Hermann. "Work, work, work. Adios, señor. See you at the club."

Hermann didn't answer. He just stood there as the Sergeant Pepper Band members ebbed and flowed around him.

We hurried to the van, cranked it up and drove slowly past the house. The poor harried city official on the front porch was still calling out volunteers' names.

"Isabella DeMoya? Isabella DeMoya?" he said into his microphone. Chica ducked down behind the wheel and hit the gas. "You out there, Chica? She's quite a hand with the joint compound, I hear. Har har."

"What did Pilar say?" Chica asked after sitting back up and heading down the street.

I mentally replayed all that I'd just seen and heard. Cripes, I needed to carry a legal pad around with me to list the myriad issues clogging my brain.

"I think that might have been her boyfriend at the Habitat house, and it looks like Hermann doesn't like him too much. I doubt he would like anyone she chose. He's so fanatical about her."

Chica nodded. "He would not like any man around his baby girl."

"Pilar said that she didn't believe Dare could have had anything to do with Randy's death, which I was glad to hear."

The real issue, however, seemed to be what had not been said.

Eighteen

The questions raised by our presence at the Habitat house celebrations faded as I stood in the middle of the ballroom beside the ladder and eyeballed the vast distance from floor to ceiling. One more of these blasted ceiling medallions to complete, along with finishing touches to the panels, and Faux Finish would have fulfilled its contract in this area of the club. Other cosmetic fixes in the corridors and restrooms needed work too, but they were minor. After that, the phalanx of wedding planners who poked their heads in every day to nag Malcolm could "enhance this dreary space," as one of them had declared, for the mayor's daughter's reception.

The last time I'd climbed this ladder was the day Randy died, but I suppressed the memory as I recalled Malcolm's stern exhortations about the timetable. I didn't want to disappoint him or my father, who'd finagled this job for my company, or Chica, who, on principle and pure cussedness, appeared to have left me the final medallion to complete.

The platform was about eleven feet off the ground, and the hand rail at the top was a couple of feet higher. Yeah. Only about fifteen feet, and that's only a little higher than a one-story building. A one-story building? Gah!

A solid wall within arm's length would have been nice, but, what the heck, procrastination wouldn't help the situation.

"If Reyshawn can hang on the rim after a slam dunk, I should be able to do this," I mumbled. Steering my thoughts into more productive channels beat agonizing over Randy's "missing" cell phone – the one now burning a hole in my pocket.

Just as I felt like whimpering, someone touched my shoulder from behind. I jumped as the ballroom slowly came back into focus.

"Don't psych yourself out," whispered Lieutenant Hendricks, shaking his head toward the ladder. "It's not that far up."

The ladder. Oh, yeah. Although my heart fluttered as I covered the pocket holding the phone, I assumed a pissed-off expression toward his belted coat and firmly planted feet.

"Lordy, didn't mean to scare you," he said as unruffled as ever, "what with the ladder doing that already. Now, if this was the ceiling at my place, you about could touch it on your tippy toes."

Chica waved at me behind his back. She cupped her hand to her ear, miming cell phone behavior, and pointed at my pocket and then at Hendricks, indicating I give him the phone. I'd told her about it this morning before leaving for the Habitat house.

I ignored Chica's advice. No way the lieutenant would get this sliver of new millennium technology until I'd chewed the cud on the possible consequences. I'd already kidnapped the laptop and was most likely accruing jail time at an alarming rate. What was one more offense?

"I'm sorry," Hendricks said as my silence lengthened. "Reckon you didn't hear me walk up. Didn't mean to scare you."

He sounded sincere, but charming Southern speech often cloaked true feelings and, being from that geographical area myself, I fancied I could detect the nuances.

Chica clucked and flapped her arms like a biddy hen, choosing not to hide her true feelings, which was what I liked about her – most of the time.

"I'm not chicken," I snapped. "Just careful on ladders is all."

"Sure you are, and can't say as I blame you," Hendricks said. "Hate heights myself. That's how I cottoned onto your state of mind."

Ack, I hoped he couldn't read it.

"Bridget is in trouble again?" Chica smiled at Hendricks like he was a brand new day.

He was momentarily struck dumb.

"Naw," he managed to say.

"Oh God, is it Dare?" I cried.

"No, no, she's good," he said. "No use to fret. I checked this morning."

"It's now or never," I said to no one in particular.

I grasped the cold, metal handrails and mounted a few rungs of the ladder. Up and up. My head swam and my sweaty hands slipped even though, in theory, the shrouded chandelier could be clutched in case of emergency. No point in dwelling on the outcome if the fixture couldn't bear the weight of a tall, well-fed, panic-stricken female acrophobic.

You're an angel on Jacob's Ladder, Bridget. Just do it.

"Giving this fear thingy another go," I blustered.

"Yes!" Chica pumped a victory fist.

Hendricks's trench coat buttons flickered in my peripheral vision.

"You'll do just fine," he said. "Look here, the brake is on. Check out the nice rails. You get this where you bought that orange hammer?"

"I will take you where we bought it." Chica was flirting beyond the call of duty.

"He can find one on his own," I muttered. Might the two of them be able distract me through this trauma against my will?

I climbed to the last rung.

"I say it over and over. It is in your mind only, amiga."

Spoken by someone not hiding crucial murder investigation evidence on her person.

"Shouldn't you tend to those panels?" I said.

"She is the cranky girl today," Chica whispered to Hendricks.

"I heard that," I said.

After a couple of deep breaths, I faked a grin. According to Honey's cornucopia of coping mechanisms, pretending to be happy during a high-altitude crisis could achieve that exalted state. Maybe.

I plucked a jar of glue from one of my pockets.

"You here to see Malcolm Jones, Lieutenant?" Was that my squeaky voice? "We've not seen him this morning, but Long Johnson is around, right, Chica?" I added to induce her guilt for dallying with the Hendricks.

"Not sure." She frowned at my interference.

"His car is in the general manager's space, so he must be around somewhere," Hendricks said over the approaching roar of an industrial vacuum cleaner. "I'll just mosey around, see what's what." He strolled from the room.

Through the panes of the French doors, the hefty cleaning woman languidly appeared, zig-zagging the vacuum cleaner toward the staff offices.

"Vaya con Dios, amiga, but you are bitchy today," Chica yelled over the noise before flouncing back to work.

"Who loves ya, baby?" I blew her a kiss.

I stepped onto the platform.

"Piece of cake," I said.

With a surge of confidence, I surveyed the room from on high. Was Honey right about fooling one's self for the better? Using the jar as a microphone, I tried to remember the words. "Once I was afraid, I was terrified…."

"What's the next line in 'I Will Survive,' Chica?"

"Ewww. I don't like that song, and your words are wrong."

The vacuum din ceased. Quiet washed over the clubhouse as I pondered on the lyrics of the big disco hit.

Then a woman shrieked over and over and over.

"Jesus Maria!" Chica cried, echoing my sentiment exactly.

I gasped and flung the glue jar in a lovely arc, reminiscent of Michael Jordan's shot to win the 1982 NCAA finals against Georgetown, and skidded backward over the rungs, flailing at the handrails. I landed bum down on the floor, gulping for air like a dying goldfish.

The cleaning woman, languid no more, burst through the French doors with her bosom flopping and arms waving, her screams reduced to gargling noises as she pounded through the ballroom.

At some fuzzy point in the proceedings, Chica began to drag me toward the front doors.

"You hurt?"

"I will be if you break my arm." I stood and planted my feet. "Stop."

"You crazy? This place is mala suerte. Bad luck. Full of Sagittarians, I am thinking."

"Hendricks," I said starting in the direction he'd taken just minutes earlier.

"OK, OK," Chica said. "I will go, too. Why are you scared of ladders and not screaming women, eh?"

"Just braver on the ground, I guess. What're you afraid of? You've been a soldier."

"It is why I am scared, idiota. Duh."

We trotted into the corridor. Hermann stood outside Malcolm's open office door with his hands behind his back, a cleaning trolley parked nearby. Something about him seemed different, but I couldn't put my finger on it.

An outer door banged open, and Long rushed in, scattering the skeleton crew of kitchen help and golf shop employees who'd gathered to investigate the commotion.

Chica and I peered around Hermann into the office.

Hendricks knelt on the floor beside Malcolm's desk.

"Yeah, we're gonna need the medical examiner," he said on his cell phone.

He snapped the phone shut and stood to reveal Malcolm lying on the floor beside his desk. He lay facing the door on his left side, his right arm flung over his head as if stretching. Papers littered the floor around him.

Long pushed past me.

"Y'all back off now." Hendricks waved at us. "And for the Lord's sweet sake, don't touch anything."

"Jesus Maria," Chica repeated softly to herself. She took a step back. "Él esta muerto. He is dead."

"You reckon it was a heart attack?" I squinted to avoid seeing the scene too clearly.

"Shot, by the looks of it," Hermann said, carefully placing his glasses on his nose and squatting next to Long to stare at Malcolm. "Small caliber. No exit wound."

I reeled as a slow-motion video of Malcolm tracking a speeding bullet played in my head.

"A gun?" Chica whispered.

"Well, it wasn't a slingshot," I said under my breath.

She gripped my elbow.

Hendricks loomed up with arms outspread, driving everyone back even more.

"Round up everyone on the premises, inside and out," Hendricks said to Long. "Put them in one of the fancy rooms the other side of the building. Now."

"Right away," Long said.

"Y'all go on," Long said to the employees gaping nearby. "Straight to the Twelve Oaks Room."

"An officer will take statements directly," Hendricks said. "Just be patient."

One woman in a white apron and hairnet opened her mouth to protest.

"Go on now," said Long. "Never mind food prep. Don't know if we'll ever reopen at this rate."

"This couldn't have happened this morning," Long said to Hendricks as the staff disappeared. "At least, not after I got here at six."

"How d'you know that?" Hendricks said.

Chica squeezed my arm, clinging like kudzu on a tree.

"Ouch," I said, which only tightened her grasp.

"Hermann arrived about thirty minutes after I did," Long added. "We would've heard something."

Hendricks flipped his notebook open to a clean page. He clicked his ballpoint pen and waited.

"Mr. Salazar?" he said.

"Nothing rum happened that I can recall," Hermann said.

"Rum?" said Hendricks.

"Means odd," Long explained. "It's his Brit-speak.

"Uh huh. What about the security guard?"

"We've got an issue there, unfortunately," Long said. "The man on duty right now started at seven this morning. He won't be of any help. And the guy last night? Well …."

"I hope you ain't saying he's the same guard was on the premises the night Mr. La Russo died." Hendricks hesitated as he looked at me. "The one who claims he sort of fell asleep in the casual bar that night because he was coming down with a bug?"

"Same guy," Long replied. "Same bug as on that night,

too, only we just found out it's the Johnny Walker Red disease. Hermann found him passed out in the men's card room hugging a couple empty bottles."

"The tosser should've been made redundant long ago," Hermann added.

"This man I know," Chica cried, releasing her savage hold on my arm. "He was very angry at A.A. last week. He was on Step Two, and then he is pfft. Adiós."

Hendricks scratched in his notebook; Long turned calf eyes on Chica and Hermann was nonplussed.

"Good to know, ma'am. We'll have a chat with him no matter if he's on or off the wagon," Hendricks said, stabbing the page with his pen. "Meanwhile, we'll seal off the club, Mr. Johnson, at least until the techs finish their job. No one enters this part of the building. Then, I'd like you to stay with the employees in the … uh … Twelve Oaks Room? Folks shouldn't discuss the case, and we'll be swabbing for G.S.R."

"Gunshot residue?" said Long, glowing with his newly acquired responsibilities despite the tragedy.

"Been watching C.S.I?"

"I like the Miami one," Long said.

"Makes no never mind to me what you watch," Hendricks replied, "but let me warn you that those guys find the killer in between commercials and wrap it up nice and tidy in about forty minutes. They have sexy lighting. The female police officers wear those high heels when investigating the crime scene. That's Hollywood. This is Chapel Hill."

That was the longest speech I'd heard Hendricks make, and Long lapped up every word. Obviously, he wasn't the only one watching C.S.I.

"But once we get started, interviewing the employees shouldn't take too much time. Just a formality, really. Then they can go home. Someone will see to their belongings and escort them to their cars."

"Check inside and out, Hermann," Long said. "Round up anyone working on the driving range or tennis courts and send them to Twelve Oaks. We're lucky we hadn't reopened yet. There aren't many people here today."

"I'd like to take your statements after I've dealt with the M.E.," Hendricks said to Long and Hermann. "Remember, no one touches anything. Anything."

"We're at your disposal," Long said. "Next door to Twelve Oaks is the Savannah Room. I'll be in one of those two places as soon as everyone is accounted for. By the way, can I use my office?"

"Not now," Hendricks said. "Let you know when."

Everyone looked solemn as the distant whine of sirens grew louder.

"I'll show them where you are," Long said and hurried off to the club entrance while Hermann headed in the opposite direction.

I grabbed Hendricks's coat sleeve. "Can I talk to you and your trench coat about how all this proves Dare's innocence?"

"You should be in that room with the others," Hendricks said, a shade distant to my notion.

"Come on, Chica," I replied in kind. "Now, don't you dare touch anything on the way or you'll get your fingers smacked."

We rounded the corner, but I dragged Chica back into the ballroom from another door. My middle name might be Eve, but lately it was fast becoming Eavesdrop.

We hugged the wall and crept up to the first set of French doors.

"¿Qué?" she asked.

"Shhhhh."

If Malcolm's murder was connected to Randy's, which seemed likely, my actions were all for a cause named Dare.

"Let's check this out. They'll take forever in that stupid interrogation room anyway," I breathed in her ear.

I squatted and peeped around the door jamb. Hendricks stood gazing down the corridor with his arms crossed. I could just make out Hermann's back through the legs of an ornate side table.

"Lieutenant," Hermann called without turning around, "might I have a quick word?"

Then he pivoted on his heel like a soldier.

Like a soldier. That was it. That's what was different about him today. If he'd been in full military regalia, his bearing couldn't have been more parade ground. Was this the self-effacing maintenance engineer, the humble, doting father?

"There was a bit of a dust-up last night," Hermann said. As he approached Hendricks, he dropped his shoulders and chin and morphed back into the graying janitor with a world of responsibilities.

"So I've heard," the lieutenant said. "Are firearms kept on the premises, by the way? Do any of the employees own a gun?"

"Suss out the security guards, lieutenant, because I haven't the foggiest," Hermann said.

"Did Mr. Jones serve in the military? Did you?"

Hermann shrugged.

Hendricks snagged a toothpick from his pocket and stuck it in his mouth.

Hopefully, it was clean.

"Not privy to his history," Hermann said. "Which, by the by, shouldn't your lot be looking under rocks to find Virgil Spoon instead of messing about with innocent folk?"

"We're onto him. As far as innocent goes, who's to say at this point?" Hendricks said. "I know what your accent reminds me of now. Some guy on that crazy public TV show my ex-wife used to make me watch. *Keeping Up Appearances* or something like that."

"Daft bunch of cows, the sisters on that show."

"Yes, well?" Hendricks locked his knees, waited for Hermann to speak.

"I was in the army," Hermann finally said, "donkey's years ago."

"You do seem to know your gunshot wounds."

"Right. That's why I don't own a gun. Keeping my girl safe, touch wood," he said, tapping his head. "I didn't fancy one in the house while my Pilar was growing up. I'm off now. See you in a bit."

Hendricks watched him walk out the door.

Without turning toward us, he said over his shoulder, "Y'all gals go get swabbed and give your statements."

Chica and I tiptoed from the ballroom and sneaked into a small powder room off the main entrance.

"How'd he know we were there?" I said, sliding down the wall and sitting on the floor. "He must have eyes in the back of his head."

"Hear me, amiga, por favor." Chica whispered. "The gun is still missing."

"I know."

I drew my knees to my chest and locked my arms around them.

"Hermann says Malcolm is shot. Not good."

"Doesn't mean it was your gun."

"It is your gun now, amiga."

"Surely, 'our' gun wasn't used. Holy Mary Mother of God. It's got be somewhere. It didn't just walk off."

"Gone." She waved in the air. "Hasta la vista, baby."

"You reckon somebody stole it? I'll shoot the bastard myself if he did. Or she. Mother will have a stroke."

"I hope it's only a…um…"

"Coincidence?" I stared at my hands and snorted. "Look at the good news. Not much chance of gunshot residue when we can't even find the blasted gun."

"Pobrecito. Poor Malcolm."

"First Randy. Now Malcolm. Who could've done all this?"

In the distance, we could hear someone pounding on the front door and screaming, so we ran back into the ballroom.

"Y'all, let me in," a woman's familiar voice screamed as a club employee wrenched open the front door and backed away from Marla Ann.

"Git your hands off me!" she screeched at the EMS guy and uniformed cop who were trying to grab ahold of her from behind.

Marla Ann booked it up the steps to the ballroom with them in tow.

Instinct born of watching Tar Heel basketball since infancy drove me after her as if she were a Duke guard on a fast break. Chica, compact and athletic, whipped ahead of both of us. I glanced over my shoulder at the medic and cop. Unfamiliar with the full-court press, they were way behind us.

"Malcolm?" Marla Ann squalled on a high C note, her face a blur of tears and mascara. "Y'all're lyin'. Malcolm, where are you?"

Her black terrycloth jogging suit fit like a second skin, which probably explained why no one had managed to get a grip on the situation. The partially unzipped jacket revealed her main handicap, the hello-there hooters bouncing so violently it was a wonder her forward progress wasn't thwarted.

But Chica saved the day by blocking out and grabbing a handful of Marla Ann's rotating haunch, whereupon all five of us slid into a heap and crashed into the French doors.

***

After handing Marla Ann over to Hendricks, passing the G.S.R. swabbing with flying colors and gabbling our statements, Chica and I finally escaped into the unseasonably warm day and ran smack into Hall Hooper as he ducked under the crime scene tape near the front entrance.

Chica rolled her eyes.

"It is you know who," she said.

"All's not quiet on the country club front, I hear," Hooper said.

"You just shut up." I poked a forefinger in his face. "Show some respect. Someone is dead in there."

He lit up like a Christmas tree. I could tell he was itching to grab a pen, a tape recorder or both.

"But of course, this is just another story for you," I said.

"Don't get your panties in a bunch." He backed up. "Just doing my job."

"You can't go in there." I spread my arms wide as I channeled former UNC forward Sam Perkins' seven-foot-six-inch wingspan.

"Says who?"

Good question.

The parking lot revealed only a couple of panda cars and the crime scene investigation van. Down at the street, an officer moved one of the barricades so an employee could leave. Officers stood blocking the other three entrances to the parking area.

Before I could answer, the door pushed me forward and Hendricks emerged still coat-clad but slack-shouldered, a sure sign of spending time with Marla Ann.

"That woman needs tending to," Hendricks said with a backward nod. "A real train wreck." He spotted Hooper. "Well, look what the cat drug in."

"Come on, cut me some slack here."

"We'll be releasing an official statement later today," Hendricks said.

"And unofficially?"

Hendricks straightened his shoulders and pointed at Hooper.

"Come by the station later."

Then he pointed at me.

"You go deal with that mixed up woman in there. But don't leave the club until I speak with you one more time. In fact, I'll meet you at the first tee when you're done with Miss Furr."

"And me too?" asked Chica, flirting as usual.

"Much as I'd like you to stay," he responded with a glint in his eye, "I only want a couple more words with Miz O'Brien, so you can go now."

***

Marla Ann peeked at me above the rim of her wine glass as I stormed into the club's "library," so called this because of the glass-fronted bookcases filled with antique leather-bound classics. However, I'm sure the polished mahogany bar was the main attraction. The only reading I'd ever seen here involved members scanning the bar menu. This was a space for glass-clinking and hard drinking. Elegantly, of course.

As I clumped toward Marla Ann, my mother's face rose in my mind's eye, aghast at what she would term my trades-man's gait in the midst of the muted lighting and dark, rich hunt colors. I shook my head to dispel the image and halted beside an end table with two goblets of red wine dregs. In the adjoining leather chair, Marla Ann huddled, feet drawn up under her like a frightened baby bird fallen from its nest. A gas fire crackled below a nearby massive oak mantel, keeping the chill in the high-ceilinged room at bay.

"Thanks for comin' back," she said so defiantly that

I was somewhat ashamed of my cold demeanor. She had swollen eyes and a shiny red nose from recent weeping.

Dabbing at her face with a gigantic ball of tissues, she said, "Seems like I'm always cryin' whenever you show up."

I nodded at the wine glasses. "A bit early for that?"

"I'm fixin' to tell you somethin' if you'd just stop judgin' me."

I relented and sat in the leather chair facing hers and waited.

"We used to be friends," she said, kind of pitifully.

"Oh Lord, Marla Ann, we still are."

"Promise not to tell anyone what I'm about to tell you."

"OK. I promise."

She flung her tissue ball to the floor and pulled a fresh one from the box on the table.

"No, I mean like we used to do when we were in school."

For heaven's sake, I really didn't have time for this.

She assumed her bulldog expression, also something I recalled from our college years.

"Don't tell me you're the murderer," I exclaimed. I uncrossed my legs and sat up straight, preparing for a quick getaway.

"I ain't tellin' you nothin' that I ain't told the lieutenant. Did I just sprout horns or somethin'?"

"Okay, okay. I swear on Dean Smith's life that I won't tell."

"Roy Williams is the head coach now," she said.

It was encouraging to know that even someone of Marla Ann's self-absorbed and limited capacity knew something of current events.

"Okay, I swear on Roy's ability to coach that I won't tell anyone. There. Satisfied? Can we move on?"

"Me and Malcolm were together when Randy was murdered." She drained yet a third wine glass and waved at the bar for another.

I gawped at her in the time it took the waitress to deliver another refill and set it on the table.

"I could use one of those, too," I said to the waitress.

I leapt from my chair and began pacing.

"Don't do that," Marla Ann said. "It gets on my last nerve."

I stopped in front of her.

"You told me you loved Randy. You cried like a stuck pig the other day. What possessed you to lie like that?"

Marla Ann wobbled to her feet and got right up in my face.

"You're such a prude, Bridget O'Brien. Maybe you're not gettin' any, I don't know. Of course I wanted Randy. Not really sure about the love thing. Whatever. The bastard didn't want me no more. There. I just admitted it. You happy now?"

I didn't dare move during that tirade, but when she stopped speaking I took a couple of steps back.

"Oh, sorry. I didn't realize that…"

"You never do," she said, flopping back into her chair. "That's exactly it. You just go off half-cocked and know-it-all."

"I beg your pardon?"

"Soundin' so snooty when you think you're right." She honked into her tissue and gave me a baleful stare so strong that I felt compelled to sit down, too.

"You know, you should check out that old red-headed Muffin woman. She and Randy were havin' a fling, I think."

"How would you know?" I asked, deciding not to reveal that I knew that already.

"I saw them out drinkin' one night. I happened to know that her husband was on a business trip and then, hot dog, I walked into the Blue Bayou Club in Hillsborough. They looked quite cozy at the bar."

"Could be," I said, "but it's not really proof, is it?" Like smelling the Chanel No. 5 she'd rubbed all over Randy's sheets at his mother's house or seeing the engraved St. Christopher's Medal she'd given him.

"It's proof enough for me. But if you don't believe that, what about that cute little Pilar Salazar waitressin' around here? I've seen them chattin' quite a bit out in the parkin' lot."

"Now you're really sounding obsessed," I said. "She's just a kid and a good one at that. Besides, she has a boyfriend. I saw him the other day at Habitat house. You were there; didn't you see him?"

"He could've just been a friend for all you know. Even if he was a boyfriend that sure wouldn't stop our randy Randy, would it?"

Good point.

"Randy called you at work about lunch time on the day he died."

"I don't know anythin' about that. My half-assed secretary probably didn't give me the message."

I decided not to tell her that I stole that message.

"He was probably callin' about a condo in Southern Village. At least he was going to give me that commission even if we were through on the datin' level."

"Enough of this," I said, glad to now believe that she probably didn't do away with Randy. After all, she did look kind of sad about him, although that pout could have been about the lost commission.

"So, if you're right, you and Malcolm appear to be off the hook for Randy's murder," I said. "If that's the case, why is Malcolm dead now?"

Marla Ann shook her head.

"Malcolm is, I mean was, somethin'. I almost forgot he even went to Duke when we were together."

"I guess the lieutenant asked where you were last night when Malcolm was... Well, when Malcolm was killed."

"Course he did. But thank the Lord I've got a cast-iron alibi for most of the night."

"You do?"

"If it's any of your beeswax, I was shoppin'."

"A bit late for that, wasn't it?"

"Yeah, couldn't sleep. I called in to QVC and got on the air. Chatted with some woman about Joan Rivers' jewelry. Bought a necklace of hers. Ain't that somethin'? I figure that cute detective can check phone records or call the TV station or whatever they do, y'know?"

"Sure," I said, knowing her shopping addiction well. "How does shopping all night help? Doesn't it keep you awake?"

"Not me, honey. I drift off on my pillow knowin' that millions of gals like me all over the world are shoppin'. It's so soothin'. You should try it."

Right.

So, if not Marla Ann, then who?

What about Mr. Ruffin or Muffin for some of these shenanigans? Could he really be jealous enough? Could Muffin be as mad as a woman scorned? I shook my head at the thought of sweet Pilar doing anything bad.

I finally walked out of the "library" in a daze, worried for the first time that Marla Ann was smarter than I was, and had been all along.

Nineteen

I walked down the hall, through the outside door that led past the baby pool and around the corner of the golf shop. The cold air was invigorating, the blue sky dotted with puffy clouds. Lieutenant Hendricks was standing near the first tee box, gazing from the ladies' tees to the flag fluttering on the green, one-hundred-plus yards away.

"I thought we could commune better in the great outdoors. I hate the cold, but today isn't too bad," Hendricks said as I walked up beside him. "I've called Davey, and he should be here shortly."

"I can't tell if I'm a suspect or not," I said, deciding not to wait for Davey, "but if I am, I can tell you right now that I didn't have time to come over here to kill Malcolm last night after you left the house. I went straight to bed where I tossed and turned 'til I was fit to be tied."

"Everyone is a suspect at this point, but there's no need to fret. I need eyewitness accounts of the argument last night, and to make sure I know where everyone was afterward."

"I gave that information inside to the officer in the Twelve Oaks room."

"There's a murderer out there somewhere, and we have stop him, or her," he said, ignoring my comment. But this gave me the opening I needed.

"You see," I said. "You think the murders are connected, don't you? Therefore, it could not have been Dare, just like I said the other night. She's locked up now because you wouldn't believe me then."

"Hey, you two," called Davey, approaching from the parking lot. "Sorry I'm late. Been working on an ugly divorce today." He looked from me to Hendricks and back to me, gauging the tension.

"No sweat," Hendricks said. "This isn't official. Just trying to figure things out. See, these two murders are so different. They could very well have been committed by two people."

My heart sank. So, Dare was still a suspect in his eyes.

"Do you own a gun, Miz O'Brien?"

My heart felt like it stopped for a moment. Despite lying my way through the past few days, it wasn't my usual modus operandi. At least not yet.

"I don't have one, uh, no, I don't actually have one." I licked dry lips and didn't look up at Davey, who had been to the shooting range with me and Chica once. I could feel rather than see him straighten up beside me. Then he squatted to examine the one of the ladies' tees. His back spoke volumes.

"What about Miz Chica?"

"She used to have one. Not sure where it is now, though," I said. Taking a deep breath, I said, "Why are you asking about that, anyway?"

"Never mind. I can ask her myself. Just wondering is all. You have to be careful with those things. They could fall into the wrong hands."

"You wanted my take on last night, didn't you? Straight from the horse's mouth?"

He laughed. "I wouldn't exactly describe it like that, but yes. I reckon I've got a pretty good handle on things, but I still want to hear what you think, even if you've already given a statement."

I told him and Davey about Pit coming in just as I was getting dizzy in the ballroom and how that's when we heard the argument in the corridor and went to check it out. I told him about Hooper coming, Virgil threatening and Hermann leaving.

No one interrupted my story. We all stood silently for a few minutes until out of nowhere Hendricks began to hum the chorus of the Carolina fight song. When he came to the end, he began again, and I joined in with the lyrics, singing softly. In this queer moment of camaraderie, Davey picked up on the next go-round in a whisper.

"I'm a Tar Heel born and a Tar Heel bred,
And when I die, I'll be a Tar Heel dead.
So I say rah, rah, Carolina – lina
Rah, rah, Carolina – lina
Rah, rah, Carolina – lina
Go to hell Duke!"

We were all a little breathless afterward, and again no one spoke for a bit. I thought about the Duke game in a couple of days. It's an occupational hazard when you are a dyed-in-the-light-blue-wool-fan. But, try as I might, I couldn't maintain that thought with so many other sad and serious matters to consider. It didn't feel like a time to worry about winning a basketball game, much as I would have loved that to be my only worry. Still, it felt good to sing. As if there was a time when all this would be over.

I couldn't lie about the gun anymore.

"We had a gun," I said up at the sky.

"Did you now?" Hendricks said. He stuck his hands in his coat pockets and gently toed the holly bushes edging the tee boxes.

"It was Chica's," I said. "Her grandmother gave it to her

a long time ago when she developed arthritis. Chica gave it to me because she didn't want anything to do with guns after her military experience."

"So, where has it been since she gave it to you?" Hendricks asked.

"Well, usually I keep it in my underwear drawer," I said, feeling my face flush. "But she got it out just lately and put it in the van in a supply box because we often work at night and thought it might be protection. That was before Randy died."

"Do you have a permit to carry concealed?"

"I didn't know you needed one for a long time. And we didn't usually carry it around anyway. I guess we should've gotten one, huh?"

Davey shook his head. Hendricks rolled his eyes and turned to Davey.

"Did you know about this gun?"

"I knew they had one a few months ago, but I didn't know it figured into anything. I'm still hoping it doesn't. Randy wasn't killed with one, so I haven't really thought about guns until now. I hope it's not this gun, Bridget."

Well, yeah.

"You said you didn't have a gun a couple minutes ago," said Hendricks, accusation ripe in his voice.

"I didn't lie. Exactly. Because I don't have it." I ploughed on, figuring I was in deep excrement anyway, wringing my hands and pacing. "I don't have it, because we can't find it. I guess I tried to lie while telling you the truth. Sorry about that. I'm not myself lately. The last time I saw the stupid thing was when we were organizing supplies to work here at the club. That would be a couple of weeks ago. Chica said she put it in the supply box along with some doggie toys. Then it just disappeared. Remember when you saw us at Sunrise Biscuit? We were looking for it in the van. Especially after Randy got killed, we decided the gun should be close to hand."

"Y'all did look like deer in the headlights when I showed up. Like you'd been caught with your fingers in the candy jar."

I hated feeling like a bad child at my age.

"So, the gun could have made its way into the clubhouse, now, couldn't it?" Hendricks said sounding like Honey during one of our shrink sessions, the psychiatrist helping me to figure things out for myself.

"We didn't think so at first. We thought it was in the van with the doggie toys, but turned out that it wasn't in that box. But yes, we now realize it could've been in the ballroom area while we'd been working."

A long silence. Hendricks had his eyes closed.

Meanwhile," he finally said.

"Meanwhile?" I answered.

"What kind of gun is it?"

"A .38 special," I said.

Davey looked glum.

"Do you think it was the gun used on Malcolm?" I asked faintly.

Hendricks shook his head.

"I'll need your extra ammunition. You have some, don't you? We can compare the bullets with the one that killed Malcolm. I'll send Officer Jones to your house as soon as possible. She'll retrieve the ammo from where you're storing it. Let her do it. Neither of you should touch it."

Great. The box of ammunition was in my thong drawer. Officer Jones should get a kick out of that.

"When can we get back in the clubhouse to finish our work? We're not done, and there's that wedding reception on Sunday."

"Malcolm Jones's office and the adjoining area will be

sealed but y'all can probably get into the rest of the club sometime tomorrow afternoon. I'll let Mr. Johnson know, and he'll contact you."

Hendricks turned and plodded back toward the clubhouse. He turned before grabbing the golf shop doorknob.

"Y'all will let me know the minute you find the gun." It wasn't a question. "If you do, that is."

Hendricks dropped his chin into his coat collar and disappeared inside.

"Lost the gun?" Davey ranted afterward as we walked to the parking lot. "How do you lose a gun? How irresponsible is that? I was wrong. This isn't an episode of *I Love Lucy*. More like a bizarre combination of *Columbo, Murder, She Wrote*, and *The Andy Griffith Show*."

"Don't leave anything out," I cried, invoking the serial-killer blood-spatter expert who murdered only guilty people. "What about *Dexter*?"

"I wish it were him this time," Davey said as he bleeped his car open with the key fob, walked around to the passenger side and opened the door. "Come on, I'll give you a ride home."

"Let's hope this isn't a serial killer," I said as he slammed the car door in my face.

Twenty

After Davey dropped me off, I left Chica and the dogs in the kitchen watching an episode of *Dog Whisperer* and went straight to bed, where I proceeded to toss and turn. Who was I fooling? I couldn't sleep.

A memory finally had broken through the dense clouds in my brain earlier in the day and was dying to be examined. In the charged atmosphere of "burglarizing" Grace's house with Chica, I'd been unable to recall something Randy once told me about a great hiding place where he'd hidden stuff from his mother when he was a boy. What was it he'd said? For heaven's sake, wasn't I too young to be forgetful? I thought of Honey's meditation instructions and tried to relax my neck and shoulders and let the recollection sharpen.

It was the day after we got married in August 1996. We'd driven down to Wrightsville Beach for a weekend honeymoon of sorts. Grace's friends had loaned us their house while my parents kept Dare. It seemed so right. A rustic beachfront cottage, the weathered shingles typical of a stilted dwelling. The living area was upstairs with a deck that faced the ocean. The garage and parking were on ground level.

Two days before the wedding, I'd mentioned bringing Dare along on the honeymoon to celebrate us finally being a family, but Randy had balked. A bad sign. I'd nagged him about it to no avail. Still, I married him. However, on the drive down to the beach, I'd fussed with him again about Dare. After we arrived at the beach house, I was still so angry that I didn't sleep with him that first night – of the honeymoon, for heaven's sake – and ended up in a lounge chair on the deck with a pillow, blanket and my journal. There was a slight breeze, a full moon and the sound of the tides going in and out. I relaxed and wrote in my journal.

My mother would have been aghast at the language swirling in my head. Well, one word, actually. F___! I didn't spell it out in my journal because I was afraid Mother might find it and for some reason I can't explain, I just would never be able to do or say some things in front of my mother, no matter how old I got.

In the journal, I'd made my language "Sarah O'Brien-friendly" and still used the bad word and all of its variations as noun, verb, adjective – but especially the verb. F___ Randy, I'd written. Still, I'd wanted this marriage to succeed. Bad enough that I'd left Marcus and hurt him. Ah, guilt. But I didn't love Marcus, so it had seemed the right thing to do.

I made a decision that night. Because Marcus still believed himself to be Dare's real father, I intended to keep it that way. I didn't trust Randy to … what? To want to stay married? To want to be Dare's father? To not hurt us both?

Some honeymoon night. Although I woke up on the deck the next morning stiff and out of sorts, my brain was calmer. While it looked a little overcast at the beach, the forecast called for the day to be breezy hot with a clear sky. I decided I could probably make things right with Randy and tucked the journal in my bag. Maybe there'd be another entry later to fix the last one and explain away my fears.

At peace with myself, I reached up to caress the diamond cross necklace that Daddy had bought when we were in Rome all those years ago. It was gone. I'd preserved it all these years by wearing it only on special occasions, like my wedding to Randy, and now I'd lost it after the vows. Here was the second bad happenstance of this new marriage.

After scouring the deck and finding only the pen I'd dropped, I gazed down at the sand through the spaces in the deck boards. I ran downstairs and began digging. Randy strolled outside and called for me.

Crying with frustration, sandy and sweaty, I looked up through the slats and told him what I was doing.

"That is the kind of thing you should keep safe," he said by way of scolding. He seemed remarkably nonplussed about my sleeping outside.

"Thanks for the advice," I sniffed. "I've only kept it safe for the past dozen years until I married you." I shuddered to think that such an incident had not boded well for our marriage, but I kept my mouth shut.

Randy wandered downstairs. He shifted sand half-heartedly with his toe in one corner where the necklace could only have fallen to if it had wings.

"Ever tell you about a great hiding place that no burglar, or parent for that matter, would find at my mom's house?" he said.

"No." I didn't really care and didn't appreciate his weak effort to cheer me up.

"You know that little round window with the slats in the attic? The one facing the street?"

I paused in my digging and looked about for a new patch of sand to attack.

"That window faces west, and in the afternoon when the sun comes through, the rays kinda point to the hiding place."

I laughed in spite of my stress level.

"Course you have to sit on top of my red rocking horse in the corner."

"Yeah right, that broken down thing? What if the rocking horse gets moved? And a hiding place for what? *Playboy* magazines and half-smoked joints?"

He frowned, and I realized he was serious.

We never did find that necklace.

***

In Chica's house twelve years later, I knew my mother would have said, "I told you so."

I'm not exactly sure what she would have been referring to, but she would have said it.

"That's it," I said in the darkness. I threw my legs over the side of the bed. "Screw the necklace and forget about sleep, Bridget."

Might as well go back to Grace's house now, I reasoned. A home invasion was easier in the dark, as I well knew, and as my flighty ex-mother-in-law had disappeared into the wilds of NASCAR and the Florida undergrowth, the house was still empty. Maybe I could come up with something important on this case without constant interruptions from well-meaning friends, loved ones and the police. I could find that hiding place without the sun setting in the West, although what would be there was anybody's guess.

I snagged Randy's appointment book, too. I could put it back in his suitcase as if it had always been there. That reminded me. I'd get Chica to do something with the laptop. Stealing and lying for a good cause was complicated as hell sometimes.

If loud snoring was an indication, then Chica was sleeping like the dead. So, I crept down the stairs, grabbed the flashlight from the kitchen, snagged the van keys and drove over to Randy's house.

Grace had never been one to maintain a lawn. She believed in natural areas with raggedy shrubbery, which meant a lot of dry sticks all over the place. Trying to avoid snapping them in the black night was challenging, but eventually I found the back steps and fumbled for the old rusty key. The hook was empty. I got on my hands and knees and shone the flashlight under the steps, patting the ground and feeling along the wooden steps thinking it might have fallen in a crack. Considering that Chica and I had been fleeing for our lives the last time we were here, I could've missed the hook.

That's when the back porch light bloomed, and the door creaked opened. A pair of crone-like feet with big bunions shuffled up at eye level. I shone the light on the toes. The thick nails had a base coat of a light cobalt turquoise – if I remembered my Winsor & Newton colors correctly – topped with little palm trees with trunks in cadmium lemon and fronds in sap green.

I gazed upward.

"Land sakes, Bridget," exclaimed Grace in her thin flowered nightgown and long gray braid. "That you down there? I'd recognize that yellow hair anyplace."

"Thank God you're home," I squeaked. Granted, it was dark, but how had I missed her RV in the front yard?

"This what yer looking' for?" she said, holding up the key. "I brought it in when old Dudley told me he thought he saw someone rootin' around in the house t'other night. I figured the only soul who could do that was you, besides my boy … my poor handsome boy."

Blinded by tears, she groped for my hand, pulled me up and hugged me so hard I couldn't breathe. Especially when I sucked in a lungful of embedded cigarette smoke from her hair.

"Oh, Grace." I patted her back and began crying too. "When did you get home? I didn't see the RV. The police tried to find you. I told them about Claire Grace but didn't remember where she lived. That race in Daytona has been over forever. Where've you been?"

"I didn't even see Claire Grace this trip," she said. "Let's go inside." She looked around in the dark before pulling me into the kitchen.

"Parked the RV down the street at a neighbor's. Didn't want folks knowing my business and that I was home," she said a few minutes later in the living room, gazing at the mantelpiece with its array of photographs. "I was fixin' to come back on the day I heard about my Randy. I'd called Dudley about some mail, and he told me. After that I just drove and drove. Not on the interstate, mind you. But on the old highways. Florida 301 up in Volusia County. We always drove around there when Randy was a boy." Her eyes darkened with memory, and I didn't want to break the spell.

We sat side by side on the sagging green sofa before the fireplace. The photos on the mantel were a shrine to Randy at various ages from babyhood to toothless first grade to a lanky basketball forward for Chapel Hill High School. The last photo in the progression was taken in front of her Christmas tree, a family pose with three-year-old Dare straddling my hip and Randy's arm around my shoulders.

When Chica and I had "entered" the house the night of Randy's death, it had been too dark and we'd been too busy being illegal to see much of the living room. I'd never seen this photo display before.

"You loved him then, didn't you, honey?" Grace asked holding my hand.

"Yes."

"He was a piece of work, no doubt about that."

She rose, chuckling as she chose the baby picture of Randy and dusted it with her nightgown. "A real piece of work. But loving."

"Yes."

Grace had been tickled pink with Dare in those days of my marriage to her son. She'd not been fooled with the fiction that the child belonged to Marcus. Dare's big brown eyes, I guess. The first time she'd seen the baby, I could tell she knew, but she never said a word. I still appreciated her going along with the fiction that Marcus was Dare's father. She realized, as I did, that it was all about Dare and her well-being.

"Who do you think …?" Her question trailed off. "I guess I should call that policeman in the morning." She put the picture back on the mantel, reached over me to the end table and grabbed her cigarette case. "Sorry, Bridget, but I have to have one," she said and lit up.

"Dare didn't do it, Grace."

"Course she didn't. Didn't believe it for a second when I heard."

Paralyzed with grief and the total inability to talk about the situation, I finally stood and told her I was exhausted and had to go.

"Why did you come over at this time of night?"

I remembered the appointment book.

"I found this when I was here before," I said, handing her the book, "and I wanted to put it back in his suitcase. But now that you're here, I want to ask you a couple of things about it."

"Ask away."

"Somewhere he mentioned 'decide about sb's.' Do you have any idea what that means?"

"Not off the top of my head. But then again, I'm old as the hills, and my memory ain't worth a toot. Let me think about it. I'll let you know if anything occurs to me."

"That's fine. He also mentioned D.D. for the week of February twenty-sixth. Would that be the Dean Dome? Did he have tickets to a basketball game?"

"I don't think so. He would've said. Of course, he could've gotten them after I left town and just didn't tell me. Not like he told his little ol' mama anything much these days, you know. Let me think about that one too. Oh wait. D.D."

Tears filled her eyes.

"Grace? Are you OK?"

"He didn't want anyone to know, honey. At least not yet."

"What?"

"I think that stood for Dr. Davis. An appointment at Duke Hospital this week. He was being treated for liver cancer." She crushed the cigarette she'd been smoking in an overflowing ashtray. Her lips trembled, and I knelt before her and took hold of her hands. We cried together, my tears ending in sniffles and hers in smoker's cough.

When I left the house, I drove home in shock, for Randy and for Dare. The cancer explained a lot of things. Why Randy moved back. Why he wanted to connect with his daughter. Why he wanted to find meaning in his life.

I'd be lucky if I ever slept again. How would I explain all of this to Dare?

When I pulled into the driveway, I remembered I'd forgotten to look for Randy's hiding place in the attic. Still and all, as dark as it was, it was probably a good idea to do it later in the day, at sunset, as Randy had told me about all those years ago.

Twenty-One

In my morning dream, someone stroked my hair like my mother used to do when I was a child sick in bed. I lay in that half-awake state, resisting the urge to open my eyes as I could tell by the birdsong that it was still early. Funny, a whiff of Joy by Jean Patou, Mother's perfume, drifted tantalizingly above my nose. Mother had worn Joy, barely dabbing it on pulse points before her vanity mirror. I associated it with maternal caresses, which lately had been absent from my life.

I mused on how nice it was to wake up like this. I opened my eyes and remembered meeting Grace the night before and the niceness was washed away by sadness, anxiety and confusion about how to get Dare home. I stretched, hoping to put off my angst even for a few seconds. Then I remembered Randy. That's when I saw my mother gazing at me. I froze in mid-stretch. My limbs locked and started to cramp.

"Jesus, what the hell?"

"What a way to greet your mother."

She was her calm, aloof self, which, when I thought about it, was downright creepy considering how I'd seen her in the past few days. Still, I was reassured somewhat to see her dressed in tasteful wool slacks and matching cardigan. Groomed, with every hair in place.

I sat up and rubbed my stiff calves.

"Is something wrong? Is it Dare? Is Daddy dead?"

I was working myself into a real lather. After last night's news, I just knew things could not be good, but I couldn't bring up the tidings about Randy at this time. Later maybe.

She eyed me. "No drama, please. Nothing's changed as far as I know, unfortunately, except for, well …."

I knew it.

"We're going on a journey."

OK. Maybe she wasn't as normal as she appeared. Not an errand or a trip or a vacation, but a "journey"? I had a painful memory of myself in high school bent agonizingly over *The Odyssey* as poor Odysseus battled Cyclops and Circe on his "journey."

"A journey, huh? Daddy going on this journey too?"

"He knows about it. I told him I was going to do this, and he totally agreed." Mother stood up and walked to the window. "So did Honey."

"Honey? My shrink?"

"I've been seeing her lately."

"For therapy? She's never mentioned that."

"Well, it's really none of your business, is it, dear?"

She sounded so like the old Sarah O'Brien that I forgot to be insulted by her uppity-ness. And of course she was right. It wasn't my business, but that was beside the point. As her daughter, I was supposed to be in her business.

"Mother, I'd like nothing better than to go on a journey with you when all of this horrible nightmare stuff is over and done with. But right now a little mother-daughter trip to Folly Beach or even the French Riviera, if that's what you have in mind, is out of the question. Between Dare's situation, murder, mayhem and my job and…"

My mother shook her head and gently put her finger to my lips.

"Hush up, Bridget. Just get dressed. I'll wait in the car. We won't be gone long, I promise." She glided toward the door in her usual debutante fashion. Turning with her hand on the knob, she said, "For where your treasure is, there will your heart be also."

I stared at her.

"Close your mouth, dear. You look like a gigged frog. Surely you remember your Bible. So, can you wear something less, um, industrial? That is, not the blue coverall?" She raised her hand. "Now, don't get het up," she added. "Jeans would be fine, but how about a nice feminine blouse? Just for me? Hmmm?"

She closed the door softly.

I looked at my watch. It was only seven o'clock. Where were we going at that hour?

I walked into the kitchen a few minutes later in slim black jeans, black ballet flats and an oversized white poet's blouse. The puffy-sleeved, floaty kind. My hair was brushed, loose and curly. My lips shone with gloss, and I'd darkened my lashes with mascara.

"Ah, Brigida la Bella," exclaimed Chica, who was sitting in the special doggy alcove leaning against Big Foot and with Bubba in her arms. "That does not look like work clothes."

I'd forgotten about work. I'd have to call to see when we could get back into the club, which seemed to be turning into some kind of morgue. I shuddered.

"What are you doing down there?" I said to Chica, as I tried to push the deaths that week to the back of my mind. I looked at the coffee pot, but wished it wasn't morning so I could have a glass of wine instead.

"I saw your mama coming down the stairs and hid with the pets. It is too early in the day to deal with Miss Sarah."

No kidding.

I spotted Randy's laptop on the counter.

"Where did this come from?" I opened and closed it. Gently.

"Not important," she said, popping up with her little fairy movement to stand beside me. "Tell me. Why are you not dressed for work?"

"Good Lord. Here we are again with his cell phone and his laptop."

"I am thinking it is a good time to give to the nice policeman," she said, pouring herself a cup of coffee.

"You're just sweet on him," I said.

"You say there is nothing bad on them, amiga?"

"Not that I could tell."

"Then give them to the police."

"I'm still trying to figure out what all that money in and out of his spreadsheet meant. Was it drug money? Bribery money? Did he win the lottery? Did he rob a bank? Let me think about it today, and I'll decide when we turn over the laptop. If not, you do something with it." I still felt there was something to be found in Grace's attic, and I intended to find out.

"Meanwhile …," I opened the oven door and stuck the laptop on the bottom rack. "Don't turn on the oven."

A tap on the doorjamb made us both jump and turn guiltily toward the sound.

"Bridget Eve, did you forget I was waiting in the car?"

Mother crossed her arms, looking me over. I was sure that Bohemian wasn't her favorite style, but she nodded approval anyway, probably glad I wasn't garbed in what she often called my gas-station-attendant's costume.

"I thought you were in a hurry," she said. "Let's go."

"I'm coming, I'm coming. Chica, I should be back in about an hour. If not, you go on to the club. Either way, I'll call."

"Miss DeMoya." Mother acknowledged Chica with a nod.

"Call me Chica, señora, please."

"Good. Come along, Bridget. As unbelievable as it may seem, I have a life, too."

Bubba clicked over to Mother's shoe and sniffed.

"I've missed you, little fella," she said patting his smooth head.

Then she grabbed my arm and said, "For pity's sake, either give Randy's electronic devices to the police or drop them in Jordan Lake, but make up your mind and do it."

"Where are you going?" Chica asked.

"On a journey to find treasure," said Mother.

I looked helplessly back at Chica as Mother pulled me through the house.

Twenty-Two

Chapel Hill seemed far behind us as we drove west into the sparsely populated countryside. Upon entering the grounds of a large walled complex about thirty miles from home, I marveled at the eerie isolation among the evergreens and bare oak branches.

Mother had not said a word in the car to clue me in on where we were headed. Stubborn me refused to prod her.

We reached the end of a long tree-lined gravel drive. A brass sign next to the double doors of a red brick Georgian structure. A discreet sign identified it as the Treasure House in the Pines.

"Is this the treasure you keep going on about?"

Mother parked in the lot beside the building, remaining silent as she cut off the engine and got out of the car. I followed her through the front doors of the Treasure House. The reception room loomed grand but aging. It looked like early Twentieth Century architecture. The artist in me appreciated the mahogany staircase and elaborate trim glowing with polish, as well as the terrazzo floors gleaming below the high ceilings. Although no one was at the front desk, we could hear a Bach toccata being played on a piano; the faint notes rippled lightly on the air.

"That's lovely, isn't it," Mother said, even as she wrinkled her nose in distaste.

The good points of the Treasure House could not dissipate the odor that filled every corner of the spacious reception area. I'd once visited the geriatric wing of a Durham mental health facility with Daddy to see my Great Uncle Albert. I knew this smell. Old sick people smell. Old people incontinent smell lashed with heavy doses of rose, lavender and disinfectant. A smell on an institutional scale along with the reek of unwashed hair and body odor.

We stood at the receptionist's desk waiting for someone to appear and acknowledge our presence. The piano music stopped abruptly, which seemed to release my tongue.

"Why are we here?"

Mother looked at me for a second and then walked over to one of the two pastel sofas in a homey configuration nearby and sat gingerly on the cushions. She indicated that I do the same.

"I should have told you a long time ago, Bridget."

"You're scaring me."

"I don't mean to. I've consulted Honey about this. Or perhaps I was trying to keep you from being as scared as I was for a large part of my childhood."

Before I could put a question to her, a female cleared her throat purposefully. At the receptionist's desk, an imposing, gray-haired woman lifted an eyebrow in our direction.

"Ah, Miz O'Brien," she said. "She's through playing and is in her room now. You can go in, but be sure to turn off your cell phones."

"Thank you, Mrs. Blair, we will. How has she been since my last visit?"

"Let me check her records," said Mrs. Blair.

She sat down at her computer and tapped on the keyboard as I turned off my phone.

"From what I can tell, she's been pretty much the same. Eating well. Enjoying her music. A bit fractious now and then but that's to be expected. I mean, we all get that way, don't we?" No doubt Mrs. Blair's deep rumble was meant to be a chuckle.

"Indeed, we do," agreed Mother pleasantly.

She stood, took my arm and nodded at the receptionist, who buzzed open the door to the lengthy wing on the left.

As we walked down the hall, I peered into some of the rooms. Two elderly men were playing cards at a small table in one room. At least one of them was playing. The other was nodding in his chair. Further on, a tiny silver-haired woman stood in her doorway smiling at nothing in particular. When she saw us, she waved enthusiastically. Mother waved back, but this caused the woman to frown and back into her room, shutting the door.

We stopped at Number 12. The typed name on the little white card read "Mrs. Blanche B. Selwyn."

I froze.

"You said she died when I was a baby," I whispered so hard I almost spit.

"I lied," Mother said calmly, as she opened the door and pushed me inside.

I knew it would be rude to slam the door or else I would have tried to bang this one shut just for the heck of it. However, I tamped down my worst instincts and took a deep breath, standing just inside the door as my mother approached the woman in a rocking chair beside the window. She had silver hair, with a memory of curl, pulled into a low bun. She was tiny, but her shoulders were erect. Cute as a button she was – in an old-fashioned flowery dress and white tennis shoes and socks.

I could hardly breathe. This was the aged profile of Nana Blanche. The lovely young woman of the sepia wedding photo on my dresser, creator of the patchwork quilt on my marriage bed and my mother's blue afghan from her college days. Blanche, the legendary, sacred person of my past, according to Mother in countless reminisces. Blanche had been a perfect lady. So, what was she doing in an institution? A grand institution as far as facades go, but an institution nonetheless.

"Mama," said my mother as she kissed Nana Blanche on the cheek. "We heard you on the piano. It was beautiful. But look, I've brought someone to see you. Do you remember me talking about our Bridget?"

Mother moved aside so my grandmother could look at me. She turned her head and smiled as if we'd just seen each other yesterday. I went all cold because her eyes didn't smile, but I walked over, knelt down and touched her arm.

"Hey, Nana. How are you today?" My hand shook as I indicated the world outside of her window. "It's a beautiful day, isn't it?"

My grandmother reached up to touch my hair. She caressed my curls with long delicate fingers.

"Yes," my mother said to my grandmother. "It's just like yours, isn't it?"

Nana Blanche screamed once. It was high-pitched and long. She closed her eyes and yanked a handful of my hair or else I would have fallen over. I tried to stand as Mother pried me loose from her grasp.

She said, "It's all right, Mama. It's all right. It's your little Bridget. You know, like the picture on your night table."

I backed away, rubbing my scalp and peered at the color snapshot in a plastic frame beside the pristine single bed. My mother and I were in our Easter hats in the riotous spring garden on Rosemary Street. I proudly held my filled Easter basket.

"Bridget? My little Bridget?" Nana Blanche said in a whisper that belied her wail of just moments ago. Trembling, she turned back toward the window and then began to rock fast and hard. Too bad we couldn't clock the miles on that chair.

There was a soft tap on the door, and Mrs. Blair poked her head inside.

"Is everything all right in here, Miz O'Brien?"

"Oh yes," said my mother, as she held Nana Blanche's hand and stroked her arm. "Mama was just surprised to see us is all. We'll be fine."

"I wasn't snooping, you know," said Mrs. Blair. "Your husband left a message for you and your daughter at the desk. He wants you to call him urgently. Why don't you two go on now, and I'll stay here with Miz Blanche to settle her down." She waved her hand as if shooing us off.

"I'm hungry," complained Nana Blanche, after we'd kissed her goodbye. As we left, she pulled Mrs. Blair down and whispered, "Who were those people?"

We hurried outside into the fresh air. I turned on my cell phone and saw where Daddy had tried to call.

"Something must be wrong," my mother said. "Why would he call when he knew where I was taking you?"

I just looked at her, wanting to scream myself. Just like my grandmother. Maybe it ran in the family. I punched in Daddy's number on my phone instead and turned to the mother whom I felt I knew not at all.

"How would I know what he's thinking when I didn't know where you were taking me or that I had a grandmother who was supposed to be dead ages ago? When will you and Daddy start treating me like a grown-up, Mother? Y'all make me crazy."

"Crazy," she cried. "Crazy. I've been afraid of crazy my whole life. You don't know what you're talking about, Bridget. For you crazy is an abstract word you can use to describe a nut of some kind. For me, it was life. It was shame, and it was something I was determined to keep hidden forever!"

With that, she raced to the car and I ran after her. We probably looked like we should have been inside of the facility instead of my grandmother.

"Bridget! Bridget!" my father was yelling from my cell phone. I'd forgotten about him. Mother zoomed out of the Treasure House driveway as if chased by demons. At this point, I didn't care what happened to us.

Finally, I put the phone to my ear.

"Daddy! You know who I just met? I bet you'll never guess. It was fascinating and…"

"Bridget. For God's sake, listen to me. Dare has run away from the youth home. No one knows if it was last night or this morning. No one knows where she is. I've called the police, although I think Mrs. Breedlove had already done that."

"Oh, my God. OK. OK. We're on our way home now," I said before severing the connection.

"What did he want, Bridget?"

"What?"

"What did your father want?"

"It's Dare. She's run away from the youth home."

"Dear Jesus."

"But why should you care?" I said.

"Well, of course I care. Don't be ridiculous."

"Why did you take me to that place anyway? This morning of all mornings? Why not next year? Why not last year?"

"As I said, I've been consulting Honey. For months now actually. She's helped me see things. You suspected me of killing Randy. Maybe even the police did. The man in the trench coat. I could tell. I was distraught. You and I have had our issues, but I was determined that you not think your mother was crazy enough to do that."

She was right, but I didn't want to admit that it had been a possibility in my mind.

"That doesn't answer why we had to do all of this family revelation stuff today of all days."

"Because you wondered where I was on the day he died, remember? And the day after he died, when you came to the house and I left you standing in the driveway. You were asking me and asking your father, and I wanted you to know where I was. I was with your grandmother. Poor crazy Mama."

"Can we talk about this later? I can't think about it right now. I'm too worried about Dare. I need to text Chica and tell her to go home if she's not still there and keep an eye out for her."

In answer, my mother pressed her foot down harder on the accelerator.

We squealed into the driveway on Rosemary Street into what looked like a gathering of the clans. Daddy had been busy on the phone.

Lieutenant Hendricks, visible through the living room window with his elbow on the mantel and the phone at his ear, was having what looked to be an intense conversation.

Honey, parked at the curb in her ancient honey-gold Toyota Camry, climbed out when she saw us arrive. With her cape flapping, she swooped over as if to protect me from harm. Oh, if I could just have stayed in her embrace with my face on her warm shoulder. But no, a grownup had to be responsible.

"Are you OK?" She held me at arm's length. "Dare will be fine. She's a sensible child."

My father appeared from around the house. In full stride, he paced back and forth in the yard with poor Davey in tow. The gravity of the situation really hit home when I saw both of them tromp through Mother's immaculate flower borders. Ordinarily, Daddy would never do that. Even more surprising

– my mother ignored their destructive circumnavigation of her handiwork. Instead, she rounded them up and waved to me and Honey to follow them inside.

"You go on," I told Honey, "I need to clear my head for a minute."

Remembering my ex-husband Alessandro's advice about deep breaths, I stood beside one of Mother's camellia bushes breathing the cold air in and out.

"Miz O'Brien?"

Pilar stood awkwardly a few feet away.

"I really need to talk to you," she said. "It's about Dare. She came to my house early this morning. I think she ran away from that place where they had her."

"Yes. Oh, my God. Was she all right? Is she there now? How did she get there?" I sat down on the driveway, my legs giving way.

"I don't know," she said, kneeling down beside me, her forehead drawn in concern. "I wasn't there. She left this note saying she would try to see me later. That she has something important to ask me. But I haven't been staying at home lately. My dad and I aren't really speaking right now. I don't know if my father has said anything to you?"

She handed me the note. I recognized Dare's scribble and lack of punctuation and smiled even as my heart lurched.

Hey Pilar I need to ask you something about Monday night it's so important please don't tell anyone about this. Thanks, Dare

"Did your father see her or this note?"

"I don't know that either. I got there at about eight o'clock. Dad wasn't there and he never forgets to lock the door, so he must have found it and left it on the table for me as it had my name on it. He was probably at work or something. The thing is, I don't know how to find Dare or if she is going to come around again. Like I'm not even sure when she left the note."

"Has your dad called you about the note?"

"No, and I wouldn't really expect him to. Like I said, we aren't talking."

"Do you have any idea what Dare was referring to? About Monday night? Did you see anything or do you think she did?"

She thought for a few seconds.

"No, not really. I dropped Dad off at the club on Monday morning. We'd had a fight. I was sick, but I had a paper to finish. So, I drove back to the house and did that. Then I packed up some of my stuff. I texted Dad that I thought we needed to be apart for a few days, but that I was fine. I drove to my boyfriend's apartment, and I haven't been back home until today."

She stood up and brushed herself off.

"I'm really creeped out about all this," she said. "First, Mr. La Russo and now Mr. Jones. I liked them both a lot, you know. Mr. La Russo was very kind to me."

"Could you do me a big favor, Pilar? Just for a few hours? Can you go back home and stay there? Dare might come back, and I've got to find her. Would that be all right, or is the situation with your father too uncomfortable?"

"I'll go home now, Miz O'Brien. For Dare. But should I say something to the police about her note?"

"I'll tell them. If they need to talk to you, they'll contact you."

She looked relieved. I hugged her. She seemed so small, and her pretty face was pale.

"But what if your father comes home?"

"It's OK. I'll handle it."

I should have pulled the lieutenant or Davey in on this immediately, but I wanted Pilar to get home and wait in case Dare came back. I could always tell them later, and maybe by then Dare would be found. I was worried, though. It seemed to be getting progressively harder to know what the right thing to do was. I folded Dare's note and tucked it into my jeans pocket.

As I watched Pilar out of sight, I saw Virgil Spoon's red pickup driving toward the house and then slowing down right in front. When he spotted me in the driveway, he gunned it and disappeared around the corner. I walked back into the house wondering why he would be so nosy. Maybe he was curious about all of the cars in the driveway and on the street.

Inside, everyone except my father and Lieutenant Hendricks was milling about in the kitchen. I elbowed my way through the crowd and glimpsed the tail end of Daddy as he wore a path through the hall. I caught up with him as he strode past Hendricks, who was still on his phone.

I pulled at Daddy's arm to stop him.

"Daddy, I don't really care why Dare ran away and don't blame her for doing it," I said, not caring who heard. "I'm glad she isn't in that place anymore. I just want her with me. Safe and sound. This instant." I stomped my foot, fully aware of my boorish behavior and unable to control it.

Daddy yanked me into the den, grabbed my shoulders and shook me hard. Out of the corner of my eye, I saw everyone else filter into the living room to find out what was wrong. Except my mother, of course, who had heard my histrionics before and was most likely ignoring them. Then I remembered our visit to my grandmother. Mother had been exposed to that and worse from Nana Blanche in the past. I felt bad for Mother, but I didn't dwell on it. No doubt she was preparing a nice pot of coffee for the mob. I myself could not have organized a glass of tap water at the moment.

"Bridget, this kind of immature behavior doesn't help," said my father, in an uncharacteristically sharp tone. "Pull yourself together."

He turned me loose and said, "The police are looking

for her. Mrs. Breedlove drove to her school and spoke to the principal and also to Dare's little friend Ellie. Honey has been up and down Franklin Street and the mall. I've been to my office and walked on campus. I went to the club, too. Long is having the building and grounds searched. Probably still doing it now. All of the staff has been alerted to contact me if they see her or find anything. We have to be patient."

I guess it was time for me to be mature. I pulled Dare's note from my pocket.

"You need to see this," I said to Daddy as Davey and the lieutenant walked into the room. "Pilar gave me this a few minutes ago. She wasn't sure whether to tell you or not. I told her I would do it."

"I need to get over there right away and speak to her," said Hendricks, off his phone now and already in motion, "and get some folks out to question the neighbors in case anyone saw your daughter."

"You could have told us while she was here, you know," said Daddy.

"She's sick, and I thought it would be better for her to go home in case Dare showed up again."

"Every second could be crucial, Bridget," Davey added. "You shouldn't be making these decisions on your own."

Good God. I'd never thought of that. And here I was polishing my detective's badge. I bit my lower lip.

"It's all right, sugar," said Daddy. "You were doing your best. Just remember, don't keep anything back from here on out."

I put my arms around him.

"I promise," I said. No more Bridget Detective Agency.

"However," Davey said, after clearing his throat and noting my contrition. "All of this information is good and will be useful for the investigation. I believe every little piece of the puzzle will solve things in the end."

I collapsed into a chair and stared out the window at the street.

I felt an overwhelming urge for an oatmeal raisin cookie, so I stood up to leave, intending to get one from the kitchen. Maybe my mother had made some, although I wasn't sure when that would have been. On the way, I looked out the living room window and saw Virgil Spoon driving slowly by the house, this time going the other way.

"Oh, my God," I cried.

"What's wrong?" Daddy said behind me.

I vaulted through the kitchen and stopped dead in the driveway. Virgil was nowhere in sight. Crap, crap, crap. I realized I didn't have a car.

Davey almost knocked me over when he barreled through the kitchen door.

"What's going on?"

"I need a ride to my house" I cried, starting to wheeze.

"All right. But, what's the matter?"

Daddy ploughed out the door, almost running into Davey.

"Sugar, what's gotten into you?"

I gave Daddy a quick hug.

"Nothing, I just need to get home. I remembered something I need to check. Tell Mother I had to run but that there had better be cookies in the freezer when I get back."

Yeah, right.

I ran to my mother's car and got my purse, hollering at Davey to hurry up.

"I need to pick something up at home and take it to Chica at the club," I lied. "We're still not done for that wedding reception. I've been living a nightmare since last Monday. Didn't know one could last this long."

I knew I was babbling and fibbing, but I didn't want to tell Davey about Virgil's suspicious behavior. I probably should have. The thing is, though, that people tended to say they'd handle things and pat me on the head. Maybe I'd seen too many John Wayne movies or listened to too much Sinatra, but I wanted to do this my way. For that I needed to appear calm to Davey.

So, the ride to Chica's house passed in silence as I hoarded my breath and my secrets. When we pulled into the driveway, Davey reached for my hand.

"Try not to worry too much," Davey said. "I know how stupid this sounds, but I feel good about this, Bridget. We'll find her soon. She's a smart little thing. She'll show up on her own."

I clung to his hand like a lifeline for a few seconds.

"I know she's smart, but she's still a child. I don't know if she heard or saw anything the night that Randy was killed. She hasn't told us everything. Or maybe she doesn't realize the significance of what she might have seen or heard."

"Yeah, I get that feeling too. According to Mrs. Breedlove, though, she didn't open up to anyone there. She wasn't there very long, though."

"Why are you looking at me with your head sideways?" he asked. "You've got the look you get when you're contemplating trouble."

"I think I should be insulted. But I'll forgive you because I really like you."

He smiled a lovely smile.

Danger averted.

I waved him a sweet goodbye, marveling at his antennae. Because he was right, of course. I couldn't just languish at home or work at the country club while the killer or killers of Randy and Malcolm roamed loose with my gun. My daughter was alone and scared out there. If she had seen anything last Monday night at the club, she was in danger if the culprit heard about her escape from custody.

Twenty-Three

I watched Davey drive away and then dashed into the foyer and up the stairs to get my inhaler from my coveralls. I paused in front of the mirror and gazed at the floaty poet's blouse, of which the sleeves were starting to get on my last nerve. I wrenched it over my head, replacing it with my favorite, holey Carolina sweatshirt that was almost paper thin from 18 years of hard use. Back downstairs, I found Chica's BMW keys in the side table before slamming out the front door to the barking of two unhappy canines.

Starting the car was another matter. It took me a while to figure out the straight drive. Marcus had tried to teach me how to use the clutch and the gear stick years ago when we were first married; he'd been a real jerk, impatient with my tears and ineptitude. A lot of cussing had ensued, and I'd refused to drive a car without automatic transmission ever since.

Consequently, I felt like I was on a bucking bronco and giving myself whiplash as I drove the five minutes to the club. If it hadn't been for dire necessity, the clutch and the brake pedal would have been beyond my comprehension.

Eventually I lurched into Magnolia Blossom's parking lot, which was almost full as the day was sunny and mild.

Golfers and tennis players were out in full swing. Through the open window I could hear golf cleats clicking on hard ground and tennis balls bouncing on the composite courts nearby. I spotted the Faux Finish sky van with little trouble. I cruised past all of the parked cars and couldn't find the club's pickup truck. Hermann must have been out on some errand. Frustrated, I banged on the steering wheel.

I parked under the portico and darted inside. Chica, bless her heart, was atop our platform ladder finishing the last ceiling medallion. She turned as I appeared breathlessly into the ballroom.

"Amiga, whazzup? I'm doing the last one. You are glad about that?"

All I could do was nod and wheeze. I dug my inhaler from my sweatshirt pocket, glad that I wasn't wearing my mother-approved outfit for the visit to Nana Blanche.

Chica climbed down the ladder quickly.

"¿Qué pasa? Retrograde Mercury strikes us again. Like lightning, yes?"

"You haven't heard?" I gasped. "Dare has run away from the youth home, and she's disappeared. Didn't you get my text?" I burst into tears.

"My phone is in the van."

Chica grabbed a water bottle and a box of tissues from a supply box and handed them to me. I wiped my face and blew my nose before wrenching off the bottle cap. The water slid down my throat. I struggled to slow my breathing and my asthma eased up a bit.

"I work like a crazy woman here," Chica said, patting my shoulder. "No one tells me anything of this."

I told her about Pilar coming to my mother's house after I got back from the Treasure House.

"Treasure House?"

"Never mind, I'll tell you later. You'll never believe it. I can hardly believe it myself. Let's just say that there was fabulous treasure there, but it wasn't exactly fun discovering it at this point in time."

She gave me a curious nod.

"Anyway, Pilar said that Dare left a note at her house sometime last night or this morning asking to speak to her about the night Randy was killed."

"What will you do now?"

"Not sure. I saw Virgil Spoon, too. He seemed to be stalking over at my mother's house. I've no idea why. Have you seen Hermann this morning?" I walked toward the ballroom entrance and peered both ways down the hall while Chica got back on the ladder.

"I came to the club after you left this morning with the madre," she said. "Hermann was in the club truck. Long was standing beside it; they were arguing, I think. When I parked, Hermann drives away. I have not seen him since then. Long I have seen." She rolled her eyes, and I figured that the poor guy was still mooning after her. "I told him I could talk to him when retrograde Mercury is all gone."

"When is that?"

"The twenty-fifth of March."

"Well, I need to speak to him before then. He'll know when Hermann might be back."

"I will hurry. To help find our baby girl."

"No. You just keep an eye out here. I'll check the ladies' locker room and have a word with Long. Please get your phone out of the truck, in case I have to call."

I turned back toward the hallway where the offices were located and saw that yellow crime scene tape still encircled that area.

"You cannot go through that way. No one can," said Chica from her high perch. "Oh, and Mr. Mike Ruffin tried to get through that way, too."

"He did? Did you speak to him?"

"Why would I do that? Should I say to him, 'Mr. Mike, are you jealous of your wife's lover?'"

"No, I guess not."

"I will go and get my phone in a minute. You find Dare now. Call me when you do or I will find you to help."

I did a quick reconnaissance of the ladies' and men's locker rooms, which were open now, in case Dare was hiding there, although I knew it was unlikely. I headed toward the entrance and heard raised voices as I opened the front door.

The overbearing designer and her young assistant who had nagged me, Chica and the club staff ever since we'd started this reception job were on their cell phones pacing under the portico.

"I don't care if it is Sunday morning after the Carolina-Duke game tomorrow, you had better have those flowers here by eight a.m., do you hear me?" said Ms. Bossy Designer. "And they'd better be fresh and organized. I don't care how late you stay out."

Her assistant, who kept a weather eye on her boss, also appeared to be arguing with someone on her phone.

"Oh my God, I told you I have to work on Saturday. This reception at Magnolia Blossom, remember? I'll get there as soon as I can," she said, exasperated. "The game isn't until nine and you said we have tickets, so what's the big deal? I'll just be a little late is all. It doesn't really matter until the last five minutes anyway."

I wished that the Carolina-Duke basketball game was all I had to worry about.

Meanwhile, Chapel Hill Mayor Elizabeth Holroyd and her daughter, Alexandra, stood nearby. The younger woman was quivering and in tears. Long patted her shoulder gingerly, and her mother glowered like a chunky thundercloud.

"Please, ladies, ladies, let's not go all to pieces out here,"

Long said, his voice a bit higher than usual. "The work is almost finished, and you'll have most of a day and tonight with the designers to create magic in the ballroom for the reception. We will be there for you one hundred percent."

Alexandra wailed, pointing toward the club. "They've had like two murders this week. I don't want to have the reception here. For all we know, the killer is running around in there right now."

"Too bad the murderer didn't take out the blasted groom while he was at it," said the mayor under her breath.

"Mama!" Alexandra stopped crying and glared at her mother. "I don't believe a word you say about the bachelor trip. He would never risk getting some tacky disease from those skanks." And then under her breath, "He promised me."

"The pictures were splashed all over Facebook, Alex," her mother whispered vehemently.

"Photoshop," Alex replied promptly, but she was starting to tear up again.

"Mayor Holroyd, Miss Alex," Long interjected to change the subject, "let me assure you that these, uh, incidents this week have nothing to do with the club or its membership."

The mayor, her daughter and I gaped at him in astonishment.

"Well," he added weakly, "Except that they happened here."

"To a club member," said the mayor, accusingly, as if it were all Long's fault.

"And the club manager," said her daughter, as if Long were an idiot.

The poor guy finally noticed me frozen on the spot and seemed to lean my way for support, but I put my head down and hurried toward the van. Long would have to handle this one himself. After all, I couldn't really disagree with the women.

There were advantages to being one of the hired help after all. I made a mental note to tell my mother this very thing the next time I saw her.

***

When I pulled up on the street outside Hermann's house, Pilar's blue car was in the driveway. I cut off the ignition and sat for a minute collecting my thoughts. By the time I got to the front door, Pilar was pulling it open.

We sat at the kitchen table, and I asked her if the police had been by to question her.

"No, I haven't seen them yet. They might have come by but I just got back from my boyfriend's house. I had to get some things, and I felt so bad that I laid down and fell asleep for a few minutes. I'm so sorry," she said, reaching over and squeezing my hand. "As far as I know, Dare hasn't been back here today. Dad was, though."

She seemed calm, but her shaking hands belied her face.

"He said he had been running club errands. Something to do with kitchen equipment and an antique chest being repaired. He's probably back at work by now."

"But he saw Dare's note?"

"Yes. It was shut into the closed screen door, he said. He said he didn't think much of it at the time and thought she must have been released. That's why he just left the note on the table. He said he was going to call me about it, but decided not to because he thought I wouldn't answer my phone when I saw his number. He didn't know she'd run away from the youth home until I told him."

Pilar sounded logical, but something about her nervous hands gave me pause.

"Are you feeling all right? I know you've been sick and stressed out."

"I'm fine," she said. "It's just that I have to figure out

what to do about my boyfriend and my dad. He's so overprotective. He still thinks I'm five years old."

"Parents are like that," I tried to smile. "I'm sure he'll come around. Just be honest with him."

"You don't understand," she said, "it's more complicated than that."

"You know best," I said. "It's none of my business anyway."

"He always tells me not to be flirty with the men at the club. I'm like friendly is all. Most of the members are too old for me anyway."

She looked up suddenly to see if I'd been offended by that remark. But I remembered thinking folks in their late thirties or forties were ancient when I was her age.

"Everyone at the club is nice to me," she added. "I like working there."

"Everyone likes you too, honey, according to my mother. Believe me, if she'd noticed anything out of line, I would have heard."

Then I remembered Marla Ann's suspicions about seeing Pilar and Randy looking too friendly.

"But you have to be careful. You're a pretty girl and something perfectly innocent could be misinterpreted."

She nodded but still looked worried.

I hugged her and walked to the door.

"Call me if you hear anything at all about Dare. Anything."

"I'll hang around here for a few hours in case she shows up," she said. "I expect the police to show up at some point."

I couldn't decide where to go next, so I drove up and down Franklin Street, through Carrboro and back, all the while checking for Dare along the way and occasionally checking my rearview mirror for Virgil's red pickup. I knew I was suppressing my panic about Dare by trying to believe she was a clever little thing, like Davey said, and wouldn't do anything dangerous or stupid. Then I'd remember her confession, which I didn't think was too clever at all, and have to suppress the panic again. Having to concentrate on the manual transmission of Chica's old BMW, while not plowing into the back of cars or mowing down a jaywalking student, helped steer my mind away from Dare's danger somewhat.

As I waited to make a left turn from Cameron Avenue onto Franklin Street, I saw the Ruffins sitting in Spanky's restaurant at a table next to the window. They appeared to be arguing. Muffin was shaking her head and her face was red and agitated. Mr. Ruffin was leaning across the small table, dangling something in her face. It looked like the gold chain with the St. Christopher's medal that Randy had returned. Whatever Mr. Ruffin was saying to her wasn't nice, as he appeared to be snarling. The people at the table next to them looked shocked.

Just then Muffin turned and saw me staring at them. She stood up sloppily and ran out the front door of the restaurant. By then, horns were blowing behind me, and I turned onto Franklin Street. I followed Muffin as she staggered down the sidewalk and crossed Franklin. I pulled up at the Henderson Street crosswalk and yelled at her to get in the car. She hesitated for a few seconds, looked back toward the restaurant and then got in my car. With Muffin in tow, I turned right on Raleigh Street, went a couple of blocks and took a left on Country Club Road and then another left on Gimghoul Road where Mike Ruffin had been living for years through his various marriages.

He had managed to keep the Tudor two-story house through multiple divorces. Randy used to tease him, saying he'd paid for the house at least three times, because he had to buy out each wife to maintain his residence in the tony Gimghoul Historic District near campus. If Mr. Ruffin didn't watch out, he might find himself buying it again if it didn't work out with Muffin. Being as I'd smelled a lot of Chanel No. 5 on Randy's pillow and on Muffin, and seen the St. Christopher's locket from Muffin to Randy, I didn't give this marriage much chance of survival.

The only car in the Ruffin's driveway was Muffin's black Mercedes convertible. I pulled in behind it. Muffin sort of rolled upright out of the passenger seat. I cut off the chugging engine and followed her to the massive front door with a brass ram's head knocker. She unlocked the door, pushed it wide open and waved me into the foyer.

"Thanks for the ride, Mother of the Year," she announced with a giggle.

"Yeah and I think you're a mother, too," I replied under my breath.

"Pardon me?" she said over her shoulder as she weaved uncertainly into what was definitely not the dark, cramped kitchen I'd last seen years ago. Evidently, she and Mr. Ruffin had spent a fortune renovating the place. I would have commented about the bright and airy spaces with pale granite and tiles and light wooden floorboards, but my mind was bent on escaping her presence as quickly as possible.

Muffin mounted a counter stool. A glass of clear liquid was sitting on the granite as if waiting for her. Somehow I didn't think it was water. She lifted it to her lips and took a big gulp.

"So, girlfriend, what's happening in your world besides homicide?" she asked.

"First of all, I'm not your girlfriend. Second, I was just wondering if you killed Randy," I said. "Thing is, I know you were sleeping with him until he kicked you to the curb, and we all know about women scorned."

To my intense pleasure, Muffin choked and spit on the glossy countertop.

"You've got to be shittin' me," she said. "What we all know is that your brat said she did it. Maybe you should ask her. Oh, and I hear she's missing, is that right?"

All I remember is lunging forward, thinking I might crack her head like an egg on the granite, when a strong masculine hand clamped onto my arm until I quit struggling and my wheezing was the only sound in the room.

"Don't do something you might regret," Mr. Ruffin growled. "She's not worth it."

That stopped me cold.

"I see you made it back from Spanky's," I gasped.

Muffin was laughing, or crying, as Mr. Ruffin frog-marched me out the front door to my car. He shoved me into the driver's seat and knelt by the open door.

"Talking to her right now would be pointless," he said. "Sorry to hear your daughter is missing. I'll keep an eye out for her."

I didn't like the way he said that, and I stared at him. He was red as a beet, with beer breath to boot. No use discussing things with him, either. Besides, if he'd heard all I'd said inside, and I believed he had, there was as good a motive as any for him doing away with Randy. Another thought occurred to me, and I shuddered. From the way he'd talked the day after the murder, he might even have other reasons I knew nothing about. Business reasons.

"Would it be pointless to talk to you then, Mr. Ruffin? Like where were you late Monday afternoon?"

"I asked you to call me Mike, Bridget, now that you're grown up."

He sounded less than friendly.

"For the record," he said, "I was in a meeting from five o'clock until I got in at about eleven. And then I was up all hours working on my taxes."

"Is that so?"

I started the car. Mr. Ruffin stood up and slammed the door. He leaned down and looked through the window.

"I believe my wife was shopping at the mall."

I looked at his agitated face and couldn't decide if he was only a cuckold or a cuckold and a murderer.

Twenty-Four

As I drove back to the club, I was determined to call Davey or Daddy to let them know what had transpired at the Ruffins' house. I scrabbled in my purse for my cell phone, but I hadn't charged it since yesterday. For heaven's sake! I'd call later. I didn't want to keep them from locating my daughter first, anyway.

When I pulled into the club parking lot, Chica was leaving. When she saw me, she reparked the van and took over driving her old BMW, to my intense relief. Although I had managed at the gear-shifting clutch thing, it had been a struggle. No telling how much I'd screwed up her transmission.

I wanted Chica with me while I searched for Dare on campus and Franklin Street. Sort of the dynamic duo theory redux. Others were handling the search, but as Dare's mother, I knew no one else could do that better that I could. Or with more conviction, anyway. Besides, I knew Dare's favorite shops and eating places and where she liked to hang out. She was, after all, only thirteen, and maybe she'd be tempted to do some window shopping or browsing.

Chica parked the car on the street in front of the planetarium – a minor miracle – and we headed straight toward town on foot.

"Where do we go, amiga? I do not think the niña would be here. Not if she doesn't want to be found. Maybe we should we go farther into campus to the Student Store?"

"No, I think it closed at 6. Let's just kick around here for a bit. It would be so easy for her to blend in with all these kids roaming around here on a Friday night before a game. I'd never forgive myself if I didn't at least check this area."

We trudged up and down both sides of the street and then crossed Cameron Avenue to continue toward Carrboro. There was almost a carnival atmosphere in town as students jostled about in school sweatshirts, getting ready for the Carolina-Duke game tomorrow night at 9 p.m. Many fraternity and sorority kids were arm in arm, singing and setting forth from their houses in packs, sporting "Beat Dook" buttons and attitude. Off-key renditions of the Carolina fight song filled the night.

No luck finding Dare, and, after a while, all of the kids in UNC sweatshirts started to look alike. Eventually, we headed toward the car. Chica was exhausted after a hard day's work, and my head felt like it was full of cotton wool. On our way back down Franklin Street, we ran smack into Pit Bullard lounging in front of the Carolina Coffee Shop.

"Just the little ladies with whom I've been wanting to conversate," he declared, taking an arm each and smiling at me and Chica. "Are you folks looking for Miss Dare? Let me assure you that I have investigated every square foot of the area between Kenan Stadium and Rosemary Street and nary missing teenager have I come upon."

"Oh, Pit," I leaned exhausted against his decrepit dusty blue suit. "Thanks so much. That's what we've been doing."

"I spoke with your father and with Attorney Davey," he said, "and I promised I would seek out the child. Unfortunately, she has proven more resourceful than most little sprites her age. Perhaps that is a good thing, and she is safe in a hidey hole of her own choosing."

"That's what I tell Bridget also," said Chica. "Her girl is so smart. She will not do the wreckless thing."

"Except confess to a crime she didn't commit," I declared, starting to tear up, my lips wobbling.

Chica put her arms around me and nodded to Pit.

"We are going now. Will you walk with us to my car, Señor Pit? I can drop you off somewhere."

I let myself feel secure and helpless, and they steered me down the sidewalk. That lasted for about five seconds until I picked out that blasted red pickup going the opposite way on Franklin Street and my blood began to boil again.

Pit saw the truck, too. It was all he and Chica could do to keep me from running it down on foot.

"No, no," yelled Chica, holding onto me for dear life. "We will follow him."

We were about half a block from Chica's BMW. She left me in Pit's charge and sprinted ahead to get the car. I finally saw the sense in that and ended up dragging Pit to the car. He shuffled as fast as his elderly arthritic legs could carry him.

"Slow down, girl. The Lord isn't sending a flood tonight. Don't fret now. I know that boy like the back of my hand," he claimed as I shoved him into the back seat and threw myself into the front. "He can seem mean as the serpent of Eden sometimes, and, I'm afraid that, due to his unfortunate background, he harbors racist tendencies, but I am mighty doubtful of any guilt on his part."

"Pit, you sure do have a lot to say sometimes."

"I abhor a vacuum, daughter."

Chica peeled off, working the gears like a Formula 1 driver.

"Turn left on Cameron," said Pit. "Most likely, he is wending his way home. He resides out the Pittsboro Road."

"Bridget says he was stalking in his truck around her mother's house today because maybe he knows that is where Dare lives."

"Yes," I agreed. "He may have heard somehow that she got away from that youth home and that she might have seen something. What if that something was him killing Randy?"

"Virgil wouldn't kill a fly," said Pit. "Why in heaven's name would he do harm to Randy La Russo? I imagine he barely knew your ex-husband. I know Virgil deports himself in an unseemly manner. Like a warthog in some instances. He surely isn't pretty or clever, but he's a real honest-to-goodness non-violent sort of creature. Why his wife has only to …"

"I've seen his wife," I said. "She's a bit scary, too. How can you say he's not violent, Pit? You saw him the other night just like I did, spitting that chewing tobacco at Martin. I wouldn't put anything past him. Besides that, he had ample opportunity to steal my gun."

"Why in all that's holy and sacred would a scattered-brained little miss like you have a firearm?"

"It's a long story."

"Please favor me with it at a more opportune time," he said, patting my shoulder.

"There is his truck up ahead," Chica blurted out.

The red pickup turned into the main entrance of the Clear Day Mobile Home Park, and Chica followed over the hard-packed dirt.

We were admitted to a trailer that had to be from the 1970s, if the avocado green and harvest gold kitchen appliances were any indication. I recognized the large woman with the red hair and dark roots that I had seen at the Habitat house eating donuts and giving Virgil what-for.

She invited us into her home with an eloquent wave of her fried chicken drumstick. We climbed the steps, and I noticed a red-and-white bucket of the southern delicacy on the kitchen counter.

"Virgil," she shouted after a mighty gnaw on the chicken bone. "Comp'ny!" She licked her fingers.

"Preacher Bullard, what do you have to allow for yourself? Don't tell me my fool Virgil has gone and done something else this week. I Suwannee, I can't keep up with his goings-on."

Chica and I settled ourselves on the threadbare sofa that had once been brown while Pit stood next to the woman and peered into the bucket. He delicately selected a wing.

"Miz Brandie, delighted as always," he declared in his inimitable bonhomie. "It has been, much to my regret, an age since I last spied you in church."

"Lordy, don't I just know it," she said. "I'm too mortified to show my face at services what with Virgil going to jail the other night and then getting hisself fired like he done. Good thing I've got my little nest egg from my mamaw or we'd be clean out of money." She polished off the drumstick and threw it in a high arc across the kitchen and into the lined trash pail. She'd make a good free throw shooter for the basketball team.

This thought dissipated as Virgil shuffled in his stocking feet into the living room with a cooing infant cradled lovingly in his arms.

"I warn't fired, Brandie," said Virgil. "I told you I up and quit.

"So you see, Miz O'Brien, I couldn't decide what to do this afternoon when I seen all of them cars parked in front of your daddy's house," said Virgil.

He tucked his baby firmly under his arm, took a bottle of formula from his wife and settled down in a worn corduroy lounge rocker.

"Brandie was right on my case about getting another job,

and your daddy has been kind and all. He called me the day after I quit to tell me he would help me find other employment."

"Daddy did?"

"God's truth." said Virgil. "Preacher here stood up for me. I told Preacher I was that sorry about what I said to Mr. Jones about being black and all. Sometimes I drink too much and get mean. I don't understand things in this life. That's why he spends a lot of time talking to me, don't you, Preacher?

"Anyhow, that's why you seen me going by your house a couple times," he added. "But I finally decided it warn't a good time to intrude."

Brandie trundled over to Virgil and kissed him on the cheek.

"You see," she said. "We had a time getting our young'un well. She was a preemie and caught a respiratory virus directly after she was born. And the bills! Virgil never was a stranger to the spirits, but when we thought we was gonna lose her, it got worse."

Beside me, Chica sighed at the Spoons' plight, and I cringed at my mistaken suspicions. I silently apologized to Virgil for thinking of him as a serial killer just on first impression the day I saw him weed whacking at the club. I would have said I was sorry aloud, but I didn't want him to know I'd thought of him as a pervert and murderer instead of an indigent husband and father under stress.

The baby finished the bottle. Virgil propped her in a sitting position on his knee, held the tiny cheeks in one hand and gently thumped her back with the other. A long satisfying burp sounded, and we all smiled.

"We have to go now," I said to Virgil and Brandie Spoon. "So sorry to have bothered you. Thing is," I hesitated as I stared at the baby, "my own girl is missing. She's not a baby.

But it's even worse because she's out there on her own. I'm worried the killer might do her harm."

Virgil handed the baby to his wife.

"I can go and look right now, Miz O'Brien," he said, digging in his pocket for his keys. "I would purely love to do that for your daddy."

We all stood, and I put my hand on Virgil's arm.

"That won't be necessary tonight, but thank you so much. Tomorrow will be soon enough, and I'll tell Daddy and Mother that you offered."

"By the way, what is the baby's name?" I asked, as I touched a tiny foot protruding from the pale pink blanket.

"Preacher told me about Ruth in the Bible," said Virgil. "I thought Ruth would be a fine name for our girl. Something to live up to, you know?"

"A fine name, indeed," I said.

Chica and I waved to Virgil and Pit as we drove away from the trailer. As Pit lived next to his Pentecostal church further out of town, Virgil had volunteered to take him home and to look for Dare in the morning.

As we drove back into town, I pulled Chica's fuzzy ponytail and sank down in my seat.

"Drop me off at my parents' house. I'll let them know what's happened today and see if there are any further developments. I'm sure Daddy will know, and if he doesn't, Davey will."

"You are coming home tonight? The doggies must be doing the bathroom thing all over the house by now," Chica said. "It's all right, though. Not a problem."

"I forgot about the dogs," I said. "The dog whisperer would be appalled. I'm staying with my folks tonight, if that's all right, Chica. Dare could show up later, and I want to be there if she does. Meanwhile, you can keep watch at your house."

"Yes, I will put a sign on the door that says, 'Dare, please ring bell. Bubba misses you.'"

I almost laughed.

I hugged Chica tightly before I got out of the car.

"I don't think I can take much more of this," I said.

"Oh no, amiga, I do not believe that. I pity this killer. We are all after him, and we will get him."

"Or her," I added.

Twenty-Five

At the kitchen counter over decaf, I told Daddy and Davey about my side trip to Gimghoul Road.

"I sort of visited the Ruffins' house. Did you know that neither of them has a viable alibi, and they both have motives?"

"Weren't they questioned?" my father asked.

"I'm not sure," said Davey. "They never signed the member register on Monday, so the police didn't know they were there."

"I'm not sure why we keep a list like that at the door, if no one bothers to sign it," I ranted for the umpteenth time that week.

"So, what are their motives?"

"Well, Hendricks knows what I think," I said. "Chica and I told him that Muffin was most likely having an affair with Randy on the side, and Mr. Ruffin could've found out about it. Muffin isn't the smartest baked goodie in the case, you know."

"He might not have gotten around to it yet," said Daddy, giving him the benefit of the doubt.

"Mr. Ruffin said he was in a meeting from five that afternoon on Monday until about eleven that night. After that he was working on his taxes. According to him, Muffin was at the mall at the time in question. If you ask me, though, that might not be the case."

With his lips compressed and frown lines on his forehead, Davey had noted my comments on his ubiquitous legal pad and said he'd check with Lieutenant Hendricks.

"Anything else you feel you can let us know so we can do our jobs and end this nightmare?" Davey asked. "Why do we have to find out this stuff after the fact?"

Even my father looked at me as if I'd let down the team, gone out of bounds as it were.

"Well, now that you mention it…."

"I knew it!"

"I was getting ready to tell you about our evening with Pit and about Virgil's redemption."

"Riddles we don't need," Davey said.

"I never considered Virgil a suspect for anything that's happened once Pit told me a few things about the man," said my father. "Malcolm could be a bit harsh, and I knew Virgil could be abrasive, but it seems we all handle adversity and our flaws in different ways."

So said my professor father, the ultimate angel man in khakis and a buttoned-down collar blue shirt.

I related the evening at the trailer park with the baby and the bucket of chicken. We all felt good about Virgil, at least.

"So, it seems that no one has seen or heard from Dare besides Pilar and Hermann," said Davey as he shrugged into his jacket to leave. "I'm going to make a copy of these notes and leave them in a confidential envelope for the lieutenant at the police station, and tell him to call me if I don't see him, that is."

Davey pulled my hair on the way out.

"Please, sir," he said to my father. "Tie her to a large piece of heavy furniture, if she even thinks about leaving the house tonight."

"Don't you worry about me," I said, stung. "I'm too tired to go anywhere, and I'm hoping that if Dare has kept hidden today, she might decide to come home tonight."

"The doors are unlocked," said Daddy. "I want her to be able to walk right in any door. Also, she knows where we hide the key. But I wouldn't put too much hope in her coming home tonight, sugar. It's pitch black out there now. In fact, I'd feel better if she waited until the daytime instead of worrying about her wandering around in the dark."

***

I cracked open an eye. A brilliantly pink and orange dawn melted into view behind the bare black branches of the oak tree of my old home on Rosemary Street. As I sat up on the living room sofa, I realized someone had slipped a pillow under my head and a huggie pillow in my arms during the night. My mother's Carolina blue afghan had been pulled up to my shoulders.

I had not intended to sleep. After Davey left, I perched on the sofa with ESPN on TV. The last thing I remembered watching in the wee hours was commentary about the legendary Tobacco Road basketball rivalry in the NCAA. The UNC-Duke game. The Cameron Crazies. The green and lovely campuses eight miles apart. Before the past week, the hype would've been my life. Now I knew life wouldn't be worth living unless I found my daughter safe and sound. The discovery of the grandmother I once thought was dead and gone seemed a blip on the horizon, even though it was amazing. Even the horrific murders had receded in my current stressed, but focused, state of mind. I had zeroed in on one goal.

Time was a funny thing. Randy and I had talked about that in our Dickinson phase, and one of her poems came to me as uncannily as if time had stood still.

"Look back on time with kindly eyes,
He doubtless did his best;
How softly sinks his trembling sun
In human nature's west."

Thankfully, my cell phone rang to rescue me before I could spend too much time wallowing in self-pity and iambic tetrameter. I eased back into the present, remembering I'd borrowed a charging cable from my parents and now had a working communication device.

As I plucked the phone from the coffee table, I prayed it would be Dare even though I knew she didn't have her phone.

"Amiga," Chica said, "Are you awake?"

"If you could call it that.

"Did you hear any news of la niña yet? She did not come here."

"Nothing."

"I will come over and pick you up," she said. "You should have a nice shower and get dressed. Long called and asked us to come to the club."

"Why didn't he call me?"

"How do I know? Maybe he thinks I am much more beautiful than you."

I smiled at her attempt to cheer me up.

"He's absolutely right," I said. "Yes, come on. I need a fresh start today."

***

After bathing and donning a fresh coverall, I felt like a new woman. Clean socks and clean hair should be written into the United States Constitution as inalienable rights. With a burst of energy, I made important calls as Chica drove us to the club.

Hendricks had no news about Dare, but he said he and Davey were poring over notes at that very moment. I didn't want to tell a veteran policeman how to do his job, so I didn't inquire if he planned to speak with Mike and Muffin Ruffin. As it turned out, he must have heeded Chica's speech of the other night about their motives.

"Davey mentioned that you spoke to the Ruffins yesterday, Miz O'Brien. I interviewed them, you know, so don't fret because they are still on my radar as are others. That make you feel better?"

I told him it did, and then I called Pilar.

"I spent the night here, Miz O'Brien. Dare never showed up, I'm sorry to say. But Lieutenant Hendricks came by and I told him everything I knew. What about on your end?"

"Nothing from Dare," I repeated, palpable depression trying to break down my positive defenses.

"I'm sure she'll turn up. I'm like an expert. I ran away from home once. Did I tell you?"

"Yeah?"

"My dad was strict about boys and dating. We got into like a huge argument when I was fifteen, and I ran out of the house. I didn't go far though. Spent the night with a friend who was house-sitting in a really cool mansion. So, it turned out all right."

"Where is your dad? Working?"

"He's off today, I think, but he was going round to the club because of that wedding reception and everything being in a mess since Mr. Jones died. I'm not sure there's going to be a wedding though, much less a reception. Seriously. Rumor has it that the engagement has been called off."

"I'm not surprised," I said. "I heard the bride and her mother discussing it yesterday."

"Like I need to go now, but can we talk later today?" She sounded worried.

"Is something wrong?"

"Maybe it's nothing," she said.

"What do you mean?" I said. But she had disconnected.

Twenty-Six

Long was pacing back and forth under the portico as Chica and I arrived at the club on Saturday morning. I spotted the club's pickup truck and told Chica to park next to it. Finally, I'd be able to speak to Hermann. We hurried over to Long.

"What's up?" I said. "I don't have time to hang around unless this has to do with Dare being missing, Long. Chica said she'd finish up things around here though, so don't worry."

"Just wanted to let you all know that the wedding is off," he said looking pained. "There's no need to start any of the smaller projects we discussed that are in limbo. Getting what is obviously unfinished cleared up is enough for now."

"Uh oh. Was it about that bachelor trip the bride and her mother were arguing about yesterday?"

"Bachelor trip?" said Chica. "Ah, the groom has cheated, yes?"

"That's what folks are saying," Long whispered. "Let's not speculate. But at least the club got a facelift out of the deal. I know Mr. Jones was pleased with your work here. He told me so before … well … before he passed. Even though he seemed to be grumpy about it sometimes to your faces. If I have my way, we'll be using your services in the future."

He'd forgotten I was standing there because he'd turned and was gazing directly at Chica. She batted her eyelashes.

"That lieutenant dropped by bright and early to give the all clear as far as club activities go," he said. "Too bad about the wedding, though. The board will be livid about the loss of revenue from the cancellation. They'll be meeting next week."

"They've got to start searching for a new manager, too," I said. "I'm so sad about Malcolm."

"I've got to untangle this wedding chaos. I'll keep my eyes open for your daughter, too. I'm sure everything will turn out all right."

"Thanks. Here's a picture of her." I handed him one of the many wallet-sized school photos I'd had made. "If someone doesn't know her, they can keep an eye out and let you know."

Long opened the front door just as Hermann was reaching for the inside handle.

"Ah, the man I was looking for," said Long. "Can you come to my office in about thirty minutes, Hermann? I've got some things to go over, and I want you to pick up something from Baron's Antiques."

"Yessir," Hermann said. "I'll be there."

"Can I speak with you a minute, Hermann?" I asked.

Long waved at us as the door closed behind him, and Hermann stepped outside.

"I've been looking all over for you," I said. He paused – pleasant, but no nonsense about getting his work done.

"I talked to Pilar earlier, and she said you found Dare's note yesterday. Did you see her or possibly see where she went?"

I was sure Pilar had told me all she knew, but sometimes people remembered things later, so I wasn't taking any chances.

"Unfortunately, the note was all I found," he said. "I had been to the shops and my hands were full of carrier bags. I did glance about the garden and into the street after I read the note but didn't see her."

He seemed to hesitate for a bit.

"How was Pilar this morning?" he finally said. "I left her sleeping."

His forehead wrinkled with worry, and I put that down to whatever he and Pilar were going through at the moment. He forced a small smile. "Did you chat for long? I know how you girls like to natter."

Now it was my turn to hesitate, and I felt the need to protect Pilar, which was silly as Hermann adored her. Dumb Bridget. He's just being a father like you're a mother. Of course you protect your own.

Still, I went with discretion.

"We only spoke for a second. I was in a hurry." I didn't mention that she had seemed anxious to have me call her later.

"Well then if you'll excuse me, Miss O'Brien, I'd better get a move on, as they say here in the colonies. Let me know if I am able to help you with anything. I was supposed to be off today, but with this canceled reception and all that has happened, I shall be in and out and running errands instead."

Hermann looked at his watch and reentered the club. Inertia grabbed hold of me, and I stood irresolute. Chica clapped me on the back.

"Stand tall, amiga. You go. Our little business will get done here. Come back in an hour, and then we will see what we can see. I will make sure no more Sagittarians enter our life before we find the little one."

Back in the van, I called Pilar to find out what she wanted to talk about, but she didn't answer her phone. So, I drove to my parent's house to park before heading back to campus for yet another search.

My father was slumped over the kitchen island, head in his hands.

"No news, Daddy?"

"No. At least nothing we should worry about at this point."

"What does that mean?"

"No, no. Nothing on Dare yet."

"Where's Mother? I didn't see her car outside."

He ran long fingers through his thinning silver hair.

"It appears that your grandmother wandered away from the Treasure House early this morning. Your mother is there handling it now. I couldn't go under the circumstances. I keep waiting for our little girl to walk in the door."

"Good Lord! Nana Blanche escaped?"

"Not 'escaped.' She's not a lunatic or a convict. She couldn't have gone far, though. She'll be fine as long as they find her before it gets colder. They said she took her coat."

He hugged me. It felt good to lean against him.

"You have enough to handle right now, sugar."

"I'm off to check every shop on Franklin Street, show her picture. Student Store, too. Maybe as far as the Dean Dome and the basketball museum, then I'll be back. Don't you think she'll want to come home for the game, Daddy?"

He tried to smile, chucked me under the chin, and checked his watch.

"I know she'd want to be here for the game, but that's not until nine o'clock, more than five hours from now. I like your plan, though. You go find her, and then we can really celebrate, watch the game together like old times."

For heaven's sake, I'd forgotten what time the game started, which had never happened before. It seemed so surreal that I felt a tad dizzy for a few seconds.

"Right," I said after a couple of beats. I squared my shoulders. "Old times. We need to find her before all hell breaks loose. If we win, Franklin Street will be a zoo with people celebrating. If we lose, heaven forbid, there'll be a million people running around afterward anyway. And a bunch of Dookies rubbing it in our faces."

I didn't mention the killer.

Twenty-Seven

I elbowed my way through the rapidly filling campus. For the first time during a game day, I cursed the hordes of enthusiastic UNC fans eating, shopping and wandering willy-nilly all over the place when my daughter was in a deadly situation.

I waved Dare's picture at student restaurant hostesses, salespeople flogging powder blue Carolina T-shirts, fraternity kids dashing out of their houses in various stages of inebriation, and glum administration folks still toiling in the emptied corridors of academic buildings. By the time I tromped back onto Franklin Street two hours later, my feet burned in my hiking boots, and I knew two things: every teenager looked like Dare and every adolescent call of "Mama" made my heart stop.

I schlepped into Starbucks and got in line for caffeine and an oatmeal raisin cookie boost. I called Chica to tell her where I was and ordered us two coffees with extra shots of espresso. I had finally managed to grab two stools in the front window when she entered the coffee shop.

"That was fast," I said.

"Hermann dropped me off," said Chica. "He looked for la niña today, too, he says."

She peered into my face.

"Amiga?"

"Was Pilar with him?"

"No."

I gazed out of the window in despair.

Virgil drove slowly down Franklin Street in his red truck, Brandie by his side scanning both sides of the street. I blew them an unseen kiss like a blessing.

Chica patted my head and went off to the ladies' room.

A moment later, a whiff of lavender floated to my nostrils, and Honey spoke up just behind me.

"She'll show up." She slid onto Chica's stool and sipped a steaming latte. "I promise."

Her honey-colored hair waved down her back, and she wore a long, gold damask tunic and jeans. She often dressed like upholstery, which I found strangely soothing to the nerves.

"I was passing by the police station and dropped in to ask about Dare's status. Told them I was her doctor. I didn't want to bother you or your parents. The lieutenant said they are out in force looking for her, and full force would have been the case anyway because of the basketball game tonight. Which is lucky for us. Don't worry, Bridget. When Dare pokes that cute little nose out of her rabbit hole, we've got her."

When Chica returned, Honey started to get up.

"Did I take your seat?" she said.

"No. Sit, please. I am too nervous to sit. Holy Madre, I need this." She reached for her coffee and took a big sip. "Café is my addiction of choice now. Drink yours, Bridget."

"Do you think it could be one of the Ruffins?" I said. "We know that Muffin was having it off with Randy recently. Mr. Ruffin could've gotten jealous. Or Muffin could have reacted poorly to the role of 'a woman scorned.'"

"Mrs. Ruffin and Randy?" Honey said in surprise. "Such a player, that Randy was."

She looked contrite when she saw my stricken face.

"I'm sorry, Bridget. I don't mean to be insensitive, but I'm flabbergasted by his revolving door of partners."

I glugged some cold coffee. Espresso was espresso, and I needed all I could get. My stomach was bunched into a knot at the moment, so I stuffed the bagged cookie in my pocket.

"No apology needed," I said, standing up to discard my trash. "Will you be here for a while? We have to tend to the dogs, and I've got to talk to Pilar."

"Sure I'll be here. This is my office away from my office," Honey said. "I find that one likes being in a crowd of people one doesn't know but feels benign toward. Very comforting. Besides, today I have a mission – to focus on the sidewalks for Miss Dare."

"By the way, as if one crisis weren't enough, Nana Blanche escaped from her nursing home this morning. I'm not sure what's happening by now, but what are the odds that two members of one family can go missing at the same time?"

Honey shook her head, pulled out her phone.

"Lord help me, what an unfortunate sequence of events," she said. "I'll call your house," (only she said "hoose" in her gentle Tidewater accent) "to ask if they need me. Your mother is at a crucial stage of her emotional awakening. I pray that your grandmother is all right."

"Daddy hasn't said much to me about it. He thinks I've got enough to handle. He'd be grateful for your advice," I said.

"Such a Southern gentleman."

"You're welcome to watch the game with my parents tonight if you want company and all is well with Nana Blanche. I'm not sure where I'll be if Dare isn't home by then. Most likely on Franklin Street."

Honey waved goodbye as Chica and I left Starbucks and

headed toward my parent's house, the blue-sky van and the road to our fractious pooches.

Mother's car still wasn't back when we got to the house, and now I really started to worry about my newly discovered grandmother. My father stood at the living room window and shook his head at us, indicating that nothing was new.

"I'll be back in a little while," I hollered at him.

Chica fired up the van. As we pulled away, Davey slid his SUV next to the curb and waved for us to stop. I cranked down my window as he walked over.

"Where you going?" he asked.

"Take care of the dogs," I said. "I'll be back later."

"I will do the dogs, amiga," Chica said. "You stay here. Run up your lawyer bill. Ha ha."

Davey looked insulted. "I'm not charging for being here."

"For heaven's sake," I said.

Chica winked at Davey, who looked embarrassed.

"When you've fed and walked the pooches, Chica, make sure the key is hidden in the usual place for Dare just in case she shows up there. Then come back with the dogs. All of us should be together tonight like we always are for basketball games."

Channel positive, Bridget.

"Om mani padme hum," I whispered with closed eyes.

"What?" Davey said. He opened the van door for me.

"She does the mantra," Chica said from the driver's seat, "because life makes her crazy."

Her brow wrinkled. "Davey is not a Sagittarius, is he?"

"He's a Capricorn."

We walked back to the house as Chica drove away. I tried to call Pilar again with no luck.

Daddy hung up the phone as we walked in the kitchen. The grandfather clock in the hallway chimed eight o'clock.

"Nothing of Dare, I assume," said my father, frown lines

seamed into his forehead. "I was hoping she would be home by now, even if only to watch the game."

I just looked at him.

"The police are doing all they can, Professor," Davey said.

"I've got some other news, though," Daddy said.

"Nana Blanche?"

"Your mother found her at Whole Foods, would you believe? Sniffing the organic bars of soap in the cosmetic area."

"How did she get there? That must be thirty-five miles."

I filled glasses of water for Davey and me and sat at the counter beside him, after plugging in my cell phone to charge.

"After searching the surrounding neighborhoods and roads most of the day, your mother just had a hunch. Whole Foods is always your grandmother's favorite place to go when they have the odd outing. She's big into organics, is your grandmother, you know."

"How would I know that, Daddy? I was kept in the dark all these years about Nana Blanche's being alive, much less her mental health. It doesn't make sense. Every family has its secrets. Why should ours have been any different? I would've been fine with it."

Uncharacteristically, he opened the refrigerator, popped the top on a can of beer and took a big swig with the door still open. He held one out to Davey, who shook his head.

"I tried for years to talk to your mother about it, but she refused to listen. Leave it for now, sugar. Let's deal with one catastrophe at a time."

"Sir, don't tell me that little old lady walked all the way from Treasure House to Whole Foods grocery store. It's not possible," said Davey.

"She hitch-hiked," he said, shaking his head. "Thank the Lord, some kindly couple saw her marching down the

Pittsboro road and offered her a lift. She told them her folks used to hitch-hike during the Great Depression. Shades of *The Grapes of Wrath*."

For a few seconds, no one spoke. If our hearts hadn't been so heavy, we would have been rolling on the floor with laughter, but all we could do was chuckle a bit.

"Here I was thinking Dare got all her cojones from Mother."

"I think that gene does run on her side of the family," Daddy admitted.

"Where are the two of them now?"

"Back at Treasure House, I imagine. They've had enough excitement for one day. Your mother is anxious to get back and find out what's going on with Dare."

"Did they ever find out why she left or how she got out?"

"Your mother hasn't told me anything yet, except to say it was all her fault. Maybe she took you over there too soon."

At half past eight, Bubba and Big Foot burst into the kitchen with Chica puffing at the end of their leashes.

"The doggies want to play with the little one," she gasped. She looked at the beer in my father's hand.

"Cerveza!" she cried.

"Now, that's one Spanish word I do know," said Daddy. He popped the top on another cold beer and handed it to her. He must've forgotten that Chica was on the wagon, so I jerked it out of her hand and substituted a bottle of water. Thankfully, she didn't protest.

Fifteen minutes until game time.

"Soon as the game starts, I'm going back to Franklin Street to look in all of the bars and restaurants broadcasting the game," I said. "The streets will be almost deserted, and it'll be easy to check all the people inside as they'll be semi-stationary."

"We will also go," said Chica, indicating the dogs who

were slurping water from one of mother's crystal bowls that I'd grabbed from a cabinet. Indeed, I was inviting the wrath of Sarah Selwyn O'Brien upon my head, but who cared at that point.

"Me, too," said Davey. "We can separate and cover more ground." He headed to the bathroom.

"Daddy, you need to stay here. Mother will need you, and Honey might be coming over too. Keep your phones nearby, in case one of us calls or finds her."

"OK, sugar. I'm going to turn all the televisions on now. For luck." He left the kitchen.

My phone rang. I almost jumped a foot in the air, but it wasn't Dare.

"Hello?" I said not recognizing the number.

"Bridget? That you, honey?" It was my former mother-in-law. Grace's usually gravelly cigarette voice seemed to be a notch higher. "I been meaning to call you all day, but I'm a bundle of nerves."

"What's wrong?"

"I wanted to let you know that the police found Randy's laptop under his mattress. They came with a search warrant. I watch *C.S.I.: Miami*, so I know all about that stuff. Lord, the house was a mess after."

"They found the laptop under the mattress?" I eyed Chica. She shrugged and looked at me with eyes full of wonder. Ha! "Glad they found it. Maybe it will help explain some things."

You could've heard a pin drop in the kitchen as Davey, Chica, and even the dogs listened to my conversation.

"Might be you could come on over after the game? I know you'll be watching it."

"Grace, you know that Dare ran away from the youth home yesterday? We're all still looking for her. I've hardly thought about the game."

"Dear God, no, I didn't know that. No one tells me a

blamed thing. My poor Randy was so looking forward to tonight. Anything I oughta do, honey? Me and old Duds can get out on the street and look for her, too."

"No. No. Stay home. You don't want to be out in the street with Dudley on game night. There'll be a mob on Franklin Street at some point. I'll call as soon as we find her."

"That explains something though," she said after a pause.

"It does?"

"Yes," she said. "Went up in the attic looking for an old photo album and found a pillow and blanket up there. Looks like someone spent a couple nights there. Maybe it was Dare. You reckon?"

"I do reckon, Grace. Wish I'd known. I wouldn't have worried. Keep your doors unlocked just in case she comes back, will you?"

"Sure will, honey. Is she in danger, now, do you think?"

"No," I lied and gulped. "She'll be fine. But I've got to go. Call you later."

There was a long pause.

"Keep an eye out for the Ruffins, OK honey?" she said softly.

"Why? What are you saying? Grace?"

But she had hung up.

Did she know about Muffin and her Randy? There was no time to call her back and find out. Besides, I was already aware of all the plausible suspects and the Ruffins were high on the list. I grabbed Daddy's jacket off a chair and shoved my phone into my pocket.

I scribbled a note telling Daddy and Davey to let Hendricks know that Dare might have spent the last two nights at Grace's house and left the note on the kitchen counter.

"I'm going on ahead," I shouted to the house. "See y'all downtown."

I paused. A last glance over my shoulder coincided with

the roar of the basketball crowd bursting into the night air and the sports announcer, Jack Allan, shouting above the crowd noise.

"With the A.C.C. tournament starting in Greensboro on Thursday, hey, let's take a step back now and just play basketball," said Allan.

"Jesus, Maria and Joseph, amiga," Chica exclaimed while trying to attach the bouncing, yelping dogs to their leashes. "I will walk the dogs up to Franklin Street."

From the television speakers, basketball shoes squeaked on the polished floor of Cameron Indoor arena in Durham.

I could hear Daddy pacing through the house in his circular basketball furrow of stress with the worry about Dare propelling him along even faster.

Then energetic sports announcer Don Visalli made excuses for Duke's star guard J.J. Redick's recent poor performances.

"You know," boomed Visalli, "when you talk about fatigue, when you talk about J.J. Redick – His numbers certainly in the last three games in a row – 18 for 59 – that is not J.J. Redick shooting – six for 26 from the three. I think it's been more emotional fatigue than physical fatigue."

"And I'm so sick of hearing about Redick," I muttered of this currently most disliked Duke player.

"Bye, Daddy," I yelled.

I heard a muffled protest from Davey in the powder room.

But when I got outside, Pilar was in her car at the end of the driveway and appeared to be crying her heart out.

I ran back in the house to let Daddy know I was leaving with Pilar instead. Visalli was still on the television waxing lyrical about Redick, for heaven's sake.

"Oh, a running jumper by Redick," Visalli cried. "Is he on fire? Wow, somebody call the fire chief. He's burning up the nets already."

A little of Visalli goes a long way, but I guess he was enthusiastic.

"Daddy, I'm going with Pilar," I shouted and sped back outside. I yanked open the driver's door and shoved Pilar over. With difficulty she lifted her feet and humped awkwardly onto to the passenger seat.

The game was on the radio, but I cut it off and gunned the little blue car toward campus. I squeezed into an illegal space in front of the Chapel of the Cross Church on Franklin Street.

"Tell me," I said to Pilar. "What's wrong?"

She mopped her face with a ball of tissues and blew her nose.

"Oh, God. Like I'm not sure. I could be wrong, and I don't know who to turn to."

"Is it about Dare?"

"Not directly."

"She's still missing, you know. Everyone is searching, including your father."

"Yes, he's out looking for her right now."

She tore her tissues to bits, pulled more out of her coat pocket.

I reached for her left hand.

"Listen, Pilar, think carefully. Do you know where your father was, late on Monday afternoon?"

"At home. At least some of the time. He'd had the afternoon off to go to the doctor. Then I think he had an odd job to do for Mr. Ruffin. They were supposed to meet at the club early Monday evening."

"They were? Have you told anyone else this?"

Franklin Street was almost deserted, but its closed store fronts and interior lights burned brightly. Certainly not a normal Saturday night. In more ways than one.

"I was afraid to. I didn't think it mattered that much at the time, and I didn't want to get my dad in trouble."

Confused, I tried to mentally collate all of this information. However, although my little gray cells were moving like a fast break, they pulled up too soon to score a basket. The UNC basketball team must not have been having that problem though, as we heard a simultaneous roaring and stamping issuing from the sorority houses across the street.

"I'm pregnant," Pilar said.

I stared at her for several seconds.

"I wondered. But then I thought you had the flu, or so your father said," I replied. "Your boyfriend knows, doesn't he?"

Then I remembered her father and his strict morals.

"Uh-oh, does your father know?"

She hesitated and then looked up and down and to the left.

"I'm not sure."

"Pilar, please think."

"The pregnancy test box was in the trash in the bathroom. I meant to empty the trash but forgot, and he might have found it. He heard me being sick some mornings. Like he might've put it all together."

"Doesn't he like your…, what's his name anyway?"

"That's the thing, Miz O'Brien," she snuffled into the tissue ball. "He doesn't really know about my Bryan. He thinks it's someone else. I know he does, and I've let him think that, because I didn't want to tell him about Bryan yet."

"Let him think what, exactly?"

But she just shook her head and started sobbing as if she'd never stop. I attributed this to fluctuating hormones and figured she was tapped out emotionally. This deserved to be a long discussion, and I felt there wasn't time for her to reveal who Hermann thought the baby's father was. I probably wouldn't know the boy anyway.

Besides I couldn't sit still any longer. Dare could be in one of the restaurants downtown getting ready to watch the game.

"We'll talk tomorrow, honey, I promise," I said. "I'll help you talk with your dad. He's probably just old fashioned about these things, as his generation is. Maybe we can get my daddy involved, too. Don't worry about it. But I need to find Dare right now. I'll get back with you."

So, I hugged her and jumped from the car and raced toward the bright lights of mega basketball night on Franklin Street.

Twenty-Eight

I slowed to a walk as I entered Four Corners Restaurant, which, as expected, was packed. Eyes were glued to the television screens. No one manned the greeting station, so I scuttled through the aisles and bar area – but no Dare and not a whole lot of joy from the diners either, as Redick had scored another trey from the corner after a Carolina turnover.

"Got it falling down," said the TV announcer, "Duke by eleven."

Loud groans from all around.

No luck here, so I exited through the front door and collided with Davey and Officer Jones.

"I told you to wait for me," he complained.

"And here I am."

He frowned, not amused.

"You should let us handle this," said Officer Jones. "You could get hurt."

I have no idea what sort of expression was on my face, but Davey held my arm and said, "Jennifer and I will go check out Top of the Hill, Bridget. Please be careful, OK?"

"Where is Hendricks?" I kept my cool.

"He's on the prowl doing double duty tonight," said

Officer Jones, "between the search for your daughter and getting ready for possible post-game chaos."

"Thanks," I said to them. Not sure if they heard me over the roar of the crowd and the even louder noise of what sounded like some maniac dogs across the street.

After an awkward pause, Davey and Officer Jones continued down the sidewalk while I decided it would make sense for me to check the opposite side of the street.

I found Chica behind the bus shelter shaking her finger at both dogs on their leashes.

"So you lie down on the ground?" She said, clearly fed up with them. She had no luck tugging at Big Foot, who was splayed out, blocking the sidewalk like a white bearskin rug. People parted for him like the Red Sea. Bubba wrenched Chica's other arm, snarling at a homeless man shuffling into the alley beside the Carolina Coffee Shop.

"I can't believe you've brought the dogs out here," I yelled.

"You told me to," she said, flashing cranky black eyes my way.

"I meant to my parents' house, not to Franklin Street."

"The dog whisperer man says to teach them the family unit, yes? Here is part of the unit." She nodded at the dogs.

"I don't think he meant to include them in a search-and-rescue mission."

"I let them smell Dare's shoes at your madre's house. You never know. They could be sniffer doggies."

"I guess so," I said slowly. "Maybe it's a good idea. With the dogs you can walk around the campus buildings and they'll get exercise, too."

"Your mama is back home, I forgot to tell you. The abuela, too."

"The what?"

"Your little grandmama."

"That's good," I said, although I wasn't really sure if it was or not. At least Nana Blanche wasn't wandering lost and alone through a cold Orange County night.

Finally, Big Foot grunted up onto his four huge feet and all three of them turned up the same alley as the homeless man, Bubba hot on his trail. I'd no doubt that Chica's arms would be as long as the rubber band man's by the end of the evening.

"Call me if you see Hermann or Mr. Ruffin? OK?"

"Why?" she shouted over her shoulder.

"They are looking, too, I think. They might find her."

"Whatever you say, amiga," she said, too agitated with the dogs to question me further.

I spent the next hour walking through every open business and peering through every window of the closed ones. I zigzagged through a three-block area, hoping that someone was having better luck and covering more ground than I was.

At Spanky's Restaurant, I rushed in the front door and ran upstairs into the back dining areas seeking my daughter's face.

Back downstairs in the restaurant and bar, I did the scary extended game of Where's Waldo?, but substituted the name "Dare." I stood at the door scanning faces and the TV screen.

I heard a bar patron say there was five minutes to go in the game and two seconds left on the shot clock.

Announcer Jack Allan said, "Hansbrough from way out – a three-pointer."

When the shot swished through, pandemonium broke out and the crowd hollered and stomped fit to be tied. Hansbrough didn't usually take a shot like that. Sounded like a herd of screaming buffalo, as if I'd ever heard one.

Three minutes and twelve seconds to go, according to the network graphic.

Visalli shouted, "Are you serious? They're celebrating on Franklin Street, baby, down in Chapel Hill on that one."

Quick shots of Coach Williams and Coach Krzyzewski showed them each ready to have a stroke.

I plugged up my free ear and called home hoping to hear my father say that Dare was back. He answered faster than I thought he would.

"Are you watching the game?"

"Yes, sugar, but not really. Not as important without my girl. No luck on your end?"

"No, Daddy. Gotta go. Love you."

Davey called.

"No luck?"

"No," I said. "And Daddy just said she's not at home either. I'm in Spanky's and going back outside right before the game's over. Talk to you later."

I disconnected and turned back to the game.

According to the clock, there were twenty-three seconds left, and the score was UNC 79 and Duke 74.

Automatically I thought the Blue Devils would have to start fouling to get the ball back. Making free throws would be key.

Back and forth, back and forth galloped the UNC boys in their powder blue road uniforms and the Duke boys in their home white. Redick had had a terrible Senior Night. At one point, he had gone thirty-two minutes with only one score, according to the announcer.

The Tar Heels were shooting with passion. No one had expected number fifteen to beat number one. Yet, it was happening.

But it wasn't even important at that point.

Through Spanky's front window, I could see students throwing wood into a pile for a big bonfire at the intersection of Franklin Street and Cameron Avenue.

Ten seconds to go, and the score was 83-76. Hansbrough had made two free throws. Everyone was screaming and hugging like maniacs, but I couldn't feel it.

It's only a basketball game.

I was so shocked at this thought that I pinched myself to see if I'd lost the power to celebrate a well-fought victory against Duke. I felt old.

I left the raucous fans in the restaurant and headed outside to get a good vantage point so I could see everyone when the bars emptied out after the game. I jumped onto a sturdy sidewalk bench. A lot of folks were already milling about, but soon the crush would commence.

A huge sustained roar emanated from the ground like a giant volcano, no doubt marking the end of the game. Like spurting lava, bodies poured out of doorways from all directions. Shouts, singing and horns echoed throughout the campus. Cars choked the roads.

Up ahead, Hermann stood on another bench and stared over the crowd of student heads. Mr. Ruffin appeared to his right and was looking in the same direction. I almost shouted at both of them, but instead followed Hermann's gaze and saw my daughter's dark cropped hair and big brown eyes. She seemed to be staring back at the two men, then she turned and ran.

Mr. Ruffin disappeared, pushing and moving in the direction Dare had taken.

As Hermann jumped from the bench, I reached him and tugged on his arm.

"I just saw Dare," I screamed. "Mr. Ruffin is right behind her."

He looked at me, unseeing at first and then he nodded.

"I will take care of it," he said and shoved his way through the crush.

"Wait," I cried.

Someone grabbed my arm. Pilar.

"Listen to me," she screamed in my ear.

We were getting knocked about like bump'em cars at the fair.

"Your dad just found Dare. I need to go to her," I struggled to loosen her grip.

But she pulled me through the mob with surprising strength for one so petite and onto the sidewalk in the wrong direction.

"No time to explain, but you need to know this. Just spoke to my dad. He does know I'm pregnant."

"You already told me that he might."

I jumped up and down to see if I could find Hermann or Mr. Ruffin in the crowd.

"Did you find out if he met with Mr. Ruffin at the club on Monday night?" I said.

"Yes," she shouted.

I couldn't believe what I heard.

"Yes, he was there early Monday evening," she repeated.

If I hadn't been forced to stay upright by the mass of bodies, I would've dropped to the ground in shock.

I turned as somebody lit the bonfire and high-powered cheering erupted.

A student began to climb the light pole on the corner of Cameron and Franklin. I bulled my way over and followed him up. I was right underneath him when I recalled my fear of heights for a heart-surging second, but immediately forgot about it because this was the best way to see in every direction.

That's when I spotted Dare. Kind of hiding behind a big guy standing in front of the bonfire. As ash and sparks flew up in the dark night air, her face glowed amber.

I don't remember shinnying down the pole but later found the bruises to prove that I had.

As I got to the bottom, Chica came up with the dogs. Big

Foot had cleared a lane and Bubba was nipping at all of the feet, causing students along his path to look like they were doing the Mexican Hat Dance.

"Señor Ruffin is over there," she said, pointing to Mr. Ruffin who stood on the sidewalk glaring toward the bonfire. "Hermann is there." She twirled her hand indicating that he was weaving through the happy, hooting crowd near the blaze.

I caught my breath. Dare was ducking behind a group of rowdy frat boys as they lined up to hop over the fire.

I started moving through the bodies toward her. Hermann reached her first. He took her by the arm and hurried off. They headed toward the darker end of Franklin Street away from the mob.

I yelled at Chica to follow me with the dogs and ran after them. A glance over my shoulder showed Mr. Ruffin close behind.

Ahead of us, Dare screamed at Hermann and tried to pull away.

"Hermann, it's OK." I yelled. "Let her go. I'm here now."

Chica seemed to become airborne as the dogs barked maniacally and took off at a forty-five degree angle from the rest of us. So much for sniffer dogs.

As I neared Hermann and Dare, someone grabbed my arm and almost pulled it off.

Pilar.

"All my fault," she screamed over my shoulder. "Dad, Dad, please."

Hermann stopped dead when he heard his daughter, but didn't loosen his grip on Dare.

"Go home," he shouted. "Go. This is not good for you in your condition."

"Dad, please. Stop."

Mr. Ruffin jogged up breathlessly with Muffin in tow. She appeared to be almost dead weight.

"What the hell?" he growled. "What's going on?"

"I am not a drunk," cried Muffin to no one in particular before collapsing on the grass in a heap.

I looked all around for help and saw Davey hurrying up Franklin Street, and I could've sworn that in my fevered imagination I spotted a trench coat somewhere behind him.

I edged closer to Hermann and Dare. The man seemed to be a bundle of nerves, unusual as he'd always seemed to be a stoic.

Don't panic, Bridget. Breathe in. Breathe out.

"Come here, honey," I said, moving toward Dare as carefully as I could even though I wanted to pounce and wrap myself around her.

"Thanks, Hermann, for stopping her. I'll take it from here."

Dare hugged me so hard I could barely breathe. But Hermann still gripped her arm.

"Baby, it's OK. Let's go home to Rosemary Street. Your grandparents are so worried about you." I tried to remove Hermann's arm.

I turned toward Mr. Ruffin, and all I could think was that he was supposed to meet Hermann at the club the night Randy was murdered, and not in a business meeting as he'd claimed.

"You did it," I said to Mr. Ruffin.

"Did what?"

"Killed Randy."

"No, Mom, Mr. Ruffin didn't do it," Dare said in what seemed like dead quiet despite all of the street noise in the distance. "Did he, Mr. Salazar?"

She looked up at Hermann, and her pent-up words spilled out. "I saw you coming out of the locker room after Mr. Ruffin had driven away."

"You shut it," he hissed, jerking her arm. She cried out in pain.

That's when I saw the gun in his other hand.

"What are you doing?" I screamed. I kicked his knee and managed to wedge in between him and Dare, but he still held onto her. "Let her go, dammit."

He held the gun over his head and shot.

We all froze.

"Dad!" Pilar ran to him. "Please don't do this." She stood in front of him, blocking the gun.

Hermann hunched his shoulders. His eyes darted like those of a trapped animal.

Pilar crossed herself and looked up at him.

"I didn't want you to know about Bryan and me, Dad," she said tearfully. "I was afraid of what you'd do to him if you found out. Randy, Mr. La Russo, was so nice. He saw me crying in the parking lot one day. He said he'd explain it all to you, and it would be fine. We talked a lot. He felt sorry for me."

Hermann's twitching jaw was his only movement.

Pilar turned pleading eyes to me.

"He saw us together in Mr. La Russo's car a couple of times. I didn't realize how it looked. He didn't understand."

"I don't get it," I said stupidly, even though the truth was starting to part the clouds in my head. Why were we all standing here in such a mess?

"Don't you see, Miz O'Brien?" said Pilar. "I let him think that Mr. La Russo was the baby's father. I was afraid for Bryan. I didn't think Dad would do anything to a club member."

So that's what she was trying to tell me in the car. It wasn't about some random male student at all. It was about Randy.

"No," yelped Hermann, in what sounded like real pain. "No."

"I was going to tell you everything, Dad," she said, "but Bryan and I wanted to get married first. I was scared to tell you I was dropping out of school."

Hermann released Dare's arm. I was pulling backward

so hard in the opposite direction that Dare and I almost fell over.

Hermann turned and ran toward the milling people in the Street.

I let go of Dare. I couldn't let him get away. He had the gun. I sprinted after him.

"Salazar," called Lieutenant Hendricks, close behind me. "Drop that gun."

That's when I heard Chica's shrill Cuban voice scream into the night air, "Arriba, arriba. Ándale, ándale."

Our bilingual canines took off with her hanging onto the leashes for dear life. As Bubba's yips and Big Foot's woofs zoomed up behind me, Chica dropped the leashes.

Hermann gazed back in terror at the dogs, and I took that opportunity to bulldoze into him with my shoulder. The air whooshed out of his lungs, and Big Foot raised up on his hind legs and knocked him to the ground.

Bubba, not to be outdone, arrived, opened his tiny maw and chomped down on one of Hermann's ankles with his razor teeth. I stomped on Hermann's wrist to make him release the gun. Hendricks snatched it up and pulled the man's arms behind his back.

"Get them off. Get the dogs off," Hermann yelled, whether in pain or fear I wasn't sure. Probably both.

Chica pulled the tire-biter off Hermann's ankle and snapped the leash on Big Foot.

"Bubba," Dare called. The little fireplug scampered over and jumped in her arms. Chica followed close behind with Big Foot.

"You were right, amiga, about that stupid dog whisperer man," she admitted to me. "He knows nothing," she declared. "I will get our money back from him. Our doggies are better than family. They are heroes."

Twenty-Nine

The red rocking horse looked like something that the Amish might have built or Grandma Moses might have put on canvas – rustic but made with love. Grace said that Randy used to rock so much he'd fall asleep on it when he was a baby.

The springs on the old rocking horse creaked but held Dare's weight. I sat on the attic floor in Randy's old home as we waited for sunset and the rays of sunlight that would tell us Randy's big secret.

"Why are we here, Mom?"

"Something Randy said many years ago about hiding places. And then, last Monday, he said something else. He said that you needed to know where to find your future."

"But what does that mean?"

It was quiet in the attic. Dust motes floated through the transparent air.

"I can't believe he told you that he was your father the night he died," I said. "I told him I'd kill him if he did that, but I didn't mean it."

"Yeah, and I thought you did. That's why I said what I said."

"You shouldn't have, though. I wouldn't have hurt a

hair on his head. Although, God help me, I wanted to often enough over the years. He could be a real piece of work sometimes."

"Like, I was so upset when he told me, Mom. I was totally mean to him. I called him a liar. I told him I hated him and that I already had a father. And then he died. I felt terrible because I didn't really hate him. I felt so guilty. It was almost like I did kill him."

She started to cry, and I put my arms around her. The rocking horse creaked.

"Oh baby, none of it was your fault. It was a terrible way to tell you. Sometimes he had no tact. He meant well, but I think because of the cancer and because I'd been so ugly that morning, he was frantic to let you know. Sometimes grownups don't mean to do things so clumsily. Please try not to think badly of him. I think he might have made a good father if he'd lived longer. Just think, you've had two fathers who loved you. And you still have your grandfather. And a risen-from-the-dead great grandmother, too."

Her sobbing slowed down with hiccups. We both got quiet and waited for sunset and its light to filter through the slats of the round west window.

The rays landed on a floorboard across the room, which seemed predictable enough, although the floorboard wasn't loose. A word to Grace and she came up the ladder with a hammer and saw. We pried up the board and in the space beneath it was an old metal box. When we opened it, there was a note in Randy's handwriting dated November 2005.

Dearest Dare,

Knowing your mother, I know you will see this note. She's really something, and nosy to boot, and she will remember about this hiding place.

Even though I wasn't there for you when I should have been and now it looks like I won't be there for you later when I should be, this will provide you with what you need to get an education and make your life easier. I found these many years ago and resisted the urge to do something with them. My grandfather started buying them for my mother and me ages ago, and then they seemed to disappear and we couldn't figure out what happened to them. We found them finally in this box and then I hid them again. I want you to have them. I think your mother should get your Grandfather Richard to handle them for you and put them into a savings account with the best tax consequences. I've also left you money in my will….

Believe me when I say that I love you and wish I could be around to see you grow up. But unless there is a miracle, I don't think that will happen.

Love, always your father, Randy,

P.S. I know your father Marcus was a wonderful dad and I'm grateful he was there for you. I was lucky that was the case because he made you happy.

Underneath the note was a huge stack of Series E savings bonds in different denominations and maturities.

At least I knew what the sb's were now.

Thirty

Randy's private memorial service took place, two weeks after Hermann's arrest, on a quiet Sunday afternoon during UNC's spring break.

Short and sweet as per Randy's precise specifications, which took me by surprise, I can tell you, because I'd never really known him to plan much of anything. But this was different as, with the cancer, he'd had to deal with death, and I couldn't imagine his courage in facing it.

As he'd requested, he'd been cremated and his urn now stood on a table in the grassy quad near the steps of Wilson Library.

We mourners stood in a semicircle. Dare, me, my parents, Nana Blanche, Grace and Old Dudley, Chica, the Ruffins, Long, Marla Ann, Honey and Davey. Lieutenant Hendricks, Officer Jones and Pilar and her boyfriend stood at a respectful distance. I wasn't sure, but through my blurred vision I thought I spotted Hall Hooper lurking near the undergraduate library.

When I turned back to the proceedings, Pit Bullard had stepped up to the table in his powder blue suit, which had been cleaned and pressed.

"According to his mother, Mrs. Grace La Russo," Pit

said, "young Randall turned inward when he realized that virulent cancer was his final summons to leave this glorious life and proceed onto the next. When he came to know the face of his illness, it was fearsome. As fate would have it, he was called sooner and maybe in a more merciful way. It's not up to us to question the Lord's methods. But all of this aside and upon reflection of his past, Randall expressed regret for all the hurt he had inflicted. He agonized over his misguided love of the material world that had left him bereft and unfulfilled. In that frame of mind, he wanted his friends and family to remember that he'd always had a good heart and was planning to redeem his life through love and good works."

Pit paused, wiped tears with a pocket handkerchief, and loudly blew his nose. Then he looked over at Dare.

"He was especially looking forward to sharing the life of his daughter and was devastated that he hadn't come to the realization years ago."

Dare and I clutched hands as if they were lifelines. I bit my lip and tasted blood.

Pit cleared his throat.

"From his college days, he learned to love American poetry. This was a little known fact about Randall that only those closest to him in his youth know. And, like many of us, he admired Robert Frost. He used to say he could understand what Frost was saying in his poetry. Or, if he didn't really understand it, he wasn't smart enough to know that."

Many in the small gathering shifted their feet and smiled at a typical Randy-ism. I could almost see his dimple as he grinned at me from the fog of our joint past.

Pit looked up and smiled at Dare, who hung on his every word.

"He said, 'Short and sweet,' so here is Frost's short but bittersweet poem, 'The Road Not Taken.' This is printed on your memorial card."

Dare and I stepped forward.

"Randy wrote this down in my journal many years ago," I said. I turned to a bookmarked page and began to read.

"Two roads diverged in a yellow wood,
And sorry I could not travel both
And be one traveler, long I stood
And looked down one as far as I could
To where it bent in the undergrowth;

Then took the other, as just as fair,
And having perhaps the better claim,
Because it was grassy and wanted wear;
Though as for that the passing there
Had worn them really about the same,

And both that morning equally lay
In leaves no step had trodden black.
Oh, I kept the first for another day!
Yet knowing how way leads on to way,
I doubted if I should ever come back.

I shall be telling this with a sigh
Somewhere ages and ages hence:
Two roads diverged in a wood, and I—
I took the one less traveled by,
And that has made all the difference."

Grace took the urn home. Later that evening, Dare and I joined her to meander through campus and scatter Randy's ashes in the green peacefulness of the arboretum, outside the soaring Dean Dome, in the woods surrounding Kenan Stadium and the Bell Tower, and in the grassy spaces hugging Franklin Street.

Randy had come home.

Epilogue

Several weeks later, the perfect April day set the tone for a Sunday brunch in the backyard garden at the faded blue house on Rosemary Street.

My father had concocted the best Eggs Benedict on the planet and proudly set the warm platter amid Mother's green cabbage majolica plates, tall glasses of mint-draped iced tea and her special sweet potato biscuits.

Nana Blanche, fetched from the Treasure House and waiting like an expectant child, committed a harmless theft; she'd folded her linen napkin into a tiny square and stuffed it in her purse, which she clung to as if it held the Enigma codes.

In a concession to Mother, I'd worn a peasant skirt, blouse and espadrilles instead of what she considered one of my "blue-collar ensembles."

Chica, in a tangerine shift and Ray Bans and looking like a movie star, sunned herself in a chaise nearby.

Big Foot sniffed through the shrubbery before plopping down under a giant purple George Tabor azalea bush.

Bubba lolled on his back in Dare's lap as she moved gently to and fro on the swing and leaned her head on the rope looking dreamily into the distance. A moment later I was running to the van for pad and pencil for a quick preliminary sketch with an eye toward that perfect elusive water color.

Finally, we all sat down to eat and began to pass dishes to the left when Lieutenant Hendricks and Davey stepped around the corner of the house.

Unbidden, Emily Dickinson's words blazed a trail through my mind: "Because I could not stop for death, he kindly stopped for me."

Davey looked embarrassed about interrupting the meal, but the lieutenant took the pleasant domestic scene in his stride.

"Sorry to interrupt your fine spread, Miz O'Brien, Mr. O'Brien. This is one good-looking table you've laid out here. We can come back later," said Hendricks, eyeing the food.

"No, no, you must stay and eat," said my mother, who jumped up for extra plates.

My father went in search of chairs.

Dare took the opportunity to retreat back to the swing with Bubba and a buttered biscuit.

When we were settled again, Hendricks dug in happily, sopping egg yolk and slurping tea. My father put food on his own plate for politeness' sake; my mother pushed an egg around and sipped her tea. The rest of us watched Hendricks eat as if it were his last meal.

"Lordy, now that's real food," he said looking up from an empty plate. "Can't remember the last home-cooked meal I've had, although I sometimes go to Mama Dips of a Sunday morning."

We all looked at him expectantly.

"I guess you're wondering why we came by," he finally said.

"Yes," said Mother, who quickly remembered her upbringing and added, "and we're very pleased that you did."

Nana Blanche began to polish a silver teaspoon with her

sweater. When she was about to slide it in her purse, my mother gently took it from her.

"Mr. Salazar wants to avoid a trial for his daughter's sake," Hendricks continued. "He has confessed to Malcolm Jones's murder, too. The prosecution and defense are arranging a court hearing to inform the judge about the agreement. Assuming the judge accepts the deal or suggests changes that are satisfactory to both sides, the judge will hear the guilty plea in open court so that it becomes part of the record. Sentencing will then take place."

I put down my knife and fork as my appetite deserted me.

Chica grabbed Big Foot's leash from her chaise and said she was going for a walk, causing Hendricks to gaze wistfully after her as she disappeared around the corner.

"Did he say why he killed Malcolm?" my father asked.

"We understand from him that Malcolm, Mr. Jones, was suspicious about Mr. La Russo's murder and threatened to tell the police. Things then got out of hand."

I made myself ask. "And the gun?"

"Taken from your van," said Hendricks.

That made me feel a wee bit better. At least I hadn't left the murder weapon in one of our crates inside the club.

***

In Mother's kitchen, I opened the freezer door and, lo and behold, there was a clear plastic bag of oatmeal raisin cookies.

"Mother," I called over my shoulder, "it's about time."

"What are you talking about?" She'd entered the kitchen with a tray full of dirty dishes.

"You haven't made my oatmeal raisin cookies for ages. I've felt so unloved."

"I haven't made them for a long time. Dare has been doing it."

"Since when?"

"For more than a year now. Your mouth is hanging open, dear. So unattractive. Dare didn't want you to know at first, in case you didn't like them. After that, she thought it was funny that you were fooled. She made this batch, too. And, if you're a good mother, she might make some over at your house, now that she's living there."

I hugged Mother and lifted her off her feet.

"For heaven's sake, don't carry on so."

But I could tell she was pleased.

I unzipped the bag and grabbed three cookies, one for me and one each for Dare and Davey. We were taking Bubba for a campus walk.

As we strolled down the sidewalk, Daddy called out to remind us to be back by three o'clock so we could watch the videotape of the Carolina-Duke game that he had made on the fateful night of March 4th. Not one of us had really seen the game that night, and it had been a great victory for the Tar Heels over the number one team in the nation. Enough time had passed so we thought we might actually enjoy it.

Dare had Bubba on his leash. The Evil One, as I liked to call him, had been putty in her capable hands ever since she'd moved back in with me and Chica. My mother, busy with caring for Nana Blanche at the Treasure House, had agreed to the new arrangement, although she demanded that Dare visit often.

"I'm going to jog a little bit, Mom. Bubba is getting a tummy," Dare said as we stepped over the low stone wall and onto the grass.

"Wait," I said. "Tell Davey what you told me. Why you confessed to Randy's – to your father's – passing." I still wasn't comfortable with this topic. Never would be.

"It was a murder, Mom. Just say it. Don't make it more or less than it was."

"Cripes, out of the mouth of babes," I muttered as Davey chuckled and grabbed my hand, which surprised me as we'd tacitly put anything that seemed like a relationship on hold for the past several weeks.

I squeezed his hand, smiled, and ran to catch up with Dare. I approached the Davie Poplar where a tall, dark-haired man stood and grinned at me.

"Bridget, il mio amore," he said, smooth as olive oil.

"Alessandro? What the...?"

I shook my head in case I was imagining the moment.

Davey trotted up just as Alessandro took my limp hand, kissed it and then gazed into my eyes, which at that point must have resembled Bubba's pop-eyed doggy stare.

"I miss you, Signora Calabria, my lovely wife," my former Italian spouse said. "I come across a big ocean to bring you back to Tuscany."

"Whose wife?" Davey asked out of breath. "Who are you?"

"But we're divorced," I cried. "You agreed to get a divorce before I left Italy."

"Ah," he said, his liquid green eyes ridiculously like those on the slick cover of a romance novel. "But I did not."

The End

DAWN DIXON (COTTER) has won Malice Domestic's William F. Deeck Grant for Unpublished Writers, as well as short story awards and publication in a mystery anthology. FAUX FINISHED is her first novel. She's written for local, regional and national publications for more than 20 years and worked as a communications specialist and financial editor in corporate America. She adores writing screenplays and really bad poetry. Dixon claims Charlotte, N.C., as home, and the University of North Carolina at Chapel Hill as her own personal utopia. She plans to hunt down her ancestors someday in Ireland, England and France. For now, she and her partner rock on the front porch in South Carolina's Low Country, where she swears the lizards and alligators roam. Visit her website at www.dawndixon.net.

CPSIA information can be obtained
at www.ICGtesting.com
Printed in the USA
FSHW021323140621
82367FS

9 781955 095006